# The Madonna
## on the Moon

### ROLF BAUERDICK

*Translated from the German by David Dollenmayer*

Atlantic Books
London

First published as *Wie die Madonna auf den Mond kam* in Germany
in 2009 by Deutsche Verlags-Anstalt, Munich.

First published in Great Britain in 2013 by Atlantic Books,
an imprint of Atlantic Books Ltd.

This paperback edition published in Great Britain in 2014 by Atlantic Books.

10 9 8 7 6 5 4 3 2 1

A CIP catalogue record for this book is available from the British Library.

Paperback ISBN: 978 1 84887 505 0
E-book ISBN: 978 1 78239 133 3

Printed in Italy by Grafica Veneta SpA

Atlantic Books
An Imprint of Atlantic Books Ltd
Ormond House
26–27 Boswell Street
London
WC1N 3JZ

www.atlantic-books.co.uk

The Madonna on the Moon

*For Louisa, Leonie, and Lutz*

*Author's Note*

The novel is set in a fictitious country. To emphasize its fictionality, the diacritics required by the Romanian spelling of the names of persons, places, and things have been dispensed with.

The Madonna on the Moon

No one in Baia Luna had the slightest doubt that the source of Ilja Botev's visions was not some luminous gift of prophetic insight, but the delusions of a wandering mind—least of all me, Pavel, his grandson. When I was a little boy, I shrugged off my grandfather's imaginings as foolish fancies, the result of the influence of the Gypsy Dimitru Gabor. Dimitru never gave much of a hoot about the laws of reason and logic. But later, as the solid ground of good common sense grew progressively thin and crumbly beneath Grandfather's feet, I myself played no small part in the old man's getting more and more hopelessly tangled up in the net of his fantasies. It was certainly not my intent to have Grandfather make himself the town idiot, the butt of everyone's jokes. But what could you say about a tavern owner who sets off in a horse and cart on a secret mission to warn the president of the United States about the rocket scientist Wernher von Braun, a mysterious Fourth Power, and an impending international catastrophe? Armed, by the way, with a laughable top secret dossier, a treatise on the mystery of the corporeal Assumption of the Virgin Mary, handwritten and triple-sewn into the lining of his wool jacket.

Today, I see my grandfather Ilja and his Gypsy friend Dimitru in the mild light of my own old age. I am aware of my guilt and know what I owe them, even though, in Baia Luna, memories of the pair are gradually fading. These days, people look to the future. If you pause to look back you're a loser. We're a democracy. There is no more Conducator outshining the sun, no more party demanding blind obedience, no Security Service throwing uppity subjects into jail. You can think and believe whatever you like. People used to write incendiary pamphlets that had to be smuggled out of the country. No more. Our borders are open to all our neighbors. We're free citizens. Our children are growing up in a free country.

Rather late in life I myself became the proud father of two daughters, begotten and born in freedom. Since then, two decades have flown by as if some crazed second hand had slung me through time. Back in the Golden Age of Socialism, we wanted for everything except time. That we had in abundance. It may be that we threw it away, wasted the best years of our lives in dreary queues. Today, time is a rare and costly commodity. It's running away from me while younger generations race memoryless through an eternal present. But when children have forgotten where they come from, how will they know where they're heading?

As things now stand, my daughters will soon make me a grandfather in my own right. In anticipation of future grandchildren, I shall turn time back to my youth in the fifties. If I'm going to tell my children and grandchildren how the Madonna got to the moon, my voice will echo those of my own grandfather Ilja and the Gypsy Dimitru. The two friends dreamed their idea of freedom, and as a final dying ember in the midst of cold ashes, that dream would be fulfilled in their final days. But I didn't come to understand that until after the historic Christmas of 1989, when our country's Age of Gold ended on the rubbish heap of history.

That was the day the Great Conductor, his hands fettered, hissed the words "pack of Judases" at his drumhead court-martial before singing "The Internationale" one last time and shouting "Long live the Free and Socialist Republic." But no one applauded. No one waved little flags. He and his wife only made it halfway to the wall in the yard of the Targoviste barracks. The president wasn't even worth the official order "Fire!" but just a couple premature bursts. Without a command. *Ratta-tat-tat.* Spent shells spewed out and danced on the cold stones. Powder smoke filled the air. Then, riddled with bullets as he was, the Conducator's knees gave way, and the Golden Age was over. Nevertheless, as the Genius of the Carpathians (celebrated in the songs of his court poets as the Sweetest Kiss of the Homeland's Soil) lay there lifeless in his own blood, his suit jacket still buttoned like a statesman's but hitched up around his armpits in some disarray, something remarkable occurred.

A spasm of horror seized the members of the firing squad.

Instead of being intoxicated with victory, they were beset by fear. Bewildered by their own deed, the militiamen didn't dare look at the fallen dictator. They averted their petrified gaze from the Titan of Titans whose wide-open eyes stared at the sky in incomprehension. A few young fellows cast furtive glances at their commander and hastily crossed themselves behind his back, then they grabbed shovels and threw a few spadefuls of dirt onto his face. Those eyes! Nobody could stand up to them except the scrawny curs who smelled warm blood. With lolling tongues and tails between their legs they crept closer. They had no appreciation for the final, frank expression on the face of a man who, at the moment of his death, revealed with disarming honesty that he really had no idea what had actually occurred on that Christmas Day in 1989.

Following the execution, Dr. Florin Pauker noted the time— 2:45 p.m.—on the death certificate. Rather accidentally, he had been present at the self-appointed Revolutionary Tribunal of National Salvation. He was a neurologist, not a coroner. Only a few days earlier the party had relieved him of his duties as director of the psychiatric hospital in Vadului and given him a new position as military surgeon in Targoviste. And since he and his wife Dana saw no point in celebrating Christmas, Dr. Pauker had switched on-call days with a colleague. And now it was his duty to officially confirm the clinical death of the Conducator and his spouse.

Florin Pauker bent over the corpse, searched for a pulse, and looked into the dead man's eyes, possibly a moment too long. He scribbled a hasty signature on the death certificate, then reached for the telephone, asked to be connected to the Athenee Palace Hotel in the capital and put through to the presidential suite. After uttering the words "It's over," he got into his Dacia and drove back to the capital and home to his wife in the Strada Fortuna. There Dr. Pauker told her that the revolutionary tribunal had put up against the Targoviste barracks-yard wall not evil incarnate, but innocence.

His wife Dana and his daughter Irisetta, their only child, stated that their husband and father changed fundamentally after this Bloody Christmas, as they called the day of the revolution. "His personality changed one hundred eighty degrees. He turned sentimental. He was no longer the energetic physician with an intellect keen as a knife to whom I'd been faithful for more than thirty years," Dana told a French journalist who was trying to reconstruct the fall of the Conducator.

"It was terrible," daughter Irisetta confirmed. "Father turned into an empty-headed, sentimental softy. He started to go out all the time—not to breathe the fresh air of freedom but intending to comfort all the unhappy brats he could find." He crammed his pockets full of American chewing gum and the multicolored lollipops that bald detective who suddenly appeared on TV always sucked on during an investigation. On every street corner children surrounded her father, and he would give each one something. But every time he spotted a kid with big eyes, he would start to shed bitter tears. She didn't dare go out with him anymore, she was so ashamed of her father's never-ending weeping and wailing.

To brighten up his melancholy mood, Dr. Pauker undertook numerous trips during the nineties. He was drawn to the holy sites of Christendom, especially the places where people said that in days gone by Mary the Mother of God had appeared. At first he visited local pilgrimage towns in Transmontania, then he journeyed to Fatíma in Portugal and Medjugorje in Bosnia. But neither in the little town of Lourdes in the French Pyrenees nor from the Black Madonna of Czestochowa did the neurologist find the relief he was seeking for his melancholy soul.

For Dana, her husband's metamorphosis into a sanctimonious sissy was almost unbearable. To her it was humiliating and even intellectually insulting that Florin brought back suitcases full of kitschy implements from these trips: plaster statuettes of the Madonna, vials of holy water and plastic rosaries, bottles of miraculous fluids, and postcards that when waggled back and forth showed first the crucified Christ with his crown of thorns, eyes downcast in sorrow, and then transfigured, lifting them up to heaven. With every new devotional object that entered the house, Dana sensed that the path her husband was on was destined never to cross hers again.

Not for lack of trying on her part. For years, Dana Pauker had appealed to his long-dormant intellectual powers. She invoked his years as the seasoned director of a neurological institute and pleaded with him to come to his senses: in vain.

As she was preparing their apartment for New Year's Eve dinner on the final night of the last millennium and ten years after the revolution, she noticed to her dismay that Florin had removed the portrait of the Conductor from the living room wall. For ten years she had fought to have his picture left in place, ten years of resistance to what she called the arbitrariness of historical consciousness. And now Florin had simply taken the portrait down from the wall and replaced it with a photograph of a statue of the Virgin. Dana Pauker knew she had lost the battle. She was alone. Their last friends from the party had turned their backs on them. The Paukers had disappeared into the void of social insignificance. Who wanted anything to do with a washed-up doctor who wandered the streets with a rosary, handing out sticky sweets?

In a final outburst of anger, Dana snatched the Madonna from the wall, threw open a window, and hurled the picture out into the street. Then she went to the medicine cabinet. While she swallowed down all the pills she could lay her hands on in a rush of blind rage, passersby on their way to some New Year's party clutching bottles of cheap sparkling wine were surprised to find lying on the asphalt of the Strada Fortuna a splintered picture frame with a portrait of the Madonna under shards of glass. She was stretching out a protective hand over the naked Baby Jesus, who sat on a globe of the world, while her right foot trod on a crescent moon.

On August 14, the eve of the Feast of the Assumption and barely eight months after the beginning of the new millennium, a grizzled but robust man in his midseventies showed up in Baia Luna asking for Mr. Pavel Botev. They sent him to me and I recognized him at once. The penetrating gaze behind his round glasses was no longer quite so keen as in the photographs I remembered from my youth, but there was no mistake: it was him. He introduced himself with some other name I've forgotten and asked me to guide him up to the Mondberg the following day, to the Chapel of the Virgin of Eternal Consolation. I agreed.

He told me his story while we climbed to the summit. Of course, I wondered why he had asked in particular for me to guide him up the mountain. Today, I think the old man knew I had already heard his story long before, not the details of it but its essentials. When we got to the top of the Mondberg, he ignored the chapel of the Virgin and strode straight toward the steep southern flank of the mountain where there was a small cemetery with five anonymous white crosses.

"Which cross is for Angela?"

"The middle one," I said.

He knelt down, said a Hail Mary, and got to his feet.

"Thank you, Mr. Botev." He extended his hand and I shook it.

"Have you reached your goal, Doctor?"

He smiled. "Yes, Mr. Botev, soon. Very soon."

Then he spread his arms and launched himself silently into the abyss, like an eagle. He flew like a king of the air who no longer wanted to be king. Dr. Florin Pauker was free.

# Chapter One

.

"He's flying! He's flying! Long live Socialism! Three cheers for the party!"

The three Brancusi brothers, Liviu, Roman, and Nico, burst into our taproom one evening about eight in a splendid mood, their chests swelling with pride and the cash to stand a few rounds burning holes in their pockets.

"Who's flying?" asked my grandfather Ilja.

"The dog of course! Laika! The first animal in space! Aboard Sputnik II! Brandy, Pavel! *Zuika* for everybody! But *avanti*! It's on us." Liviu was playing the big shot, and I could foresee I'd have to run myself ragged the next few hours.

"Gr-gr-gr-gravity has been co-co-conquered! Now nothing can hold back pr-pr-progress. Sp-Sputnik beeps and Laika b-barks all around the w-w-world," Roman stammered, as he always did when his tongue couldn't keep up with his excitement.

"Progress, yes sir," Nico, the youngest Brancusi, fell in with his stammering brother. "A toast to the Union of Soviet Socialist Republics! Side by side we will be victorious! We will conquer the heavens!"

"You can keep your schnapps to yourselves." The Saxons Hermann Schuster and Karl Koch threw on their coats and left the taproom.

Trouble hung in the air that November 5, 1957. It was a Tuesday and the eve of my grandfather Ilja's fifty-fifth birthday. I was fifteen. In the mornings I reluctantly attended the eighth (and final) grade, in the afternoons I killed time, and evenings and Sundays I helped my grandfather, waiting on his clientele in our family's tavern. I should mention that it wasn't an inn in the ordinary sense of the word. Ilja, my mother Kathalina, and Aunt Antonia ran a shop by day whose inventory provided the housewives of Baia Luna with the basic necessities. By night, we moved a few tables and chairs into the shop and transformed it into a pub for the men.

All I understood of the Brancusis' blabber about progress was that a dog was zooming across the sky in a beeping Sputnik that managed to do without jet engines and rotating propellers and had nothing in common with ordinary airplanes. At the price, however, of never being able to return to earth. Satellites had escaped the rules of gravity and were on their way to eternal flight in space.

While the men in the bar were getting hot under the collar discussing the whys and wherefores of the newfangled airships, my grandfather Ilja was unmoved: "Weightlessness—not bad. My compliments. But the Russian beeping won't fill my belly."

Dimitru Carolea Gabor stood up and took the floor. Some of the men lowered their chins in contempt. After all, didn't people say the Gypsy had his feet in the clouds and thought with his tongue? Dimitru clutched his right fist to his heart as if taking an oath. He stood there like a rock and swore that the chirping flying contraption was the work of the Supreme Comrade of all Comrades, Joseph Vissarionovich Stalin himself. While still alive, he'd ordered a whole armada of Sputniks to be built. "Sly machines camouflaged as harmless balls of tin, under way on secret missions, and now they even have a dog onboard. I don't quite get the point of that yapper among the stars, but I'll tell you something: those aluminum spiders aren't poking their antennae into the sky just for fun. The Supreme Soviet has something up its sleeve. That beeping, that cosmic cicada, robs peaceful human beings of their sleep and of their sanity, too. And you know what that means? If you're crazy, you turn into a zombie, and the world revolution just goose-steps right past you. And then, comrades"—Dimitru stared at the three Brancusis—"then you've finally achieved the equality of the entire proletariat. The idiot among equals thinks everyone's smart."

"In your case, the beeping seems to be working already." Liviu tapped his finger on his forehead to mock the crazy Gypsy. "You Blacks are nothing to write home about, anyway. Why don't you do something productive for a change? Under Stalin, you all would've been—"

"Right! *Exactamente!* What'd I tell you?" Dimitru interrupted him. "Joseph was a sly dog. But he had problems getting everyone proletarianized. Big problems. Because his policy of state control just couldn't achieve the equality of all the Soviets. Sure, the Supreme Comrade really tried hard: bigger jails, higher prison walls, bread and water, half rations. He tried to rub out the last vestiges of inequality with more and more gallows and firing squads. But what did that achieve? Joseph had to keep expanding the labor camps for the unequal. The boundaries of the prisons grew incalculably vast. Today no one knows who's in and who's out. What a dilemma. The Supreme Soviet can't keep track of it all anymore. That's why they need Sputnik. The beeping eliminates the mind and the will. And where there's no will, there's no—"

"Who needs this bullshit?" yelled Nico Brancusi. Purple with rage, he jumped up and glared around at the assembled company. "Who wants to hear this crap, goddamnit!" From way back in his throat he hocked up a loogie and spat it onto the floorboards with the words, "Gypsy lies! Black talk!"

Dimitru drummed his fingers nervously on the table.

"It's the truth," he said. "If my calculations are correct, Sputnik will be flying over the Transmontanian Carpathians between the forty-sixth degree of latitude and the twenty-fourth degree of longitude in the morning hours of my friend Ilja's special day. It'll be beeping right over our heads. I'm telling you, Sputnik is the beginning of the end. And you, Comrade Nico, you can offer your naked ass to whoever you want, that's your business. But I'm a Gypsy, and you'll never find a Gypsy in bed with the Bolsheviks."

Nico went for the Gypsy's throat, but his brothers held him back. Dimitru emptied his glass, belched, and after whispering to grandfather, "Five on the dot. I'll be waiting for you," left the tavern without a backward glance.

I didn't know what to think about all the excitement. I went to bed but had a hard time falling asleep. The Gypsy had probably catapulted himself out of the track of logical thought again (as so often in the past) with his hair-raising speculations about the beeping Sputnik.

But my bedtime prayer (which admittedly I usually forgot) suddenly gave me pause. "Our Father, who art in heaven, hallowed be thy name. Thy kingdom come . . ." Now, at fifteen, I was already clear that the kingdom of heaven was not about to arrive in the foreseeable future, at least not in Baia Luna. But it was different with the Sputnik. The kingdom of heaven might not be expanding on earth, but on the other hand, man was heading for the heavens. Or at least an earthly creature was: a dog. Surely the beast would soon be dead of starvation. But what was a dead mutt doing in the infinity of space anyway? Up where the Lord God and his hosts reigned, as our aged parish priest Johannes Baptiste thundered from his pulpit every Sunday.

Night was already drawing to a close when the floorboards in the hall creaked. I heard cautious footsteps, as if someone didn't want to be heard. Grandfather was taking great pains not to wake up my mother Kathalina, Aunt Antonia, and me. The footsteps descended the stairs and died out in the interior of the shop. I waited awhile, got dressed, and stole downstairs, full of curiosity. The outside door was open. It was pitch black.

"Fucking shit," hissed a voice. "Goddamn crappy weather!" It was Dimitru.

"Be quiet or you'll wake up the whole village."

"I prayed, Ilja, I mean I really beseeched the Creator to make short work of it and with one puff of his almighty breath sweep away these goddamn clouds. And what does he do when just once a Gypsy asks for something? He sends us this fog from hell. We can forget about hearing the Sputnik in this pea soup."

I hid behind the doorjamb and peered outside. Dimitru was right. It had been raining buckets for days, and now the fog had crept down from the mountains. You couldn't even see the outline of the church steeple. Five muffled strokes of the clock penetrated the night. Ilja and Dimitru looked up at the sky. They cocked their heads, put their hands behind their ears, and listened again. Obviously in vain. Disappointed, the two shuffled back into the shop. They didn't see me.

"Ilja, I'm wondering if it wouldn't make sense to go back to bed for a while," said Dimitru.

"It does make sense."

Then the Gypsy's gaze fell on the tin funnel my grandfather always used to pour the sunflower oil delivered in canisters from Walachia into the bottles the village housewives brought.

"Man, Ilja, that's it! Your funnel. We'll use it as a megaphone, only in reverse. You've heard of the principle of the concentration of sound waves—*sonatus concentrates* or something like that? We can use it to capture even the faintest hint of a noise."

The two went back outside and took turns sticking the tin funnel first into their left ear and then their right, hoping to amplify the sound. For a good quarter of an hour they swiveled their heads in all directions.

When at last I cleared my throat and wished them good morning, they gave it up.

"So, Dimitru, you're going to let Sputnik steal your sanity?" I ribbed him.

"Go ahead and laugh, Pavel. Blessed are those who neither see nor hear but still believe. Let me assure you, it's beeping. *Evidentamente*. We just can't hear it."

"No wonder," I pretended to be sympathetic. "The November fog. It swallows everything up and you can't hear a thing. Not the calves bleating, not even the cocks crowing. To say nothing of Sputnik, it's so far away. Beyond the pull of gravity, if I've got it right."

"Good thinking, Pavel! You're right, when it's foggy the Sputnik's not worth much. The Supreme Comrade didn't think of that. Between you and me and in the cold light of day, Stalin was pretty much of an idiot. But don't spread it around. That can get you into trouble nowadays. And now, forgive me, but my bed is calling."

Grandfather looked a little sheepish. It made him self-conscious to be caught holding a funnel to his ear out in front of the shop on his fifty-fifth birthday.

"Pavel, go with Dimitru so he doesn't break his neck on the way home. You can't see your hand in front of your face."

Out of sorts, I groped my way with Dimitru to the lower end of the village where his people lived. At the doorstep of his cottage he put his hand to his ear again and listened.

"Give it up, Dimitru. What's the point?"

"*Sic est*. You're right," he said, thanked me for my company, and disappeared inside.

Was it mere coincidence? No idea. But just as I set off back through the village, the roosters began to crow, and across from the Gypsy settlement a weak light shimmered through the fog. For the second time on that early morning I let myself be driven by curiosity. The light was shining from the cottage of Angela Barbulescu, the village schoolteacher. This early in the morning! "Barbu," as we called her, usually slept till all hours. She seldom showed up for class on time, and once in front of the class, she often stared at us from swollen eyes because the brandy from the previous evening was still having its effect. I left the street and peeked through her window. She was sitting at the kitchen table with a warm wool blanket thrown over her shoulders. Incredible! She was sitting there writing something. She lifted her head from time to time and looked at the ceiling as if seeking the right word. Much more than the fact that Barbu was apparently getting something important down on paper at this ungodly hour, it was her face I found astonishing. In the last few years of school, I had come to think she was disgusting. I never looked at her except with contempt, if not revulsion.

Yet the Barbu I saw early on the morning of November 6, 1957, was different. She was bright and clear. Beautiful, even. Someday in the not-too-distant future I would understand what was happening in Angela Barbulescu's cottage that morning, and it would plunge me into the abyss. But how could I have known it in that dreary November dawn?

Pavel, you're not going to tell Kathalina about that dumb idea with the funnel, are you? Your mother is not amused by that stuff."

"I didn't see anything. Especially not on your birthday. Word of honor."

That took a load off Grandfather's mind, whereupon I shook his hand, wished him happy fifty-fifth, and gave him a package wrapped in shiny red paper.

As she did every year, my mother (and Granddad's daughter-in-law) had asked Adamski the mailman to purchase a box of cigars in Kronauburg, the district capital. Ilja unwrapped his present, knowing full well he would soon be holding a wooden box with sixty Caballeros Finos, each thick as his thumb. Sixty cigars were the precise number Grandfather needed for his systematic smoking habits, plotted out for the year ahead. Sixty cigars were exactly enough for one every Sunday, one each for the parish fairs on the Feast of the Assumption, the Feast of the Virgin of Eternal Consolation (the patron saint of Baia Luna), and two or three other holidays. When he added in the birthdays of his closest friends and compensated for the doubling that sometimes occurred when a religious or secular holiday such as All Saints', Christmas, or the Day of the Republic fell on a Sunday, then the inevitable result was that one final Caballero remained for his birthday, just before he opened the box for the following year.

Ilja thanked me and, contrary to his customary procedure of smoking only in the evening, decided to allow himself then and there the pleasure of a Cuban, as he called his cigars. He pulled out his last Caballero and lit up. "America"—he sighed and blew a few smoke rings into the air—"America! What a country!"

Of course, my mother Kathalina and I knew that Ilja's Cubans had never seen the hold of a transatlantic freighter. The Cyrillic letters on the cigar bands betrayed the fact that the tobacco had been rolled in a Bulgarian factory near Blagoevgrad and probably transported across the Danube on the new Bridge of Friendship between Ruse and Giurgiu in a diesel rig. But Mother's lips were sealed, leaving her father-in-law with the conviction that Cuba was the most marvelous among the United States of America.

By the age of five or six, I had already guessed that Granddad could barely read. Up to then I had hung devotedly on his lips when he told me stories or pretended to be reading one from a book. But I began to notice that sometimes he got the plot hopelessly tangled up, mixing up persons, places, and times and very seldom turning the page. Once I started first grade, my suspicions were confirmed. So as not to embarrass Grandfather I didn't tell anyone about my discovery. And since Ilja could juggle numbers with great facility and my unmarried aunt Antonia, who had set up her digs in the garret upstairs, took care of the bookkeeping for our family's shop, Ilja's defect remained for many years hidden from the rest of the village and even from the Gypsy Dimitru.

My father Nicolai, on the other hand, certainly had no problem reading and writing when still alive. I gathered that from the underlinings and marginal notes he had made, as a young man, in a volume of poetical works by Mihail Eminescu. The only other things of any value he left me were *Das Kapital* by Karl Marx and a beat-up chess set with the stub of a candle replacing the missing white queen.

I had no memories of my father. For me, Nicolai Botev was a stranger who existed only in a framed photograph standing in the glass-fronted cabinet in the living room. It showed him as a soldier on leave and a note on the back dated it to December 1942. With his thin cheeks, Nicolai sits next to my mother in a sleigh in front of the snow-covered slope of Cemetery Hill in Baia Luna. I am about one year old and stand between his knees, wrapped in a scarf and with a Kazak cap pulled down over my ears. There was something unsettling about this family photo that always caught my eye. It was Father's hands. They lay on my shoulders limp and lifeless, incapable of providing support.

On winter evenings, my mother would take the photo out of the cabinet and sit silently in her chair holding it on her lap. She could sit that way hour after hour until sleep wrote an ethereal smile on her face. She never talked about my father. I think she wanted to hide the fact that she thought about him constantly so I wouldn't be reminded that he was gone. But his absence seemed quite natural to me. Besides, Grandfather made sure that nobody in the village could complain that I didn't have enough paternal oversight.

In the 1950s two hundred and fifty people lived in Baia Luna, distributed among thirty houses. To the southeast rose the Mondberg with the pilgrimage Chapel of the Virgin of Eternal Consolation, to the west the village was bordered by the mighty cliffs of the Carpathians, while the village fields and pastures extended in a northerly direction until one's gaze was lost in the landscape of the

distant Transmontanian hills. Below the Mondberg flowed the Tirnava. After the spring thaw the river became a raging torrent, but in
the hot, dry summers the Tirnava shriveled to a thin, foul-smelling
trickle, and the fish jumped onto the bank so as not to suffocate.
Following the river downstream, one came to a wooden wayside
cross in memory of the tragedy that occurred during the blizzard
of 1935, and continuing on foot, one could reach the neighboring
village of Apoldasch in an hour and a half.

The ascent of the Mondberg took three hours. Once my legs
were strong enough to survive the climb without whining and
whimpering, Granddad regularly took me along to the Virgin of
Eternal Consolation. As we entered the chapel, we crossed ourselves and presented our compliments to the Mother of God. As
a child I always found the Madonna a bit creepy. Her face, carved
from red beech centuries ago by a sculptor of manifestly modest
talent, was anything but beautiful. The Queen of Heaven stood
on a pedestal, and when I looked up at her, I found her expression
more tortured than majestic. With files and chisels, the artist had
set about his work quite coarsely, so that Mary's gentleness only
touched me on second or third glance. The right foot of the Mother
of God peeked out from under her enveloping cloak and trod on a
crescent moon. Obviously the sculptor had no sense of proportion.
He made Baby Jesus, who sat on the globe with Mary's protective
hand above his head, too small. By contrast, the Madonna's imposing breasts were too big, as was the crescent moon. Generations
of believers interpreted the foot on the crescent as a symbol of the
Virgin's victory over the Turks, who under the sign of the crescent
moon had tried by force to turn Europeans into Mussulmen. But
which—thanks to the heavenly intervention of the Virgin of Eternal Consolation—they failed to do in Baia Luna.

After paying our respects to the Mother of God, Grandfather
and I sat on the rocks among the juniper bushes. With the stock
phrase "Then let's take a look and see what Kathalina has packed
up for us," Granddad would open his rucksack and take out a ther-
mos of sweet black tea, hard-boiled eggs, tomatoes, bacon, and
ham sandwiches. After lunch Ilja stretched out on the warm grass,
napped for a half hour, and awoke refreshed. Then we sat awhile
longer, gazing out over the countryside.

If, like the Mother of God (who is known to have ascended bodily into heaven), one could take off from the Mondberg, Grandfather explained, one would at some point settle to earth in America. And he stretched out his arm and pointed in the direction where he thought the skyscrapers of a city he called "Noueeyorka" were located. According to Grandfather, that splendid city would obviously be the only logical goal of such a flight. Dimitru had also assured him it was so and declared that the geographic space between the towns of Baia Luna and Noueeyorka was like an electromagnetic field between positive and negative poles in which one pole without the other would be reduced to a void of nothingness. Seen in this light, the American Noueeyorka owed its very greatness to the existence of Baia Luna. From Grandfather I learned that, thanks to an independent disposition, an American never concerns himself with petty details and on principle always thinks on a gigantic scale. The Americans build the tallest buildings in the world, roll the best cigars, and in honor of the Mother of God erected the most colossal of all statues of the Virgin at the gates of Noueeyorka, surrounded by water on all sides. Mary guarantees the inhabitants of the skyscrapers peace, prosperity, and protection from enemy attack. The burning torch in her hand not only shows the way for ships from all over the world, but the broken chains at her feet also promise new arrivals freedom from all forms of servitude. That's why seven beams of light emerge from the crown on her head, each beam bigger than the church steeple of Baia Luna. Dimitru had interpreted the number 7 as Mary's seven closest confidants, of whom the Lord God, the Son of God, and the Holy Spirit represented the Fields of Heaven, while the four Evangelists were in charge of earthly affairs.

I couldn't find a city with the name Noueeyorka on the globe at school, but the story about the giant Madonna and her blazing torch seemed to be true, for at my school-friend Fritz Hofmann's house I had seen an impressive poster of Mary hanging on the living room wall. I stared at it openmouthed. There she was. I was surprised to find a picture of the Madonna here in the house of the photographer Hofmann, since Fritz and his parents Heinrich and Birta were ethnic Germans with no interest in the Catholic religion and were the only people in the village not to attend Mass.

It was also strange that the statue stood not in Noueeyorka but clearly in New York, as one could read on the poster in black and white. Since Herr Hofmann had a photographic studio in the district capital of Kronauburg, it seemed logical to ask if he had taken this impressive picture with his own camera. The only response I got was a gruff "No!"

Fritz Hofmann and I were the same age, and in the mornings we attended the village school, crammed together in one classroom with sixty boys and girls between the ages of seven and fifteen. There were enough seats for everyone, however, because the Gypsies seldom or never sent their children to school. Angela Barbulescu was the teacher for everyone. At the beginning of the fifties, the Ministry of Education had sent her to Baia Luna from the capital—under compulsion, it was rumored, although the reasons for this measure remained obscure. I had overheard the men in Grandfather's tavern say that she used to be quite good-looking and took care to conceal her tendency to drink too much. But at some point, she'd lost all sense of shame. The village women, however, maintained that Barbu could never have lost her feel for when the bounds of decency had been overstepped, since she'd never had a woman's natural instinct for propriety in the first place. After all, when she went up to the altar to receive the Body of the Lord on her first Sunday in the village, everybody at Mass had seen her hands. Her fingernails were painted a garish blood red. Kora Konstantin even reported that the obscene trollop had prevented her from listening to the priest's words in the proper spirit of devotion. Kora put into circulation that Barbu had something called a "nimmfomaniac" character defect and had been banished to the mountains to cure this inclination. I hadn't heard any gossip about her for a long time, however. Angela Barbulescu's nail polish had cracked and peeled. And besides, the wives and mothers behind their curtains gave her no chance to go more than three steps unobserved.

In my last year of school Barbu shuffled to class every morning wearing rubber boots and a dark blue dress with shiny grease stains and a smell like rancid butter. Often she would stand unsteadily at the blackboard, struggling to stay on her feet. While she waved her pointer around to direct the national anthem, we had to stand at attention, put our hands on our hearts, and crank out all eight verses. After that she quizzed us on local history. The younger kids sat and listened while we older ones sang the praises of the deeds of Michael the Brave, conqueror of the Turks, rattled off historic dates from the Dacians to Gheorghe Gheorghiu-Dej, and explained for the millionth time why Catholic Baia Luna had not joined the Protestants in the previous centuries and had never been captured by the Turks. Then we sang the song to the Virgin about the patron saint full of grace and her protective cloak. Then it was time for math.

Grades 1 to 4 added and subtracted columns of figures from zero to a hundred. Grades 5 to 8 had to multiply four- and five-place numbers and calculate the percentage increases in the quotas for milk production and fattened hogs since the collectivization of agriculture, even though the farms in the district of Kronauburg had yet to be nationalized. Luckily, Barbu never gave our results more than a cursory glance. That's why my neighbor Fritz Hofmann and I finished the assignment in a flash by writing down fantastically inflated numbers.

But when Miss Barbulescu was sober and having a good day, she sat on her desk, smoothed out her blue dress, and told us about life in the Paris of the East, which is what they called the capital. "A glittering gem of Western culture," she often repeated. She praised the powerful voices of its nightclub singers and the grace of the "chorines of *Swan Lake,*" waxed ecstatic about the mirrored halls of culture, the temples of dramatic art, and the moving-picture palaces where top stars of the American silver screen enchanted audiences with their art. So poignant was her depiction of two lovers named Rhett and Scarlett that I found myself listening closely and feeling a twinge of sympathy.

In the moments she spent gazing pensively out the window, the teacher dreamed herself into the world of "ahpray culture." Something like that was what she called high society's habit of going to the very best restaurants after they've been to some cultural event—not to eat or even to dine but rather to enjoy a "sumptuous repast." I had no idea back then what a sump had to do with the most elegant form of taking nourishment. As for cultivated drinking, she told of waiters in tails gliding silently around four-star establishments with a hundred different glasses on hand for a hundred different cocktails, which particularly astonished me, since in Grandfather's tavern we had one kind of glass on offer. But as I listened to Barbu praising the men in evening dress dispensing wine a few splashes at a time into crystal flutes and carefully dabbing up the drip with white linen napkins and at the same time looked into the brandy-ravaged face of my teacher, it was clear to me that something had gone wrong in her life.

That's why the good days in school were outweighed by the bad days when civics was on the agenda. The regime had also started requiring a pledge of allegiance to the fatherland combined with an oath of loyalty to the Workers' Party everyone was talking about back then. Every day the *Kronauburg Courier* reported the founding of new local chapters. In Baia Luna it was especially the Brancusi brothers and the blacksmith Emil Simenov who grabbed the initiative in the effort to persuade the farmers to join the party and welcome collectivization as the wave of the future, which met with little enthusiasm but no open resistance. What could you resist, after all? The puffed-up Brancusis who made propaganda speeches in the village but were otherwise big nobodies? The party big shots way off in the capital who passed laws but didn't check to see if they were being followed in Baia Luna? So people just waited things out in the conviction that if the collectivizers ever showed up someday in the village, they'd show them what was what. And sometimes I got the impression from Barbu, too, that she only grudgingly taught us the precepts of the party. Sometimes it seemed to me she was exaggerating the party blabber so much in order to provoke disgusted boredom in her pupils.

"Maybe she's settling a score," I'd suggested to Fritz. "For something that happened to her in the Paris of the East. A bitter disappointment, possibly, or a cruel injustice."

"Hard to imagine," Fritz had answered. "So you think she forces party slogans down our throats just to make us barf? No, Barbu isn't that crafty."

So the only obvious explanation for Barbu's Socialist blabber was the schnapps that had interfered with the rhythm of her brain waves. Anyway, only someone with brain damage would get the idea of having defenseless schoolchildren copy out the poems of Alfred Margul-Sperber. We must have had to copy the poem "The Party" a dozen times:

> Now look about. Where'er you bend your gaze,
> Appears a new world struggling to be born,
> And what you see now only through the haze,
> Shall be completed long before the morn.

That's the first verse. Printed in black and white on page 5 of the state anthology, right after the portrait of President Gheorghiu-Dej.

Since copy work bored Fritz to tears, he'd gotten into the habit of modifying the text of the poem. One day in class, he slid his notebook over to me. I read:

> Now look about. Where'er you bend your gaze,
> Another party idiot is born,
> And our Miss Barbu's daily drunken daze,
> Shall be in progress long before the morn.

"Are you crazy?" I whispered. "Put that away!" It wasn't the rebellious words that frightened me but the cold-bloodedness with which Fritz had written the rhymes in his good notebook. Any fear of discovery by Barbu, however, proved unfounded. Since she evinced no zeal in checking our copybooks, she seemed never to notice Fritz's insubordinate poetizing. Which only emboldened him. With growing enthusiasm, he inflated his parodies of the party to insane levels of grotesqueness. Until his father Heinrich discovered his copybook, that is. After that, Fritz Hofmann didn't appear in school for two weeks and then showed up with a letter his mother had written excusing him from physical education. Fritz didn't say a word about what had happened at home.

From my visits to the house of my school friend I gathered that despite his very Germanic name, Heinrich Hofmann held no stock in the traditions of his fellow Germans. Among the Saxons whose ancestors had settled in Baia Luna generations ago, the Hofmann family was the only one that didn't live from farming or raising livestock. There weren't even any chickens clucking in their yard.

Hofmann avoided contact with the villagers, and people left him alone. I only saw or heard him once in a while, roaring off to Kronauburg in black leather on a big motorcycle of Italian manufacture that no one else in Baia Luna could have afforded.

During the week Heinrich Hofmann was the proprietor of a photographic studio in the district capital. People used to go to Herr Hofmann when they needed a souvenir picture of their wedding or a photo for their identity cards. But in the fifties he earned his money as an "artistic studio portraitist." That's what Fritz called the occupation that must have earned his father a considerable income. At least to me, the Hofmann family seemed quite well-to-do. Fritz's mother Birta was the only woman in the village who didn't need to heat up a wood-burning stove to cook. She put her pots on electric burners that glowed with heat at the turn of a Bakelite knob and set a teakettle whistling in a matter of seconds. Birta was a woman in her midthirties with short blond locks and steel-blue eyes. When she laughed, white teeth shone between red lips. But I noticed that she was only relaxed and jovial when her husband was in Kronauburg. On the weekends, when Heinrich Hofmann sat in his reading chair beneath the poster with the Virgin of the Torch from New York and next to a bookcase containing many volumes by a certain F. W. Nietzsche, then Birta always made a nervous impression on me. She chewed her fingernails, and her laugh seemed forced. Fritz also fell instantly silent as soon as his father entered the room. Unlike in school, he kept his cheeky remarks to himself and restricted his utterances to a curt yes or no.

I couldn't stand Fritz's father. When I entered the Hofmanns' living room and went to shake his hand politely, as I had been taught to do, he lowered whatever Nietzsche volume he was reading for a moment and gave me a sharp look over the top of his reading glasses. Then he gave a brief twitch of his head like someone shooing off an annoying fly and applied himself to his book again. At some point, I promised myself to ignore Herr Hofmann, and I kept that pledge until just before the fall recess in October 1957.

In the last hour of school Barbu instructed us older students to calculate the increased quotas for the export of fattened hogs to the Soviet Union. As so often before, Fritz and I made a bet on how abstruse we could make our results and still have Barbu nod and check them off. I put down a seven and then fourteen places after the decimal point on my paper. When Fritz upped the stakes to twenty-three, Barbu patted his shoulder. "Accurate, very accurate. Your precision will be a great advantage to you, Fritz. An incalculable advantage."

Fritz looked up at her, nodded in feigned zeal, and said, "Thank you, beautiful Miss Barbulescu."

I was surprised that Fritz didn't even grin. Personally, I couldn't control myself and had to laugh out loud. Everyone in the class knew what the consequences of a laugh like that were. Barbu stared at me and picked up her hazel pointer. She raised her arm and I cringed.

At that moment, something unexpected happened. I only hoped the pointer would miss me, but Fritz jumped to his feet. He grabbed Barbu's arm and held it fast. With a cold stare, he spoke calmly, almost whispering: "Go ahead! Hit my friend if you want my father to make your life a hell."

I didn't understand this brazen threat against the teacher. Although it protected me from her blows, it seemed outrageous to me. Shocked, Barbu turned from me, and her face went white as cheese. Fritz let go of her arm, and for a moment it looked as if she was lowering the pointer. But then she struck. Again and again she rained blows on Fritz, more in desperation than in fury was my impression. Fritz just stood there without uttering a sound. He grinned while she turned red as a turkey. Then the stick broke and, exhausted, she stopped thrashing him.

As I grabbed my satchel and was heading for the door at the end of the hour, she called, "Botev! I'm giving you an hour's detention! Copy work!" She pronounced this harmless punishment not like an order but a request.

I lounged insolently on a bench in the empty classroom and registered the fact that Barbu was more upset than I was. She was pacing up and down by the blackboard while her hands fiddled with a piece of chalk. Finally she said with feigned strictness that it hadn't escaped her I was bored by class and found schoolwork very undemanding of my talents.

"Just tell me what I'm supposed to copy out," I grumbled.

"You don't have to copy out anything."

"So why am I here?"

The teacher swallowed hard, looked at the ceiling, and chewed her lips as though trying to keep an unconsidered word from slipping out.

"Pavel, I thought . . . you and Fritz, you're friends . . . and maybe, I mean, Fritz's father is . . ." She put her hand over her mouth and fell silent.

"You're just afraid of Herr Hofmann!" I said cheekily.

The chalk between her fingers snapped, and white dust trickled onto her blue dress.

"Yes," she replied. "Yes, Botev, your Barbu is afraid."

I bit my tongue. It took me awhile to stammer out in consternation, "But why? 'My father will make your life a hell.' What did Fritz mean by that? I thought he was just trying to be a big shot like always. He's always got such a big mouth, that's just the way he is."

Angela Barbulescu looked out the window. "Fritz will be like his father." She said nothing more, but it was enough to let me know I was just a boy of fifteen, not a man. What separated me from the grown-ups was their knowledge of secrets I didn't have the slightest inkling of.

"Your detention is over," she said suddenly.

I made no move to get up. "Herr Hofmann won't hurt you," I said spontaneously.

She gave a pained laugh. "And you're going to protect me. You mean well, young man. Better go home now."

"No! I won't go until you tell me why you're afraid of Herr Hofmann!" I was surprised by the resolution in my own voice.

"Believe me, Pavel, you're too young to understand."

I bent down and picked up a piece of the broken chalk. "It's true, I'm young. Just like Fritz. But he's old enough to make his teacher go white with fear. Your face was as white as this chalk."

She looked at me. "Not here. Not in the school. Come see me tonight after dark. And don't tell anyone where you're going."


With the excuse that I had to go over to Fritz Hofmann's for something, I left my mother, Aunt Antonia, and Grandfather sitting at the dinner table. In the shadows of twilight I dawdled up the main street of the village. Just before I reached the Hofmanns' front gate I turned around, saw that no one was watching, and quickly ducked down along the massive wall of the church. Behind the church, I hurried off in the opposite direction past Cemetery Hill to the lower part of the village where Barbu lived in a wooden cottage across from the Gypsies.

She opened the door before I even had a chance to knock. I went in and took off my shoes as one does when entering someone else's house. She took my jacket, led me into her overheated parlor, and offered me a seat on her sofa. To my surprise, she wasn't wearing the grubby dark blue dress she'd had on that morning in school. Instead, she'd put on a fresh, airy summer dress with yellow sunflowers on it. The dress smelled like a field of roses, and her parlor made an unexpectedly neat and clean impression. Yet I felt uncomfortable. On the coffee table, a candle was burning on a round brocade doily. Next to it stood a bottle of the plum schnapps we call *zuika* with a cork in it. There was no glass in sight. Next to the bottle, a well-worn book lay open and facedown. To have something to do, I picked it up. It was a book of poems by Mihail Eminescu.

"Mind if I have a look?" I asked to hide my embarrassment.

"You're too young for those poems."

I ignored the remark. Someone had underlined verses in pencil: "And one more thing I ask you, / please grant that I may die / upon that distant shoreline, / red evening in the sky." I caught sight of a few other phrases: "cool evening wind," "trees bare of leaves," "moonlight on gravestones." I quickly clapped Eminescu shut.

Something had slipped out of the book and landed on the table. It was a square photo with a scalloped white border.

"Go ahead and have a look, my boy," said the teacher and she handed me the picture.

"I'm not a boy anymore," I protested. "You were going to tell me about Herr Hofmann now that I'm here."

She picked up the bottle, pulled out the cork, and drank.

"Not a boy anymore! We'll see about that."

I said nothing and stared intently at the photo.

"You can see that I wasn't such a bad catch."

I had to admit to myself that Barbu was right. The photograph showed her with a man who had pomaded and combed back his dark hair in the style of a university student. He wore his sport coat open and his tie was loosened. He had a cigarette in the corner of his mouth and displayed what I thought was a roguish grin for the camera. Maybe even rakish. Between the middle and ring fingers of his left hand he casually swirled a big-bellied glass such as I had never seen in my grandfather's taproom. Mr. Pomade's right arm firmly encircled Miss Barbulescu's shoulder, while only one side of her face was turned toward the camera. Unlike this evening, in the photo she had long blond hair that she had gathered into a ponytail and tied with a scarf. Although her eyes were closed, she was beaming, and her puckered lips were a fraction of a second away from kissing the cheek of the man at her side. If I wasn't mistaken, in this black-and-white photo she was wearing the same sunflower dress in which she now sat next to me on the sofa.

"Taken in the capital?" I asked, studiedly casual.

"Yes, and guess who pressed the shutter release."

"Heinrich Hofmann?"

"Correct, boy. Exactly right. It was Hofmann."

"And the man in the photo? Your fiancé?"

"He had many fiancées." Barbu laughed. It was a laugh that scared me. As the tavern gofer I was familiar with various kinds of laughter. Mischievous chuckles, malicious grins, idiotic guffaws. I knew the shy smile of the embarrassed, the laugh salvos of the jokesters, and the caterwauling of the drunks. I could gauge by their laughter the level of intoxication my grandfather's customers had reached. But I had never heard a laugh like Barbu's before. It alienated and confused me. I longed to get far away from it, back to Grandfather Ilja, back to my mother and to Aunt Antonia. I had just left their supper table, and I'd lied to them.

"He's a sorcerer." Barbu's laughter broke off suddenly. "He can cast spells. He changes wine to water and turns fields into deserts. The photographer Hofmann is his right-hand man. Be careful, boy. Watch out."

Before I could grasp the insanity of her words, she snatched the photograph from me and held it over the burning candle. The flame flickered blue and ate into the paper. When the picture was half consumed, she pulled it away and blew it out with a few strong breaths. Flakes of ash drifted through the room. The man at her side had been incinerated. She handed me what was left of the photograph, her kiss now aimed into nothingness.

"Take it. It's for you."

I resisted. "What would I do with it?"

"Take it! Take it as a reminder that your Barbu was once Angela Maria Barbulescu."

Unwillingly I put the picture in my pocket. She sat down next to me on the sofa and put the volume of Eminescu's poems into her lap. Without opening it, she recited, "A whisper from your lips so warm has veiled my eyes in gentle night. Encircled by your icy arm I die, succumbing to its might."

She drank from the bottle and hitched closer to me. The fragrance of roses was lost in her sharp alcoholic breath. She was drunk. My thoughts froze as she ran her fingers through my hair.

"Are you afraid, boy?"

"No," I whispered.

Suddenly appalled at her own attempted seduction, she withdrew her hand and smoothed out her dress the way she always did when she sat on her desk in school and told us about the Paris of the East. I sprang to my feet.

"Forgive me, Pavel, please, I'm sorry," she begged. I was already in the hall putting on my shoes. "Pavel, things are different than they seem. And believe me, people are, too."

But I was already out the door and heading up the village street. I tripped over my shoelaces, fell, got to my feet, and ran.

Next morning in school everything was as usual. National anthem, blue dress, percentages, party poems. In the weeks that followed, winter was approaching, and school days passed in the same monotony, except that I refused to participate in class at all. Barbu left me alone and avoided calling on me until the day in November that began with my grandfather Ilja and his friend Dimitru trying to capture the beeping of the Sputnik with their tin funnel.

"More *zuika*, Pavel! A bottle of Sylvaner! Pavel, my glass has a hole in it!" The customers would be yelling for me, and I would have to scurry as I did every year on November 6, Ilja's birthday. After school I would shove aside the crates of vegetables, tubs of sugar syrup, and heavy sacks of potatoes, put away the cash register and the decimal scale and iron weights, and drag in the wooden tables and wicker chairs from the storeroom. Once the bottles of plum brandy and wine were lined up on the counter, everyone would trickle in. Hardly a man in Baia Luna would not want to pay his respects to the storekeeper and tavern owner Ilja Botev on his special day. Hans Schneider was never one to refuse a glass of schnapps, nor his fellow Germans Hermann Schuster and Karl Koch either. Alexandru Kiselev and the bilious blacksmith Simenov would stop by for a more or less extended hour. The Hungarian Istvan Kallay would stumble home to his wife in the middle of the night, falling down drunk, and Trojan Petrov would most likely introduce his seventeen-year-old son Petre into the circle of grown-up men for the first time. Of course the hothead Brancusis would also put in an appearance, and it goes without saying that Dimitru the Gypsy would be there, too. The only uncertainty was whether the ancient priest Johannes Baptiste at almost ninety would find his way to the tavern again this year.

As I gave Grandfather his box of cigars wrapped in red paper that morning, the thought went through my head that it was going to be a long day. While Granddad was enjoying his Cuban, my eye fell on the clock. I had to go to school. "You haven't eaten anything yet!" my mother called after me as I slung my schoolbag halfheartedly over my shoulder and left the house. I wished the hours on the hard wooden school bench were already over. Eighth grade—my last—seemed like it was dragging along so doggedly it would never end. One more long winter, one more spring, then I would finally have sat out the boredom of school. As I ambled down the village street on that morning of November 6, 1957, I had not the faintest foreboding that when the school bell rang, it would ring in my last day of school.

Angela Barbulescu showed up promptly at eight. She was transformed. She wasn't staring from reddened eyes. Her gaze was open and clear, just as it had been when I spied her sitting at her kitchen table in the wee hours and writing something. She was holding a gray package under her arm. I already knew what was in it, but I didn't know that its contents would derail my own life.

The previous day, in a pouring rain, a messenger had arrived in Baia Luna. He came into our store, identified himself as a courier from the district administration, and asked after the teacher Barbulescu. Grandfather offered the man an umbrella, which he gratefully accepted.

"Must be something important in that package," Granddad opined, giving the messenger an opening to let off some steam.

"This is my last delivery, thank God! Three hundred village schools in two weeks. My bones are weary, let me tell you. My sacroiliac is killing me. And this shitty weather. Two whole hours it took me to get to this godforsaken hole. My diesel got stuck in the mud three times. Three times! They whine and complain in the office when I don't keep to my schedule, but no one tells them that the roads up here are a joke. Potholes like bomb craters."

I was listening with only half an ear when the courier started talking about a new party secretary in Kronauburg, a capable man with a bright future whose portrait was to be hung in all the schools of the district. I think that afternoon was the first time I heard the name Stefan Stephanescu. At any rate, the courier intimated that the new secretary wasn't one of your puffed-up party hacks and bullshit artists, know-it-alls without a clue.

Barbu dispensed with the national anthem. Instead, she unwrapped the gray package and took out a framed photograph. Although there were boys who were better than me with tools, I was the one she chose to put a nail in the wall and hang it up immediately to the right of the energetic visage of President Gheorghiu-Dej, whom the men of Baia Luna referred to respectfully, with a hand discreetly covering their mouth, as "Little Stalin." Sullenly, I walked to the front of the classroom and climbed onto a chair. Restlessness spread through the class. Angela Barbulescu handed me a hammer and the portrait in its matte gold frame. I bent down to take the photograph from her. The same fragrance of roses reached my nostrils as on the terrible evening on the sofa in her parlor. She whispered something to me. It took me a moment to grasp the force of her words. Just two short sentences. I heard them distinctly despite the jumble of voices in the classroom. But there was a time lag as their meaning sank in. I held the picture up to see where I should place the nail. Then I recognized the man I was about to nail to the wall.

"Send this man straight to hell! Exterminate him!"

The hammer slipped from my hand and banged my toe. The sharp pain made me wince. I fell off the chair. The classroom roared with glee.

*Send this man straight to hell! Exterminate him!*

I knew the person in the picture. I had seen the man looking at me with a winning smile once before. Only now his hair wasn't shiny with pomade, and his tie was properly tightened. Along the bottom edge of the picture was the saying CHILDREN ARE OUR FUTURE. It was the man with many fiancées. The man for whom Barbu had puckered her lips in happier days. The man she had burned out of the photo whose surviving half was in my room, stuck between the pages of *Das Kapital* by Karl Marx.

"Quiet! Be quiet!" Barbu shouted, breaking the spell that had shocked and paralyzed me. "For this masterful portrait we are indebted to the eye of a photographer who has done so much to advance the art of making pictures with light. As you all know, his son Fritz will soon have to find his own way into the world of adulthood, and perhaps one day he will follow in his father's footsteps."

Everyone's eyes flew to Fritz Hofmann. Slowly he leaned back in his chair and pretended he was about to yawn. With the exclamation "Bravo, bravo, bravo!" he clapped his hands. Barbu ignored the provocation and explained that the person in the picture was the new party secretary of Kronauburg, Dr. Stefan Stephanescu, honors graduate of the university in the capital and a specialist in economic administration.

"But remember: not everything that's framed and glitters is gold." The class grew quiet. "To distinguish the genuine from the fake," she continued, "requires the greatest wisdom of heart and brain. Perhaps someday Dr. Stephanescu will meet a person who's up to the job."

"Amen!" called Fritz.

I slunk back to my seat with a blue and swollen toe. I was surprised to discover that my fright was fading, and in its place I felt a previously unknown clarity. *Exterminate this man!* That demand had knocked my legs out from under me, but I was on my feet again, calm and collected. *Send him straight to hell!* Only a crazy person, a drunk who had drowned her mind in *zuika,* could have whispered such a mad assignment into the ear of a fifteen-year-old, into my ear. Me, Pavel Botev? I'm supposed to exterminate this Dr. Stephanescu? What a joke! A man I don't even know, who looks anything but unpleasant in his photos. No. I wasn't about to let a lunatic recruit me for some dirty business. Never.

"Barbu is nuts. Stephanescu is a good guy, a close friend of my father's."

Fritz's words sounded like a casual remark, but I pricked up my ears. Heinrich Hofmann! My silent misgivings about Fritz's father's questionable pretentions to artistry immediately found new and bitter nourishment. My mistrust grew to a dark suspicion but was still obscure, since except for a large dose of personal dislike I found no basis for it whatsoever. Only one thing was clear: Barbu and Stephanescu had a common acquaintance. But "acquaintance" was much too weak a word. Fritz's father Heinrich must be a friend of this doctor, who in his turn had been my teacher's lover in earlier years. Something must have happened between the two of them, something unpleasant, malign even, or why would Barbu reduce to ashes the face of a man she had once kissed? And so what if Barbu still had a score to settle with this guy? That was her business! But what did Herr Hofmann have to do with it? He'd taken Stephanescu's picture at least twice, once when he was a student and now again as the Kronauburg party secretary. Hofmann frequented higher circles. He had influence. He exercised power. And with that power he had it in for Barbu. Before fall vacation, Fritz had threatened that his father would make her life a hell. The teacher's face had blanched deathly white. She was afraid. But why? I was wider awake than ever before, burning with curiosity.

Suddenly it made sense to me that Fritz had been explaining his lack of interest in school by saying that his days in Baia Luna were numbered. "Father's looking for a house in Kronauburg, and once he's found a suitable piece of real estate we're out of this hick town." I couldn't believe Fritz was serious. The very thought of voluntarily moving away would never have occurred to Germans like the Schusters or the Schneiders. But once the picture of Herr Hofmann's friend Stephanescu was hanging on our classroom wall, I realized that Fritz had been telling the truth. Soon he would turn his back on Baia Luna. I looked over at him. As always, he was sprawled on the school bench—and suddenly for me he was no longer a friend but a stranger—looking cool and unapproachable. But the coldness of alienation didn't just emanate from Fritz. The chasm separating us yawned within me, as if it had always been there and only now became visible.

"Reader, page eleven," announced Barbu. "The patriotic poem by Hans Bohn. Julia, please begin!"

Julia Simenov, top student in the class, stood up and recited in a clear voice,

> *"I love the land of the Carpathian forests,*
> *So rich in natural beauty and so vast,*
> *The land of new construction and of heroes,*
> *Where each new day is better than the last."*

We were told to get out our notebooks. While everyone except Fritz and me was writing down the words of the patriotic poem, Barbu leaned against the wall at the back of the classroom. She tugged at her blue dress and rubbed her chin while I chewed on my pencil. I didn't notice her advancing until she had almost reached us. She walked up to Fritz. She ran her hand over his head. It seemed to me a dreamy, strangely absentminded, and almost involuntary gesture. I heard her say, "Tell your father it's over. Barbu isn't afraid anymore."

Fritz looked her right in the eye. Mockingly. Then he rose from his seat and walked up to the blackboard cool as a cucumber. He picked up a piece of chalk and wrote,

> *When Barbu whispers in my ear,*
> *my thing gets hard and out to here.*

I felt hot and cold all over. Although shocked by Fritz's impudence, I was impressed by his daring. I was sure the older kids would burst out laughing. But it stayed quiet. Someone in the first row dropped a pencil. Barbu walked quite slowly up to the front. In a second she would pick up her stick and start whipping him and screeching, striking again and again. And Fritz wouldn't bat an eye. He would grin like always when Barbu cut him into kindling, screamed herself into a fury, and finally collapsed in exhaustion. But Barbu didn't strike. She wiped the blackboard clean with a rag and then blew her nose into it and rubbed her eyes. The chalk dust mixed with her tears and smeared her face.

"You can go home now," she said softly.

Her voice sounded infinitely weary. But everyone stayed seated. Only Fritz hastily packed up his schoolbag and disappeared. Then the bell rang. Angela Barbulescu took Stephanescu's picture down from the wall and shuffled out of the classroom in her rubber boots.

# Chapter Two

●

## HONEST GYPSIES, PIOUS SAXONS,

## AND THE STUDIES OF THE BLACK PHILOSOPHER

*Send this man straight to hell! Exterminate him!* Whatever Barbu had meant, it exceeded my powers of imagination. Go to hell! Devil take you! How often I had heard those curses in the barroom. Even Father Johannes Baptiste wasn't any too choosy when thundering imprecations against the enemies of the faith from the pulpit. But exterminate someone? Forestall the Last Judgment? Never!

Exterminate! What did that mean anyway? You exterminated weeds, annoying insects, and rats when they got to be a plague. And enemies, of course, but only in war or in self-defense and only if you were a hero. Father Johannes Baptiste warned us repeatedly in his sermons to beware of all exterminators whose titles ended in "-ist." The Hitlerists exterminated the Jews, the fascists murdered the Socialists, the Stalinists sent their enemies to die like dogs in Siberia, and even the capitalists were exterminators who drove their competition into financial ruin and plunged working families into poverty and misery.

But not in Baia Luna. No one here to my knowledge had exterminated anyone else, and nobody had ever been exterminated. Sure, the Brancusi brothers were Communists and always talked big about how they were going to wipe out the moneybag landowners and the parasite bourgeoisie. That did sound like extermination. But Liviu, Roman, and Nico Brancusi were basically not such bad guys. I couldn't imagine they would ever really kill anyone.

Of course from time to time, there were nasty incidents in the village. Occasional arguments flared up, heated words that sometimes ended in fistfights. But what got people worked up one day was usually settled by a handshake on the next or forgotten by the day after that. I was never aware of any signs of deep malignity or irreconcilable enmity in the village. To my fifteen-year-old self, Baia Luna seemed a peaceful place where the indigenous population lived with the Hungarians and Saxons who had settled here centuries ago in an unspoken compact not to make life difficult for one another.

The Gypsies held to that as well. When people referred to them, they always called them the Blacks, as was customary in Transmontania, even though among the Gypsies in our village were a couple of flaxen-haired, blue-eyed children who didn't fit the stereotype at all. The Gypsies didn't call us the Whites in return; they referred to us as *gaje,* which means "strangers" but also "fools" or "dummkopfs."

Nevertheless, we *gaje* considered the Blacks in Baia Luna to be poor but honest folk. They belonged to the Gabor tribe and their ancestors had lived in Hungary. The men wore black trousers, black jackets, and wide-brimmed black hats. The women dressed in red skirts and braided gold coins and colorful ribbons into their hair. When I was little, I thought the women simply chose colors they liked, but then I asked Buba Gabor during recess if they meant anything. Buba was pretty as a picture and the only Gypsy girl in the village who through her own stubbornness and with the encouragement of her uncle Dimitru obtained her family's permission to attend school at least on uneven days, Monday, Wednesday, and Friday. She told me that among her people, you could tell from the color of the ribbons if a girl was single, already engaged, or married. I blushed and asked what her own status was in this regard. Buba answered pertly that she wasn't allowed to tell that to a *gajo* like me. Then she brushed a black lock out of her eyes and warbled sweetly, "Only a man with beautiful hands can win me." Whereupon I stuck my hands into my pockets quick as a flash, who knows why. Buba laughed and ran off.

On summer days, the Gabors strolled up and down the village street or sat in front of their houses playing cards and smoking unfiltered Carpatis. Their proudest possessions were their numerous children and two dozen powerful Percherons they pastured at the edge of the village. In October they went to the horse market in Bistrita where they used the meeting with other tribes to matchmake for their sons and daughters and change the color of their ribbons. When the Gabors returned to Baia Luna, they celebrated noisy weddings for days on end before returning to their bleak everyday existence. In the village the Blacks' idleness was regarded with suspicion but accepted without open hostility, even by the Germans, whose industrious character included deep contempt for any kind of idleness.

The fact that the hearts of the Saxons weren't paralyzed by zealous piety was due to the influence of Pater Johannes. I knew only the vague outlines of his story. What was certain was that in 1935, two years after the Hitlerists had seized power in Germany, the abbot of the Benedictine monastery in Melk had dispatched Baptiste from the Danube into the mountains of Transmontania. The order probably hoped to get rid of Brother Johannes in his old age, since he was already approaching seventy back then.

Once Johannes Baptiste had moved into the empty rectory in Baia Luna with wagonfuls of theological books and philosophical writings, the most fantastic rumors began circulating in the village, spread mainly by the sacristan Julius Knaup, the overweight Kora Konstantin, and her equally fat mother Donata. People said Johannes Baptiste had fathered a bastard child with a Viennese hooker. It was also rumored that despite tortures of self-castigation he had been unable to keep his hands off the boy sopranos in the monastery choir. Even worse for the Catholics was the accusation that Baptiste had been banished to Baia Luna for delivering heretical sermons abusing the Holy See in Rome and even Pope Pius himself.

These poisonous rumors must have left my grandfather no peace. On a Sunday in the autumn of 1935 he screwed up his courage and asked the priest over a Sunday-morning glass of wine in the tavern, "Reverend, are the things people say about you true?"

Johannes Baptiste's answer would enter the annals of the village as "the tavern sermon."

First Pater Johannes burst out laughing, slapped his thigh, and claimed he hadn't created just *one* bastard with the strength of his loins but dozens of them. Then, however, the pater turned very serious.

"Yes," he said to the assembled men, "they sent me to you in the mountains because I followed my conscience and not my vows to the order and the Holy Father in Rome."

Then Pater Johannes told about a contractual agreement called a concordat between the Vatican and the German Reich, whose chancellor was about to plunge the world into a yawning abyss. The evil handwriting was long since on the wall, legible for everyone, but his Austrian homeland had deteriorated into a land of the blind. His countrymen were bedazzled by their pride in knowing that pure Aryan blood flowed in their veins, drunk on the idea of being part of the Germans' Thousand-Year Reich. Instead of resisting this madness of the blood with all the power of papal authority, the Vatican was eating humble pie before the German gangsters and courting the goodwill of the Führer so he would treat the church kindly.

"But I'm telling you, the Lord God didn't permit his Son to be nailed on the cross so that something like this could happen. Not for a church that's asking the devil to be nice to the clergy and leave its priests alone. If you do business with Satan, you've already got one foot in hell. Just like the people here in the village who sit in front of their radios in the evening listening to that loudmouth from Berlin promise to bring them home to the Reich."

Grandfather told me the young Saxons Karl Koch, Anton Zikeli, and Schneiders' Hans got all hot under the collar when he said that, smashed their glasses against the wall, and came that close to laying hands on the priest. Which they would all come to bitterly regret later, after the war. Back then, however, the ethnic Germans accused Pater Johannes of getting mixed up in worldly affairs instead of looking after people's souls as a priest should. An accusation Johannes Baptiste let go unanswered.

"Either you're a Catholic or a Hitlerist! They're mutually exclusive. Heaven or hell, it's your choice! Either we love our neighbors as ourselves, or we destroy those we've declared to be our enemies. And mark my words, the Hitlerists are going to be the worst destroyers that evil has ever brought forth. First the Germans will kill the Jews, then the Gypsies, and then anyone else who isn't like them. The Catholics won't cry out in protest when the killing begins. They'll keep going to Mass on Sunday, crossing themselves, and singing 'Praise the Lord.' But not me. I'll keep reminding everyone that our Lord Jesus Christ himself was a Jew. If his people had not taken on the heavy burden of nailing him to the cross, how could he have redeemed us? Without Golgotha, no Ascension. History will show if I'm right or wrong. And believe me, I pray every day that the good Lord will make me wrong. Even if I have to pay for my disobedience toward the Holy Father in Rome with eternal damnation."

After these words, my grandfather Ilja never again doubted the honesty of the man of God. Anybody who raised his voice against the Benedictine was banned from Ilja's tavern on the spot. And that's how Johannes Baptiste became the most respected priest who ever preached from the pulpit in Baia Luna, even though in my youth he had already lost a lot of his Bible knowledge. Unforgotten among the congregation was the previous year's Christmas sermon in which he placed Judas among the three Wise Men from the East and sent him hurrying to Bethlehem where the repentant traitor paid back the thirty pieces of silver with interest.

The Gypsies loved their Papa Baptiste. It was thanks to him they hadn't been driven out of Baia Luna. Dimitru's people turned up in the village late in the summer of 1935, just when the rumors about Pater Johannes were particularly rank. Their *bulibasha,* Dimitru's father Laszlo, had asked the village council to permit his tribe to stay. As their leader, he proposed that they could move into a location below the village, on the banks of the Tirnava, where a few tumbledown stalls had fallen prey to high water in earlier years. As compensation for a residency permit the Gypsy men offered to help the farmers with their harvest in the fall. In addition, they knew everything about horses of all breeds. And last but not least, he, Bulibasha Laszlo Carolea Gabor, personally guaranteed that no one from his family had ever been accused of burglary or been taken to police custody for unjustified inebriation. The village council, consisting of four indigenous, four Hungarians, and four Saxons, considered the proposition briefly behind closed doors. Then they informed Laszlo that the Gypsies had until Sunday to make themselves scarce.

As the men, women, and children of Baia Luna set off for church on Sunday, the Gypsies were still there. Johannes Baptiste celebrated Mass as usual. From Grandfather I know that the Gospel reading for that Sunday was the parable of the miracle of the loaves and fishes and the feeding of the five thousand, but the priest didn't stick to that. He read from the Christmas story. Four months early. Only he didn't announce the good tidings of the birth of the Lord but the less-good tidings about the pregnant Mary and Joseph, the father of her child, desperately looking for someplace to stay. The scandal came after Johannes Baptiste had consecrated the bread and wine for the Eucharist. The faithful rose and moved forward toward the communion rail. They knelt and stuck out their tongues but waited in vain for the host. Baptiste refused them the Body of the Lord. Instead, he splashed the congregation with a cascade of holy water while crying out, "And Jesus said, 'Inasmuch as ye have done it unto one of the least of these my brethren, ye have done it unto me.' And now go to the Gypsies and think about that commandment."

Even now my grandfather couldn't suppress an impish smile when he related what happened then. Fat Donata collapsed at the altar in a faint with her yammering daughter Kora trying in vain to hold her up. Some men had their noses so put out of joint by the priest that they stormed out of the church and on the spot composed a fiery letter of protest to the bishop of Kronauburg. The indignant postman Adamski even called for a schism and demanded that the whole congregation join the Protestants. Then Hermann Schuster emerged from among his outraged fellows. He called for quiet, and since he was and still is a respected person in the village, the crowd in fact calmed down after some grumbling.

"We have to do what our priest has ordered us to do. We must bear our cross just as the Redeemer had to bear his." No one dared to contradict Schuster's words. Then Grandfather Ilja's young wife Agneta emerged from the door of the family's shop. In her hands she held a golden-brown Bundt cake she had baked to have with coffee that afternoon. She strode right through the crowd and straight as an arrow to the lower end of town where the Gypsies were encamped. Ilja followed her. Hermann Schuster and his wife Erika as well as a dozen other inhabitants of Baia Luna joined them, while it suddenly occurred to others that they had a sick cow, or the women said the Sunday roast had to come out of the oven right that minute.

When Laszlo Carolea Gabor saw the little troop approaching, he walked slowly out to meet them. Agneta presented him with the cake. A big tear rolled down the *bulibasha*'s cheek and disappeared into his huge mustache. Then he started to weep uncontrollably. His family at first stood silently around the cake until the men began to cry, too, then the women, and finally the children. All together they spilled veritable torrents of snot and water so that their wails of joy reached the other end of the village. Then Laszlo Gabor snapped his fingers, and the river of tears subsided.

"Slaughter three sheep and prepare a feast!" he ordered. Immediately, the whole clan broke out in shouts of joy, and the men began whetting their knives. The Gypsies brought out their cymbals, fiddles, and drums and marched through the village making an earsplitting racket. Despite their parents' strict prohibitions, the schoolchildren were the first to start following them, then came the first hesitant adults, until finally both Hungarians and Saxons had joined the column. At last, the sole concern of every household was not to be the only villager to miss this extraordinary event.

By early afternoon everyone was dancing on the village square. Johannes Baptiste strolled around, his face beaming with delight and his hand stretched out in benediction. He contributed a cask of Lake Kaltern red from the rectory cellar and twenty bottles of fruit brandy he had brought with him from Austria on his diaspora. Only the Konstantin family cowered behind their curtains and prayed the rosary until they were so hoarse they couldn't anymore.

By midnight, when the last inhabitants were wending their way home unsteady in step but steadfast in faith and old Adamski shouted at the top of his voice that the Protestants could just piss off, everyone in Baia Luna thought it was the best party the village had ever had. The Gypsies could stay.

To make sure the miraculous feast would never grow pale even in the most distant chambers of memory, Pater Johannes declared an annual and onerous day of penance for the preventive purification of stubborn hearts. Moreover, he had them build a wooden chapel on the Mondberg to be the new home for the Virgin of Eternal Consolation whose statue had stood in the Baia Luna church for generations. From then on, the Mother of God would not just remind us of the victory of Christendom over the Mussulmen but also preserve us from coldness of spirit. And nothing seemed to the priest better suited to that purpose than a penitential hike into the mountains in the frosty midst of December, on the twenty-fourth, the day of Mary's desperate search for shelter for her unborn child.

The reason I never knew my grandmother Agneta was a blow of fate that struck my grandfather in the winter of '35. A week before Christmas he hitched up his nag and drove to Kronauburg with Agneta and the two children: my aunt Antonia and my father-to-be Nicolai. While Ilja restocked his inventory, Agneta and the children visited some distant relatives. Since the early dusk made a return trip on the same day difficult and, in addition, the first snow began to fall, they decided to spend the night in town and leave for Baia Luna early the next morning.

By noon the next day their heavily loaded wagon had already reached Apoldasch. Following the road along the Tirnava upstream, the weary horse would have them home in an hour.

That's exactly what the Gypsy Laszlo and his son Dimitru also were thinking. As luck would have it, they also had business in Kronauburg. They had ordered five hundred medicine bottles with corks from György the druggist. Not until two decades later did I learn the purpose of those mysterious brown bottles. But I don't want to get ahead of myself. At any rate, Laszlo and Dimitru had packed their horses with the cases full of empty bottles and also started out for Baia Luna. Beyond Apoldasch they caught up with Grandfather's family, and they all decided to travel the rest of the way together.

As far as I know, the storm came from the southwest, out of the Fagaras Mountains. It was upon them in a matter of minutes, first as thick gray clouds, then high winds, and finally as a blizzard. Laszlo and Dimitru sprang from their horses. The two Percherons immediately lay down on their sides with their backs to the wind. Grandmother Agneta, my twelve-year-old father-to-be, and his six-year-old sister crept under their wool blankets in the back of the wagon while Granddad tried to quiet the skittish horse. Panicked, the animal reared up and thrashed his front hooves against the oncoming storm. Grandfather was just calling for help from the two Gypsies when the nag took off into the gray wall of snow and straight into the icy river. At the last minute, Nicolai succeeded in jumping out of the swaying wagon. Laszlo rushed toward the vehicle, but before he could get hold of Agneta and little Antonia, the iron-clad wagon wheel struck his forehead so hard that blood spurted from his mouth and nose and he fell into the snow as if struck by lightning. Without a moment's hesitation both Grandfather and Dimitru jumped into the river. Blinded by the wind-whipped snow, they fought their way through the icy chest-deep water toward the screams of Agneta and Antonia. While the nag thrashed around to keep from drowning and just got more and more entangled in the harness, Grandmother held on to the wooden stanchions of the wagon for dear life with one hand and pressed Antonia to her with the other.

When Grandfather and Dimitru finally reached them through the biting cold, Antonia hung stiff and blue from her mother's arm. The men expended their last bit of strength and pulled the two of them to the bank. Dimitru immediately tore Antonia's wet clothes from her body and wrapped her in a horse blanket. "Rub, rub!" he shouted to Nicolai. "Rub your sister warm or she'll die!" Then Dimitru's eyes fell on his father. Laszlo lay dead in the snow, a blood-red wreath spreading around his head.

"God give me a long life to mourn you," Dimitru cried out and turned to Ilja and Nicolai. "Take the horses and get mother and daughter into bed at once!" He clapped his hands, and the Percherons got to their feet. "Ilja, take your daughter, and you, Nicolai, take your mother. Mount and ride home! I'll come on foot."

"No," Ilja protested. "We're not leaving you and your father here alone."

Dimitru didn't listen. Instead, he raged and howled the soul out of his body, uttering curses so foul that the shivering Agneta blushed red and was infused with a moment of warmth. "Leave me be!" the Gypsy screamed and clapped the horses' flanks with the flat of his hand, sending them trotting off. Dimitru struggled out of his stiff frozen coat and took off his shoes and his pants. Then he started running. "A Gypsy is tough!" he screamed into the storm. "And I'm a Gypsy. A Gypsy! I'll live forever! Live to mourn my father forever. Father, dear Father!" Then his voice was swallowed by the storm.

Thanks to the endurance of the Percherons, Grandfather's family arrived safely in the village an hour later. Neighbors hurried over to wrap the half-frozen family in thick feather comforters and brew gallons of peppermint tea.

Amazingly it was little Antonia who was up and about first. By the next morning she was completely recovered, and Ilja, too, aside from a powerful head cold, seemed to have survived unscathed. But his wife was so thoroughly chilled that she couldn't warm up despite a double goose-down comforter. For three days her body was shaken by frightening chills so that it was all Grandfather could do to get a spoonful of hot elderberry juice into her mouth. Around the clock, Ilja and Nicolai watched by Agneta's bedside, rubbing her hands to get them warm and laying hot towels on her forehead.

After a while, Grandmother seemed to get better. She even sat up a bit and was able to lift a cup of honey-sweetened milk to her mouth with her own hand. But then the cold in her body turned to heat. Agneta was burning up, and the mercury in the fever thermometer rose above one hundred four degrees. She groaned, was racked with chest pains, and could hardly breathe. She coughed and vomited. When they finally called Dr. Bogdan from Apoldasch, he diagnosed acute pneumonia. The only hope for Agneta was a new drug called penicillin. He didn't have any himself, but some could almost surely be obtained from György the druggist in Kronauburg. Hermann Schuster leaped into the saddle. When he returned ten hours later with the promised tablets, my grandma had just died in Granddad Ilja's arms.

Foresters found Dimitru in Apoldasch at the place where the road to the Schweisch Valley and Kronauburg forks off. In the blizzard he had run in the wrong direction, gone in a circle several times, and finally completely lost his orientation in the darkness of the night. The foresters wrapped his frozen body in sheepskins and took him to the Apoldasch forge where the young blacksmith Emil Simenov was working at the time, before getting married and taking over the smithy in Baia Luna. The grumpy Simenov was known to be no great friend of the Gypsies'. But actually, he was no great friend of anybody's. Whenever the men in Grandfather's tavern reproached the gruff fellow for his sour mood and lack of human kindness, Simenov would always answer, "And who was it who saved the Black blabbermouth in '35? You or me? He was a block of ice when they carried him into my forge, and if I hadn't put Dimitru Carolea Gabor next to the fire he never would have thawed out. And who loaned the Black a warm shirt, overalls, and hobnail boots and never got them back? Me or you? With my own hands I schlepped that miserable weakling back to Baia Luna, him and his idiotic little bottles. Those Blacks are nothing but trouble."

When Emil Simenov saw the three Brancusi brothers nodding in agreement, he cooled off and shut up again.

Johannes Baptiste scheduled the joint burial of my grandmother Agneta and Dimitru's father Laszlo for the forenoon of December 22. As far back as anyone can remember, that burial in the year 1935 was the biggest in the history of the village. Dozens of delegations arrived from Bessarabia and the Bukovina, from the Banat and Walachia, from Dobruja and even the distant Budapest to pay their last respects.

At the wake following the interment there were so many mourners to serve that the Gabor tribe ran up debts for years to come and had to sell all their gold jewelry and horses. No one in Baia Luna would fail to be at the cemetery, and the brass band from Apoldasch played so soulfully that the mourners' breath stood still and their tears froze to icy pearls. The villagers certainly felt sympathy for Laszlo the Gypsy, but more for my grandfather and the half orphans Antonia and Nicolai. In acknowledgment of their part in the death of the young mother, even the wholesaler Hossu brothers from Kronauburg showed up. They promised Grandfather to replace the wares swept away by the Tirnava for free, and they kept their word.

On the day before the double burial, Johannes Baptiste had seen to it that there wouldn't be a scandal. While inspecting Cemetery Hill he saw that the hired grave diggers had already finished a hole in the ground. Then he heard quiet voices coming from beyond the cemetery wall. The organist Marku Konstantin and the sacristan Knaup were sinking a hole in the frozen ground with pickaxes and shovels while Konstantin's sister-in-law Kora looked on.

"What's the meaning of this?" asked the priest.

"This hole's for the Gypsy," answered Julius Knaup. "He's not baptized."

The Benedictine flushed with righteous anger. Not even for a second had it ever occurred to Father Johannes to wonder whether Laszlo Gabor had a baptismal certificate. Nor would the thought ever have crossed his mind to scrape a hole for the upright Gypsy in unconsecrated ground.

"You have five minutes," he thundered, "exactly five minutes. If not, I'm going to pray every morning, noon, and night that your dirty souls will be crawling through the filth of hell to the end of time."

Two minutes later, as Grandfather loved to relate with a grin, the hole was filled.

As far as I know, Laszlo Carolea was the first of the Gabor tribe whose mortal remains found their rest in consecrated ground. Full of gratitude, the Gypsies went en masse to the priest's house after the burial of their *bulibasha* and insisted that each one get to kiss the blessed hand of the man of God. Then, led by Dimitru, they asked to receive the sacrament of baptism, and their request was granted. Without protest, Dimitru allowed Pater Johannes, with both hands, to push his bushy head three times—in the name of the Father, the Son, and the Holy Ghost—into the holy water of the baptismal font, which gave Kora Konstantin another chance to be indignant to the marrow.

Once the Gypsies had celebrated their new role as children of God for three days, the church of Baia Luna would almost burst at the seams on Sundays. A half hour before the bells tolled, the Gabors were already waiting in front of the entrance, intent on receiving the Body of Christ. In the course of time, however, their zeal for the sacred magic cooled rapidly. Once they discovered that, despite incense, holy water, and the blessing of the priest, their everyday cares continued undiminished, the rituals of the Mass began to bore them.

Except for Dimitru.

I cannot remember ever not seeing him in church on Sunday except in the summer when opaque business dealings forced him to travel. Whenever Johannes Baptiste ascended to his pulpit, Dimitru sat in the front pew next to his friend Ilja with his mouth agape. I watched Dimitru practically ingesting every word that fell from the pulpit, unlike Grandfather, who sometimes nodded off during the sermon.

With the tragedy at the river, a friendship had developed between the two men, a spiritual fraternity which—if I may be allowed to anticipate—would survive the storms of time, even if Grandfather didn't know very much about Dimitru's life.

"By the way, can you swim?" he had asked the Gypsy years after they had jumped into the icy Tirnava together.

"I should hope so," Dimitru answered. "I was already a fish in my mother's belly." Yet everyone in the village knew that the scaredy-cat Dimitru even feared splashing some puddle water into his shoe when it rained.

Grandfather was of the opinion that Dimitru had developed a serious streak while mourning the death of his father, while I thought his flightiness prevented it from being very well grounded. Nevertheless, baptism must have activated a real passionate impulse to pursue life's most basic questions.

And certainly the paternalistic friendship of Johannes Baptiste was also a contributing factor. The Benedictine made the books he had brought with him from Austria to Baia Luna available to all in a kind of public library in the rectory, which was almost never used by the villagers. And if anyone ever did use it, they didn't go to the priest to ask for permission but to Dimitru, who in the course of two decades advanced to the post of Lord of the Library.

In summer you could see him lying on the green grass of the rectory garden with his nose in a book; in winter a light burned in the library even at night because Dimitru was pursuing his studies by the shine of a kerosene lamp. To make it easier for him to read, Johannes Baptiste had had an old red divan and a warm featherbed moved to the library.

When the men of Baia Luna called him the Black philosopher, it might have sounded like an expression of respect but was closer to mockery. That didn't bother Dimitru in the slightest. He served himself generous portions from the pots of human knowledge, sampled here, snacked there, and in the end mixed it all together as he saw fit. He cared nothing for logical coherence. "Either/or" didn't count for much with him; he preferred "both/and." Whenever he got hopelessly tangled up in logical inconsistencies, he would cut the Gordian knot of his contradictions the very next day from some new vantage point. Something that was true today could be false tomorrow and vice versa. Dimitru learned by heart the most important sayings of the great scholars without caring a fig about the correct sequence of thinkers and their thoughts. It was Liviu Brancusi who dubbed him "the blabbermouth" after Pater Johannes had taught Dimitru a few scraps of Latin. Grandfather Ilja had advised his friend not to throw around such difficult terms so much but just slip one in from time to time to give people the impression they were dealing with an educated man. Dimitru took the advice to heart but continued to confusticate (one of his favorite words) often.

When Grandfather wanted to chat with Dimitru undisturbed, he visited his friend in the library. When I was little, he would sometimes take me along, but then he stopped because the smell of musty paper made me sick. In the fall of 1957, when I was fifteen, I often sought refuge in the library, not to read as my mother Kathalina thought but to escape chores at home. I took into account that Dimitru would talk my ear off.

Since Johannes Baptiste gave the Gypsy a free hand in the library, Dimitru had arranged the books according to his own system. "There's got to be order, Pavel, or it'll start to look like a Gypsy camp in Moldavia." He was happy to tell me that his rise to head librarian had begun with unpacking the books from their crates and putting them on the shelves. "It was a challenge, Pavel." Even twenty years later he groaned at the thought. "A real challenge for any intelligent person. First I arranged the books by size, from thick folios to slim pamphlets on self-improvement, then according to the color of their spines, from dark to light. Then by their year of publication. That number is up front on the first pages, you see. Now the books are all standing as they should be: alphabetically from Augustine to Zola. Emilio Zola—you must have heard of him in school?"

"No."

"What do you actually learn from Miss Barbulescu? Zola! That's literature. Not that junk by party hacks that's in your readers. That's trash. How can I send my Buba to school with a clear conscience? By the way, Zola wrote a book about Lourdes. Lourdes—at least you know what that is?"

"Never heard of it."

"Never heard of it! Even though you *gaje* go on penitential pilgrimages to the Virgin of Eternal Consolation. You *gaje* are funny people, dumbskies. Why don't you have the Mother of God in your hearts? Then you could spare yourselves the hike. Like in Lourdes. They don't pray to a wooden statue. Mary the Mother of God appeared there in the flesh. In the flesh, Pavel! You know what that means? Think that over for a while instead of filling glasses with schnapps every night. Don't misunderstand me: I've got nothing against *zuika* and nothing against the honest calling of tavern keeper, but you? You were meant for something higher. What am I saying—you have a calling!"

Dimitru got on my nerves. His flattery was embarrassing. I should have left. But I didn't and asked instead, "Mary appeared in the flesh? How's that possible?"

"See, I knew you were a smart boy. How can Mary, who has shuffled off this mortal coil, still appear in the flesh? That's the question! You just have to turn it around with dialectical logic, understand? Then the question becomes: Where does someone have to rise up to in order to return to earth after death and show themselves to people?"

I felt sorry for the Gypsy. How could anyone think such screwy thoughts? "I don't understand what you're getting at, Dimitru. Where's the problem?"

"You're still young, Pavel. But I'm tortured by this question. And I'll tell you why and since when. I miss my father Laszlo of blessed memory. Since the moment I closed the lid of his coffin, there's only one thing I want to know: how can a person get to heaven? I mean, not just your soul but your body, too. The resurrection of the flesh. I mean the whole person."

"It's not possible, Dimitru. If I understand Christian teaching, up to now only Jesus has succeeded in the resurrection of the flesh."

"But it also worked with Jesus's Mother. Mary was also taken up into heaven body and soul. Pope Pius himself made the announcement. How did the Assumption work, exactly? Body and soul? What happened to them? When I know that, Pavel, I'll know everything."

"Why don't you ask Johannes Baptiste? He'll be able to solve your problem for sure."

"I asked Papa Baptiste already. 'Dimitru, my son,' he said, 'to find that out would take an entire lifetime. Maybe even longer.' But I don't know if I have that much time, Pavel."

What was time? Except for the wish that my dreary school years would end, time played no special role in my life. In Baia Luna, today was like what yesterday was and tomorrow would be. Even Margul-Sperber's propaganda verses could not change that. "Now look about, where'er you bend your gaze appears a new world struggling to be born." Nothing struggled to be born in Baia Luna. At least not for me.

Until my grandfather's fifty-fifth birthday.

Ilja had smoked the last Cuban of the previous year and was waiting for customers in the shop while my mother Kathalina was getting lunch ready in the kitchen. Aunt Antonia was still dozing in bed. From time to time, as always, she would stretch out her arm for a nougat praline from the nightstand, then let the chocolate melt in her mouth as she fell back asleep.

I sat in school, where no one else guessed that the woman in the blue dress would never again make us copy out Hans Bohn's patriotic poem about the beautiful land in the Carpathian forests on its way to a grandiose future in which "each new day is better than the last." Up to now, the poems in our schoolbooks had struck me as just empty blather, but no more. Today was no longer like yesterday since Angela Barbulescu had whispered the incomprehensible assignment into my ear, *Send this man straight to hell! Destroy him!*

What did she mean? Was Barbu's plea a demand to kill the Kronauburg party secretary? She couldn't possibly have meant that. She would never have made such a request given the fact that she'd always praised the sacredness of the Ten Commandments in religion class. "Thou shalt not kill." That was the sin of sins. Any halfway-intelligent person knew that even without Moses. The teacher surely was not asking me to commit murder. It was out of the question! Of course, there were ways and means to send an enemy to the other side without getting one's own hands dirty. If you believed in witchcraft.

The Gypsies were said to understand something about black magic. I considered mixing potions of pulverized pubic hair, menstrual blood, and cat shit to be nothing but humbug. And Buba Gabor gave me to understand with a wink that I was right. Rumor had it that her mother Susanna had access to occult powers. "We listen to people, understand their worries, make a little hocus-pocus, and cash in. Sometimes it works, usually not, but we have enough to eat for a few days." I believed Buba because she had such a wonderful laugh, because she was beautiful, and because a witch couldn't possibly smell so good.

Angela Barbulescu, on the other hand, was superstitious. Clearly. Burning the image of her former lover out of a photo, however, seemed not an effective piece of magic but a pointless gesture of helpless misfortune that didn't testify to Barbu's secret power but merely to her helplessness There was no doubt this Dr. Stephanescu had done her wrong. Rejected love, probably. Maybe that's why she had drunk herself into a ruin. She wished this man dead, not alive. But she was too weak herself. Now I was supposed to deliver a man to hell for her, and all I knew about him was that he used to smoke unfiltered cigarettes and drank *konjaki,* and was now a big-shot party functionary. Anyway, only people like the dumb Konstantin still believed in hell. Why should I go do battle for Barbu? Declare her enemy to be mine? Stir up bygone filth and get my own hands dirty? Clearly this Stephanescu was a heartbreaker, a creep. But you didn't just wipe out a Ph.D., a big shot in the state and the party. Especially if you had no plan and no idea as to why and wherefore.

"Send this man straight to hell"—after school, while I poked listlessly at my lunch, something had changed. I had changed. Not because of the crazy assignment, but the picture! That photo that I had hung up in school! Something was wrong with it. Why had Barbu taken it down again and carried it away? While my mother admonished me, "Eat something! Put some meat on your bones! You're getting a chill," I could still see Stephanescu smiling.

# Chapter Three

•

## ILJA'S BIRTHDAY, THE FLIGHT OF THE SPUTNIK,

## AND PATER JOHANNES'S BURNING CONCERN

The dreary weather continued the entire day and hardly a house-wife in Baia Luna found her way to our shop on November 6, 1957. Grandfather dozed behind the counter while I huddled shivering by the stove. Around three, the widow Vera Raducanu entered, a flaxen-haired woman in her midforties. It was said in the village that she had cornered the market on being insulted and outraged.

Instead of wishing Grandfather happy birthday, Vera pointed to her spattered shoes and complained about what a morass the village street was. As always, she examined our stock suspiciously and asked for Luxor in gold foil, a snow-white soap scented with essence of roses, although she knew very well we didn't carry such luxury items. Granddad kindly offered her a bar of chamomile soap instead, whereupon Vera called him a vulgar huckster, turned on her heel, and flounced out the door.

Shortly thereafter, Elena Kiselev came in with her four-year-old twins Drina and Diana, who curtsied prettily and wished Grandfather many happy returns.

"Your order is here," said Ilja while I fetched the brand-new suitcase of brown leatherette from the storeroom.

"It's a present for my husband." Elena inspected the suitcase with shy pride. "For his new job when he takes the train to Stalin-stadt on Sunday."

The news had already circulated through Baia Luna that Alex-andru Kiselev had found a job assembling transmissions in the new state tractor factory. But the fact that from now on her husband would bring home three times as much money in his pay envelope as he earned on their farm couldn't diminish Elena's heartache at soon having to live apart.

While she paid for the suitcase, her daughters eyed the glass candy jar on the counter with eager expectation. Grandfather unscrewed the lid and pressed into each extended palm a piece of genuine chewing gum in silver foil, thereby displaying not only his understanding of the little raptures of childhood but also his passion for America. It was his hope that, someday before he died, a ship would carry him across the Atlantic to the homeland of the Virgin of the Shining Crown.

It's going to be a birthday like any other, I thought on that November 6. The men would talk themselves into a state. First about harmless, uncontroversial topics. They would probably start off with rabies. At some point Avram Scherban the shepherd would curse the wolves and bears that grabbed his sheep at night because he couldn't defend himself against those hungry thieves without a rifle and he didn't have a rifle because only party officials were allowed to go hunting. Avram would bitch and moan. And drink. First the new Sylvaner: one carafe and then another and then another after that. Then the men would ask for *zuika*. Goes down nice, that brandy, that's what they'd say. I'd have to rush back and forth, and they'd start getting louder. Work up some Dutch courage. Ready for anything. They'd thunder about the sinking price for milk and meat and the steady devaluation of the currency. They'd have nothing more to laugh about then, those comrades, those collectivists. "Down with the Reds!" the Scherban boys would holler while their drunken father shook his hands in front of him: *ratta-tat-tat, ratta-tat-tat*. But Avram Scherban wasn't about to bump anybody off. He couldn't, because he had to turn in his gun. They'd confiscated all our firearms, those fat-assed pencil pushers. They'd stolen the men's pride, and that fanned their anger, but they had to swallow it. Until they were falling down drunk. Then they'd sleep it off the next morning. The only one who wouldn't have a serious hangover would be the host and birthday boy, my grandfather Ilja. He didn't drink.

And there was a reason for that.

..............

There's a saying in Transmontania: Poverty teaches you to pray, but even more to drink. The old people tell the story that during the severe famine of 1907, shortly before Ilja was to start school, he fell into one of the vats of mash in which the village farmers ferment their rotten potato peelings. Luckily, the moonshiners had discovered the boy at once and pulled him out of the slime. Nevertheless, Grandfather was poisoned by the undistilled spirits and suffered a delirium that lasted several hours. He suffered no visible permanent harm, and the incident was soon forgotten. Only the pious and gossipy Kora Konstantin, his former schoolmate, was always making nasty remarks about how Ilja Botev had been a complete washout at learning his letters and she didn't see how someone like that could be an honest shopkeeper with no debts.

I had had enough experience behind the bar to see Kora Konstantin's bitchiness for what it was. She was one of those women with a chronically empty household account and a half-dozen squalling brats who used to get more whippings than bread from their father. That is, they did until Holy Week in 1956, when Grandfather vowed never to serve Raswan Konstantin another drop, whereupon the lush called the whole village together and threatened to break Ilja's neck and torch the shop of that whole Botev clan. But it never came to that.

When Kora returned home from confession on the day the Lord was crucified, her children stormed screaming out of the house. Raswan lay dead in the front hall. People say his fly was open, and his hand still held a well-worn and detailed drawing that Kora threw into the stove on the spot. After she had straightened the clothes on the body of her unloved husband, she made known his death by beginning to weep and wail. Since the police had to be notified in a case of unexpected demise, the young Plutonier Cartarescu was called over from Apoldasch. Although he was reputed to be overly punctilious, he had no experience with corpses in front halls and ordered an autopsy in the Kronauburg hospital. A few days later the deceased returned to Baia Luna in a simple spruce coffin on the bed of a horse-drawn cart and several pounds lighter, curiously enough. The cause of death was determined to be heart failure caused by a very high level of arousal. They said that as a result of the engorgement of the inner organs, Raswan's liver (a liver, by the way, big enough for an ox) had squashed his myocardium.

Instead of giving Grandfather credit for trying to rescue Raswan from drink, Kora laid into him at every opportunity. As for Ilja's weak reading skills, however, what the nasty widow had said was true. The wheels of Grandfather's mind turned slowly, and the logic with which one usually recognizes connections and discovers contradictions was not one of his strengths. Numbers, on the other hand, were never a problem for Granddad. By the age of nine, he reportedly could multiply and divide multidigit numbers in his head without ever making a mistake. So that the other young men of Baia Luna didn't take him for a weirdo because of this talent, he would now and then take a sip of strong drink. But he gave it up because even a thimbleful of *zuika* could leave him with a pounding headache, chills, and memory loss. I for one had never seen Grandfather drink a drop.

They all came. Earlier than usual they gathered in the taproom as if they couldn't wait to get out of the cold, wet November weather. They congratulated Ilja with a brisk handshake, put down the bottles they'd brought as presents, and found a place to sit. Some of the men just sat dully in their seats while others asked me for dice or cards.

"What's the matter, Pavel?" asked Karl Koch. "Your face is more miserable than the weather. Trouble in school?"

I didn't answer. The more I tried to banish thoughts of Angela Barbulescu from my mind, the more urgently they crowded forward. Why this crazy assignment? Why was I the one who had to hang the party secretary's photo on the wall? Why should I keep the half-burned photo of the kissing Barbu as a memento? Herr Hofmann had shot both photos, and he probably knew exactly why Barbu's life had gone off the rails. Worlds lay between her sunflower dress in the Paris of the East and her grubby blue dress in Baia Luna. Moreover, Herr Hofmann possessed the means to make her life a hell. It was a certainty that Barbu wasn't in the village voluntarily. Yes, she was a terrible teacher. But she hadn't always been that way. And then there was Fritz's nasty rhyme about his thing out to here. The more I recalled that day in class, the more sympathy I felt for my teacher.

"Don't pull such a long face, Pavel! Chin up, boy!"

I tried to smile, but my thoughts were a heavy drag.

Hermann Schuster took the floor. He dispensed with the usual detour through the rabies problem and got right to the point: the party's newest five-year plan. Now the trouble begins, Grandfather was saying to himself—I could tell from his expression. But the Saxon Hermann spoke quite calmly. He talked about what they had inherited from their fathers, about tradition, honor, and home-land, and said he wasn't about to toss his ancestors' centuries of hard work into the jaws of a state collective. "Everything for the party, nothing for us," he concluded. "My answer is no, no, and no again."

Hans Schneider agreed and told of plans to erect a series of gigantic industrial-type hog farms not far from Apoldasch.

"All for the export market, all for the Russians," Hermann Schuster added. "The kolkhoz will be our undoing."

Amazingly enough, the volatile Brancusi brothers reacted with remarkable objectivity to the attacks of Schuster and Schneider. Liviu Brancusi defended the planned state takeover of agricul-ture and the industrialization of Transmontania as the footprint of progress. "We must emerge at last from the shadows of obsoles-cence." Following the Soviet example and under the leadership of the Central Committee, Liviu declared, ninety percent of bour-geois property had already been returned to the people. Industry and banking, transportation and wholesaling, had been successfully transferred into the hands of the working class, ditto the hospitals, theaters, and movie houses. Then he began to rattle off statistics about rising quotas for milk production and feedlots in the regions of Prahova, Covasna, and Buzau until he threatened to drown in a sea of numbers.

Hermann Schuster took advantage of Liviu's pause for breath. "But now let's have a toast to our birthday boy!"

Just as the men were raising their glasses, somebody started kicking against the door with heavy boots.

Grandfather opened it. There stood Dimitru the Gypsy, wet

through and through, panting, and holding a huge crate covered by a dripping wool blanket with both hands.

"Room, make room!" he called, gasping for air and pushing into the taproom with his crate. The Scherban brothers jumped up and pushed aside the bottles on the bar while the muscular Karl Koch gave the skinny Dimitru a hand. Together they heaved the box onto the bar. Dimitru was panting like a dog and collapsed into a chair while the others looked on in curiosity. Then he proclaimed ceremoniously, "By the blessed hump of Simon of Cyrene I swear this damn technology breaks your back. Give us a glass, Ilja."

Granddad grinned and filled a glass with his own hand. Dimitru drank. Everyone was staring at the draped box in anticipation. The Gypsy rose, tapped Grandfather on the shoulder, and urged him to unwrap his birthday present. "For you. On your special day."

Ilja hesitated in embarrassment.

"Go ahead," said Liviu Brancusi, insulted that his propaganda speech had been cut short by the muddleheaded Gypsy, someone he considered totally incapable of helping to construct the New Nation. Grandfather stepped forward. Cautiously he pulled the wet blanket from the box. The awestruck men froze where they were. Before them stood a brand-new television set.

It was a gigantic apparatus with tubes and a polished glass screen, a case of fine wood, and ivory-colored knobs and push buttons. Speechless, Ilja examined the TV, tears of joy running down his cheeks.

The thought flashed through my head that not even the Hofmanns had such a luxurious piece of equipment. I absolutely had to show Fritz the TV. He would be amazed. I ran off to his house, and he didn't need any persuading. "Gotta see that," he said.

When we returned, Grandfather was still standing silent before the imposing tube. Then he tentatively pushed one of the buttons. Nothing happened.

"Current," said Dimitru. "You need electric current."

"Here," called young Petre Petrov. Under the shelf with jars of pickled cucumbers he had discovered an outlet. Petre pulled a wooden stool in front of the shelf. Carefully Karl Koch and Alexandru Kiselev lifted the heavy appliance onto the stool while Petre plugged the cord into the outlet.

"You turn it on," Grandfather said to Dimitru. The Gypsy put down his glass and took up a position in front of the new acquisition while the men formed a half circle behind him.

"All right then," said Dimitru, raising his right index finger theatrically, and then slowly lowering it onto the power button. There was a crackling noise. After a while, tiny flames flickered up in the glass tube behind the screen and then a little lamp shimmered greenly. "That," the Gypsy solemnly intoned, "is the Magic Eye."

Instantaneously the screen brightened, and millions of teeny points of light flickered like snow crystals, interrupted by a black bar running repeatedly down the screen from top to bottom. From the loudspeaker emerged a soft rustling that swelled and swelled until it was a farting, earsplitting rattle. Petre Petrov turned down the volume knob.

"We have to find a channel," he said.

Dimitru nodded in agreement. "That's right. No reception without a channel and no picture without reception."

Petre fiddled for a while with all the buttons and dials but couldn't coax a picture from the machine. "The antenna! Dimitru, where's the antenna?"

"Oh shit!" The Gypsy clapped his hand to his forehead. "What a disaster! My cousin Salman, the blockhead. I told him ten—no, twenty times, 'Just don't forget the stupid antenna when you arrange for the TV.' And what does Salman do? He forgets it. May he drown in the Flood, that certifiable halfwit. What time is it?"

"Almost five," answered Petre Petrov.

"Oh holy shit! At five on the dot, you'll see that your Black philosopher Dimitru is no ignorant blabbermouth. Sputnik, I tell you. State TV is broadcasting a program about Sputnik. At five on the dot. Oh no, no, no," the Gypsy moaned. He pushed all the buttons, twirled all the dials, and banged the box with his fist. "Madonna, help me!" he cried. "Almost five and no picture. My cousin, the idiot, that fart-faced jerk!"

"Thou shalt not curse!" Everyone turned to the door. With shuffling feet, a cane in one hand and a present wrapped in brown paper in the other, Johannes Baptiste came into the room. The men immediately offered him a chair. The priest presented Grandfather with his present and sat down. Then he raised a hand as if in blessing. "May I have a glass of water? And don't let me interrupt you, brothers."

Dimitru crossed himself. "Forgive me, Papa Baptiste." The Gypsy grasped the priest's hand, planted a kiss on it with his moist lips, and stammered, "Papa Baptiste, please help. The power of your consecrated hands can drive the crafty devils of technology out of this box. A single word of blessing, a quick prayer, a splash of holy water."

Before Johannes Baptiste could answer, someone called out, "Forget that pious mumbo jumbo and find some wire."

Everybody stopped short and looked over at the person who'd uttered those words: Fritz Hofmann. A schoolboy! The snotty photographer's son! What could he have to say to a group of grown men?

"Get a piece of fence wire for the antenna. That'll work."

The men were speechless. Only Pater Johannes remarked, "The boy is right."

Hermann Schuster and I disappeared into the storage room, where we cut a few yards from a bale of barbed wire. I pulled the wire through a cracked-open window and wrapped the end around the roof gutter while Schuster took the other end and improvised a connection to the antenna socket on the TV.

Suddenly the sound of a string orchestra emerged from the speaker. The men applauded and pounded one another on the back. Dimitru beamed, knelt down, and kissed the screen, but then jerked back in horror.

"Electricity," he cried and rubbed his lips anxiously. "The whole box is full of electricity."

"We can use the box as a radio," Petre Petrov decided.

Dimitru calmed down. "*Bene bonus.* A TV with sound is better than a radio without a picture anyway." No one disagreed.

It beeped a few times, and then a gong sounded. "Five p.m." Then a sonorous male voice announced an address by the first secretary of the Communist Party of the Soviet Union. While the screen flickered snow, we heard the voice of Nikita Sergeyevich Khrushchev overlaid by the voice of an interpreter.

"From this day forward the history of mankind must be rewritten. With Sputnik a new era has begun. And it is we who have rung in this new era. Who has any more interest in that TV dog Lassie when our Laika has already circled the world a hundred times? America has been defeated."

Grandfather jumped up in outrage. "Never!"

"The Union of Soviet Socialist Republics," emerged from the box, "has won a decisive victory over the United States of America in the race to conquer space. The Union of Soviet Socialist Republics has mobilized the elite of its proletarian intelligentsia to overcome the forces of gravity for the first time in human history. The Union of Soviet Socialist Republics is the shaper of the future."

"Turn off that crap," cried Hermann Schuster, whose blood started to boil at the very mention of the word "Socialist," ever since he had returned to his Transmontanian homeland from the coal mines of Donezk six years after the end of the war, reduced to nothing but skin and bones.

"Hear, hear! Proletarian intelligentsia! Creator of the future! Just like we've always said," called Liviu Brancusi.

"Until today no nation in the world was in a position to catapult living beings out of the powerful gravitational pull of the earth. But soon we will be sending not just satellites but our cosmonauts into weightlessness to raise on the moon the flag of the Union of Soviet Socialist Republics in testimony to the accomplishments of our productive powers. American transcontinental bombers are already ripe for a museum. With the thrust of their engines they can just barely . . ." Then the loudspeaker began to chatter.

Impatiently Ilja twirled the station dial, but gurgling and squeaking noises kept interfering with isolated scraps of the speech until the signal became clear again.

". . . brown cocaine-lemonade, drug addiction, and the terrible dissonances of jazz music will lead to the downfall of the bourgeoisie. Their young people waste their time in movie theaters and shady bars. They act like animals in their uncultured dances and trade obscenities on public thoroughfares. Instead of studying science their children chew sticky gum from morning to night that turns the human face into the stupid visage of a cud-chewing cow."

Some of the men laughed and pointed to Grandfather's candy jar. He cut them short with a harsh "Shut up." Then we heard barking from the loudspeaker. It wasn't translated. The commentator explained that the barking was an original recording of the bitch Laika who, shot into the weightlessness of space with the power of a half-million kiloponds, was now circling the earth in the space capsule Sputnik 2.

"Unbelievable," cried Alexandru Kiselev, the future transmission assembler in the Stalinstadt tractor factory. "Simply unbelievable. A half-million kilos. What power!"

"That's equal to the power of sixty-six thousand six hundred and sixty-six horses," Grandfather calculated.

"Bunch of crap! Lies and propaganda! Russian bullshit!"

Flushed with anger, Hermann Schuster jumped up and yanked the cord from its socket. The TV gave a pop, and the screen went black.

"Shit on the Russians." Petre Petrov flew into a rage, too. "They shoot millions into space, and down here on earth people have to eat grass. We're going to end up just like their damned collective farmers."

"What about the new tractor factory? Who built that if not the party, you greenhorn?" replied Alexandru Kiselev. "Tell me how I'm supposed to keep the bellies of my wife and six children full here in this hole. Tell me how I'm supposed to earn a living from two cows and a couple of sows. Now that winter's coming. If you know a way out of this misery, youngster, then say so. Otherwise keep your fresh mouth shut."

Petre whispered to me that if Alexandru wanted to do something about being poor, he should stop popping buns in his old lady's oven. But Petre well knew that a seventeen-year-old had no business saying such a thing out loud in a gathering of men.

The Brancusis and the blacksmith Simenov loudly applauded Kiselev's words. "We refuse to accept progress, and we defend our backwardness," said Liviu. "Everybody in the village plows his own field, and the harvest barely keeps us alive. We kill ourselves toiling behind our draft horses while the party has been building tractors for years. We have excellent grazing land, but we don't sell a single quart of milk. Where would we sell it? There's only a rutted field road to Apoldasch, yet the party's building new roads all over the country. We're the only ones still walking; everywhere else they've got buses. Not even to mention our school. Sixty, seventy kids in one classroom, taught by a teacher who's ideologically suspect.

Yet children are the future. Do we want our young people to end up like Americans, chewing gum, selfish, lazy, and spoiled rotten? Comrade Khrushchev is right."

Liviu Brancusi sensed that his training course as a politcadre was bearing fruit. The mood in the tavern was swinging in his favor.

"Why don't we follow the example of our successful neighbors? Why would we want to stay on the side of history's losers? Why not stand side by side with the winners? I'm telling you, learning from the Soviet Union means learning to win! The Sputnik is the result of their glorious struggle for progress."

With that, Liviu's brother Nico took up the cudgels.

"Listen up, you blabbermouth," he smugly addressed Dimitru. "Here's what I have to say to you with your reactionary palaver about Sputnik last night. 'The Sputnik's beeping robs people of their sanity.' That's about the stupidest thing I've ever heard."

*"Quod erat demonstratum,"* replied Dimitru caustically.

"Hold your tongues! You quarrel like the blind arguing with the sightless!" The men looked over to Johannes Baptiste.

"Next Sunday," he announced, "I shall address the pressing questions of today from the pulpit. And I expect to see every one of you in church, Catholic, Communist, or heathen." Johannes Baptiste pointed to Ilja's television. "What we've just heard from this apparatus is the beginning of the end. Pandora's box is open and I say to you that a line has been crossed. Space travel of any kind—by a dog or a man—should be banned *in principio* and *ex cathedra*. Excursions into space are per se a mortal sin against the spirit. Man has no business in the infinity of the universe except to seek his Almighty Maker."

*"Sic est,"* Dimitru agreed. "Truly, a truer word was never spoken."

"The Socialist riffraff don't give a fig for the Lord's command-ments," roared the Saxon Schuster. "They test God's patience," he shouted. "To hell with the Communists." Whereupon Roman, the middle Brancusi brother, couldn't keep his seat a moment longer.

"You tra-tra-tra-traitor!" he screamed at Schuster, stammering as always when he got overexcited. He rushed over to the Saxon and with the words "Da-da-damned Hitlerist!" shattered an empty

Sylvaner bottle on his head. Schuster gave a brief twitch, then keeled over like a wet sack. While a few men came to the aid of the unconscious fellow and carried him outside, Grandfather managed with quite a bit of difficulty to keep the outraged guests from going for the Brancusis.

"You haven't heard the last of this," the three of them cried defiantly before making a quick getaway.

Hermann Schuster slowly regained consciousness, still woozy from the bang on his skull. Kristan Desliu, Karl Koch, and I helped him drag his way home through the rain. Erika Schuster blanched when she caught sight of her husband with a big bruise on his forehead. She put up water for tea and wrapped his head in moist towels, but Hermann tore them off, pushed the chamomile tea away, and pretended nothing special had happened in the taproom.

The tavern emptied out after the fight. Most of the men went home sober and cranky. By the clock it wasn't even seven yet. Ilja's fifty-fifth birthday celebration was over before it had really begun.

Grandfather was at a loss. "Satellites circle the earth, and we humans have gone off the tracks. Believe me, Pavel, the world is out of joint. The maelstrom of evil grows strong again."

I could read Grandfather's thoughts. I knew exactly what was on his mind at this moment: his son, Nicolai, my father. Grandfather had already witnessed the fatal pull of perdition when the rabid tirades of the Führer in Berlin had lured the Saxons to their radios, and even his peace-loving neighbors had gotten fired up for the mad idea that their chancellor would bring them home to the Reich of their ancestors. It didn't turn out that way. Instead, there was a war that cast its shadows even over Baia Luna, and my father joined the wrong side. He lost his life because he thought it was the right one.

In the fall of 1940, Wehrmacht units had marched into Transmontania, their ally against Stalin. The boys had run off, the best young men in Baia Luna, led by Karl Koch, Hermann Schuster, and Hans Schneider. And Nicolai Botev. They had all volunteered for the imminent campaign against the Soviets. They intended to achieve a glorious victory over the Bolsheviks, melt down the tanks and cannon of the godless troops of the red star, and recast them as bells that would ring in the victory of the Cross over Communism.

The war had left no trace in my memory. I was three years old when it ended. But for my grandfather, it had never ended. He lived with his loss. He had lost his future, Nicolai, his only son. I don't believe a day went by when Ilja didn't think of him, even though he still had his daughter-in-law Kathalina and me. And of course his daughter Antonia, too. I know that Grandfather wished Antonia had left his house long ago. With his whole heart he longed for her to find a decent husband. But the prospects weren't good for him to acquire a new family and more grandchildren. A train wreck of a love affair that no one would talk about had derailed my aunt's life to such an extent that she sought refuge in indifference and laziness. She conscientiously took care of the bookkeeping and paperwork for the store, but that was the extent of her household duties. Most of the time she lay in bed, salving her sorrow with chocolates and pralines and otherwise watching indifferently as her ample proportions increased with each passing day.

I was now fifteen and soon would have school behind me. Grandfather was asking more and more often what I had in mind for the future. I didn't have an answer.

"Innkeeper, another drop?"

Dimitru pulled us back into the present. He was sitting in the corner beside the stove next to Johannes Baptiste and my school friend Fritz. Granddad set up Sylvaner and *zuika* while I went to the storeroom to get the broom and dustpan. I swept up the shards of the bottle Roman Brancusi had smashed on Hermann Schuster's hard skull and then sat down with the mixed company.

"Pavel, you can take the rest of the night off," said Granddad. "The bar is closed."

I looked over at Fritz, but he indicated no desire to go home.

"We'll hang around a bit," I said. "It's still early."

Fritz nodded, and Father Johannes said, "I always like having young people around." Grandfather didn't object.

I heard the ticking of the clock whose hour hand had just passed seven. Johannes Baptiste was twiddling his thumbs, a habit that always meant he was looking for a good opportunity to start talking. Then he cleared his throat.

"So Dimitru, you think there's a shady story no one can see through behind this Sputnik?"

"Absolutely!"

"And what dark plot do you see at work?"

Dimitru fumbled around looking for an answer. "I'm very close to a *conclusio,* if only—"

"So you know nothing," Baptiste cut him off. "Does the name Sergei Pavlovich Korolev mean anything to you?"

"A Russian, I'm guessing."

"A Ukrainian," said Johannes Baptiste. "A luminary of rocket technology. The best. For years, Korolev has been developing a secret program of manned spaceflight with thousands of engineers working for him. Bad, very bad. And today we've learned"—Baptiste pointed at the television—"that the Sputnik is only a first step toward the illusion of human omnipotence. The way things stand now, the Bolsheviks have really managed to overcome the powerful gravitational forces of the earth. Against nature. First a dog, then a chimp, then a man. But I tell you that according to Holy Scripture, an ascension into the heavens is reserved for the Lord Jesus. Besides him, according to God's design, only one other person of flesh and blood has been granted bodily admission into heaven. And as you very well know, Dimitru, it was Mary the Mother of Jesus. That's how Pope Pius in Rome laid it down in a secret dogma in 1950."

*"Sic est,"* agreed the Gypsy.

"Back to Korolev. What does this crafty Ukrainian have in mind? That's the question that preys on my mind. In fact, it's a burning question. What's the Soviet Engineer Number One looking for in the vastness of the firmament? It's a riveting question. And the answer is much more riveting." The priest took a swallow of water. "You heard it today from this flickering doomsday box. From Khrushchev's own lips. The Soviets want to send cosmonauts into the heavens and raise the Communist flag on the moon."

"So what? Let them do it," Fritz interrupted the priest in a snotty voice.

"And you would be Fritz Hofmann, the lad who just had the idea of using wire for the antenna? A clever fellow, no doubt, although I've never seen you in church. But you should keep quiet, Mr. Know-It-All, when an old man is talking about things you haven't got the foggiest notion of."

Fritz tried to conceal how much this reprimand had hurt him as the Benedictine continued. "If my information is correct, Korolev is working with a man by the name of Yury Gagarin. When Khrushchev was elevated to first secretary last year, Korolev and Gagarin got personal audiences in the Politburo. They spread their rocket plans out on Khrushchev's desk and asked for money for a titanic space program. A lot of money."

"And they got it," Dimitru interjected. "Probably double what they asked for. I suspect the army raised the ante a fair amount."

"In any event, Korolev can build his rockets—as many as he wants. But only under top secret conditions somewhere out in the steppes of Kazakhstan and only on condition that he never uses the word 'ascension.' He's only allowed to refer to it by the code name 'the Project.' If he doesn't"—and Baptiste made his fingers into scissors—"they'll cut out his tongue."

"But why would the chief of all the Soviets want to cut out people's tongues," Grandfather put in his oar, "just on account of a Russki flag on the moon that nobody's going to see from down here anyway?"

"Forget the flag," replied Johannes Baptiste. "That's just to taunt the Americans and rub their noses in Soviet superiority. Pure vanity. That's also why the Sputnik sends out those signals. From a scientific perspective, the *beep-beep* makes no sense. Basically, the Sputnik is just announcing, Listen up, listen up. I exist. I'm up here. Of course, that's how Khrushchev drives his opponent Eisenhower stark raving mad and demonstrates to the Americans that the Bolsheviks' engineers are faster, smarter, and further along. Remember, we're in the world political phase of a Cold War that sometimes produces quite heated skirmishes. Even in Baia Luna, to which the ringing skull of our doughty Hermann Schuster can attest. Without a doubt the Kremlin wants to win the race against the capitalist system of the USA. But that's not the heart of the problem. The essence of an ascension is something completely different. And I claim that Korolev knows what it is."

Pater Johannes paused to ask for a refill of water, and I guess also to give us listeners a chance to ask questions. No one had any, so he continued: "I don't see the world with the eyes of a politician but of a pastor concerned with the spiritual needs of his flock. All the more so since I can feel that my days are numbered. And what

I see concerns me. Really concerns me. Where do we come from and where are we going? Those are the fundamental questions of human existence. The world knows only one answer: ashes to ashes and dust to dust. There is no God and no heaven. But I believe in the Trinity of Father, Son, and Holy Ghost. I believe in heaven and that there's someone up there."

"Laika the dog?" I interjected.

"Forget about that yapper. No, Pavel, I'm talking about a woman. I already mentioned that mysterious Vatican dogma of the corporeal Assumption into heaven of Mary the Mother of God. Is it beginning to dawn on you why Korolev is building rockets? The reason that the Soviets plan to shoot cosmonauts into the firmament is so top secret that only Khrushchev, Korolev, and this Gagarin fellow are in on it. They're looking for an answer to the question: Does God exist?"

"Oh my God." Dimitru groaned and hammered his fist on his skull. "The Bolsheviks simply fly up to the stars and take a look. Pure empiricism! The ultimatoric proof of God's existence! No more Thomas Aquinas!"

"You could see it that way. And I'll wager that in the near future, when the first cosmonaut returns from space, there's only one thing Khrushchev and Korolev will want to know—"

"Did you see God up there?" Fritz chimed in.

"You're no dim bulb, Hofmann Fritzy, but you're not a good listener. You think you've got nothing more to learn, not in church and not about church. Wrong, boy, big big mistake! If you'd only think back, you upstart whippersnapper, then you'd know what Korolev's question would be and can only be: Did you see Mary up there?"

I registered a nervous tic in Fritz's face. Not even Barbu's pointer could shake his composure, but Father Johannes had unnerved him. He chewed his nails in silence. It was clear to me that, privately, Fritz was determined to pay the priest back for his humiliation. He just didn't know how yet.

"And why won't Korolev ask after God himself?" I chimed in.

Baptiste patted my shoulder. "Put yourself in his place, boy. Try to think like he does! Korolev is a researcher—measuring, weighing, counting, testing—a materialist, a self-declared atheist for whom only the scientific theory and its proof are valid. Nevertheless, he isn't stupid. Of course he is aware that if God really does exist against all expectations, his cosmonauts would never be able to see him. The Almighty is invisible, as the Jews already knew. He is invisible not only for the human eye, but for optical instruments of any kind whatsoever. Ditto the Holy Ghost. The *spiritus sanctus* escapes every pupil for the obvious reason that he's a spirit. With Jesus Christ, it's a little more complicated. He lived, suffered, and died as a man, and he rose from the dead as the Redeemer. As such he is obviously visible in the form of the consecrated bread and the gleam of the Eternal Flame in the sanctuary lamp that attests day and night to the presence of divine omnipotence in our church. But what about Mary? Mary was a human being, and she remained a human being in death and after death. That's what Pope Pius (whom otherwise I don't think much of) recognized so fittingly. In 1950, five years after the war, he issued the Apostolic Constitution Munificentissimus Deus. It says more or less, 'We proclaim, declare, and define it as a dogma revealed by God that the immaculate, eternally virginal Mother of God Mary at the end of her earthly life was assumed body and soul into heavenly glory.' That means not only Mary's spirit but also her flesh and blood are in heaven. Now just imagine what this Vatican dogma means for a materialist: it's the supreme challenge, pure and simple. If the dogma is true, then this Jewess from Nazareth beat Korolev to it. The first spaceflight in history, the first conquest of gravity. Without a rocket. That's why the Russians are firing cosmonauts in among the stars. They have to find the answer to the all-important question about God. If the visible Mother of God exists, then logically the invisible Creator of All Things exists as well. And no one knows that better than Engineer Number One."

"Oh holy shit!" howled Dimitru. "This doesn't look good. Bad news for the Catholics. And worse news for Gypsies. Mary is our Mother, our queen, our advocate at the heavenly throne, *Mater Regina* of the miserable! Without her, no deals with the Lord God. Uh-oh, I'm telling you, if Korolev finds the Madonna, then God have mercy on us. Didn't I give early warning that Sputnik would spell disaster? But nobody listens to a Black. Didn't they laugh at me, slander me, mock me, spit on me? But I predict here and now that what began as a beep will end in *desastrum*."

"Hang on, hang on. Not so fast," Grandfather jumped in. "There's a way to stop Korolev."

"I'm unable to see such a possibility," Pater Johannes objected.

Dimitru took a swallow and agreed: "Where nothingness reigns, even the seer is blind."

"It's simple," Grandfather continued undeterred. "The Americans have to get in ahead of the Russians. They can't let this Sputnik beeping drive them crazy. They've got to keep a cool head and build their own rockets. Better ones than the Russians. Rockets that fly higher and farther. After all, the United States of America has certain obligations to the Virgin Mary, who protects the city of Noueeyorka from enemy attacks. So it's high time for the Yanks to give Mary some protection of her own."

Dimitru rose slowly to his feet, swaying slightly. He stumbled, caught himself, and fell into Ilja's arms.

"Tha's it! America'll build rockets and save th' Madonna! And the Soviets'll bite their own asses. Why di'nt I think've it myself? That'd be th' answer!"

Ilja felt entitled to correct his friend: "That wouldn't *be* the answer, Dimitru, that *is* the answer."

# Chapter Four

•

## THE ETERNAL FLAME, BLOND HAIR IN THE WIND,

## AND A THREE-DAY DEADLINE

"Time to go," said Johannes Baptiste, picking up his cane. "Until Sunday. In church. It's time to confront the collectivists."

He tapped the television set with his stick, grumbled something about an *apparatura diavoli non grata* whose presence transformed every tavern into a brawling dive, and gestured toward the birthday present wrapped in brown paper that Ilja had set down next to the cash register.

Grandfather gave the priest his arm and offered to accompany him back to the rectory, but Baptiste waved him away grumpily before his weary steps receded into the blackness of the night.

Fritz and I stood up, too. I yawned but wasn't tired. I felt like getting some exercise and fresh air. Fritz was silent, his lips clamped together tight as a vise. He was nursing his grudge against the priest for the dressing-down he'd been given.

Dimitru reached for the bottle of *zuika* and held it up to the light from the ceiling lamp. It was empty. He spied the full glass of wine Pater Johannes had left behind and slurred, "What th' sainted hand disdain z'good 'nuffer th' Gypsy." Then he tossed off the Sylvaner and staggered out onto the porch. His hands groped for the railing but found only thin air. Dimitru slipped, fell over, slid down the slippery steps on his belly, and landed headfirst in the mud. He moaned pitifully, cursed Saint Joseph (the patron saint of carpenters) and the disasters associated with wooden steps in the rain. Then he ran his hands along his thighs, knees, and calves while the mud dripped from his hair.

"Morphine," he groaned, "need morphine."

Grandfather scolded him, "Don't carry on so, you big baby."

Dimitru shut right up, his mouth still wide open and his face distorted in such a painful grimace that I couldn't help grinning in schadenfreude.

"Pavel! Fritz! Help Dimitru get home." Whining, the Gypsy pulled himself to his feet and leaned on my arm. Then we set off, he limping, cursing, and crying while he sagged on my shoulder like a wet sack of corn. Fritz trotted along behind us. The clock in the church tower was tolling nine thirty when we reached the gypsy's cottage at the lower end of the village. His niece Buba took delivery of her drunken uncle. Dimitru dropped onto the rug, pulled his knees to his chest like a fetus, and fell asleep at once. Buba took off his shoes, shoved a pillow under his head, and covered him with wool blankets and sheepskins.

"Uncle Dimi gets a chill easily. He must have been a block of ice in an earlier life." She laughed and extended her hand. Although the girl with the unruly black curls was usually ready with some cheeky remark, she thanked us for our help and asked if we'd like to stay a bit.

"I've got something to take care of," Fritz declared.

I shrugged my shoulders apologetically. "Maybe some other time."

Buba insisted on shaking my hand again, then she smiled and brushed my cheek lightly with her hand. The smell of her hair wafted over to me. No, Buba's locks didn't just smell good; they were fragrant with the tang of fire, smoke, and damp earth. I blushed and felt suddenly warm.

Then a voice screeched, "Bubbah! Bubbah! Is somebody there?"

"My mother's calling. See you in school," and the Gypsy girl disappeared.

In school! It seemed to me that an eternity had passed since this morning in school when the teacher Angela Barbulescu had assigned me to hang the likeness of the party secretary Stephanescu on the wall. I could still hear her demanding, *Send this man straight to hell! Destroy him!* but as a thin sound from a gray distance. Nevertheless, I could picture Barbu again, standing before me. Standing before the class in her rubber boots with Fritz's sentence about his "thing" on the blackboard. And how she wept into the dusty rag for cleaning the board.

Silently Fritz and I left the Gypsy settlement. On our right,

just where the village street began a slight rise, stood Angela Barbulescu's wooden cottage, the cottage I had dashed from, head over
heels.

"Why's there no light in Barbu's house?" I asked.

"How should I know?" Fritz sounded annoyed.

"A light ought to be on. Barbu always goes to bed late." I stepped
toward the house and saw that the curtains weren't pulled closed.
"She's not at home," I concluded. "She's always in her house, otherwise. She never goes away."

"She probably tied one on and went to sleep. Like that chuck-
lehead Gypsy," Fritz answered.

I shook my head without replying. We went back into the village. When we reached the wall of the church, I turned off to the
left. I wanted to go to bed. Then I changed my mind without
knowing why.

"I'll walk you home," I said.

Fritz stopped. He glared at me in hostility. Then the dam broke.
The resentment that had been building up in him all evening came
pouring out. "You want to walk me home? I haven't got a home
in this hole. Get that through your head! I just live here with my
parents. Unfortunately! Everybody in this village is crazy. The
crummy priest, the idiotic Gypsy, your stupid grandfather, and you,
too. You're one of them, one of the idiots. You people don't understand anything! The party, Barbu with her shitty poems, Korolev!
Sputnik! The whole idiotic pile of shit. Mary in heaven, what a
joke! Absolutely ridiculous." Fritz was working himself into a rage.
"There is no heaven," he screamed, "and there's no hell either."
Then he aped Pater Johannes: "'We proclaim that the immaculate virginal Mary, Mother of God, was taken up into heavenly
glory body and soul at the end of her earthly life.' Shit on Mary.
Shit on the whole thing. She isn't anywhere. And God isn't any-
where either. God is dead. Your stupid God is dead, you blind fools.
You're all clueless, chuckleheaded idiots."

To my surprise I realized that I wasn't afraid. I was only taken
by surprise. I'd never seen my schoolmate like this. Furious, trembling with outrage. All the tirades Fritz had fired off certainly hit
me, but they bounced off. Bombs without fuses, ineffectual duds.
But now our fight had finally arrived. I'd always been afraid of a

moment like this, had sought ways of avoiding conflict, but now it was here. And I was astonished at myself. The fight didn't make me fearful or hesitant. The sluice gates of anger had been opened, and I was awake, alive, courageous. And calm.

"Tell me something I don't know. It's been in the cards for a long time that you would leave Baia Luna someday. You aren't really one of us. You don't belong here. But I also know you'll pay a price for leaving. You'll have to pay it."

"I don't have to do anything!" Fritz's hot anger turned into defiance. "I don't have to do anything for anybody."

I laughed in scorn. Only when I was ripe in years would I realize why I was being unfair to Fritz by goading him on. "Five minutes ago you had to do something. You told Buba you had something to take care of. Right this minute? At this time of night?"

Fritz looked up at the church. The hands of the clock in the steeple were invisible in the darkness.

"You always talk like a know-it-all, but nothing happens." I kept on provoking him. "Go to Kronauburg! I'm going to bed."

"Wait!"

Fritz walked over to the stone wall, the thick wall that was said to have once protected the church of Baia Luna from the assaults of the Mussulmen. He went along the wall to the oak portal leading into the churchyard.

"Come on!" he called to me.

"What are you going to do?"

"Come on," Fritz repeated. "You want to see something happen, don't you? So I'm going to prove something to you."

"What?"

"That Nietzsche is smarter than you pious Catholics. Your church is nothing but a crypt for your God. Are you coming or not?"

I followed him. Without hesitating. Led not, as one might suppose, by Fritz Hofmann's imperious tone but by some vague instinct. Nietzsche! I had no clue about all the things that graphomaniac had committed to paper. But my curiosity had been piqued. I had read the name several times already, F. W. NIETZSCHE, stamped in gold on the spines of dark brown leather bindings. The books stood in a bookcase in the Hofmanns' parlor next to the poster of the

Virgin of the Torch. Fritz's father got something out of Nietzsche. But what? I didn't give a hoot for Nietzsche, but I was interested in something else: the shady existence of Heinrich Hofmann. He was the only person in Baia Luna who had to know something about the past of the teacher Barbulescu. Fritz had said his father and Dr. Stefan Stephanescu were good friends. Hofmann had taken the studio portrait of the party secretary of Kronauburg for display in classrooms and government offices. In the Paris of the East, moreover, he'd taken that snapshot of the pretty Angela soulfully puckering her lips for Stephanescu. I hoped perhaps to learn more about Heinrich Hofmann from Fritz and from Nietzsche. About his opinions. Maybe this Nietzsche fellow concealed a piece of the puzzle that was this man I didn't trust, without being able to say exactly why Herr Hofmann struck me as suspicious.

As we stood below the church tower, the clock struck the hour. I counted ten strokes. In their courtyard the Schuster family's German shepherd started up, first with sharp barking and then with threatening growls until he finally stopped. At the same time, it got dark as it always did at ten o'clock, when the power plant in Kronauburg shut off the current for the streetlights in all the district villages.

Fritz pressed down the latch of the church door, which was never locked on Pater Johannes's orders.

"Why is it so dark?" hissed Fritz.

"Try pushing the curtain aside," I suggested sarcastically. I groped my way past him and felt for the heavy velvet that on cold days protected the congregants from drafts. I pulled it aside, and we ducked into the nave.

Fritz Hofmann was in a church for the first time in his life. The stale air crept into our nostrils, a stuffy mixture of cold incense, melted wax, and human perspiration.

"Does it always smell this bad?"

I didn't answer, just stood still for a moment until my eyes adjusted to the weak light. It flickered from an oil lamp on the wall to the right of the sanctuary and bathed the interior of the Lord's house in a warm red shimmer. I looked around. Everything was in its place: to my right the steps up to the choir stalls, baptismal font, and pulpit; to my left two rows of pews, one for men and one for women, the kneelers for receiving Holy Communion, and beyond them the chancel, lectern, the high altar with the Holy of Holies and the image of Christ Pantocrator, then the carved side altars with the damned and the saved at the Last Judgment. I knew that on the bas-reliefs the damned were tearing their hair and grinding their teeth while the righteous exulted and rejoiced. Every detail so vividly visible when I attended Mass on Sunday was there, discernible only as a shadow in the dull glow of the Eternal Flame. I had been taught that the light testified to the presence of Christ and was a pledge of his existence in the form of the sacred bread in the tabernacle, though I'd never paid much attention to the lamp in the daytime. But now, at night, the small red lamp drew all my attention to itself. Silent and unobtrusive, the oil lamp burned as if it had no intention of illuminating the world but only of taking away a bit of its darkness.

Fritz strode up the center aisle to the front of the church. His leather shoes clacked on the stone floor and echoed from the arches. He stopped at the baptismal font and flicked his fingers in the water. Some drops moistened my face. Then he plunged both hands into the font and made crazy gestures with his left hand meant as a parody of crossing himself.

"See?" he said, "I'm baptizing myself. With water, stagnant $H_2O$."

"Of course it's water," I answered quietly. "Let's go."

"Just a second. Just one more little demonstration. Watch this. I'm going to show you how dead your God is inside this tomb. And he won't even notice, I promise."

Before I could grasp what he had in mind, he had vaulted the communion rail into the chancel. He climbed the steps and picked up one of the chairs where the altar boys sat during the sermon. He pushed the chair under the cast-iron bracket from which the red glass sanctuary lamp was suspended on delicate chains. I saw the light falling on the hymn board whose wooden numerals directed the congregation to number 702 in the Catholic hymnal. "Almighty God, We Praise Thy Name" was the last hymn that had been sung in church.

"No lamp burns forever," cried Fritz. Then he drew in his breath and blew. The little flame flickered for one or two seconds as if warding off death. Then it went out.

I remember that at that moment the Gypsy girl Buba popped into my head, her chapped hand on my cheek, her fragrant hair, and the screechy voice of her mother, "Bubbah, is somebody there?" When Fritz Hofmann's breath extinguished the Eternal Flame, the thought of Buba flared up for a brief instant. I was again astonished. I felt that in the midst of the darkness, I was watching myself with the eyes of a stranger who was simultaneously an intimate friend. I saw all the possibilities: I could yell, call Fritz crazy, rush forward, grab the defiler of the temple, beat him up, apply my fist to his belly, his face. I could run away, call the priest, ring the bell. All those choices were open to me. I could choose, but I didn't. I followed my feet and simply left. With my eyes closed, the way I had gone hundreds of times before, every Sunday since I could walk. As the church door creaked, a cry reached my ears. A voice broke into falsetto, the echoes multiplied and overlapped in the darkness. "Hey, wait for me! How am I supposed to find my way out of here?"

I tossed and turned in my bed. Grandfather Ilja and my mother were asleep, and from the next room I could hear the regular snores of Aunt Antonia, too. Sleeping was out of the question for me. My heart was pumping the blood so powerfully through my body that my neck veins bulged and my head felt like it was going to burst. This had been going on for two or three hours.

I got up, opened the window, and looked out into the night. Inhale, exhale, inhale, exhale. Turn off your thoughts. Calm down. I registered the silence lying over Baia Luna but couldn't become part of it. This stillness was deceptive. It had no location. Came from nothingness.

Fritz Hofmann hadn't merely blown out a burning wick; he had overstepped a limit. He had violated a prohibition that was so unquestionable, so indubitable, that it had no need to be named or voiced. The boundary was invisible but real. It was *the* boundary, the hidden threshold that only reveals itself at the moment it is violated. A threshold beyond which there was no going back.

If only I hadn't gone along. If only I had grabbed hold of Fritz, torn the chair from his hands. Then I could go to school in the morning, calculate percentages, willingly copy down everything Miss Barbulescu assigned.

On the other hand, why should I feel responsible or guilty for the deeds of others? Fritz is Fritz and I'm me. That was my exoneration, the absolution from my gnawing sense of guilt. But I had allowed Fritz to act, left him alone with his Nietzsche. With cool calculation I had used him just to make something happen so I could find out about his father.

I pulled on my sweater and stepped into my pants. Carrying my shoes, I stole silently down the steps. In the store I grabbed a box of matches. Then I slipped out the back door, tied my shoes, and ran to the church. The gate was still open. It was so dark I almost tripped over the heavy velvet curtain, which had been pulled off its rod and lay on the stone floor. I lit a match and went down the middle aisle to the chancel. Cautiously I approached the sanctuary. The chair Fritz had stood on was still there under the extinguished lamp. There was a smell of scorched oil and singed wick. I stuffed the box of matches into my pocket and crept up the altar steps in the dark. In a few moments everything would be back the way it had been. I straightened up, and the top of my head banged hard against something. The lectern fell over with a crash, and my body shuddered at the sharp pain. I put a hand to my head and felt warm blood wetting my hair and dripping onto the floor. Then someone pushed open the door from the sacristy. Someone entered the chancel slowly, with a heavy tread, carrying a petroleum lamp in one hand: Johannes Baptiste. He came toward me and held the lamp up to my blood-smeared face.

"Pavel!" the priest cried in shock and disappointment. "You, Pavel! What are you doing here? What have you done?"

"I . . . I only wanted to . . ."

"Get out! Get out of the house of God!" thundered the priest. "You shall never, ever enter this house again."

By the time I realized the shattering enormity of his words,

Johannes Baptiste had disappeared into the sacristy with a final "Go to hell!" I left.

At the edge of the village square I bent over the hollowed-out tree trunk that served as a watering trough and washed my hands. I plunged my head into the cold water and rinsed the sticky blood from my face and hair.

What should I do? Who could I talk to? Grandfather Ilja would certainly take the side of the priest. I could also forget about my mother. And Johannes Baptiste himself? Should I seek him out during the coming day and explain the misunderstanding, protest my innocence to a blustery old man who had banned me from God's house without the slightest question about the circumstances? A man who had cursed me, damned me to hell, me, who only wanted to restore order? Fury rose up within me. Who did this priest think he was that he could make himself the judge over good and evil?

No, I would not go see him. Even though from this night on, Fritz Hofmann was dead as my friend, I would not betray him. I would never become a Judas in order to beg absolution from this self-righteous man of God, absolution for something I hadn't done. Never.

I was about to turn sixteen. I was stuck in a swamp halfway between a boy and a man. As I washed my bloody face in the cattle trough on the village square of Baia Luna in the middle of the night, I understood I was alone. For the first time I felt the pain of not having a father, felt empty and abandoned. I had never missed my father. The photograph was enough for me, the one my mother took out from behind its pane of glass on winter nights when she sat in her chair and dreamed her way back to her husband, to my father Nicolai Botev. A stranger. Now I longed for that stranger who had gone off to war and never returned. He had taken something from me, something that lay cut off and withered in distant Russia, a piece of my roots, a source of confidence. I longed for a firm hand, a strong arm, and the reassuring belief that everything would turn out all right in the end. And yet I felt not just pain, not just sorrow and anger. An unknown feeling sprouted within me, pushed its way into my consciousness, grew larger, stubborn at first, but then powerful and strong. On the night the Eternal Flame was extinguished in Baia Luna, I learned that I stood alone in the world. And that knowledge produced an appetite for life. Back in my bed in the predawn twilight, I wept bitter tears of happiness. I felt free.

I was still asleep when the school bell rang. Mother and Grandfather let me sleep, so I didn't know Buba Gabor had come into the store shortly before eight. Before leaving her house she had checked on her uncle Dimitru, still fast asleep under a mountain of sheepskins after his fall down our porch steps. Buba later told me that she was surprised to discover that her uncle had turned around in his sleep and his feet were resting on the pillow. She didn't tell me that she had hurriedly searched his jacket pockets and swiped a few coins.

"What's wrong with you, boy?" exclaimed my mother as I came down the stairs shortly before nine. I had dark circles under my eyes, and my hair was in matted hanks. "Sit down!" she commanded and immediately began examining my head wound. There was a gash on my forehead above the hairline. Mother said I was lucky the laceration wasn't too deep.

"What happened?" she asked. Grandfather Ilja was concerned, too. I waved them off and said I had banged my head against a low lintel down at Dimitru's when I took the drunken Gypsy home last night. Satisfied with this explanation, my mother fetched some gauze for a bandage and ordered me to bed. I gruffly refused to be nursed.

"Oh, before I forget," said Mother, "you had a visitor this morning. Buba was here. I think she wanted to walk to school with you."

"You think so, or did she say so? Buba's never done that before."

"She asked for you. I told her you were still asleep and maybe had a cold. You were so cold yesterday, and you sat by the stove half the day. Anyway, Buba seemed disappointed. Then she bought a handful of chewing gum. It was amazing. She tore off the silver foil and stuffed it all in her mouth."

"I have to go to school," I said, threw on my jacket, and was out the door. It had turned cold overnight. Although the sun was breaking through the clouds, you could feel that winter was close at hand. There was already some snow on the mountains. The cries of children drifted over from the school yard. I looked up at the church tower. The clock said nine fifteen. There was no recess at that time of the morning. The teacher hadn't shown up for school, and I had no doubt whatsoever that she wasn't going to. Never again would Barbu teach in Baia Luna.

"No school today! Barbu's not there!" Buba had seen me coming and ran up. "I thought you were sick with a cold."

"Where did you hear that?" I pretended my mother hadn't told me about her visit.

Buba tapped her forehead. "The third eye. You should know by now that Uncle Dimi and I have second sight. I hope you realize what an honor it is for a *gajo* like you to even hear about that. 'Cause we Gypsies . . ."

"Where's Barbu?"

Buba tossed her hair back.

"I don't know. She's just not here."

"And what does your third eye see?" I mocked her.

Buba bowed her head and closed her eyes.

What is this, some act? That's what I wanted to say, but the words stuck in my throat. Buba stood there frozen, like a statue. Then she folded her hands and slowly, slowly lifted her head toward the sky. I hardly dared to breathe. She looked wonderful: dirty and beautiful. Her tousled hair, handsome face, her velvet skin, and full, dark lips.

Suddenly Buba started shaking; then just as abruptly, she stood stock-still and stared at me with eyes like saucers. "I'm afraid," she whispered.

A chill ran down my spine. "What do you see?"

"I see flowers, bright yellow sunflowers."

"Anything else?"

"Her hair, Barbu's hair blowing in the wind."

Buba started running toward the lower end of the village, where her people lived.

I walked after her, not hurrying. I could never have caught up with her anyway. On my way to the Gypsies' I saw that Barbu's curtains were still not pulled closed. When I got to Dimitru's house I clapped my hands.

"Enter, please," called a strange voice, "and leave all cares behind."

I slipped off my shoes and went into Dimitru's room. He wasn't there.

"Don't be afraid," said a Gypsy with a huge mustache. "I am Salman, Dimitru's cousin." Salman was sitting on a stool that was missing one leg. In his lap was a wooden board and on it a frying pan full of onions and mutton, dripping with fat. He offered me a piece of bread and held out the pan for me. "Dip it in and chew it slowly. It will banish the spirits of the night."

I declined. "Where's Dimitru? Where's Buba?"

"Dimitru is in the library. Urgent studies. Just don't ask me what's the matter with him or I'll have to start worrying. 'Where are you going so early?' I asked him this morning. And you know what he replied? 'If I don't rescue Mary I'm a lost soul.' That's what he said. Can you beat it? What Mary did he mean? Yesterday he was quite cheerful, and now this woman has turned his head. Something must have happened yesterday, at that birthday party. And I'll tell you: whatever it was, it wasn't good."

"And where's Buba?"

"In school, where do you think?"

"There's no school today. The teacher has disappeared."

Salman furrowed his brow. "Where could a teacher disappear to in this Podunk?" Without waiting for an answer, he put down his pan, wiped his greasy mouth on his shirtsleeve, and got to his feet. The stool fell over. Soon Salman returned with Buba in tow. He eased down onto the rickety stool again and offered us a seat on Dimitru's bed.

"Buba, I have to know what else you saw at Barbu's," I begged. "Please tell me."

"Only yellow sunflowers and her hair in the wind."

"But Barbu has short hair. I can't imagine it blowing in the wind."

"I don't know either. But that's how I saw it: long blond hair. I'm sure. And her hair was tied up in a kerchief, like a ponytail."

"Like on my photo" slipped out.

"What photo? Did some girl with blond hair give you a picture?"

I could see she was jealous, but I didn't answer her question about a blonde. "When did you see Barbu last? She lives right next door to you."

"I wasn't in school yesterday, so day before yesterday" was her brief answer. "Not since."

"Barbu?" Salman chimed in. "You mean Miss Barbulescu?"

"Yes, do you know her?"

"I don't. Never seen her. But yesterday I gave some guy a ride. I drove my wagon over from Kronauburg with that television for Dimitru. I picked up the man on the way here, after I'd passed Apoldasch. I felt sorry for him, on foot in such shitty weather. So I took him along. Should have thought twice about it, though. Talked my ear off the whole way, he did. Who'd I know in Baia Luna? Did I know the schoolteacher? (How would I?) Then the guy followed me right in here as if he owned the place and asked Dimitru like some cock of the walk if he would be so kind as to identify the domicile of the village schoolteacher Miss Angela Bar-bulescu. 'Right over there,' was all my cousin said. Wham, the guy is gone. Not even time for a word of thanks. He could at least have helped me unload that heavy TV."

"What'd he look like?"

"Big guy, I'll tell you, six-six if he was an inch. A tank. Long brown coat, hat, mustache—like mine, but lighter. Mid- to late thirties, I'd say, if somebody can guess the age of you *gaje* at all. A suspicious character, believe you me. Had a wart on his cheek. The right one. No, hang on . . . the left one from my vantage point . . . a big fat one, I'm telling you. It looked funny, and I asked myself, Why doesn't he get that thing removed? Just a little cut and it'd be gone. Anyway, the guy didn't thank me. Didn't like Gypsies. A Black like me can smell that."

I stood up.

"Where are you going?" asked Buba.

"To Barbu's house."

"I'm coming, too."

There were already some men and women from Baia Luna gathered in front of the teacher's cottage. Hermann Schuster Junior had told his parents about Barbu's absence. His father had asked his wife Erika to look in on her because his head was still hurting from the blow with the wine bottle. Now Erika and her son Hermann were at a loss. They were standing in front of Barbu's house along with Julia Simenov and her father Emil, Julius Knaup the sacristan, and about a dozen schoolkids. The widow Kora Konstantin stood a little off to one side, rosary in hand and mumbling the first Ave Marias of the Joyful Mysteries.

"What are we waiting for?" asked Simenov urgently. The blacksmith had shouldered his sledgehammer and pushed Barbu's garden gate open with his boot. "We may have to break open the front door," he muttered as I pushed past him. I pressed on the latch, and it wasn't locked. The key was in the lock on the inside.

"Out of the way. Beat it. Get lost, kid," said the smith testily.

"She's my teacher and not yours," I responded and stepped into the hall. "Miss Barbulescu?" I called, "Miss Barbulescu?"

"Hello! Is anyone here? Please say something," Erika Schuster joined in. No one answered. "We'll have to take a look," said Frau Schuster. Boldly she opened the door to the parlor.

Barbu wasn't there. The room looked just like I remembered it from my only visit. Neat and clean. A pile of firewood was stacked by the stove. Hermann's mother felt the stove. "Lukewarm. She didn't build a fire. She must not have been here last night."

"She's been drinking again," remarked Simenov, "and not just a drop."

On the table stood an empty bottle and a glass. I picked up the glass.

"Give it here!" The blacksmith grabbed the glass from me and gave it a quick sniff. "*Zuika!* What'd I say?"

Something wasn't right. I remembered that ill-fated evening when Barbu came on to me on her sofa. She'd been drinking then, too. But with the practiced eye of a bartender I had noticed immediately that there was no glass to be seen anywhere. Barbu drank straight from the bottle. This glass in her parlor could only mean that in her last hours in Baia Luna, Angela Barbulescu had not been alone. Someone had been drinking with her. I kept this hunch to myself.

"The whole bottle!" was Erika Schuster's shocked suspicion.

"She must still be so drunk she's wandering around somewhere. And in such cold, with frost on the way. We should look and see if she took a coat with her."

Emil Simenov took a look around the front hall. "A black coat with a fur collar?"

"Yes," called Frau Schuster.

"It's still here."

Erika Schuster opened the door to the bedroom. "Oh, she makes her bed!" The Saxon housewife seemed genuinely surprised and then proceeded to peer into every corner. With an energetic "I guess it'll be okay," she pulled open the door to the closet. "One, two, three. Three wool sweaters," she counted out loud.

"We have no more business here," the smith decided. "Let's go. She'll turn up again."

"One skirt. And two blue dresses!"

Frau Schuster still had her nose in Angela Barbulescu's closet. I looked over her shoulder. The closet smelled like roses. I knew what I was looking for and guessed that I wouldn't find it. One hanger was empty. The dress with the yellow sunflowers was missing. I looked around and couldn't spot the framed portrait of Stephanescu either.

As the gossips would later whisper, when I walked out the garden gate onto the village street I looked like the Grim Reaper in person. Schoolchildren apparently shied away at the sight of me, and Kora Konstantin broke her rosary, whose beads then hailed down onto the heads of the little gawkers. The Gypsy Susanna Gabor exclaimed, "We're going home right this minute!" She grabbed her daughter Buba by the hair with one hand while pointing at Barbu's house with the other: "Bad luck lives under that roof."

All I remember is that I fell into bed exhausted with Buba's words in my ear, "Sleep, Pavel, you need sleep."

In the following days, the rumor pot boiled over in Baia Luna, and everyone had a spoon in it except for the Gypsy Dimitru, who never left the rectory library. He didn't even touch the food Buba left on the doorstep for him. The largely subsided discussion of Angela Barbulescu's obscure origins was revived. Kora dropped hints about Barbu being a "nimmfomaniac" who had been lured back to the capital, while Scherban the shepherd was absolutely convinced he had heard Barbu howling with the wolves up near Fagaras the night before. Probably stark naked, too, Erika Schuster suggested. At least, it was strange that not a single thing was missing from Barbulescu's closet.

The sacristan Julius Knaup also added fuel to the rumor that diabolical powers could have played a part in the disappearance of the teacher. Aghast, he told everyone about the furious struggle that had taken place in the church. First he discovered the curtain torn down at the entrance, and next he saw that someone had knocked over the lectern on the altar. And the blood! Blood everywhere! Smeared on the steps to the altar, on the lectern, in the nave. Some men had immediately run off with Julius Knaup to follow the trail. It petered out by the watering trough, where they could only find hoof prints, which Kora Konstantin's brother-in-law Marku interpreted as an infallible sign that the Goat-Footed One himself had emerged from the mouth of hell to defile the church and on his way back home simply took Barbu along into the Realm of Darkness. Neither Marku Konstantin nor the sacristan Julius Knaup mentioned the fact that inside the church the Eternal Flame was no longer burning.

Father Johannes Baptiste could have shed some light on the darkness of rumor, but he had withdrawn into the rectory to work on his sermon for that coming Sunday. He had his stalwart housekeeper Fernanda turn away anyone who rang his doorbell. The news that the priest had explicitly ordered even Communists like the Brancusis to come to church on Sunday had already spread through the village, and everyone expected some fireworks. But several people doubted the weight of his words, for Johannes Baptiste's senility was growing more obvious by the day. He was getting grayer, wearier, and more confused. And next Sunday? Would he once again thunder combative words from the pulpit? Go up against the Bolsheviks on the Sputnik question? How would he react to the party's plans to collectivize the farmers in a kolkhoz? When the dispossessors arrived, would he demand unquestioned obedience to the state? "Render unto Caesar the things which are Caesar's" was one of his favorite sayings. On the other hand, Pater

Johannes had always been a friend of the farmer. But was he on their side now? Would he call upon them to disobey, resist, even revolt?

Only later did I hear all about these questions and the whole brouhaha. I was sleeping, and my mother Kathalina and Grandfather Ilja left me in peace.

When I woke up refreshed on Friday morning, I came to a decision: nothing would prevent me from finding out what was behind Barbu's disappearance. But first I had to free myself from the burden of damnation the overbearing priest Johannes Baptiste had heaped on my head. My deep resentment of the old man had been transformed while I slept. The heat of my anger had given way to cool calculation. I was unjustly suspected of a grave offense. To violate the Eternal Flame could cost a Catholic his salvation. But I hadn't committed the crime. I wanted nothing more to do with Fritz Hofmann, ever. But betray him? I would never do that. There was only one way out of my dilemma: confession.

In contrast to my original resolve never to honor the priest with another word, I would go and confess to him. It was surely a great violation to intentionally conceal a sin in the confessional, but could the opposite possibly be wrong? Could it be sinful to confess to a shameful deed even if you hadn't done it? Was such a person a bald-faced liar? A sinner? Or wasn't he really a sort of martyr—a saint like those early Christians who preferred being torn apart by lions in the Colosseum to kissing Caesar's image on a coin. I would admit that in the midst of an inexplicable blackout of my faith, I had extinguished the Eternal Flame, and I would repent and do penance for my sin. And then the crime would be gone from the world and my inner peace restored without me ratting on Fritz Hofmann. After Sunday Mass I would wait for Pater Baptiste outside the sacristy and ask for the sacrament of absolution.

On Friday, November 8, the second day after Barbu's disappearance, they called Plutonier Cartarescu over from Apoldasch, less out of real concern than not to leave any stone unturned.

That afternoon a gray four-wheel-drive vehicle with grimy windows and a dented fender pulled up at the cattle trough on the village square. To everyone's surprise there were two men in the car with Cartarescu. A uniformed policeman from Kronauburg squeezed out of the jeep after Plutonier, a heavyset guy with a full beard and grizzled, wiry hair sticking out under his cap like a bird's nest. He lit up a Carpati and shook hands with the men of Baia Luna but ignored me and Petre Petrov. The third man remained in the backseat awhile. At first all I saw were his shiny black shoes peeking out the door, and I got the impression that this classy footwear was hesitating to step into the mud of the village street. But then he emerged: Major Lupu Raducanu, in plainclothes. His brown coat had obviously been made to order of the finest material and was draped casually over his shoulders. He cut an elegant figure, although it contrasted disconcertingly with his soft, beardless face. Chubby cheeks gave him a more prepubescent than masculine appearance. Lupu Raducanu was in his midtwenties but looked markedly younger, which didn't exactly make him seem predestined for his high position in the Securitate. Because of his bored and apathetic manner, some cadres had been disgruntled to learn of his promotion to major in the Security Service. They'd tried to block it, in fact. But their reservations melted away once word got around that this officer possessed interrogation methods so crafty and unconventional that he could bring any opponent of the Republic to the point of talking—or, as Karl Koch muttered, of silence. Nobody in Baia Luna knew any details, just enough to know that it was better to have nothing to do with the Securitate in general and Lupu Raducanu in particular.

Raducanu looked around, impassive except for a restless glitter in his eyes. I saw how the men who had just been jovially greeting Cartarescu and the stout policeman suddenly folded their arms across their chests. The women lowered their voices. Intimidated by the oppressive atmosphere, the shouting children fell silent.

"My son, my fine boy! It's been so long!" With outstretched arms the widow Vera rushed toward Lupu. She hadn't heard from him in a year. All she'd had was a package delivered by a military supply truck the previous Christmas. In it Vera found a salami, genuine ground coffee, a bar of Luxor soap in gold foil, and a slip of paper with three meager words on it: "Happy Holidays, Lupu." But for the moment, her disappointment seemed forgotten. She flew to her son, who was standing on the village square with ostentatious calm.

"Lupu, my son, don't you know how much your mother has missed you? You never visit me. Why don't you get me out of this miserable hole? Why so ungrateful?"

Vera née Adamski had married Aurel Raducanu, a high-ranking officer of the Security Service, at a young age and with her chin in the air had moved from Baia Luna to an imposing villa on the Klosterberg in Kronauburg. There she lived until, one night three years ago, she discovered her husband lying in the bathroom next to the toilet bowl like a dead pig with a yellow face and a swollen belly. A diagnosis of putrefied liver made the rounds. And then Vera Raducanu began her free fall into the abyss. Her pension was canceled, and she had to clear out of the house on the Klosterberg. To escape the humiliation (for a woman of her social position) of wasting away in a shabby apartment block on the outskirts of town, Vera had preferred to take refuge in Baia Luna in the house of her cousin Adamski the mailman. Only for a short time, as she repeated on every possible occasion. Because her son Lupu, treading in his father's footsteps and pursuing a brilliant career with the Securitate, would soon fetch her back to town and restore her social status.

Major Lupu Raducanu dismissed his mother's reproaches with a curt "I have work to do" and turned to the onlookers. "Does she live down there?" He pointed in the direction of Angela Barbulescu's cottage and was rewarded with a nod. The security agent gave a brief jerk of his chin, which Cartarescu and the elderly policeman from Kronauburg took as a signal to follow him.

For ten or fifteen minutes the three of them looked around in the teacher's house and came to the conclusion that a minute forensic investigation was unnecessary. Plutonier Cartarescu merely impounded the empty schnapps bottle and the glass. These objects were regarded as evidence that, once again, alcohol had driven a person to commit a desperate act.

On the village square the elderly policeman explained that just in the district of Kronauburg, four hundred people were reported missing each year. Half of them showed up again in a week, and a good portion of those had taken off in the first place to escape familial or conjugal duties or had disappeared with a lover or mistress, while two or three dozen of the disappearances were alcohol related.

"Those drunks are awful, just awful," Cartarescu corroborated his superior's words, "and we have to identify the bodies, mostly in the spring when they emerge after the snow melt. First the suicides fill up on booze, then they freeze to death in their sleep. Remember last summer, that case with the false teeth?"

"Don't remind me," groaned the fat guy and he stuck another Carpati in his mouth. "Three gold teeth. Who's got that many? We found the skull first—up in the Fagaras Mountains, below the Ortuella Chasm. Just the naked noggin with a couple tufts of hair still on it. And the bones, all mixed up: arms, ribs, thighbones. No surprise: the wolves and bears make a mess of everything, like a Gypsy camp. We knew where the scene of the crime was once we found the bottle. The cork was still in it. Drink yourself silly and then neatly cork up the bottle, your male suicides never do that. And the bottle was only half empty. You want to know why? It was a woman! We were thinking we'd have to go knock on every dentist's door in the whole district, but we found the right one pretty quick. He said right away, 'I know her. Three gold teeth, two in the upper-right quadrant, one in the lower left.' The wife of Dascalescu, second in command at Kronauburg Electric. A randy old goat, let me tell you, after anything with skirts. Must have gotten to be too much for her, being the wife and always last in line. Killed herself instead of her old man. She was missing without a trace for two whole years. Scratch that: nobody disappears without a trace. It's just a question of when we find the remains."

Plutonier Cartarescu added that for now we shouldn't worry too much about Miss Barbulescu. "She'll turn up again for sure. Unless she's holed up somewhere with a secret lover." Cartarescu snorted a laugh, glanced over at the silent Lupu Raducanu in embarrassment, and then offered the opinion that a person's love life was fundamentally a private matter and therefore not the object of official scrutiny. But since in Miss Barbulescu's case it was a civil servant who was involved, her absence from the school would be punished as a serious dereliction of duty, although at the present time no search would be initiated.

The fat policeman nodded and ground out his cigarette with

his shoe. "There's no point searching now when it's already snowing in the mountains."

Cartarescu enjoined us to keep our eyes and ears open and report anything whatsoever unusual to the police station in Apoldasch. Then he tugged at his cap, saluted, and opened the driver's door of the jeep.

"Just a moment! We're not in such a hurry."

The whole time I'd been getting the feeling that Lupu Raducanu had just as little interest in the fate of missing drunks as in the disappearance of a village schoolteacher. Now he turned to the men of Baia Luna.

"Just a few more questions," said the security agent. Then he looked around and walked up to the Saxon Hermann Schuster. Everyone could see the goose egg on his forehead. It had turned dark violet since the party member Roman Brancusi had shattered a bottle on his head on Grandfather's birthday.

"You should have that examined in the hospital," said Raducanu. "An undiagnosed concussion can cause permanent damage."

"It's nothing worth mentioning," the Saxon replied.

"Doesn't look good, though."

"Like I said, not worth mentioning."

Raducanu dug a white pack of cigarettes out of his coat pocket. Kents: a brand unknown in Baia Luna. The major flipped open a silver lighter, took his own sweet time lighting his cigarette, and then inhaled the smoke.

"I hear you had a little disagreement a few days ago?"

"Me? No. I can only repeat, it wasn't worth mentioning." Schuster seemed ill at ease.

"That's right. Just a little misunderstanding." Liviu Brancusi and his brothers Roman and Nico emerged from the crowd of men and came over to Raducanu and Schuster.

"J-j-just a mi-mi-misunderstanding between two m-m-men," Roman repeated. "A m-m-minor mi-mi-misunderstanding between two m-m-men who had ma-ma-maybe a little too m-much to drink. You can see, M-m-major, the argument's been se-se-settled already."

Roman Brancusi ostentatiously extended his hand to Hermann Schuster. The Saxon shook it.

"Well, well. The argument is settled. How nice. Very pleasant to hear. So now you're in agreement?"

Schuster and the three Brancusi brothers nodded cautiously.

"Very good. I hear tell that the argument was about the implementation of the government's five-year plan and the upcoming collectivization of agriculture."

"Who told you that?" asked Schuster.

"It doesn't matter, does it? Now that you, a Saxon, an ethnic German, and the comrades Brancusi are in agreement."

Hermann Schuster didn't reply.

Major Raducanu turned to Roman. "Comrade, I understood you to say that this difference of opinion is really over and done with?"

"Ye-yes indeed, Co-co-comrade Major."

"Very good. That means we can proceed immediately to transfer private landholdings in Baia Luna to the possession of the Commonwealth?"

Liviu Brancusi piped up, "It's possible there's a little more persuading that needs to be done. But our side has the best arguments. Baia Luna needs progress."

"So, Comrade Brancusi, that means the work of persuasion has yet to be completed?"

"But soon will be, Comrade Major! Very soon."

"I don't understand. You were just talking about being in agreement. But now? Do people have a problem seeing the necessity for progress? Is there stubbornness? Protests? Resistance?"

The onlookers saw party member Liviu getting red in the face. "Protests? Resistance? Here in the village? No, no, one wouldn't put it that way."

"One damn well would put it that way!" Karl Koch pushed his way to the front. "And I will put it that way. Loud and clear."

Koch looked Major Raducanu straight in the eye.

"After the war your father Aurel sent us off to the Russian mines even though you people cheered for the Führer just as much as we did. We Saxons did the dirty work for you. When we came home you'd taken our land, our houses, even the right to vote, a right every citizen has. We had a long struggle to get everything back that belonged to us. And now you want to dispossess us again. Let me tell you something, you little snot! I'm not giving up anything. Nothing! You Bolsheviks aren't getting anything out of me. Over my dead body!"

Lupu Raducanu kept calm, even nodded. "You're an upstanding fellow, an honest soul, Herr . . . Herr . . . ?"

"Koch," said the Saxon, "Karl Koch."

Raducanu lit up another Kent. "Our country needs people like you, honest men, Herr Koch. People who say what they think."

The Saxon was completely nonplussed.

I was standing off to one side and got a fright as Lupu Raducanu suddenly stretched out his arm and pointed at our shop. "Herr Koch, there must be paper and pencils in that store?"

"Of course," answered the confused Saxon. "Why do you ask?"

To Karl Koch's surprise Raducanu took his wallet out of his coat and fished out a bill. Before Koch knew what was happening, the major had stuck the money into his jacket pocket.

"Herr Koch, you will go into that store and buy paper and a pencil. Then you will sit down in your parlor and write down everybody's name. Just the men in the village, in two columns. To the left the names of the ones who want a kolkhoz and to the right the names of the men who refuse to accept progress. I know you're an honest man. You won't forget anyone. You have three days. Then I want to see the list. I think we understand each other. Three days."

Raducanu flipped his cigarette onto the ground.

"I'll do shit-all, pretty boy."

Koch spat onto Raducanu's shiny shoes and tore the bill into little pieces. The major grinned, turned on his heel, and got into the car.

The fat policeman gave a brief shrug, which I interpreted as a gesture of regret, then Cartarescu started the car. The motor revved to a shriek, and the tires spun. As the cloud of diesel exhaust dissipated, I corrected an erroneous impression. I always thought a Securitate interrogator made people sweat, but Lupu Raducanu gave me a chill.

# Chapter Five

●

## A PRIEST'S LAST DAY, SILENCE, AND A MISSING COFFIN

I saw Karl Koch through the eyes of a boy, but everything I had seen convinced me the courageous Saxon would never draw up that damn list. It was November 8, a Friday. On Monday the Securitate major would show up in Baia Luna again and demand the list. On the left the names of those who wanted the kolkhoz, on the right the names of those opposed to the nationalization of their land.

As the gray jeep sped off in the direction of Kronauburg, some of the men clapped their German neighbor on the shoulder and expressed their admiration for his blunt words and the guts it took to say them.

" 'Pretty boy'! Not bad!" said Istvan. " 'Fatface' would've been even better."

If I had to guess, I'd say the Hungarian would be on the right side of the list that Karl Koch would definitely not be turning over. Same for the Petrovs and the Deslius. And of course the Scherban brothers and Grandfather Ilja. On the left the three Brancusis, all of them stout comrades. Certainly their father Bogdan as well, who didn't till his land anyway, just let it go to seed. Simenov the blacksmith would also be on the left. I wasn't sure about the Konstantins and the sacristan Julius Knaup, nor about Alexandru Kiselev. As a future employee of the state tractor factory, would he dare to have his name on the right side? There was no question where the Saxons stood, except for the photographer Heinrich Hofmann. The Gypsies didn't even enter into the picture, since they had nothing to collectivize.

"Man, Karl, have you gone crazy?"

Hermann Schuster shoved the shoulder clappers aside and

started rebuking his fellow Saxon. "Did you have to call Raducanu a pretty boy? The man is dangerous!"

"I'll say whatever I want to. A pretty boy is a pretty boy."

"Of course," replied Schuster, "but it was a mistake to call Raducanu that to his face, a really dumb mistake."

Hans Schneider put in his two cents: "Not here in the street. Let's go to Ilja's where we can talk it over in private." Some agreed and started off toward the tavern—but only those whose names would have been on the right side.

I was still preoccupied with my fears about the extinguished Eternal Flame and the mysterious disappearance of Angela Barbulescu and so only grudgingly followed Grandfather's summons to help him out in the tavern. As I was about to open a bottle of *zuika*, the men signaled me not to. Those who had just been congratulating Karl Koch for his resistance to Lupu Raducanu now admitted ruefully that Koch's public protest against the Security Service had been extremely unwise and could have unforeseeable consequences.

Hermann Schuster's reproach couldn't be ignored: "If you hadn't provoked Raducanu, the idea with the list of names would never have occurred to him."

"You shouldn't ever tangle with the Securitate, especially not that Lupu. He's nothing but trouble," remarked Alexandru Kiselev, whose only dream was to install transmissions in Stalinstadt.

"Do you realize what you've done, Karl?" Hermann Schuster asked his friend with growing urgency. "You know what it means to have the Securitate as an enemy? It means paragraph one hundred sixty-six: resisting state authority, threatening national security. For that you get two years, five years, maybe even seven years. Off to Aiud or Pitesti. They mess you up. Is spitting on an asshole's shoes worth that? If you make this list, we'll all be in trouble. If you don't, they'll just come and get you."

"Fuck the list," replied young Petre. "With it or without it, either way they're going to force us into the kolkhoz. If not today, then tomorrow. And if Karl doesn't make the list, somebody else will. The Brancusis or Simenov or whoever. The main thing is they want to divide the village. If we're fighting each other, it's easier to dispossess us."

"They're not going to collectivize me!" Karl Koch banged his fist on the table. "You can quote me. I've been on the wrong side once already. Never again! I must have been crazy to run and join that fucking war. I cheered along with everybody else for that strutting rooster and his Third Reich. And I did things I should never have done. Never, never again! I'm not going to let these crooks turn me into their stooge. Black, brown, or red, I don't care. Over my dead body."

"Okay, okay, Karl. We were all stupid." Hermann Schuster put his arm around his friend's shoulders. "But man, it's not just about you. It's about all of us, all of us who want to live here together in peace. It's about your wife and children, too, Karl. Think about Klara, think about Franz and Theresa."

Karl Koch was silent.

"But it's true. Petre is right," Hermann Schuster continued. "Raducanu wants to drive a wedge between us. We can't let him do it. We need unity."

The men sat together awhile longer but didn't make much progress toward deciding what to do about the disunity threatening the village. The only sure thing was that Karl Koch was not going to make a list of names. No one, however, had a useful suggestion for how the Saxon should behave when Lupu Raducanu showed up again on Monday. More stymied than purposeful, they all agreed to wait and see what Pater Johannes would say in his sermon on Sunday. But then because of the urgency of the situation, they decided to seek the priest's advice the next morning. With the authority of the clergy behind them, they hoped it would be easier to resist the power of the Securitate.

I was shocked when Karl Koch got up to go home. He looked tired and gray, older by several years and smaller than usual. Suddenly I understood what fear is. Without being afraid myself, I saw what fear can do to someone. Hermann Schuster's appeal to think of his wife and two little children had awakened it in him. He was disabled by a power that snuck up on him with the question, What will happen if . . . ?

I tried to imagine what Karl Koch must be thinking. What would happen if he didn't write down the names? What if on Monday he just went and hid out in the woods for a few days? Raducanu would leave, empty-handed. But the major would be back again sometime with ten or twenty of his people. They would come looking for him but wouldn't be able to find him. But what then? What would happen to his wife and his children? Who would look after them? What about the others in the village? Would the Security Service interrogate Karl Koch's friends as accessories to an enemy of the state? And what if Koch stayed in the village and confronted Raducanu with the words: Fuck your list, Fatface, write it yourself! That would mean Aiud or Pitesti. I didn't even know where those two towns were, but I knew there were big prisons there. People said that anyone who made it out of them was never the same again. After two or three years in the clink, the wives no longer recognized their husbands nor children their fathers.

That Konstantin woman is nuts," said my mother Kathalina at the supper table. "She really believes the devil himself's been running around the village at night. Sometimes I have to wonder what kind of place this is, anyway."

"Whoever pays attention to anything Kora says is beyond help. Best thing is just to let it go in one ear and out the other," Grandfather replied. "But it is a funny thing about that blood. Everyone in the village is scratching their heads about the trail of blood from the altar to the horse trough. I'd sure like to know what went on that night."

I was relieved. No one seemed to have the least inkling that Fritz and I had anything to do with what happened. Strangely enough, no one said anything about the Eternal Flame being out. Could it be burning again? Had Johannes Baptiste or the sacristan Knaup relit it? I'd have to take a look. Next morning, when the delegation of men paid the priest a visit to confer about Karl Koch's list and how to get out of it, I'd go into the church.

Even though the modest flicker of the red lamp was hardly noticeable in the daylight, I saw immediately that it wasn't burning. But nobody else had noticed. With the little box of matches still in my pocket I could reestablish order.

But I didn't. It was Fritz Hofmann who had blown out the light, not me. And it was up to him to straighten things out insofar as that was possible. Surely the Christian God was merciful and forgave every sinner: every liar, every thief, perhaps even every murderer, as long as he truly repented. But there probably wasn't much that could be done about someone who blew out the Eternal Flame. Fritz would be punished. Maybe not today or tomorrow, but sometime or other he would pay for his sacrilege. On the other hand, what if God was in fact dead, as that Nietzsche guy claimed? Then Fritz Hofmann had nothing to fear, for a dead God cannot punish. But could God be dead? Could he die at all? If he's dead, I reasoned, then he must have been alive at some point. But if he was once alive, then he had to be both almighty and immortal, because a god who wasn't almighty and immortal was no kind of god. The true God, however, could obviously not be dead because of his immortality. Accordingly, Nietzsche was wrong. But was that thinker really so limited that I, a simple barroom gofer, could overturn his declaration that God was dead with a few logical arguments? I had to discover what Nietzsche really meant and, while I was at it, find out something about Heinrich Hofmann—what he believed, what he thought.

There was no way I was going to ask the photographer directly. And Fritz was dead to me in any case. Under other circumstances, I might have asked the priest for advice, but if I approached Johannes Baptiste with the riddle of the death of God after the incident with the Eternal Flame, he would deny me absolution until the end of time. The only remaining possibility was Dimitru the Gypsy, Lord of the Library. Maybe its collection included even the works of Nietzsche. If so, Dimitru was sure to have studied them.

I left the church and set off for the library. Winter was on its way—a good time to read, which I otherwise never did.

If it had snowed during the night on Friday, then the four men who gathered on the village square on Saturday morning to visit Pater Johannes would have noticed the strange footprints on their way to the rectory. But the first snowfall of the winter of '57 didn't begin until midday. Karl Koch, Petre Petrov, Kallay the Hungarian, and Hermann Schuster stood at the rectory door, and the latter pushed the bell. Fernanda the housekeeper would surely let them in, although in the last few days she had turned every visitor away from her Johannes's door so he would run no chance of being disturbed while preparing his Sunday sermon. But the men were determined not to let themselves be brushed off. They had a more urgent need for their pastor's advice than ever before.

"I'm going to see Dimitru in the library," I explained, hoping to forestall any suspicion that I wanted to get mixed up in the adults' business.

"You can forget the library. Nobody's opening the door," said Petre. "We've been ringing the bell the whole time." Karl Koch belabored the heavy wooden door with his fists. Hermann Schuster had just suggested calling Simenov the blacksmith, who knew how to crack any lock, when Dimitru came shuffling up to the rectory on his way to the library.

"Oh! You here? Blessed are those who seek words of wisdom, for—"

"Nobody's answering the door," said Karl Koch. "Something's wrong."

Dimitru produced a key. "Did you ring?"

"Do we look like idiots?" snapped Petre. "We've been ringing the bell for half an eternity."

"Then there's something wrong." Dimitru unlocked the door.

Everything was quiet on the ground floor and in the library. Following the Gypsy, the men climbed the stairs and found the door to Johannes Baptiste's private apartment cracked open. When they called out his and Fernanda's names and got no response, I followed them. No one paid any attention to me. Hermann Schuster pushed the door and met with resistance. "The rug must be jamming it," he said. They all pushed the door together. They had to push aside something heavy: Fernanda. She lay in the entrance hall in her white apron. There were no signs of injury on her. Karl Koch knelt down and felt for her pulse. The housekeeper was cold and stiff.

Immediately it became clear that the men would never be able to seek the priest's advice again. He would never preach again. Prepared for the worst, they entered the parlor, and when they didn't find Johannes Baptiste there, they proceeded to his study. I stayed in the background as they came upon a scene of devastation. Books had been tumbled off the shelves, drawers pulled out of the chests. The typewriter lay smashed on the floor. The rug was strewn with sheets of paper and notes. And in the midst of it all sat Johannes Baptiste on his desk chair. The thing that was terrible was not that the priest was dead but the way he had been killed. Johannes sat there naked with his hands tied, his head bowed, and his chin resting on his blood-spattered chest. When Karl Koch gently raised his head, a horrific wound opened up. Someone had slit the priest's throat.

Dimitru just stared in dumbfounded disbelief. Then he ran to the door. Again and again he hammered his head against the doorpost. In silence.

The others rubbed dry tears from their eyes. No one said a word. All words were dead, expired even before they were thought.

"What's that?" asked Petre quietly. He pointed to something that looked like a piece of gray string.

The men looked at one another, perplexed. The string was hanging out of the priest's mouth.

"A shoelace?" Hermann Schuster finally said the word. "What's a shoelace doing there?"

When Karl Koch hesitantly took hold of the gray string, he could feel it wasn't a shoelace. Hermann Schuster nodded to him, and Karl pulled. Hanging from the string in his fingers was a dead mouse.

"Who would do such a thing?" whispered Istvan Kallay, pressing his hands against his eyes.

"This is nothing you should be seeing." Hermann Schuster took my arm and tried to hustle me out of the study. But I was rooted so firmly to the spot that the Saxon couldn't move me even an inch. I stood petrified before the naked old man on the chair. I felt nothing, but I saw everything. Every detail. I was transformed into a machine, a photographic apparatus that could fix events in an image but felt nothing. Something in this image caught my attention, something that burned itself onto my retina. It wasn't the pastor or the gaping wound, not the blood or the men covering their faces with their hands and not wanting to believe what they saw. In the midst of the books and papers on the floor there was a little white piece of torn paper. There were only a few words on the handwritten note. I was too far away to read them. The only word I could clearly make out was a name: "Barbu."

That name broke my rigid spell. Whatever else had happened in this room, my one thought was: I have to have that note.

"We've got to report this." Hermann Schuster turned to go. Kallay and Koch followed, walking backward and still staring, fascinated by the gruesome scene. Petre, who had never paid me much attention before, took my hand. Like a longtime intimate. "Come on, Pavel. It's not good to stay here."

My eyes were glued to the piece of paper. I wanted to just pick up the note but I couldn't. No, I had to. Right now. Once the police started to examine everything it would be too late. Something crashed in the stairwell. Hermann Schuster's knees had given way, and he'd fallen. "Petre! Come quick and help!" Petre Petrov jumped for the stairs. A few steps, and I shoved the note into my pocket.

The men decided at first to just announce to the village of Baia Luna that the priest had died. This was absolutely not the time to make the circumstances of his death public, especially because it would frighten the women and children. That afternoon they would call an assembly, but first they had to do what was always done whenever a villager passed away. Karl Koch hunted up Julius Knaup and instructed the sacristan to toll the mourning bell. Within two minutes the village square was filled with people shaking the snow out of their hair and wondering which of the old folks the bell was for. When the name Johannes Baptiste made the rounds, everyone gasped. The women broke down in tears. The men bowed their heads or stared helplessly into the silent descent of the snowflakes and didn't know what to do with their hands. Then someone finally extended his hand to a neighbor who passed the handshake on until all the men and women were walking around in silence, consoling one another. Even the Brancusis, for whom hostility to the church and clergy was a revolutionary article of faith, mixed in with the mourners, genuinely moved by the pain at the loss and realizing that Johannes had always been their opponent but never their enemy.

Karl Koch made the mistake of warning everyone not to enter the rectory under any circumstances until the police in Apoldasch had been notified. After this warning a tense silence prevailed until people realized what the Saxon was saying. When Avram Scherban called out, "What do we need the police for? Our good shepherd was almost ninety and now he's dead," shock and fury gripped the mourners. People at the edge of the crowd started saying that the pastor had not died a natural death. Everyone began talking at once; some even shouted angrily that Karl Koch should tell them what was going on. At last Petre Petrov couldn't control his emotions any longer and shouted, "They slit his throat. They killed him. Him and Fernanda. They murdered him, silenced him—silenced him for good!"

Petre stumbled over to his mother and broke down. While Aldene Petrov bent over her son, everyone else, men and women, rushed to the rectory. Only the Gypsies stood off to one side of the square, shivering in their thin clothes and the silent fear that, from now on, Baia Luna would not be a good place for them.

Schuster, Kallay, and a few other strong men tried to keep the advancing crowd from entering the rectory. They didn't succeed.

The first who rushed the building pushed their way forward to the scene of the crime, where their yelling ceased. Silence filled the room, spread to those pushing in from behind, in the halls, on the stairs, on the village square. Slowly, gradually it became quiet. You could hear the snow falling.

"He's an angel now," a voice suddenly called. Everyone looked at Dimitru. "And he should look like an angel. And so should his Fernanda." Everybody stepped aside to make way for the Gypsy. Dimitru was bringing a stack of snow-white bedsheets.

At the stroke of four Julius Knaup and Marku Konstantin started pulling the bell ropes and hung on them into the night, ringing themselves to exhaustion. Six men carried Fernanda Klein on their shoulders, six Johannes Baptiste, three on the left and three on the right, and all of Baia Luna followed. With infinite slowness the procession moved through the village, through the first snow-fall. Flakes fell on white linen, on two dead faces carried on strong shoulders that were still too weak, white flakes on dark coats and on blond, brown, and black heads that didn't shake them off. Every man, woman, and child held a candle in their left hand and cupped their right around the flame to protect it from the wind.

We reached the church, and the pallbearers laid the bodies on the altar, where they slept in white like an elderly couple. There was singing but no loud prayers, no murmured rosaries. Only the tolling of the bells and sometimes a cough from the chilly pews. The church was bright with all the candles held in hands onto which hot wax dripped, so bright that no one noticed the Eternal Flame was no longer burning.

I sat up front on the right side of the nave beside Grandfather Ilja and Dimitru. The women sat on the left. Around midnight the children were asleep in their mothers' arms, the candles had burned down, and the bells had fallen silent.

When Hermann Schuster and Istvan Kallay were just reaching the police station in Kronauburg with their team of horses, the first inhabitants of Baia Luna were returning to their homes, filled with sorrow and wondering fearfully who would do such a thing. Whatever evil lurked behind the murder of two human beings, it had done more than just kill them. That most silent day Baia Luna had ever experienced ushered fear into the village. I wasn't sure, but on my way home I thought I had seen Fritz Hofmann and his mother Birta among all the shadowy faces streaming out of the church.

The note: since I had snatched the piece of paper from the devastation in the study and under the nose of the murdered priest, it had been knocking around in my head, but I hadn't been able to think clearly about it. The image of the naked Baptiste on his chair raged in my brain, loomed larger, more powerful, threatened to burst my skull, and left no room for anything else. I sat on my bed. The note was on my nightstand in the lamplight: "6.11. A. Barbu, library key. Return!!!"

That's all that was on the scrap of paper, hastily scribbled in pencil. What was clear was that only a man had such angular, spiky handwriting. The housekeeper Fernanda hadn't written it, Johannes Baptiste had, and obviously on November 6. Not until I reviewed the events of that day did I understand how the note came to be written.

November 6 was the previous Wednesday. I'd gotten up earlier than usual, caught Grandfather holding a tin funnel to his ear, and given him the Cubans for his birthday. Then I went to school, listless as ever. "Send this man straight to hell! Destroy him!" Angela Barbulescu had whispered in my ear. At noon I'd seen the teacher for the last time, when she shuffled to the blackboard, took the rag and wiped out Fritz's sentence about his "thing." In the afternoon Dimitru's cousin Salman from Kronauburg had driven the television to Baia Luna in his cart, picked up some ugly guy on the way, and given him a ride to the village. Probably Barbu had known the stranger and had a drink with him in her parlor, she from the bottle as always, he from a glass. After that she'd disappeared. But the note revealed that before she did, Angela Barbulescu had paid a visit to the pastor on that Wednesday afternoon, before three o'clock. Because at three, Dimitru was already lugging the television into the tavern. While the men were admiring the appliance I'd run off to tell Fritz Hofmann about my grandfather's birthday present. Fritz had come right back with me. And right after that, Johannes Baptiste arrived at the tavern where he remained until late that evening. Thus there was no time later than the early afternoon, after school, when Barbu could have been at the priest's.

"Library key." The pastor had given Barbu the key to the library. Normally Johannes Baptiste had nothing to do with the rectory library. Whoever wanted to borrow a book would go to Dimitru. But at that particular time he wasn't in the library because he was busy with the television. Pater Johannes—everybody knew his memory was increasingly letting him down—had given the key to "A. Barbu" and made a note to himself: "Return!!!" The note was supposed to remind him not to forget to retrieve the key in case the teacher (with her reputation as a slattern) didn't return it herself. Had Barbu returned the key? The question seemed to me of secondary importance. Much more important was, What was my teacher looking for in the library? And on the afternoon of November 6, of all days! Couldn't she have waited until the next day, when Dimitru would be lying on his red chaise longue again, whiling away the hours with his studies? Which book was so important to Barbu that she had to bother the old pastor that very afternoon for the key? And where was that book now? If a book was missing from the library, there was only one person who would know: Dimitru.

But was it right to visit him alone? I needed an ally, a friend. Fritz was dead to me. Hermann, the son and namesake of the Saxon Schuster, was a decent guy but much too clueless for me to explain the whole story to him, beginning with Barbu's sunflower dress and ending with what happened to the Eternal Flame. What about Petre Petrov? Petre had taken me by the hand in the murder room, and for a moment we had been partners in pain. But I hardly knew Petre. He was two years older and beginning to enter into the world of the men. He usually didn't have much to do with younger boys like me. I only knew one person I would want to tell everything to: Buba, except I didn't see her in my mind's eye, couldn't conjure up her image. I knew about her eyes, her open laugh, her cheeky remarks, soft hands, and the smell of earth and smoke in her hair. But I couldn't see or hear or taste her. And I wouldn't see her or taste her as long as the picture in my head and heart, the image of the naked Pater Johannes tied up on his chair, left no room for anything else.

Something evil had come over Baia Luna. It had stolen Fernanda and our Good Shepherd from the village and introduced fear. A knife through the throat had not just silenced the pastor but also made him deaf for all time. Pater Johannes would never listen to anyone again. That was what caused my despair. *Out of the house of God! Go to hell.* Those were the last words I had heard from the priest's lips. Johannes Baptiste had died in the mistaken belief that I, Pavel Botev, had extinguished the Eternal Flame. And the priest would never ever hear, No, no, no, Pater Johannes. It wasn't what you think. I bit my pillow in the night to keep from crying out in grief.

On Sunday morning Hermann Schuster, Istvan Kallay, and their haggard horse returned from Kronauburg. They had driven all night. "The police are on their way to investigate the murder," said Istvan while Schuster unhitched the nag.

They arrived at midday. Two jeeps and a black hearse. In one jeep sat Plutonier Cartarescu and the fat policeman, in the other six uniformed officers.

"What a fucking pain," complained the fat cop with the bird's nest of hair. Despite the cold he was dabbing sweat from his brow. He clamped his cap under his arm and introduced himself with rank and name: "District Commissioner Captain Patrascu. Never had been to Baia Luna in my whole life, and now I'm here again, twice in three days! Things are really poppin' up here. First a teacher disappears and now this." He lit up a Carpati. "Where's the crime scene?"

Kristan Desliu pointed toward the rectory. "But the deceased are in the church."

"What? The bodies are in the church! Who took them there?" Plutonier Cartarescu was livid.

"We did."

"Are you crazy? That's a serious offense: interference in police work! Crime scenes are not to be touched under any circumstances. How are we supposed to investigate now that you've tampered with the evidence? Who was responsible for this unauthorized transport?"

"Calm down, calm down," said Patrascu. "Let's take a look first."

While some of the policemen waited on the village square, the commissioner, Cartarescu, and two officers walked to the rectory. Since the door had fallen shut, they called for Simenov the black-smith who broke it open with a powerful jerk of his crowbar. An hour later the officers returned from their inspection.

"Complicated, complicated," Patrascu said and took a drag on his cigarette. "Thousands of footprints—in front of the house, on the stairs, everywhere you look. Nothing to be done about it. Kind of a mess up there. What were we going to find? We don't even know what to look for. You can see the perpetrators were looking for something, too. But the way they threw stuff around they probably didn't find anything useful either."

"What do you mean the perpetrators didn't find anything?" Cartarescu didn't understand. "How can you tell?"

"Experience. Burglars only throw things around when no one's home. But if someone's there, there's a different procedure. Believe me, if I hold a straight razor to your throat you're gonna tell me where everything is: money, jewelry, booze, important papers, whatever. You're gonna spill the beans in a flash, voluntarily—if you can call it voluntary under the circumstances. Unless there isn't anything hidden. In which case the boys will turn everything upside down until they realize there's nothing to be found. Then if they're smart crooks they just beat it. But I'll tell you what: if they're pissed off, they'll slice you open. That's what we got here."

Cartarescu gave a surly shrug and urged his superior to inspect the victims themselves.

"You fellows do it," said Patrascu. "I'm retiring on the fifteenth, so why should I inflict that gruesome stuff on myself? After forty-five years on the job, I've seen enough."

When Plutonier Cartarescu and two sergeants finally returned from examining the corpses in the church, the other policemen were still questioning men and women from the village. Suspicious persons? Strangers in the village? Personal enemies of the pastor in his private life? What about clerical opponents? Unusual occurrences? A lot of money in the rectory? Religious art? Gold objects? They asked about the relationship between Fernanda and the priest, wanted to know everything about his habits, penchants, dislikes. Until finally Karl Koch had had enough.

"He was against the party, against your goddamn Communism. And you know exactly who's behind this cowardly murder. Your fucking Securitate! They knew very well that Johannes was going to preach against the kolkhoz in church today. So they killed him and Fernanda. That fatface Lupu Raducanu is behind this. The Security Service craps a load of shit, and then the police make sure no one steps in it."

The district commissioner's Carpati sailed into the snow. He put on his uniform cap. "Do you have any proof of that?"

"Proof? Fuck your proof! Those guys are all criminals, disgusting crooks!"

"Bunch of crooks! Socialist hoodlums!" Now Petre Petrov and Kristan Desliu were also shouting. Petre's father Trojan raised two clenched fists, and Avram Scherban the shepherd, who had been drinking already, rushed the Brancusis in a blind rage. "You Commie bastards," he bellowed, grabbed Roman by the neck with both hands, pushed him to the ground, and started choking him. Of all people, it was Hermann Schuster, the guy Roman the stutterer had given the bird's egg to, who pulled old Scherban off. Hans Schneider snarled at Schuster, "First you let him hit you and now you're putting your tail between your legs?"

Liviu Brancusi's forehead was dripping with sweat. "We had nothing to do with this! Why don't you believe us?"

The Brancusis' frightened cries were drowned in a hail of punches and shouts. Commissioner Patrascu looked over at his men and reached for his belt. The cops pulled their pistols and fired into the air. The crowd scattered, and calm was restored in an instant. Cartarescu shepherded the Brancusis to one of the cars and opened the tailgate. "A police measure for your own protection. It will be good for security in town if you disappear for a while." Plutonier had hardly finished his sentence before the three brothers were huddled in the back of the police car.

The policemen were still pointing their pistols at the sky when the commissioner announced that they were under orders to take the bodies to Kronauburg for autopsies. The driver of the hearse grumbled that he'd only been instructed to pick up one body; there'd been no mention of a woman. Didn't any of the gentlemen at headquarters stop to think what it means to pack two dead bodies, heavy and stiff to boot, in just one hearse? It couldn't be done without more bruises and contusions. What kind of meaningful information could you get from an autopsy anyway under the circumstances? For him personally, God knows, a proper autopsy was extremely important because as the driver and last link at the arse end of the chain, he'd get the blame if anything went wrong.

"Shut up," said Patrascu. "You think I don't know how fucked up this is? We're just cleaning up the shit ourselves. But next week I'm gonna put up my feet and keep my ass warm." Then he turned to Karl Koch. "Let me give you a piece of advice. You people shouldn't talk so big. Keep your flame turned down, or you'll have a fire on your hands that will burn you badly."

One of the sergeants who'd been in the church must have overheard the word "fire." "You're Catholics here, right folks? You should go to church more often and make sure the Eternal Flame stays on in the house of God."

My fear that Kora Konstantin's hour had now struck was confirmed.

"The light is out! Johannes murdered! *It* has returned! Now *it* is back!" Kora ran around like a madwoman. In horrified rapture she trumpeted the return of the Apocalypse, shrieking, "The devil, the demon, the Beast from hell!" She threw herself on the ground, wallowed in the snow, and grunted like a pig. Julius Knaup started babbling about the return of the Antichrist, blood down the altar steps and out to the trough. "The hooves, the hooves!" cried the sacristan. "You all saw them. The Beast has returned! It lives! Johannes is dead. The light is out. The end is near!"

The villagers, some rigid with shock and others repulsed, failed to respond to the sacristan or Kora's swinish twitching, and the excitement gradually subsided. Supported by her brother-in-law Marku on one side and Julius Knaup on the other and panting from the exertion, Kora staggered off to her house.

"You ignoramuses. Have you all gone mad? Didn't any of you listen to what Papa Baptiste said?"

Dimitru had emerged from his library and seemed to me the only sane person in this hour of insanity. I knew that the Gypsy had soaked up every word from Pater Johannes's pulpit like a sponge. It was well known that the priest was exceptionally knowledgeable about the differences in the spirit world. He knew the fine distinctions between Beast and devil, Lucifer and Beelzebub, among ghosts, demons, and evil incarnate. Now Dimitru proved himself to be an apt pupil. He informed the assembled villagers that neither the Beast of the Apocalypse nor a demon could have been the cause of the evil events of recent days. The Beast fled at the mere sight of a church and avoided the Eternal Flame like the plague, so how could he have put it out? And whoever murdered Brother Baptiste, it was certainly not a demon.

"Demons only spread fear. But they can't kill, since they have neither feet nor hands nor knives. They wander around looking for a human husk that's hollow inside, and when they find one and settle in, they smile continually because they're happy to have someone to carry them."

"We gotta go! Pack up the bodies," Commissioner Patrascu ordered his cops, "and then back to town as quick as possible."

Toward evening Istvan Kallay the Hungarian, Schusters' Hermann, and Trojan Petrov came to my grandfather's to buy pencils and paper. The three of them were going to go house to house. Karl Koch wanted desperately to be part of the delegation, but they had refused, saying he'd had enough trouble in the past few days and should stay with his wife and children and rest his raw nerves. Lupu Raducanu would show up tomorrow demanding the list. And he would get it, devil take him, but not from Karl Koch. He needed to stay out of the line of fire.

That evening I learned an important lesson. I wanted to find out if I could influence people to do something for me against their will. It wasn't hard. Just as the three men were ready to march off and visit all the families in Baia Luna, I hit myself on the forehead and cried out, "The hooves, the hooves, the blood on the altar!"

That was all it took for them to rush back in concern. I felt terrible about it, but that was the price I paid.

"The boy has seen too much. He needs fresh air," said my mother. Everyone agreed, even Grandfather.

I turned to Hermann Schuster, "I don't want to go out there alone. Can I come with you? I'll carry your paper and pencils."

And so I was with the delegation wading through the snow. None of the three was for the kolkhoz, but they had no choice. Fear had done its work. It had evoked the bitter realization that you had to be reasonable and accept the inevitable. To protect the village from further scares, every head of a household would add his signature to a list with no left and no right column. There would just be a list with the names of all the families. The question "Do you want the kolkhoz or do you want calamity to return?" was no longer necessary after the murder of Johannes Baptiste.

We started at the lower end of the village. No signature was needed from the Gypsies. The Blacks didn't own any land, they just leased the pasture for their horses from the farmers. First Avram Scherban, old Lopa, and Vasili Adamski signed, and, as expected, Bogdan Brancusi, whose three sons were in Kronauburg waiting for the turbulence in Baia Luna to quiet down. Simenov the smith signed, saying it was "an act of common sense in difficult times." We found Julius Knaup at the home of Marku Konstantin and his sister-in-law Kora. They were sitting around the kitchen table and even laid their rosaries aside to document their agreement. Of the

Saxons the Schneiders, the Zikelis, and the Klein family signed with grim, dyspeptic expressions. When Karl Koch went to put his name on the paper, he was grinding his teeth, and the pencil broke.

We finally reached the Hofmanns' house in the upper village. I felt queasy. When I simulated the psychotic attack it hadn't occurred to me that I'd encounter Fritz, my friend turned enemy. Hermann Schuster knocked. Birta opened the door and invited us in. Except for me none of them had ever crossed that threshold before. They admired the roomy parlor and the poster of the mighty female with her crown of light beams and torch against a background of gigantic buildings. Schuster explained to Birta that they had come about a serious matter and asked to see her husband.

"Heinrich isn't here," she said and Fritz added sarcastically, "And he isn't coming back either."

Perplexed, the men looked at one another. Heinrich Hofmann was always in Kronauburg, and no one in Baia Luna took notice of his absence, but the three of them couldn't get it through their heads that he would never again drive his Italian motorcycle through the village. I couldn't either.

"Isn't coming back? What do you mean?" Hermann turned to Birta.

"I've put in my application! For papers. For myself and Fritz."

"What about your husband, Birta?" asked the dumbfounded Hermann. For him, applying for an exit permit was an incomprehensible act.

"Heinrich's staying in Kronauburg," she answered in embarrassment. "Fritz and I are leaving. For Germany."

"But without your husband? How can that be, Birta?"

"Just so you know"—Fritz gave me a poisonous look—"my mother is getting a divorce. High time, too. As soon as we have the papers we're out of here."

Birta Hofmann blushed. Her son's frankness was as painful to her as his cheekiness.

"Yes, that's how it is. Heinrich is currently trying to sell the house and the lot, but who's going to buy property that may be expropriated or purchase a house in a village that has no future?"

The men responded to that last remark with a halfhearted "Well, we'll see about that," but after what Birta had said, the delegation could dispense with Heinrich Hofmann's signature and hers as well.

As the steeple clock was striking nine, only one name was still missing from the list, but Kallay, Schuster, and Petrov would have no problem collecting it. Or so they thought. It was my grandfather's. We walked back down to the village and headed for the back door, since the tavern was closed in mourning for Baptiste and Fernanda.

My family was not affected by the impending expropriations. We owned only an insignificant piece of pasture that fed a few sheep and was so small it was under the minimum size for private land to be transferred to the collective. Besides, it didn't make any sense to collectivize a little tavern and a couple of tables and benches and declare a small shop that supplied the village with only the bare necessities to be the property of the people.

My aunt Antonia stood in the hallway, swathed all in black from the pain of losing the beloved pastor. With tear-reddened eyes she said only that Ilja and Dimitru were in the shop.

"Pardon the interruption," said Hermann softly. "Ilja, just sign and we'll be on our way." Schuster handed him the pencil and the list of names. Granddad looked at the paper and gave the impression he might refuse to sign.

"I've got to find my glasses in the parlor."

Hermann Schuster was surprised because he'd never seen Grandfather wearing spectacles. I wasn't surprised. Granddad didn't have any.

He plucked at Dimitru's sleeve. "Come with me," Grandfather whispered to his Gypsy friend.

Ilja handed Dimitru the paper and pencil. "Quick, write my name on it!"

"You . . . you can't write?" Dimitru sounded sympathetic, not reproachful. "I always guessed it, but now, my friend, you know that your friend knows. From now on there are two of us." Then he signed with a swift, sure hand.

"Did you find your glasses?" called Schuster.

Grandfather didn't answer, just handed Hermann the list of names. At the very bottom, clear and legible: "Borislav Ilja Botev."

Kallay, Petrov, and Schuster thanked him and left. "Pray for us when that Raducanu comes back tomorrow" were the Saxon's parting words. Grandfather nodded.

But Lupu Raducanu didn't come. All day you could feel the tension in the village. What would happen when he showed up? It took the men who were shoveling the graves for Fernanda Klein and Johannes Baptiste many times longer than usual for this sad job. Again and again they would pause, lift their heads, and gaze in the direction of the road to Apoldasch on which the jeep would appear. But it didn't. Not on Monday, not on Tuesday, and not on Wednesday either. On Thursday afternoon the villagers hurriedly gathered when, from Cemetery Hill, Margitha Desliu spotted a black dot in the snowy distance. Once she could identify the slowly advancing vehicle, she ran down to the village. "The hearse! The hearse is coming back!"

It stopped on the village square. The driver was different from the one who had transported Fernanda Klein and Johannes Baptiste to their autopsy in Kronauburg. He wore a black suit as did his young assistant. Both bid us a more formal than friendly good day and tried to look pious.

The village had been anxiously awaiting the coffins, and it was decided to lay them out in the church and inter them the following day. When a priest died, the bishop or auxiliary bishop of the diocese usually officiated at the funeral. But since it was an open secret in Baia Luna that relations between Pater Johannes and the Kronauburg clergy were marked by mutual aversion, they asked the priest from Schweisch Valley to administer the last rites and see to the proper interment of his fellow priest and the housekeeper, and he had agreed.

As a mark of respect, the village council had decided not to bury the deceased on Cemetery Hill as usual but in the churchyard. There was disagreement at the council meeting on what to do about the extinguished Eternal Flame. Some urged the solution of just relighting it with a match, but then someone suggested they could ask the pastor from Schweisch Valley to light a candle from his own Eternal Flame and carry the sacred fire to Baia Luna. In the end, this idea was also rejected, and they passed a resolution that the extinguished light would not burn again until the dastardly murderers had been apprehended.

"Now we will carry the coffins into the church," Hermann Schuster addressed the driver, who looked at him blankly. "What coffins?" He opened the tailgate of the hearse. There was only one.

"There's got to be two," several voices called out. The men waiting to carry the caskets hurried over to peer into the black vehicle. "Only one coffin! He's right, there's only one. Have you taken leave of your senses?" The driver and his companion didn't know what to say except "Quiet please!" and "Must be some misunderstanding." But once people realized the obvious error couldn't be corrected by making a fuss, they settled down.

The chauffeur dropped his pious manner. "We had the clear order to transport a coffin with one body from Kronauburg to Baia Luna." He pulled out a piece of paper. "It says so right here: 'Cleared for transport: Johanna Fernanda Klein, d.o.b. July fifteenth, 1886, in Trappold, single, deceased November ninth, 1957, in Baia Luna. Signed, Dr. Petrin, Institute of Pathology, People's District Hospital, Kronauburg.' One deceased. One coffin. Those are our orders."

"Fernanda is not deceased, she was murdered!" Petre Petrov flew into a rage, and others joined in. "Where's our pastor? Where's Johannes? Where is he?"

"We don't know anything about a priest," reiterated the chauffeur and his assistant. "There must be some misunderstanding, some error in the planning. Happens all the time. The problem's in Kronauburg. Best thing would be for one of you to come back with us and clear things up right there."

The assistant explained that, unfortunately, the hearse only had two seats, one for the driver and one for him. But they were happy to take two or three people back to Kronauburg as long as they didn't mind sitting in the back. It smelled a little, but everything was clean—guaranteed. They just shouldn't think about whom that space was normally reserved for.

"Doesn't matter to me," Petre spoke up. "I'll come along." The other men hesitated at the thought of spending a good three hours bumping through the mountains in the back of a hearse, but they were also unwilling to send an impetuous seventeen-year-old to poke around the police station and the district hospital in Kronauburg.

"You're too young, Petre," objected the Hungarian Istvan.

"So go yourself then!" said Simenov the smith in a nasty voice. Istvan thought it over for a moment. "Okay, I'll do it."

"But I'm coming with you," Petre stubbornly insisted and left no doubt he was not to be dissuaded.

"I'm going, too!" People turned around and looked at me with a combination of surprise and disapproval.

"I forbid it!" My grandfather's voice had never sounded so stern.

"It's out of the question, Pavel." Hermann Schuster backed up my grandfather. "I'll go instead."

While Erika Schuster made a sour face at her husband for once again putting the village before his family, I answered my grandfather, "Every day all I hear from you is 'Pavel do this, Pavel do that, Pavel you're old enough to know,' blah blah blah. So now I'm old enough."

Since Granddad didn't have a ready answer, Karl Koch took his part. "What will you accomplish by going to town, Pavel? Nobody's going to take a greenhorn like you seriously."

"Exactly," I said. "Nobody's going to pay any attention to a twerp like me. And that's our chance to find something out about Pater Johannes. If his missing coffin really is just a misunderstanding, it can be cleared up easily. But if something else is behind it that none of us can see, then I could—"

"What the hell could be behind it?" the chauffeur interrupted me. "It was a mistake. As usual. In October we had seven bodies, and there wasn't a driver who knew where they belonged. You wouldn't believe how we had to wander all over the countryside. And all because of an insane bureaucracy where the right hand doesn't know what the left hand's doing. But eventually you dig your way through the paperwork and finally see the light. Every deceased finds his place at last. We'll find your pastor for you."

"Then there's no objection to my keeping Istvan and Petre company," I added.

Since nobody but Grandfather objected it was decided: Istvan Kallay, Petre Petrov, and I would go to Kronauburg to discover the whereabouts of Pater Johannes's earthly remains. The coffin with Fernanda Klein was unloaded, and the three of us ducked into the back of the black car.

The driver proved to be a speedster. Although by now there

was eight inches of snow on the ground, it was only a good hour until he was pulling up before a new tin sign with raised letters: PEOPLE'S HOSPITAL—HEALTH OF THE FATHERLAND—DISTRICT OF KRONAUBURG.

"You can't miss it," said the assistant as we three scrambled out of the hearse and breathed in great drafts of town air. Although the air was heavy with the stink of thousands of coal-burning dwellings, the smell of tar and ashes was like a fresh breeze. Istvan, who never smoked, asked the assistant for a cigarette to get the stale, sweetish scent of the hearse out of his nostrils.

"A word before we go in there, Pavel: you keep quiet. Let me do the talking," he said.

Then we walked briskly to the hospital entrance and headed straight for the registration desk. Istvan asked a fat woman in an apron dress where we could find Dr. Petrin.

"In pathology. It's in the basement, down three flights, and then keep turning right. What's your business? May I see your papers? Do you have a clearance?"

But we were already on our way downstairs. We kept turning right past dozens of yellowed doors and through strange odors I couldn't identify except for ammonia in a cleaning solution. But they all seemed to be trying to drive out bad smells with even worse smells. In the last corridor a young woman scurried by, the tails of her lab coat flying.

"Miss? Excuse me?" Istvan called after her. "Could you help us? We're looking for Dr. Petrin."

The lab coat stopped flying. "Do you have an appointment?"

"We've come from Baia Luna."

"What? So far? Is it snowing up there yet? They say it's the end of the world. But the mountains must be beautiful in the summer. What do you want with Dr. Petrin?"

"We'd like to speak with him personally, to clear up a misunderstanding," the Hungarian replied.

"We're looking for a corpse. Our dead priest has disappeared. You can understand—it's urgent," I burst out.

"Shut your trap!" hissed Istvan.

"No, young man, I don't understand. But I'll see if Dr. Petrin has any time for you. You've come so far, all the way from Baia

Luna! But just a few minutes at most. I can't promise you more than that."

I was annoyed at being called "young man." She wasn't that old herself, but the way she strolled ahead of us, hands in her lab-coat pockets, her shoulder-length hair lying on the white material, and with such a gentle swing to her hips, I realized that the ladies in town were put together in a different way from the girls in Baia Luna.

She stopped at one of the yellowish-brown doors with peeling paint and opened it without knocking. We'd overlooked her name tag: DR. MED. PAULA PETRIN, SPECIALIST FOR INTERNAL MEDICINE. The pathologist sat down at her desk.

"What can I do for you?"

Petre's jaw dropped, and so did mine. Istvan Kallay cleared his throat and pretended nothing in the world could surprise him. "So you're Dr. Petrin? Forgive me, but I was actually expecting a man."

"A man, that's right. Me, too," Petre managed to say.

"Well, you weren't far wrong. My father was head of pathology until just recently. But now he's enjoying his retirement—although I think winter on the Black Sea can't be all that cozy. But please, what is it you want?"

With a quick frown Istvan let Petre and me know we should keep our mouths shut. "May I be frank?"

"Please do, go right ahead. But I don't have much time."

Paula Petrin listened intently as the Hungarian described the events in Baia Luna clearly and precisely, with no digressions or dramatic flourishes.

"So you say two people were murdered. Afterward they were brought here for an autopsy, and only one of the bodies was returned to your village. Very strange indeed. I haven't been here long, but if such a thing had happened before, my father would surely have told us about it. Let me look this up."

Paula Petrin opened a file drawer and her fingers glided over the index cards. She's never peeled potatoes, I thought to myself. No girl in Baia Luna has such slim, well-formed fingers. Not even Buba.

"The bodies were picked up last Sunday?"

"Yes."

"Then they must have reached our morgue that evening. But no one's here on Sunday. So we should look at Monday. There's always a lot going on on Monday because cases from all over the district build up over the weekend and have to be worked through. I've found it. Baia Luna. On Monday. Yes, you're right. There must have been an unresolved death in your village."

"No, two!" protested Istvan and Petre simultaneously.

"Hang on . . . here!" Paula Petrin laid an index card on her desk. "Fernanda Klein. Yes, I remember: an elderly woman from Baia Luna. I recall her quite clearly. Sometimes you can tell from the body what they were like when still alive. She must have been a pleasant person. Single, but terribly inquisitive, am I right? Angina pectoris. No doubt about it. Her heart wasn't getting enough oxygen. Arteries clogged by calcium deposits. They build up over the years, and it's a frequent cause of death in people of Mrs. Klein's age. If I look at the data, the lady must have been living the last few years with enormously high blood pressure. Very likely her heart wasn't up to some heavy exertion, and then—"

"Fernanda never had to exert herself," Istvan interrupted the doctor.

"Well, it wouldn't have to be some demanding physical activity. Sometimes a sudden emotional stress can cause an angina."

"You mean a big shock?"

"Yes. You can't rule that out. In an extreme situation—let's say in a panic or threatened by danger—the human body reacts with increased blood flow to the heart. But if the vessels are narrowed by arteriosclerosis, the heart muscle doesn't get enough oxygen. But what in heaven's name could have given dear Mrs. Klein such a fright?"

"The murder of our priest," said the Hungarian. "Fernanda Klein was our pastor's housekeeper."

"And that's why we're here," Petre added. "Those guys slit Pater Johannes's throat in the rectory."

"That's right," confirmed Istvan. "The police picked up his corpse as well as his housekeeper's to get them autopsied, but only Fernanda's coffin came back to be buried."

Paula Petrin chewed her lower lip. "That's really strange. But I give you my word, no murder victim with a slit throat was ever on my operating table. I can swear to that on a stack of Bibles. I can't be of much help in your search for your pastor's body. He definitely wasn't here. Who investigated the case in Baia Luna?"

"A fat, elderly policeman with a thatch of hair. I think his name was . . ." Istvan rubbed his forehead.

"Patrascu!" exclaimed Paula Petrin.

"Exactly," said Petre. "And this Patrascu didn't give the impression he was going to bust his ass for anybody in his sunset years."

"He seemed unmotivated, you mean," Dr. Petrin corrected him with a smile. "But Patrascu is a good cop. The commissioner has been a friend of my father's ever since I was a kid. Patrascu is a stand-up guy even if he maybe—to put it crudely—can't get his ass in gear so easily anymore. Why don't you go see him? The police station's not far from here. I think Commissioner Patrascu can help you. Buy him a pack of Carpatis and tell him best wishes from his little Pauline. That's what he always calls me." Paula Petrin shook our hands. "Good luck! Let me know when you've shed some light on this dark business."

Twilight was already falling, and the streetlights flickered on as we entered the Kronauburg District police headquarters ten minutes later. Istvan greeted one of the sergeants who had been in Baia Luna after Pater Johannes's murder, the one who had asked about items of value in the rectory.

"Ah, a rare visit from the mountains. Got something to report?" The officer acted like an old acquaintance.

"We'd like to see Commissioner Patrascu."

"You're too late. The chief's been gone since yesterday. I mean, the former chief. Finally retired after forty-five years. But you can make your report to me."

Istvan hemmed and hawed. "We had business in town and thought we'd come see if there's any new developments in the disappearance of our teacher Miss Barbulescu."

"And I thought you were here because of that awful thing that happened to your pastor. We're on the case, I can tell you that. And now you say your teacher has disappeared, too? I don't know anything about that." The cop turned to his colleagues. "Have you heard of a teacher gone missing up in Baia Luna? Name of Barbulescu?"

Head shakes all around until one of them remembered. "Patrascu was up in the mountains twice last week, wasn't he? Maybe he knows something about the teacher."

"As you can see"—the policeman turned back to us—"no such incident has been reported here. You have no idea how many people disappear and then show up again. There's no way we can go looking for all of them. But if you want to ask the old man, no problem. He lives up on Castle Hill, Alte Schanzgasse 3, a yellow house with blue shutters. Can't miss it. Buy him a pack of Carpatis, and he's happy. And best wishes from his colleagues."

On the market square in front of the police station, the illuminated façade of a shop caught our eye. To judge from its blinding white stucco, it must have just recently opened. Over the glass entrance hung a huge banner with red letters proclaiming THANKS TO THE REPUBLIC! THANKS TO THE PARTY! and beneath that something about the inevitable progress of Socialism and world-class products for the people. Petre suggested we detour into the shop to buy cigarettes for Patrascu.

As I entered through the double doors, I could hardly believe my eyes and nose. The only shop I knew was my grandfather's store, where the smell of stale tobacco smoke mixed with the odor of fermenting sauerkraut. In this place, on the other hand, all the fragrances of the world reached my nostrils simultaneously. I recognized rose oil, baking bread, and fresh paint. Behind what seemed an endless counter stood a dozen pretty girls in white aprons. I caught a whiff of arrogance in the smug way they were dealing with the customers. I was floored by the variety on the towering shelves behind the counter. I spotted four different brands of toothpaste and twice as many kinds of soap, including the expensive Luxor with essence of roses that the stuck-up Vera Raducanu always asked for to make Grandfather look like a fool. Where Ilja had only one shelf of canned goods to offer (and even then you weren't quite sure what was in them), the Socialist People's Market was piled high with attractive pyramids of cans without number containing every vegetable imaginable. In contrast to our village store where we put out apples and pears in battered old baskets, the apples here were polished to a high gloss, displayed behind glass, and carried sonorous names like Golden Delicious and Jonas Deluxe chalked onto little black slates. Next to them were whole mountain ranges of glowing bananas, until a closer look revealed they were displayed in front of a clever system of silvery mirrors that optically multiplied the tempting fruit. But the peak of luxury was represented by three examples of a curious brown fruit spotlit on a white cloth inside a glass case. They reminded me of royal heads with a crown of prickly green leaves. The three fruits came from Hawaii, about which the only thing I could vaguely remember from Miss Barbulescu's geography class was that it never snowed there. When I read the price for one of these so-called pineapples I almost had a stroke: as much as my grandfather earned in a month. I elbowed Petre in the ribs and pointed at the price tag. "Take a look at that!"

When we finally got to the head of the line, the brunette salesgirl asked pertly, "May I help you?" while eyeing my threadbare jacket with suspicion.

"A pack of Carpatis please, Miss," said Istvan with exaggerated courtesy.

The girl went to the cigarette case, took out a pack, and slammed it onto the counter. "Anything else?"

Istvan didn't answer. He fished a couple of aluminum coins from his pocket and tossed them across the polished surface with a flip of his wrist. While the indignant clerk retrieved the money from the floor, Istvan strode out with his head held high.

As we climbed the slippery wet cobblestone street to Castle Hill, I felt ashamed—of our pathetic shop back home, of Grandfather, of Baia Luna, of myself.

By the light of a streetlamp the yellow paint of the retired commissioner's house did in fact stand out. It was in a row of other lopsided medieval façades that managed to stay upright only by leaning against one another. An iron lion's head with a ring in its nose was mounted on the blue wooden door. Istvan knocked on the wood three times. We soon heard the rattling of keys, and Patrascu opened the door. A Carpati hung from his mouth, and he was stuffing his shirt into his pants with both hands.

"Good evening, gentlemen. What's up?" Patrascu stared at us. His grinding lower jaw revealed his memory was at work. My face and Istvan's apparently meant nothing to him, but he recalled Petre Petrov.

"You're one of the crazy guys that went for Brancusi's throat after what happened to your pastor."

"That's exactly why we're here, Commissioner. Kallay, Istvan Kallay, if I may."

"You could have saved yourselves the trip. I'm not on the force anymore, and I don't have the remotest desire to be reminded of anything that has to do with my time in the service of the fatherland. Understood?"

"We bring greetings from your colleagues at the station," the Hungarian attempted to alter the atmosphere.

"Maybe I didn't make myself clear . . ."

"And from your little Pauline, greetings from her, too," I interjected. "Pauline . . . I mean, Dr. Petrin thought for sure you would be able to help us with our problem."

Patrascu flipped his cigarette into the street and ran his fingers through his thatch. "You talked to Paula? What in heaven's name did you want from that angel? Was it about the priest?"

We nodded.

"Didn't I tell you to turn down your flame? Didn't I say you'd get your ass burned otherwise?"

"Better get burned than freeze," I blustered.

Patrascu couldn't help laughing. "Funny, Pauline always comes out with stuff like that, too. All right then, come on in. But I'm afraid I really won't be much help. Besides, I have nothing to offer you. Since my wife died there's not much going on in here."

As far as I could judge in air dense with Carpati smoke, Patrascu's parlor made a neglected impression. Our foreheads beaded with sweat in the sticky humidity. We took off our coats; Patrascu got out four glasses and poured us some *konjaki* Napoleon.

"None for me." After all, I was only fifteen.

"If we're going to discuss something among men, then act like a man. Cheers!"

I clinked glasses with them and drank. Istvan told him about the transfer of Fernanda Klein from the hospital in Kronauburg to Baia Luna and about Johannes Baptiste's corpse and how neither the driver of the hearse nor Dr. Paula Petrin knew anything about it.

"Commissioner, you were there when the chauffeur drove the two of them from Baia Luna to Kronauburg. How come one corpse was autopsied but not the other one? First our priest is murdered in cold blood, and then his body disappears. We have to at least give Pater Johannes a decent burial, you understand."

Patrascu stroked his beard and dragged on his cigarette. "It's a nasty business, but I don't know where your priest is either."

"And if you knew?" I asked, emboldened by the alcohol.

"I'll be honest with you." The commissioner was silent for a while. "I'd keep mum about it. Yeah, I'd keep my mouth shut. And here's why: I've worked my butt off for this country for forty-five years, and let me tell you: I've never seen so much nasty shit as in the last few years. And if an old geezer blabs too much—you people from Baia Luna have seen for yourselves how somebody like that is silenced nowadays. But this is all hypothetical, remember, only if I really had any idea where the priest's body might be."

I was trembling with excitement. If I was supposed to drink like a man, then I wanted to talk like a man, too. "If Dr. Petrin knew that Commissioner Patrascu took his own fear more seriously than justice, do you think little Pauline would have sent her best to you?"

Patrascu stubbed out his cigarette. You could have cut the air with a knife. I had violated the rules of respect toward a man who yesterday was still the highest police officer in the Kronauburg District. But contrary to expectation, Patrascu addressed me in a positively paternal way.

"Pavel, is that your name? I'll tell you what, boy. You don't understand what you're getting into here. I don't know what happened to the priest's body, and I don't want to know. I'll just say this much: up there in your mountain backwater you don't seem to understand that international politics are involved. Your Johannes Baptiste had the makings of a real, hundred percent martyr. Get this through your heads! This is a Communist state. There's a priest in the mountains who's against it? Okay, slit his throat. Not good. Listen, people, there are certain circles far beyond the borders of our country—for the sake of simplicity let's call them strictly Catholic and anti-Communist—that have a massive interest in such martyr figures. You want my personal opinion? Even though I think all this religious folderol is so much nonsense, these martyrs are going to bring down our idiotic collectivized Socialist delusion. Not today and not tomorrow, but someday. That's the logic of history. One delusion replaces another. Royalists, Iron Guards, fascists, Communists, clericalists! What do I know? And if you can just grasp the fact that there are also certain circles in our republic that have no interest at all in seeing martyrs from the wrong camp, you'll also understand why corpses disappear. The memory of people whose blood has been spilled is always dangerous. Martyrs' blood causes trouble. But if these figures simply disappear like the melting snow in spring, then it's all over. Over and done with, forgotten. No grave, no flowers, no temple, no gods. No grass grows as fast as the grass on the grave of an unknown soldier."

"And the fact that in Baia Luna we have no grave to remind us of our priest," said Istvan Kallay hesitantly, "for that your Security Service is to blame."

"You should leave now." Patrascu pushed himself wearily to his feet.

"When spring comes the snow melts," I said in farewell. "You're right about that, Commissioner. But in the winter new snow falls."

"You weren't listening to me, boy. That snow will melt, too. That's the wheel of history. You're young. You want to stop the world from turning. To do that you have to get real close to the wheel. And then it will crush you."

We descended Castle Hill in silence. The evening bus to Apoldasch had left Kronauburg two hours ago. We decided to spend the night in the waiting room of the train station and take the first bus in the morning. Istvan put his hands deep into his coat pockets to warm them. He took out a pack of Carpatis. That night I smoked my first cigarette.

## Chapter Six

●

*FRITZ HOFMANN'S DISCOVERY, DIMITRU'S HEADSTAND,*

*AND A PERSON WHO WAS SOMEONE ELSE ENTIRELY*

That night it snowed again in the mountains. We would have a long march on the footpath from the last bus stop in Apoldasch to Baia Luna, especially under the cloud of our failure to find out anything about the location of Johannes Baptiste's body except for the disheartening realization that its disappearance was no mere oversight of an incompetent bureaucracy. Behind it rose the shadow of an obscure and ominous force for which I had no name. After our conversation with Patrascu, Petre and Istvan also had no doubt that the wheels of that force would grind up anyone who interfered with their turning. "Keep your flame turned down." The old commissioner's sentence kept going through my head, and I was scared.

To our surprise, it was extremely easy going along the footpath beside the Tirnava. We were able to follow in the tracks of a truck with chains that had broken a trail to Baia Luna early that morning. In the track of the tires we discovered another comparatively narrow one: the track of a motorcycle. The police in Apoldasch drove such vehicles and the photographer Hofmann also owned one. Istvan was worried. Tire tracks heading for Baia Luna had not been a good sign lately.

We reached the village at midday and saw that the tracks in the snow led to the Hofmanns' house. The truck was a make seldom seen on Transmontanian roads. The hood ornament was a three-legged star, and the country code on the trunk was *D*. Under the muddy splashes on the license plate you could make out the letter *M*.

"Munich," said Istvan.

My former comrade Fritz Hofmann's last day in Baia Luna had dawned. In his black leather getup, Heinrich Hofmann stood next to his motorcycle and was giving instructions to two furniture movers. Fritz and his mother were nowhere to be seen.

"Thank God you're back safe and sound." My mother's relief and happiness were written on her face, while Grandfather betrayed no emotion. I had ridden to Kronauburg in the hearse against his wishes and gotten mixed up in things that weren't any of my business, in his opinion. Granddad only jerked his thumb toward the bench next to the potbellied stove. "You have a visitor."

Fritz was sitting in the corner. "I've been waiting for you."

I took off my coat. "What do you want?"

"I want to talk to you. I have something important to show you."

"Maybe for you, but not for me."

"You don't get it, man. It's very very important! And we're leaving in an hour at the latest. You think I'd be waiting here for hours if it wasn't important?"

"I've never heard you talk like this before. Usually you're too busy desecrating churches and not needing anyone for anything. We're all such idiots here in Baia Luna."

"Stop it, Pavel, please! I'm serious."

"Then show me what you have to show."

Fritz turned his head and saw Grandfather and my mother. "Not right here. Can we go to your room?"

We sat on my bed. Fritz sat up straight and took a deep breath to get the excitement out of his voice.

"You remember last week when you ran over to my house to show me the new television?"

"You mean the same day you blew out the little flame like such a hero and then took off like a chicken?"

"Man, cut it out. Please, Pavel! You wouldn't believe how happy I was to finally get out of the house that afternoon when you came to bring me to your grandfather's birthday party. I was suffocating in there. My father and mother were having another fight. Now they've separated. My father's going to move to Kronauburg, maybe even to the capital. My mother and I are going to Germany."

"To Munich, I guess."

"Yes, to Munich. Anyway, my father came home day before yesterday to pack up the stuff he's taking to Kronauburg before the move. He filled two crates and said we could do what we wanted with the rest of the junk. Throw it away or burn it, he didn't care. He left the two crates in the upstairs hall and threw a blanket over them, then he told me and my mother to keep our mitts off his stuff."

Fritz took a breath. I said nothing.

"But you know me. He tells me not to do something, and it makes me hot to do it. And yesterday when the old man was back in Kronauburg and Mother was saying good-bye to some people in the village, I went through the crates."

"And so?" My pulse started racing.

"Here's what I found." Fritz reached under his sweater and pulled out a photograph.

"I don't believe it!" I gaped at it in shock, shame, and arousal. Although the woman's face was hidden by a man's naked, out-of-focus behind, I knew at once who was lying there on the table with her legs spread. Her breasts were bare and her dress had been pushed up around her waist, the dress with a sunflower pattern. Five or six men were standing around Angela Barbulescu and grinning. Some of them had dropped their pants around their knees, others had erections jutting out through their open flies. I recognized one of them immediately. He was the only one standing there over her naked flesh who wasn't beating off. He wore his hair slicked back, had an unfiltered cigarette between his lips, and was spraying sparkling wine from a thick-bellied bottle into Barbu's crotch.

"You know the guy with the cigarette?" asked Fritz.

"Sure. This is crazy. I nailed him to the classroom wall last week."

"Exactly. The picture must be ten years old, but it's clearly the new party chief of Kronauburg, Dr. Stefan Stephanescu, and his randy buddies. Photographed by my father."

"Unbelievable!" I exclaimed. All the enmity between Fritz and me melted away. Instead I felt a bond of intimacy I never would have thought possible. "And now I'm going to tell you something. Do you know who that woman is?"

"How would I know? You can't see her face. Maybe a street-walker or something. You know what? My old man took more like this. They were in one of the crates, well hidden among piles of old wedding portraits. Only young women in the pictures. All pretty and all blond. I'm telling you, you can see everything. Really hard core. All the men are older. What do you think would happen if this stuff got out? I looked through all the photos, but this is the only one you can recognize Stephanescu on."

"That's Barbu lying there."

Fritz caught his breath. "You're crazy! How do you know? You can't see anything . . . I mean, her face."

"I just know it is. A hundred percent guaranteed, believe me. But I don't have time to explain."

"Holy shit," groaned Fritz. "I never understood what Father meant a couple months ago. One weekend he asked me how school was going, and I told him how Barbu was always blabbering about the Paris of the East and how civilized it was and all. Father just said the teacher should teach us something useful instead of digging up the past or he would make her life a hell. Pavel, I'm sure there's something really nasty going on here, but I don't know what. And I'm leaving for Germany soon."

"You always said you were going to move to Kronauburg. Is it because of the dirty pictures you don't want to live with your father?"

"I decided long ago I didn't want anything to do with my father."

"But why? I always thought you two got along well. You both swear by that Nietzsche guy."

Fritz stood up and unbuckled his belt. When he dropped his pants I bit my lip so as not to cry out in anger. His thighs were covered with welts, some blue-violet, some black. He showed me his scarred backside.

"The last beating I owe to those party verses. The old man didn't like me improving on that stupid poem."

Instantly I grasped why Fritz had stopped participating in gym class. While my classmates and I were still being sent off to school in short pants, I had secretly envied Fritz as the only student in Baia Luna who wore long pants even in the summer. His father Heinrich had bought them at a haberdasher's in Kronauburg. What made Fritz so grown up in my eyes did nothing more than conceal the evidence of his father's abuse. I thought of what my teacher Angela Barbulescu had called after me as I stormed out of her cottage: "Pavel, things are different than they seem."

"Fritz! Your mother's waiting for you!" Kathalina called up the stairs.

"I have to go, Pavel. Keep the photo and do something with it. Put some stones in the road of those scumbags."

I hid the picture under my mattress. Birta was waiting in the tavern. I went outside with Grandfather and my mother to say good-bye to Fritz and Frau Hofmann. The Mercedes stood there with its motor running. Parked beside it was Herr Hofmann's motorcycle with two crates strapped to the rear seat. Herr Hofmann walked over to his son and put out his hand. Fritz put his hands in his pockets.

"See that you make something of yourself in Germany." Hofmann put on his helmet and mounted his bike without a second glance at his wife and Fritz. Birta was so embarrassed she didn't say a word. She just shook our hands.

"Good luck," said Fritz. "Too bad I have to go. And about that thing with the light in the church: I'm really sorry if you got into trouble for that. But what difference does it make if there's a little lamp burning in this Podunk or not?"

As I went back inside, it started snowing again. The flakes drifted to earth, heavy and slow. The calendar showed Friday, November 15, 1957. Winter had definitely arrived. Baia Luna was facing long months when the village would drowse away in deepest isolation. With so much snow no one could get out of Baia Luna and no one could get in. But there was also something soothing about the loneliness. The security officer Raducanu still hadn't come to pick up the list of names. Until spring Karl Koch would be spared the sight of the pretty boy.

November 6, A. Barbu, library key. Return!!!"

I put the note in my pants pocket. I told my mother I was bored and I was going to the rectory library to see if Dimitru could recommend a book to me.

"You want to borrow a book?" asked my mother in astonishment.

Even Grandfather, dozing behind the counter in the absence of customers, woke up. "Don't let Dimitru pawn off any trash on you." He handed me a bottle of *zuika*. "Books won't warm you up. Tell Dimitru not to drink the bottle all at once, and he should show his face sometime."

I pressed the bell at the rectory, but it didn't ring. However, since Simenov the blacksmith had done such a thorough job of breaking the lock, it was easy to push the door open. I could hear wild ranting and raving from the library. At first I thought Dimitru was arguing with someone from his tribe, but then I realized he was alone and quarreling with himself. The noisy Gypsy didn't hear me knocking. I pushed down the latch. As I crossed the threshold I instantly had to duck to avoid being hit by a folio.

I was shocked. Dimitru's forehead was wrapped in cloth rags, since he'd beaten it bloody against the door when he saw the murdered Papa Baptiste. With his pathetic bandage he was the timeless image of a defeated soldier after a lost battle. Then he saw me.

"Oh my goodness! What an honor, what joy, what happiness! Is it really you, Pavel? Come to the place of intellect?"

I couldn't fend off Dimitru's hugs and noisy kisses. I freed myself from his embrace, and he picked up the tome he had just hurled across the room. He rapped his knuckles on the leather binding. "This here is the handbook of the universe. I tell you, Pavel, the cryptological language of these researchers of the heavens will be the death of me yet. Formulas as long as your arm, gravitational laws, centrifugal rotations, parabolic accelerations. Everything multiplied by pi. Nothing but uneven numbers and mathematical horrors."

"Is that why you're so angry? You're letting this shopworn old doorstop about the universe get you all steamed up?"

Dimitru put his hand on the bandage. "A hothead can always find a reason to get hot. As if a yummy apple in Eden can help it if that idiot Eve takes a bite. No, Pavel, those astronomical bureaucrats aren't driving me crazy with their calculations. It's just, it's just . . ." Dimitru rubbed his eyes so he wouldn't cry. "It's just that I miss Papa Baptiste so much. He's gone. I'll never be able to ask his advice again. Never, you understand?"

Dimitru finally calmed down. I got up the courage to ask him if his problem had anything to do with the beeping Sputnik and the Assumption of Mary the Mother of God.

"Absolutely!" Dimitru's eyes shone like a child's who feels himself understood. Then he sang the praises of Papa Baptiste, extolled the wisdom and foresight snatched from humanity in general and the Baia Lunians in particular by those cowardly killers. He complained that the burden of knowledge now rested solely on the weak shoulders of a single poor Gypsy.

"But what is the problem?" I asked earnestly. "How would Pater Johannes help you out of your dead end?"

"That's the exact word, my boy. Even better: a double dead end. There's no going forward, and the way back is blocked, too. And you know where the dead end ends?"

"No idea."

"I'll tell you: the dead end of my research ends far away. More precisely, I'm stuck somewhere between heaven and earth."

"In outer space? Up in the sky?" I didn't understand. "Where did you get such an idea?"

"Listen: let's assume that the corporeal Assumption of Mary the Mother of God is a fact. Vatican dogma, infallibly proclaimed by Pope Pius, and, despite that, completely correct. With me so far?"

"Yes."

"Good. Rising bodily from the dead isn't a matter of just hopping on the *spiritus sanctus* and zooming into the firmament. Rising bodily from the dead—for a person, especially a woman (and after all, that's what our Mother of Jesus was)—means the whole of you goes up to heaven, thighs, buttocks, breasts, and all."

"Sounds logical," I agreed. "So where are they? I mean, where's the entire Mary?"

"That's the sixty-four-thousand-dollar question I've been working on, and I may be on the brink of a decisive breakthrough."

"What do you mean? Haven't you had a clue up to now? Didn't you know where the Mother of God was?"

"Do you think I'm an idiot? Of course I had a clue. But a clue doesn't count. What counts is proof. I've been collecting evidence, making hypotheses, and counting on the power of logic. 'Stick to facticities!' That's what Papa Baptiste always advised, not once, but a thousand times. And that's what I stick to. Fact is, the Russians want to go to the moon. Determined to. But that's suspicious. More than suspicious, I'd say. The Russian president promised his people not vodka and pork chops but a moon flight. Preferably on the anniversary of the Revolution. The Bolsheviks aren't about to mount such a gigantic operation with their rockets just to look at some old rocks on the moon and put up a pathetic flag that can't even flutter. Not a fart's worth of wind up there, you know." And Dimitru rapped on the handbook for the far reaches of the universe again. "It's all in here. You just have to replace the word 'atmosphere' with 'intestinal wind' to more or less understand it all."

"You mean to say that the Russkies are such idiots they'd fly to the moon just to look for Mary? You believe that nonsense that Johannes Baptiste said? He thought the Russkies were looking for the Lord God in outer space, too."

"But what if it's not nonsense, Pavel? What then?"

"Assuming the pope is right and Mary literally rose up to heaven, why would she land on the moon? She could just as well be God knows where—on Mars or Venus. Or sometimes in one place, sometimes in another, floating weightlessly among the stars."

Dimitru acted insulted. "You didn't have enough schooling, Pavel. You don't understand the essence of dialectical deduction. But I'll explain it to you. Thesis: Mary is on the moon. Antithesis: Mary is not on the moon. And now for the *conclusio* . . . but that's the problem. There isn't one, at least not as long as the truth of the thesis has not been proven by the verification method."

I nodded. "I sort of get it."

"Assuming—and that's exactly what I mean: *assuming*—the thesis is true and Mary is literally on the moon or anywhere else in space, what do you think would happen, Pavel, if Korolev's cosmonauts discover where the Madonna is and get their sights on her? It doesn't take much imagination to know. Pavel, do you seriously believe those atheists would say, 'Oh, what a surprise, dear Mother of God! Very sorry we made a mistake. Please forgive us that we didn't believe in you. Just a misunderstanding.'"

"Don't get mad, Dimitru, but I'm afraid you've made a pretty big error somewhere in your brain."

Dimitru crumbled like a dry leaf. "Why do you say that, Pavel? That's exactly what makes me so desperate. An erroneous deduction, one tiny fohpaw, and whoops! Your logic is down the drain. A locomotive's racing through my brain. Will it reach its goal? Has it gone off the tracks? But where? A thinker has to see with a thousand eyes, look at all sides of the coin, solicit contradictory opinions, test, weigh, test again, up to the bitter end of the *conclusio correcto*. Wrong turns are lurking everywhere. And there's only one person on earth who could keep me from taking those false turns. Just one, and he's dead! And I don't even know where his earthly remains are. Why wasn't I in the rectory when the murderers came? Why was Papa Baptiste alone with Fernanda? Why didn't he call for me? They could gladly have assassinated me. I'm just a Gypsy. But not the good Papa Baptiste. Oh, how I miss you, Papa Baptiste! How I miss your wise advice! You must know, Pavel, that in all heavenly matters, no one could put one over on Papa. No one! What have you got there under your coat, by the way?"

I took out the bottle of *zuika*. "Best regards from Granddad."

Dimitru spread his arms and made to launch another attack of affection, which I escaped with a quick sidestep, so that he ended up kissing the bottle instead. "The world," he soulfully declared, "isn't on the brink of the abyss just yet." Then he pulled out the cork, threw it into the corner, and drank.

Outside of school I hardly read anything at all, and I hadn't entered the library intending to change. My curiosity was not for all those books standing on the shelves but only for the single, ominous book that my investigation still needed. But I was unsure if this was the right time to ask Dimitru which book the teacher Angela Barbulescu had borrowed from the library. Instead of taking Baptiste's note from my pocket, I asked, "Dimitru, do you have the writings of a certain Nietzsche in your library?"

The Gypsy jumped up as if stung by a hornet. His hand flew from forehead to chest to shoulders and back as he crossed himself repeatedly. He tipped up the *zuika* and glugged half the bottle at one go. "That's nothing for a boy of your age! If you ask to read his lucubrations I'm compelled to refuse permission in my capacity as director of the library."

I counterattacked. "You're just scared, Dimitru. You don't want me to read that God is dead. You're afraid that that Nietzsche told the truth. Because if God is dead all your hypotheses are nonsense. Then there's no Mary in the sky. Am I right?"

He closed his eyes and then stared fixedly at the ceiling. I regretted attacking Dimitru so hard-heartedly. It seemed like an eternity until the Gypsy gave an almost imperceptible nod. Then he opened his eyes and tore off his bandage. His blood-encrusted forehead shocked me, and then he uttered the most deliberate sentences I had ever heard from Dimitru Carolea Gabor.

"We come from God and we return to God. Alpha and omega, the beginning and the end. I would never have dared to doubt that, Pavel. Never. Not until I saw Papa Baptiste, saw that old man on a chair and so much, so much blood. There was no more heaven. Only earth, nothing but earth. Dust to dust without beginning or end. Since then I've been afraid, Pavel. Yes, you're right, I'm afraid. Not of the devil and not of that Lupu Raducanu and his gang of thugs that everyone in the village fears. I'm afraid that we come from the void and return to the void."

Dimitru paused for a long time. Then he asked if the teacher Barbulescu had told us about Friedrich Nietzsche in school.

I said no. "It was Hofmanns' Fritz who talked about the death of God and claimed the churches were just God's grave. And Fritz's father had a lot of books by Nietzsche in his living room, a whole yard of them, at least. I never read any of them. But what's so dangerous about them?"

"Books are never dangerous, just people who understand them the wrong way."

"Do you pray a lot?" I asked suddenly.

"Very often, my boy. A Gypsy prays day and night. And if you want to know if my prayers were ever answered, I'll tell you: no. God is a poor partner when you want something from him."

"Then it doesn't matter if God is alive or dead, like this Nietzsche says."

"No, Pavel, it does matter. Remember this: people who understand Nietzsche right go crazy. And people who understand him wrong have no more boundaries. And whoever knows no boundaries thinks he has a license to do anything he wants. If heaven is dead, there's only earth left. And the earth doesn't care about anything. Mother Earth is a bad mother. It's all the same to her. Sow your seed, groan, give birth, eat, die. Dust to dust. In between just a fart from the ass of life. That's all there is."

Dimitru tipped the last of the schnapps into his mouth. The empty bottle fell from his hand onto the floor. Then he said the odd words, "God dies because we can't bear it that we're killing him."

With an effort he got up from his chaise longue. Grief and schnapps had left their marks on him. He staggered to the bookcases. He was falling-down drunk, but he pulled out just the book he wanted, opened it, and handed it to me. I sat down and began to read the story of the crazy man who lights a lamp on a bright morning and runs into the marketplace crying, "I'm looking for God! I'm looking for God!"

Outside in the hall someone kicked against the door. I put Nietzsche aside and opened it. Buba stood there, a jug of fresh water in one hand and in the other a pot with hot polenta.

"Sorry, I didn't have a third hand to knock with." She smiled at me. "I've got dinner for Uncle Dimi. He always forgets it when he's with his books."

Dimitru was asleep on his red chaise longue, his mouth open and snoring. Buba put his supper on the floor, straightened his jacket, took off his shoes, and covered him with a blanket.

"Haven't seen you in a long time, Pavel. Didn't even know you were paying Uncle Dimi a visit. D'you like books?"

I seized the opportunity. "Do you have some time?"

"For you? Have you got something to tell me?"

Buba tried to conceal her beaming smile, sat down, and leaned her back against a bookcase. I sat down and slid nearer to her, and all the thoughts that had been oppressing me during the preceding days came flowing out. I talked about the missing coffin, the search for the dead priest, the trip to Kronauburg, and the meeting with Commissioner Patrascu. Via Fritz Hofmann and his mother's move to Germany, I arrived at the story of the Eternal Flame. Then I pulled the priest's note from my pocket and explained the real reason for my presence in Dimitru's library, talked about my concern for Angela Barbulescu and my suspicion that on the day of her disappearance the teacher had borrowed an important book from the library. And since I understood Buba's silence for what it was—the expression of her wonderful gift as a listener—my heart became lighter with every sentence so that I had no hesitation in telling her about our teacher's shady past as well, about the lewd photographs and the whippings Heinrich Hofmann gave his son, and about his friend, the party secretary Dr. Stephanescu, and Barbu's affair with him, which must have ended very unhappily for her. When I told Buba about her mysterious assignment that seemed to me more and more like a desperate plea, she took my hand, so that I decided not to tell her about the evening when a drunken Angela Barbulescu in her sunflower dress had made a pass at me.

When I had talked all the tribulations from my soul, Buba said, "And I thought you didn't like me anymore." After a quick glance at her uncle assured her he was asleep, she kissed me on the mouth. "You're my boyfriend now. And I'm your girlfriend. Don't do anything foolish without me anymore."

The drunken Dimitru tossed from side to side on his chaise longue. Then he muttered something in a singsong that sounded like old women mumbling litanies in Latin. "Uncle Dimi talks in his sleep when he's been drinking." Buba laid her hand on Dimitru's injured forehead, gave him a kiss, and put out the light. "It's better we wait until tomorrow morning to ask him what Barbu was doing in the library, when he's slept it off. If you want me to be there, too, that is."

"No more foolishness without you."

On the way home I was glowing so much I could have melted the snow. My weakness had vanished. The shadows of the last few days were no longer a threat but a challenge—a darkness demanding illumination.

The next morning I was up before seven. I washed with cold water and, contrary to my usual habits, I also brushed my teeth thoroughly. As I approached the library I was happy to see Buba waiting for me at the door of the rectory. Despite my fear that Dimitru would be unapproachable after his bender the previous evening, we found him not with a pounding headache but in the best of spirits. He put aside his pot of cold polenta, wiped his mouth on his sleeve, and offered his niece and me a place on the couch.

"I've been thinking since our disputation last night." He turned to me. "First about God, then about Nietzsche, and finally, in the sense of synchronous research, about both of them. Seen in the light of day, the question is, Who's the smarter of the two, the evangelist of God's death or the Creator of all things? Which has the most staying power, the everlasting breath of creation and salvation or an ephemeral work by an admittedly clever philosopher?"

"Who's Uncle Dimi talking about?" Buba looked at me.

"Let me guess," I said without answering her question. "God is smarter than all the thinkers combined. In the long run. But only if he isn't already dead."

Dimitru clapped his hands in delight. "Correct, my boy! But God is not dead. God is a hedgehog."

Buba rolled her eyes in exasperation because she couldn't follow the twisting course of her uncle's inspiration. But I feared the *zuika* of the night before was still having an effect. The comparison of God to a hedgehog, I remarked grumpily, was pretty far-fetched.

"Not at all," Dimitru disagreed. "You know the tale of the race between the hare and the hedgehog. The hare is swift as the wind but as dumb as a board. The hedgehog has short legs, but he's slyer than a fox. So he uses the *principio duplex,* the law of doubles. Father Hedgehog stands next to the hare at the starting line. Ready, set, go! Longears zooms along the furrows as if the devil himself were at his heels. At the finish line, there's Mother Hedgehog waiting for him. 'What's been keeping you? I got here long ago,' she calls. The hare in his stupidity demands an immediate rematch. The same thing happens. Only this time, Father Hedgehog calls out, 'Where've you been? I've been waiting for you!' The hare almost goes berserk, demands another race and another and another and another. End of story. He collapses on the field, run to death. Earth takes him back. *Exitus finitus.* Dust to dust."

"An illuminating story," said Buba. "But if the double hedgehog is God, who's the hare? You mean people like your cousin Salman, always on the road on business but never really getting anywhere?"

When her uncle answered, "I mean Nietzsches' Friedrich," Buba was disappointed. "Never heard of him."

"There's a catch in your story, Dimitru," I said. "Your hedgehog God puts one over on the hare. Your God is a swindler, a cheater, who only pretends he's always there waiting without ever really moving from the spot while the poor hare—or that Nietzsche, for all I care—runs himself to death honestly and with no cheap tricks."

"Exactly," Buba agreed. "The hare dies of exhaustion 'cause God double-crosses him. It's a dirty trick."

Dimitru cleared his throat. "It's youth who are mistaken in this case. The hare doesn't lose because the hedgehog double-crosses him; he loses because he wants to be the first at any price. He'd rather kick the bucket than accept defeat."

I took Buba's hand. She returned my gentle squeeze.

"Dimitru," I said, "will you help me?"

"Gladly. Anytime."

I took the note out of my pocket and handed it to him.

"'A, period, Barbu'! It's his handwriting! Papa Baptiste wrote this!" Reverently, as if holding a sacred relic in his hand, Dimitru examined the piece of paper. "Six, period, eleven, period. Pavel, you know numbers are absolutely not my strong suit, unlike your good old granddad Ilja."

"It means the sixth of November. On that day, the teacher Barbulescu was in the rectory. And it looks as if Pater Johannes gave her the key to the library."

Dimitru knit his battered brow. "Now it's beginning to make sense to me. I never forget the sixth of November. It's your Grandfather's birthday. On this November sixth I wasn't here in the library. I was at home on tenterhooks all morning, waiting to see if my chuckleheaded cousin Salman would get here with the television on time. Salman arrived after noon, with the machine but without the antenna. Instead he brought that Hun with a mustache and a wart on his cheek, the guy who asked after the domicile of the village schoolteacher Miss Barbulescu in such a stilted way. I didn't return to the library until the next day, the day after Ilja's birthday. When I came in here, I said to myself right away, Dimitru, something's not right here. It all looked the same as usual. But"—Dimitru tapped his index finger on his nose—"it smelled different. At first I thought someone had left me flowers, but I couldn't find any. I swear it smelled like roses. Imagine that, in the middle of a frosty winter! How can it smell like roses? But I'm not crazy—I'm never crazy."

"Barbu has a perfume that smells like that," I explained.

"Then she was here!" Dimitru looked at Baptiste's note again, turned the paper this way and that, and held it up to the light. "Miss Barbulescu was here, hundred percent guaranteed. And since one of the duties of a librarian is to protect the books from unauthorized access, I always lock the door when I'm not here. She must have gone up to Papa Baptiste. There are two keys: one's always in my pocket, and the other hangs on a board next to the coat closet up in the pastor's apartment. You see how empiricism comes in handy? Test your theory and monitor the results!"

Dimitru hurried up the steps. Quick as a flash he was back down and opened his palm: there were two keys.

"They're both the same," I remarked.

"They're identical," he corrected me.

Together we concluded that Angela Barbulescu had asked the pastor for the key to the library in the early afternoon of November 6. Johannes Baptiste had handed over his key and noted it down on a little piece of paper so he wouldn't forget. Barbu went to the library, left behind a scent of roses, and returned the key, which either Baptiste or the orderly Fernanda had returned to its hook on the rack of keys. We could deduce the chain of events up to that point.

"Now we have to find out what Barbu was doing in here among all these books," Buba summed up.

"Usually you go to a library to borrow books," I said.

"Or to return a book you've already borrowed," Dimitru added.

"Had Barbu borrowed a book?" I asked eagerly.

"No, never. She never crossed the threshold of the rectory. I would know if she had, since she lives right next to us Gypsies. When she moved to the village, I often invited her to come to the library. 'The welcome mat's out to the world of knowledge,' I told her more than once. Umpteen times, in fact—she was a teacher after all. She always said, 'One of these days I'll come see you, Dimitru. Promise.' But as we know, woman is a fickle creature."

"Not true!" objected Buba. "She was here on November sixth, but you weren't."

"But what did she want? Dimitru, can you find out if a book is missing?"

The Gypsy closed his eyes. Buba put her finger to her lips and signaled me to keep quiet.

"No book is missing," Dimitru announced after a pause. "However, something in this room has changed."

To my astonishment Dimitru walked toward one of the walls of books, got a running start of two or three steps, and swung himself into a handstand. His steadied his feet against a shelf and explained his strange behavior: "We look but we don't see. Things reveal themselves when you stand the world on its head."

I was silently amazed. At first I thought that Dimitru's skinny arms would not support him for long, but then I realized that he had fallen into a strange state of semiweightlessness. Dimitru held himself upside down against the bookcase for more than an hour. With his eyes open. But then he suddenly crumpled sideways like a sack, looking bewildered and apparently without any memory of his eccentric behavior. At last he spoke.

"All the books that belong in this room are here. Angela Barbulescu did not remove a single one. She did the opposite: she took nothing, but she gave something. Seek and you will find it. Somewhere in among the other books. It's a green notebook. On the front cover there's a picture of a red rose. But the picture may already be worn away. Forgive me, but I'm very, very tired now. I have to lie down and take a nap."

Buba supported her uncle the few steps to his couch. A few minutes later she removed the notebook in question from one of the shelves.

We sat on the floor against the bookcase where we had sealed our friendship the night before. With trembling hands Buba opened the autograph book bound in green cloth. On the cover there were remnants of dried glue. Schoolgirls like Julia Simenov and Antonia Petrov possessed similar albums and passed them back and forth. But this album belonged to a grown woman. Inside the front cover were some faded pencil lines drawn with a straightedge. On them was written in a schoolgirl's hand, "This book may be read only with the permission of Angela Maria Barbulescu. Strada Bogdan Voda 18, Popesti."

"Popesti!" Buba exclaimed. "I know Popesti. It's near the capital. That's where Uncle Salman lives when he's not traveling on business."

Buba opened to the first page. The first entry was dated September 17, 1930. *Early blooms wilt all too soon. Your friend, Adriana.* Three days later a certain Juliana wrote the rhyme *Love makes us into royalty; lock up your hate and lose the key.* And a *best best friend* by the name of Alexa advised, *If I'm away and so are you, remember always: I love you.* Dated October 2: *Pray and hope without a frown, even when your luck is down. Your teacher, Aldene Dima.* We skimmed over the aphorisms that followed, written into the autograph book by schoolmates, friends, and aunts. One was dated December 24, 1931, and signed *Your Mother: Hope for nothing and you won't be disappointed.* "That's not right, Pavel," said Buba quietly. "Whoever hopes for nothing is not a flesh-and-blood human being."

I guessed that Angela Barbulescu must have been about ten or twelve in the year of the first entries and had gone to school in Popesti. A quick calculation brought me to the unexpected discovery that if Barbu was about ten in 1930 she must be somewhere in her mid- to late thirties today. "She always looked a lot older up in front of the class."

"She was worn out," Buba surmised, "because she didn't catch a man."

"Or she caught too many."

The next entry, still in a schoolgirl's hand, was not dated. *At home we always just sit around. Mama doesn't want to go out or see other people. It's all too much for her. She never wants to do anything. And Papa always makes promises he doesn't keep. Why couldn't I be lucky and have parents like Alexa's and Adriana's? They go to the mountains in the summer. Papa says he'll take me to the seashore sometime. He won't, though!* With these lines the character of the green notebook had changed. The autograph book of her girlhood became a diary that Barbu kept only sporadically. There were years when there were no entries at all, followed by little notations and occasional long passages in which her handwriting lost its girlish roundness and became more and more rough and uneven. Words were often distorted to the point of illegibility, and when Barbu did write something in a neat hand, she would often cross it out with brutal slashes, which led me to speculate that the teacher had been drinking heavily when she wrote, while Buba argued that she must have been very desperate.

"Let's take a look at what she wrote more recently," I urged.

"Not so fast." Buba stayed my hand. "I want to read it through in order and find out what happened back in those days in the capital."

If one could trust Angela Barbulescu's notebook, her father had died in 1942 in an accidental explosion at the Ploiesti oil fields where he was a guard. There were no remains left to be buried. Her mother Trinka seemed unaffected by the loss of her husband. In any event, one got the impression that her dull life continued to run its joyless course. Since there was no mention of either brother or sister we could assume that Angela grew up an only child. If she had already suffered under her mother's melancholy while her father was still alive, after the war Trinka Barbulescu's loathing of anything lively or joyful grew ever stronger. Angela must have tried from time to time to escape the prison of her mother's gloom, but Trinka had obviously reacted to each of her attempts with clever stratagems to keep her daughter tied to her apron strings. It wasn't easy to know whether the different illnesses that beset her—from migraines to fevers to a heart attack—were genuine or merely simulated. At any rate, Angela felt tethered to the cramped and stuffy maternal apartment except for a few mornings a week when she attended a training program for elementary schoolteachers at the new party academy in the capital. *My courses would be easier if I could study with the other student teachers. Why does Mother have to make everything so hard for me?* she wrote in March 1946.

On August 14 of the same year (she was already twenty-five or twenty-six years old), she wrote down some sentences that for the first time give evidence of her yearning for happiness. A young man named Fabian from the party academy had sent Angela a postcard with the picture of a red rose and asked her to the summer ball of the party youth group. *I've never danced, but Fabian promised to teach me all the steps. He's so friendly and I'm so excited!* When her mother found out that Angela was going to learn the pleasures of dancing, she must have remained silent for days on end, which Angela didn't take as permission but not as a clear prohibition either. *Alexa is sweet*, she noted in the book. *Even though we hardly see each other anymore she's going to lend me her blue summer dress.*

As we read the next entry, Buba wept tears for the first time onto the diary of our former teacher.

*August 20, 1946. I hate her. I hate her. Why did I have to come out of her belly!!!*

On the afternoon of the ball Angela had already applied some of Alexa's red lipstick and put on her friend's dress. Then she sat at the window, waiting. When Fabian rang the doorbell Trinka walked over to her daughter with a bread knife in her hand. She smiled, turned her left hand palm up, and drew the knife across her wrist. Blood spurted onto the borrowed dress. The doorbell kept ringing and ringing. Angela's throat constricted at the sight of what her crazy mother had done, and her scream was silent. She threw herself onto her bed and bit her fists and was still lying there hours after the bell had stopped ringing.

She never saw Fabian again, and Alexa had stuffed the blood-stained dress into the garbage can.

*I want to replace it*, the diary recorded, *but Alexa says the dress isn't even worth burning because it reminds her of a certain scumbag. Sometimes Alexa's pretty coarse, but she's a nice person.*

Alexa had offered to share her small apartment in town with Angela. *I have to get out of here. Mother is crazy and just lies in bed all day. I spend all our money in the pharmacy, but even with all her pills Mother doesn't get better. She's a lost cause, but why should I be, too?*

Angela apparently didn't accept her friend's offer, and another year went by with almost nothing in the diary.

I flushed with excitement when under the date September 2, 1947, I finally spotted the name I had been looking for the whole time: Stefan.

"That must be our Kronauburg party secretary," I whispered to Buba.

"The friend of Fritz Hofmann's revolting father?"

"Exactly."

My guess was confirmed. At the beginning of October, Angela had learned from Alexa, a certain Stefan Stephanescu was to receive his Ph.D. in economics. First there would be a ceremony with university dignitaries to which they weren't invited, but that evening Stefan was planning a party and had invited a bunch of amusing people.

*September 7, 1947. I don't have a dress but I'm going anyway, even if Mother . . .* The sentence broke off. Angela was certainly determined to go to Stephanescu's party with Alexa. Although she continued to run to the pharmacy for her mother in the following weeks, she apparently bought cheap vitamin pills instead of the expensive heart tablets. *Mother doesn't notice the difference. I ought to have a bad conscience, but it hasn't piped up at all. Soon I'll have saved enough for my dress. I would have liked the one with a rose pattern, but it's gone from the shop window. But the one with sunflowers will be lovely, too, and maybe Alexa's right that the brown accents go better with my blond hair now that fall has come.* On September 11, 1947, Angela wrote, *First installment paid! It will be mine in three weeks.*

Only later, when I'd read the diary several times, did I notice that from that point, Angela's mother never appeared again. Not a single word about what had become of Trinka Barbulescu.

After the party at Dr. Stefan Stephanescu's house Angela moved in with her friend Alexa. Her entries lost their melancholy and tortured tone. Suddenly they sounded not like those of a grown-up woman but of a dreamy girl.

*October 3, 1947. He danced with me. It was so wonderful. I always thought I couldn't dance. But with Stefan I can do anything. When we're dancing and he's holding me in his arms, I'm light as a feather. I'm floating. He so attentive and not at all like what you'd expect from a doctor of economics—boring and strict. And he's not stuck-up either. He's funny and popular and makes everybody laugh, especially me. He wants to see me again—soon, when one of his friends has a birthday party. His name is Florin and he's a brand-new doctor, a specialist for nerve problems. Stefan wants to take me and wants me to wear the dress with the sunflowers again. He likes it. He likes me. Life is wonderful.*

*October 11, 1947. The party was nice, because Stefan was there. His friends are really interesting even though I'd rather avoid Florin, he has such a penetrating gaze. Heinrich even came over from Kronauburg for the party. He's a little older and married already. He brought his camera along and took lots of snapshots. One of Stefan and me, too, giving each other an affectionate kiss. I hope I don't look stupid in the picture. I'm sure I had my eyes closed. Heinrich promised to bring me a print next time, since he's going to have things to do in the capital. I don't get some of Stefan's friends, though. Maybe because they're so free and easy. But that Koka guy is really obnoxious. Alexa says Koka's a puke, but she flirts with him. She says she's choosy, but she kisses everyone. Stefan says life holds a thousand possibilities and I've only tried one or two of them. He's right. He wants to show them all to me. I have to learn not to be afraid to live.*

*October 28, 1947. This noon another guy came out of Alexa's room. She's so nice, but why doesn't she fall in love with the right guy? She says she's waiting for someone who has more to offer than just his . . . I don't like it when she talks like that. How can I tell her I can't sleep when she's squealing so loud in the next room? Stefan's been traveling for two weeks. On party business. Waiting for him was awful. Does he miss me, too, this much? Really got sick and could hardly eat. Still went to class and forced myself to do the reading. Alexa thinks I'll sail through final exams the way I study. But it's hard for me. Stefan says good teachers are needed now that the war is over. But I don't know if I'll really be a good teacher for the children. Learn from the past, plan for the future, enjoy the present. That's what Stefan always says. The party has big plans for him, Heinrich says. That makes me happy.*

*November 2, 1947. Didn't go to the cemetery yesterday. Stefan asked me out, to his apartment. At last. Alexa was starting to joke about how long I intended to keep running around as a virgin. She talks so frankly. I thought it would hurt, but Stefan was gentle. Didn't know how many places you can be kissed on. I'm getting warm just thinking about it.*

The following entries from 1948 suggest that Angela Barbulescu invested a lot of effort in her training as a teacher but was enjoying herself at the same time. She spent the weekends with Alexa and Stefan's clique, often partying all night long. Sometimes she and her beloved (as she called him) spent all day in bed. Some evenings they went to the new movie palace on the Boulevard of the Republic. After evening cultural events Stefan took her to elegant restaurants. *Paris couldn't be more beautiful.*

In the summer of '48 Angela Barbulescu passed her exams at the teachers' college. Attached to her certificate was a memorandum recommending regular courses offered by the party to consolidate her ideological foundation. The day after graduation she left with

Stefan for two weeks on the Black Sea in Constanta. During the day they swam in the blue water. In the evening they strolled arm in arm along the harbor promenade before dining at Rapsodia. At night they churned up their bed in the elegant Palace Hotel, and Angela's notebook revealed that even before she'd had any breakfast she wanted nothing but to feel Stefan inside of her.

"I want to go to the seashore, too," Buba blurted out. I blushed.

Nothing in the entries of 1948 suggested that Angela's carefree happiness was the least bit endangered, except for one small hint of uncertainty at the end of their vacation on the Black Sea: *Asked Stefan about all the money this wonderful trip must have cost. He just laughed. The man earns and the woman spends. Alexa says his parents are loaded, but why doesn't he introduce me to them?*

*December 23, 1948. Not looking forward to Christmas. On party letterhead Koka invited us to an Oh Unholy Night celebration. That's his idea of humor. Stefan's been traveling a lot lately on account of collectivization. Some of the farmers resist progress, he says. But he'll get the job done. He can persuade people. If only he wouldn't drink so much on the weekends. He has me, isn't that enough? Alexa says I shouldn't worry about the Christmas party at Koka's. Drink enough and he'll seem nice, she says. Oh, well, Alexa and her liqueurs. Stefan doesn't even listen when I say I don't want to go to Koka's. He admits that Koka's a stupid bungler and a windbag to boot, but he's also an acting deputy of the Central Committee with excellent contacts with President Gheorghiu-Dej. You can't turn down an invitation from someone like that, Stefan says. Alexa thinks so, too. She suggested exchanging dresses for Christmas Eve. Me in her striped one! Why not? Even though everybody says the sunflowers go so well with my hair.*

*December 26, 1948. It was all a bad dream. I can't go on like this. He once asked what I would do for him. Anything, I said. I would jump off a bridge for you. He doesn't deserve it! It hurts so much when someone betrays you. He didn't stand up for me. What shall I do now? Alexa just lies in bed. She's hiding from me. I'm so ashamed!*

The party in Koka's luxurious apartment had apparently started out pleasantly enough, although Angela was hurt that she couldn't persuade Stefan Stephanescu to attend Christmas Mass with her beforehand. The host had spent a fortune to entertain his dozen or so guests, half of them men and half women. The buffet in the dining room was groaning with dozens of delicacies: Caspian Sea caviar, lobsters and oysters from France, Atlantic scallops. Then came venison and pork terrines and a huge grilled ham with an oversize fork and knife stuck in it. There was Russian vodka and French cognac to drink as well as American bourbon that Koka always cut with genuine Coca-Cola. Silver ice buckets kept the champagne cold, and on a sideboard stood bottles of local Tarnava Riesling and red Murfatlar from Dobruja in addition to fruit cordials especially for the ladies. Alexa started right in with the motto "Don't study 'em, drink 'em!"

Since Angela Barbulescu was obviously utterly despondent as she wrote about what happened that evening, Buba and I had difficulty deciphering her handwriting in some places. Angela had crossed whole passages out or written over them so that I had to fill in the gaps with my imagination to reconstruct that 1948 Christmas Eve party in the home of a certain Koka.

The mood must have been very boisterous. Contrary to her usual habit, Angela had drunk a few glasses of champagne. Alexa stuck to her cherry *exquisit* and flirted with everyone, male or female, while Stefan alternated cognac with red wine. All the women were tipsy and the men high. Then Koka and a guy named Albin made a bet to see who could drink the most "Russian piss" in a minute. Stefan counted off sixty seconds while everyone else shouted encouragement. They both more than half emptied a bottle of vodka, and put side by side, you couldn't tell a bit of difference between the levels. But Koka was declared the winner anyway, because he claimed Albin had taken one more swallow after the time was up. Which probably wasn't true. Angela called the bet a stupid little boy's game and said it had ended in a tie. Koka took that as an insult to himself as host and called her a cheap Catholic cunt who should keep her mouth shut in his house. *Everybody stopped talking,* she wrote in her diary. *Stefan pretended he hadn't heard.*

After this lapse on the part of the host, things started to get out of hand. At some point Koka jumped up, slapped his thighs, and danced the polka to liven things up. The others hesitated at first, then all started to clap in rhythm. Except for Angela, who wanted to go home but couldn't muster enough resolve to bestir herself. Koka was getting more and more crude and obscene. He grabbed the champagne bottle and poured it down his gullet. His guests laughed and choked and spluttered as they drank from the bottles Koka forced into their mouths. He jumped onto the buffet and bellowed, "Silent night, holy night." To her horror, Angela saw him drop his trousers and take out his penis. Then Koka peed on the oysters to the howling approval of the others. "Ladies' choice," he roared, jumped down from the buffet, took the tray of oysters, and offered them to the young ladies. Lenutza and Veronika grabbed some and swallowed them down. Lenutza shrieked and let the slimy stuff drip between her breasts. She boasted that the juice reminded her of something else she couldn't get enough of. "Show us how much you need it, show us!" screamed Florin. The others joined in the chorus. Lenutza knelt down in front of the host and went to work on him. The drunken Alexa pushed her aside, eager to finish with her mouth what Lenutza had started with her hand. Koka pulled away from her, saying that Alexa was so hot she needed more than one man. Stefan looked on grinning while Albin, Heinrich, and the young doctor Florin cleared the buffet. Alexa pulled the dress she was wearing—Angela's dress—off her shoulders and down to her waist, took off her stockings, underpants, and bra, and lay down on her back on the table. She spread her thighs while the men unbuttoned their pants. Except for Stefan Stephanescu. He shook up a champagne bottle and sprayed the foam between Alexa's legs. While Heinrich Hofmann took flash pictures of the scene and the men masturbated onto Alexa, the front door slammed, and Angela Barbulescu wandered lost through the Christmas Eve darkness.

"Barbu makes me sad," said Buba quietly. "What kind of person is this Stefan, anyway? He tramples on her heart." She shivered and pressed closer to me. "Will you put your arm around me?" She sighed, but I had already hugged her to me.

"She was a different person than when we knew her," I said softly.

Despite my shock at Angela Barbulescu's confessions, I was secretly happy about one thing: the naked woman in the photo under my mattress was not my disappeared teacher.

We heard Dimitru's even breathing from the red chaise longue, interrupted from time to time by incomprehensible babbling—for Buba a sure sign that her uncle was deep beneath the ocean of dreams from which he would not emerge in the foreseeable future.

*December 29, 1948. Alexa acts like nothing happened. She seriously asked me where I wanted to go on New Year's Eve.*

*December 31, 1948. He sent me a letter. I burned it unopened.*

*January 3, 1949. Comes with flowers. He absolutely must speak to me. As if there was anything left to say.*

*January 5, 1949. S. rings the doorbell for all it's worth. Never want to see him again.*

*January 10, 1949. Day after tomorrow moving to a furnished room near the Piata Romana. A job? Money for the rent?*

At some point during those days Angela Barbulescu must have received a letter inviting her to come to the Ministry of Education for the assignment of teaching positions for the school year 1949–50. *I ought to go,* she wrote, *but what's the point? I don't want to be a teacher anymore. I don't want to do anything.*

What happened next in Angela Barbulescu's life remained obscure because there were no entries for the following months. To my and Buba's complete surprise, however, she suddenly wrote a half year later, in July 1949, that she was getting married. Buba cried out when she gathered from the diary that Dr. Stephanescu might become Angela's husband.

"If she marries him, I'll cut off my curls." Buba was trembling and had apparently lost sight of the boundary between past and present. She'd forgotten that we were watching events unfold of many years before.

"Your curls stay on your head," I commanded.

"And why?"

"Because I like the way they smell."

"Okay. But she mustn't marry a man like that—ever!"

The entries on the following pages suggested that something had happened to Stephanescu, an accident in which he was badly injured. First we thought it must have been an automobile accident, but later Angela gave the impression that someone had tried to assassinate Stephanescu during the collectivization campaign in Walachia. The only certainty was that the party functionary had spent a long time in the hospital. And Angela sat at his bedside around the clock. Her past wounds seemed healed, as she wrote repeatedly of false friends that Stefan would now avoid—especially Koka. *Stefan's a new man. He's talking about marriage, family, children! I can hardly believe it.*

"If she marries that man, it will kill her." Buba sighed again and lowered her eyes. I had already seen Buba throw some kind of invisible switch that allowed her to see with her "third eye," something I would never make fun of again. I watched my sweetheart. She was crying from closed eyes and humming quietly, the sound light and airy like delicate singing that moved through her from some bright realm. Then she came back.

"Buba, what's wrong?" I asked in concern and wiped away her tears.

"If she doesn't marry this man, then she doesn't have to die, because she's already dead."

*July 6, 1949. I missed my period—it's been ten days already.*

*July 18, 1949. Dr. Bladogan says it's too early to tell for sure, but the symptoms are clear. I'm going to have a baby!!! Should I wait to tell Stefan? Yes. I want to be completely certain.*

*July 31, 1949. I'm sure! Dr. Bladogan says I'll be a mother by April 1 next year. We're going to be parents! Maybe now I can get Stefan to come to church. It's not nice to get married at the registry office.*

*August 1, 1949. Haven't slept. Stefan didn't come, although he promised to pick me up. Heinrich called at ten, sent a thousand kisses from Stefan; he had to make an urgent trip to Walachia. Trouble with the farmers again because of relocation. Stefan will be gone for two weeks. But he ought to be taking it easy. Politics is horrible.*

*August 2, 1949. I'm completely confused. What am I to think? Since Heinrich was here, I'm sure that Stefan is hiding something from me. He's lying. I had to get out of here yesterday, I felt like I was suffocating in this tiny room. And so hot outside. Then who should I run into in the park? Alexa! I haven't seen her since I moved out. She throws her arms around me and is all wound up. She talked and talked and talked. Acted like my dearest friend. I think she'd been drinking, although I didn't smell anything. She had on a new dress and nice leather shoes. She says she's with Albin now and she thinks the wart on his cheek is really cute, not like before when she couldn't stand him. Everything is different now. Koka has also calmed down. He married Lenutza, that stupid cow who was so hot for the oysters.*

*Heinrich often comes over from Kronauburg. Koka even loaned him money for a brand-new motorcycle, since he has such a long trip, and he also lets him use the big apartment as a photo studio. Alexa works with him there. I asked Alexa what she knew about cameras. "Are you kidding?" She made fun of me. "I don't take pictures, I let him take pictures of me," she said proudly. For a fee. Some men pay a lot of money to see the pictures. "Some pay even more"—she laughed—"so nobody else sees them."*

*I'm so stupid!!! Why did I have to blab to Alexa that I'm expecting a baby? Maybe I just wished somebody could share my happiness. But Alexa isn't the least bit happy for me. I don't understand her anymore. She used to want a whole house full of children and now she's so fidgety, so agitated. Her hands can't keep still. She hardly listens at all, and I also told her that Stefan doesn't know about the child yet because he's in Walachia dealing with the troublemakers there. Alexa looks surprised. "In Walachia? Aha. Didn't know that Stefan had put a bun in your oven. He never said anything about it. Oh, well, accidents happen." How can Alexa say something like that? How could she tell me that if I want to get rid of it, I should go see Florin—Dr. Pauker. It would all be private, sterile, and no big deal. "Man," she said, "really had no idea that Stefan planted one in your belly, too . . ." I was startled. What did she mean by "too"??? Alexa bit her lip, said "Take it easy," and was gone. My head is spinning. I'm screaming. I black out. I only recall that I must have fallen down. What do I do now?*

*August 16, 1949. Stefan is back, at my door with flowers yesterday. He went to put his arm around me, but I held back. He takes me out to the street and shows me his new car. He saw right away that I wasn't happy. He asks what's wrong. I told him about running into Alexa, asked if it was true what she said about other women. My knees were shaking, it was terrible. How can he say such crude things, tell me I can kiss a wedding good-bye, since I'm snooping around behind his back and listening to that cheap slut Alexa. Why is he so nasty? Said I could earn my own rent from now on, spread my legs and let them take pictures, like Alexa. I didn't dare tell him I was pregnant. How could I say we're going to have a child? He's a bad person. He doesn't want me. I'm afraid of him.* "Me, too." Buba was trembling all over. "I'm cold." At that moment no embrace in the world could have warmed the girl beside me. Least of all mine, because I was also cold as ice. Outside the tower clock struck noon.

"My God, Pavel, it's so late. I've got to go home. My mother's sure to be looking for me."

She gave me a fleeting kiss on the cheek. I replaced Angela's green notebook between the other books. Buba dashed off. We'd continue reading as soon as we could.

Dimitru stirred on his chaise longue, crawled out from under his blanket, and rubbed his eyes. He stared at me as though returning from some immensely distant world.

"What are you doing here, Pavel? Do you know if Papa Baptiste has left already? Is he still mad at me?"

"What are you talking about, Dimitru? Father Johannes is dead."

"But he was just here a second ago."

"You were dreaming, Dimitru. Try to wake up."

"But I saw him. Papa Baptiste came through that door. He came toward me shaking a stick. 'What are you doing, Dimitru?' he scolded. I was going to ask forgiveness and shake his hand, but zip! And he was gone. Disappeared!"

"No, Dimitru. Johannes Baptiste was murdered. He couldn't disappear because he wasn't here."

"He was here! And he was scolding."

"Scolding you? What did he say?"

"He said, 'Dimitru, my arrogant son! Keep faith with the earth! Keep faith with man! Like your father Laszlo! Shall nothing remain of your father's legacy but dust and bones? Turn around! What did I teach you? Where two or three are gathered together in my name, there am I in the midst of them. But you, Dimitru Carolea Gabor, you're satisfied to be by yourself.' That's what Baptiste said. He disowned me, Pavel! I'm a prodigal son, disowned for all eternity!"

"But you know the father loved his prodigal son most of all, more than his obedient sons who were so well behaved all the time. That's what Baptiste always preached."

"But the prodigal son returned to his father, Pavel. Don't forget that."

# Chapter Seven

●

## *AN INVINCIBLE PAIR, A BROWN CROSS,*

## *AND THE LAST PROCESSION TO THE MONDBERG*

I was still cold. Since reading Angela's diary with Buba, I couldn't get warm. I took pillows and wool blankets and sought out the warmest place in the house, the bench next to the tiled stove in the tavern. Here I could hold out against the cold. My mother took good care of me. She fried blood sausage with polenta, brewed peppermint tea double sweetened with honey, and stroked my hair, which she hadn't done for years, since I always reacted so crossly. I lay awake with my eyes open and listlessly watched Grandfather Ilja half dozing behind the counter of the store. A daily calendar hung above his head and proclaimed Wednesday, November 20, 1957. Only fourteen days had gone by since Granddad's fifty-fifth birthday, but he had aged in those two weeks.

Dimitru stomped in at twilight. He'd come back down to earth. When he called out, "A customer, barkeep, with a full heart and empty pockets," Grandfather's eyes opened and his gray face took on some color.

"Sit down," he told Dimitru. "Nothing's happened around here for days. I could just as well close the joint."

"And let your Gypsy friend shiver his behind off out there in the frost? What kind of friend is that?"

Ilja gave a pained laugh. "*Zuika* or Sylvaner?"

"The honor of my people forces me to say—both." Granddad took out two glasses and placed the wine and the schnapps on the table. Dimitru didn't touch the glasses.

"First you order and then you don't drink. What's the matter?"

"I mustn't drink alone anymore. Ilja, you've got to keep me company and have a little glass, too," urged Dimitru, although he knew very well that Grandfather couldn't drink any alcohol since his childhood fall into the vat of mash.

"Why mustn't you drink alone? It's not against the law. You usually booze alone."

"That's just it. But no more. I can't drink alone if I want to toast our dear departed Papa Baptiste. To have him in our midst, there has to be two of us. At least. Otherwise it won't work."

"Well, if that's the way it is, I can't leave you in the lurch."

I saw how Grandfather could hardly keep himself from bursting out laughing. Even though Dr. Bogdan from Apoldasch had warned him of the effects of even the smallest amount of spirits, to which his delicate constitution was likely to react with the shakes and memory loss, Grandfather took a glass of Sylvaner and drank. "To our Father Johannes."

"What's wrong with your Pavel, anyway? Is he sick?" When Dimitru spied me on the stove bench beneath my down pillows, I closed my eyes and made a couple of snoring noises. That's how I overheard the conversation of two men as earnest as they were peculiar.

Grandfather must have experienced the speedy effects of the unaccustomed glass of wine as beneficial. His weariness fell from him. His tongue was loosened, and he felt light enough to share the weight of his worries with Dimitru.

"Dimitru, you know I've always dealt fairly with everyone as a shopkeeper and tavern owner. But I just don't know anymore who I can trust in the village and who I can't."

The Gypsy didn't reply, which I took as a sign he was ready to listen.

"Nasty rumors are making the rounds, rumors that worry me. I find myself unable to tell the difference between truth and falsehood. When Pater Johannes was murdered, people in the village thought at first that the Communists and possibly even the Brancusis had blood on their hands. Those brothers are hot-blooded comrades for sure, but such a horrible crime against Pater Johannes—no, no Brancusi could do such a thing. The police have witnesses who confirm that: the brothers weren't even in the village the night of the murder. They were in Apoldasch taking a class for party cadres. Then there's this strange business about the body disappearing. No one still has any idea what became of our dead pastor. The Saxons are whispering that the Security Service is guilty of the murder. The Securitate is supposed to have silenced Baptiste forever because he was going to preach against the kolkhoz. Now there's a completely different story. The rumor is going around that Baptiste's murder is connected to the teacher Barbulescu. Kora Konstantin claims to have seen Barbulescu sneak into the rectory before she disappeared, a few days before Pater Johannes's murder. I don't know whether to believe that blabbermouth Kora. But she swears that Barbulescu went to see the pastor in order to confess mortal sins that she's been piling up since the very beginning of her dissolute life. That Konstantin woman is spreading it around that Barbu's vices are so enormous that Johannes Baptiste was not able to grant her the sacrament of absolution, since the measure of her sins exceeded his authority to forgive."

I flushed under my pillows; I was all ears. Dimitru said, "Tell me more."

"If what Kora is telling everyone is true, then this is how it went: Pater Johannes listened to Barbulescu's confession but then refused her absolution. And now Kora's claiming that a confession without absolution is invalid, and Baptiste was no longer bound to keep it confidential. You know as well as me, Dimitru, that Pater Johannes never betrayed anyone's confidence. No one had to fear that he would ever say even one word about it."

"He'd have cut out his own tongue first!"

"But did Barbulescu know that, too? Anyway, Kora claims she knows that Johannes asked Barbu to leave Baia Luna. She says it's not proper for a slutty person like her to be teaching children. And now both the Konstantin woman and Knaup the sacristan claim that Barbulescu had something to do with the murder of Johannes Baptiste. What exactly it is, they won't say. But Kora's trumpeting that it won't be long before they do."

Since Dimitru said nothing, I opened my eyes a crack and saw him running his hand through his tangled hair. He took a swallow of *zuika,* shook himself, spit, and pushed the glass away. "When not even your schnapps tastes good anymore, Ilja, then believe me, things are at a serious pass. Especially when people start listening to madmen."

Grandfather nodded in agreement. "Then you don't believe what Kora Konstantin says either?"

"My dear friend Ilja, I'm just verificizing. First of all: Papa Baptiste never sent a repentant soul packing without absolution. Never. Secondly: women always act on pure emotion *in principio*. They can hate, oh boy can they ever! Just as they can love, and I speak from experience. But a hating woman would never tie a naked old man to a chair, turn a whole room upside down so it looks like a Gypsy's house, and then cut his throat. And thirdly: what does this Konstantin woman say? What sins did Barbu supposedly commit, for heaven's sake?"

"Matricide and killing the fruit of her womb."

Dimitru was silent. My blood was boiling.

"There is one strange thing," Dimitru said slowly. "It's true that Barbulescu was in the rectory. It was on your birthday, when we were sitting in this very room listening to Khrushchev's Sputnik speech. According to my modest fund of information, she didn't want to confess to Papa Baptiste but only to borrow the key to the library."

"The key to the library? From the pastor? But everybody in the village knows that you have the key to the books. Why would she bother old Johannes for it? Why didn't she come to you? She lives right near you."

Dimitru didn't respond immediately. "Maybe I should ask myself the same question sometime. But I know one thing *sine dubio*. Whatever Miss Barbulescu has on her conscience, it's absolutely not our good Papa Baptiste."

The stairs creaked. I recognized the heavy tread of Aunt Antonia. She greeted the two men, and I heard her go to the shelf where the chocolate was kept. She bid them good night, and the stairs groaned again.

"There's one more thing that's been knocking around in my head," Grandfather resumed after this interruption. "Dimitru, do you think Baptiste was telling the truth about the Project of this Korolev guy? Do you really think it's possible the cosmonauts would go flying into space and then tell Khrushchev if they've seen God and Mary?"

"Ilja, my friend! To prevent that very thing is why I'm sitting here! We have to do something. By the breasts of the Blessed Virgin, the Project must be sabotaged as truly as I'm a Gypsy. We're going to throw a regular monkey wrench into Korolev's works. I . . . just don't know how yet."

"I tell you, if anybody can stop Korolev it's the Americans."

"But the Yanks are blind. They don't realize what the Soviets are cooking up. And not a voice to warn them. And Korolev is rubbing his hands with glee. America fell for his Sputnik trick and is boiling mad about that stupid beeping. Meanwhile time is running out. I would guess Korolev and Khrushchev are just counting the days until the real countdown begins."

"The real what?"

"It's the period between a point in time $x$ and the rocket launch," Dimitru explained. "When the cosmonauts have overcome gravity and are on the moon, the order will reach them, 'Fan out and find Mary!'"

"And if they don't find the Madonna, they'll announce to the world that there's no God . . ."

"And you know what that means?"

I heard Grandfather refilling two glasses before he answered, "Not exactly."

"I'll tell you: if there's no God, it means the United States of America is done for. *Exitus.* Up to now the Yanks were always superior to the Soviets in everything. Higher buildings, bigger cars . . ."

"Bigger statues of the Madonna and better cigars," Grandfather added.

"Exactly. Everything in America is better. But without God, it'll be all over. Then the Americans will have to pulp all their money. Without God, all those lovely dollars are worthless. *In God we trust!* That's English, and it's written on every American bill, on account of the parable of Jesus about the master and his servants and the talents. If you have a talent, make it two. If you have a lot of money, make even more. That's what an American does. Like in the Bible. I know about it from my cousin Salman. He once tried his hand at currency trading. But if there's no God, then you can't trust in him, much less in a currency that puts its trust in something that doesn't exist. Without God, America might as well burn its dollars. Then comes the ruble."

"I understand," said Ilja. "That's why the Americans have to act fast. Faster than the Russians. Another shot?"

"I'll never say no!"

"Someone should warn the president of the United States. But how?"

"*Sic est*. But it's still too early for an intervention. First we need to know if Mary really went up to heaven. Otherwise we'll make a laughingstock of ourselves. Why do you think I study so much? I'm testing if it's possible that the infallible papal magisterium is fallible. If it turns out that Pius in Rome made an *error fatal* in his dogma or, worse, knowingly misled the faithful, then we can close up shop. There'll be nothing left of Jesus's Mother but dust and bones, scattered about somewhere in the Holy Land. There'll be nothing left but to verificize: forget the Assumption! That's how I see it."

"That must be how it is," Grandfather confirmed. "Exactly how I see it, too."

He refilled their glasses and stood up. The cash-register drawer squealed. Besides drinking, Grandfather was obviously breaking another habitual rule. He took out the new box of cigars I'd given him for his fifty-fifth birthday.

"Here, Dimitru. Have one. Nothing beats a good Cuban."

Matches scratched and flared. The powerful aroma of tobacco permeated the still air. Then Dimitru said something long overdue, ever since the day when he lent my grandfather his hand to write "Borislav Ilja Botev" on the list of names demanded by Raducanu.

"Your Cubans are classy, Ilja. The Bulgarians understand a thing or two about rolling cigars. But why they write the letters backward in their Cyrillic scribble isn't clear to me. No one who knows Latin can make heads or tails of it. By the way, it's time you finally learned your letters."

"I know, Dimitru, I know. High time."

"Starting tomorrow you're going to have lessons, taught by yours truly. An hour per day. As a restaurateur you can afford the innocence of ignorance but not as my ally on this most tricky mission. How are you going to stand up to that sly fox Korolev if you can't even write your name on a piece of white paper?"

"And you won't tell anyone?"

"What a question! I'm your best friend! I'm pledged to silence. Feel better now?"

Grandfather laughed. "Much better. But there's something else . . ."

"Out with it!"

"Well, even if that box only works as a radio, believe me, Dimitru: your television was a wonderful present and makes me very happy. But sometimes I think the pleasure of owning such an apparatus is too great. The present must have cost a fortune, and you Gypsies have nothing saved up for a rainy day. I think now that we're not just friends but allies, you can tell me where you got the money for the TV. Not that I think you organized the acquisition—how shall I put it?—outside the bounds of the law, but . . ."

"Good Gypsies don't steal!"

I was sure Dimitru was about to jump up and curse and cancel the friendship. But things stayed calm. I opened my eyes and saw the Gypsy struggle to hide his emotion.

"Dimitru," asked Granddad in a worried voice, "what's the matter?"

"What a time you picked to remind me of my dead father Laszlo!"

"But Dimitru, the accident by the Tirnava was twenty years ago. Your father's been dead a long time and I'll never forget the way he tried to pull my Agneta and Antonia out of the wagon. I'll never forget how you jumped into the icy water with me either. But what in heaven's name does the television have to do with Lazlo's death?"

Dimitru was sobbing. "It was Father's idea—I don't mean the television, but the way we would earn some money. Like Americans: if you don't have any money, go where the money is. That's how we came by all those little bottles."

"I remember. You'd bought bottles in Kronauburg, a whole lot of bottles."

"Not just bottles, *little* bottles," the Gypsy specified, "tiny brown glass bottles with even tinier corks, brown for light protection, if you see what I mean."

"I don't see anything!"

"All right, all right. If you insist, I'll explain the whole thing to you." Dimitru downed his *zuika* and started his story. "The Gypsies' fate—lack of money—had inspired my father to more and more elaborate methods of obtaining cash. One fine summer day in 1935, shortly after the tribe's arrival in Baia Luna, Laszlo was lying on his back in a pasture on the edge of the village. Not idly, as one might assume: he was studying the farmers' cows and thinking about how you could make money out of other people's cattle without anyone suffering a loss. Not like the idiot *gaje* rustlers who steal horses and cattle all over the place and get caught red-handed at the next cattle market. Laszlo Carolea Gabor had a much better idea: milk! Before the farmers' children drove the cows into the barns every evening to be milked, you'd only need to secretly draw off a little milk. Not much—just a shot glass's worth at the most."

Dimitru pointed to his empty glass. Ilja uncorked another bottle and remarked that a few drops of milk would never make a man rich.

*"Exactamente!"* That was precisely why Dimitru's father had the idea of a clandestine premilking into tiny bottles. That's why they'd borrowed some investment capital from relatives in Walachia and purchased five hundred bottles from the Kronauburg pharmacy.

"But the business with the milk never bore fruit, since my good father lost his life in that blizzard. I waited for three times seven years of mourning and then came the hour when the son was able to put his father's brilliant idea into action. That hour arrived last summer. And now? Has anyone in the village complained about not getting enough milk from their cows?"

"Not that I know of."

"You see!"

For weeks, Dimitru confessed, he had been secretly crawling on his belly through the pastures, relieving the village cows of a little milk before they went into the barns, then, following the law of *principio duplex,* he'd doubled his take with water from the Tirnava. Then he'd bottled it in the little brown medicine bottles, corked them, and sealed them with the wax of a red votive candle from the parish church. "And then the reliquaries were ready! The best I ever had."

"What reliquaries?" It wasn't only Grandfather who didn't understand where the Gypsy was heading with this story. Neither did I.

"Milk from the breasts that once nursed Baby Jesus."

"You're crazy!"

"Not at all," objected Dimitru, and explained that a few drops of milk from the Holy Virgin Mary were a highly prized devotional object that the Crusaders had once brought back from the Holy Land as a souvenir and excellent protection against the devil's animosity. Which of course had its price, especially since the milk that nourished the Son of God was much more effective than a splinter of the true cross or a thorn from the crown Jesus wore for his Crucifixion. This piece of wisdom had unfortunately been forgotten by Catholics during the long years of Enlightenment, but not by the Orthodox.

"But you're a swindler! You're not selling people the Madonna's milk, you're selling cow's milk and water!"

"Hang on, hang on! When you receive the host in church, what are you eating?"

"The Body of Christ," answered Grandfather without hesitation.

"Correct. Only heathens, Bolsheviks, and people who don't know what they're talking about would claim all you are eating is a stale piece of bread. Faith transforms things. Water and flour just the same as water and milk."

"But bread was sacred to the Lord," Granddad objected. "Jesus passed around bread at the Last Supper. And wine, of course. He changed them into his flesh and blood. But there's nothing in there about milk. You're swindling the Orthodox."

"I protest! I'm no crook! According to the laws of negative dialectics, a swindler who swindles other swindlers is no grifter; he's a champion of justice. Look here: who's going to believe a Gypsy? Nobody! But the Orthodox will believe anything a priest in gilded robes says. Every word. If a Black sets up on the market square and starts hawking bottles of Madonna's milk, people will just laugh at him—if he's lucky. If he's unlucky, stones will start flying. That's why my father already knew that you only make money with the people who want to make money themselves, with the greedy. So last summer I loaded up my cart with bottles and set off for Moldavia. Let me tell you, it was just one monastery after another. On the way, thousands of Orthodox were streaming into the monastery of Humor. I came right on the heels of the pilgrims with my wares. At first the head pope didn't want to receive me. So I sent him a message that the Gypsies wanted to donate a new watertight roof for the basilica and money for the restoration of the frescoes of the Last Judgment, and I got an audience. I offered him fifty-fifty if he hawked my bottles."

"And was he in?" asked Grandfather.

"Was he ever! The milk was sold out in two hours. People almost came to blows over it. The ones who got a bottle were happy as angels. The pope even served me a meal, the best of everything, and he opened a fine bottle of red wine and said if I come next summer and bring more reliquaries, he'd be honored to have me as his guest. Believe me, with that money the priest could have put three roofs on his church. And I was able to pay back my relatives with double interest, and I gave my cousin Salman my share to buy you a good television. There was enough money for ten antennas, but what did that chuckleheaded idiot do? He does an American: wants to increase his yield and plays cards with those crafty Gypsies at the Kronauburg train station."

I'm sweating so much next to the tile stove that I throw off the feather bed and sit up. Incredibly enough, the two of them still don't notice me.

"Here, you Doubting Thomas." Dimitru fished a crumpled piece of paper out of his pants pocket. "Everything on the up and up," he said to Grandfather, handing him the receipt for the television. "It's for you. Take good care of it."

As Ilja was stowing away the receipt underneath the coin tray of his cash register, the amount the set had cost jumped out at him. His head reeled.

"My God, Dimitru, you're a sly dog, damned sly. Like David . . . David in battle with . . . what's that giant's name again?"

"Our giant is Korolev. He's our Goliath. We have no armor and no army, so we have to be smart. The stone in our sling is our cunning. That's our weapon."

"And we're not alone!" Grandfather twisted the cork from another bottle of Sylvaner. "We can depend on America. The Americans will build better rockets than the Soviets. The Yanks don't want rubles . . . Oh, you're awake, Pavel! Feeling better? Then bring us another stick of chewing gum, okay? I'm telling you, Dimitru, the real American kind is the best."

I'm going out to get a breath of fresh air. I'm still feeling a little low," I said. My experience was that this always gained me permission to disappear for a while. There was no one looking after the library in the rectory. Dimitru had already started to squint a bit and certainly wouldn't be returning there for the next couple hours. I threw on my coat and left the house.

I waded briskly through the snow to the Gypsies' settlement. When I reached the clay hut where Buba lived, I regretted not having agreed on a secret signal to let her know it was me. I guessed it was about nine, too late to call to her. Cautiously I lobbed a snowball against the windowpane I figured was my girlfriend's bedroom. It seemed like an eternity until the window opened and a voice whispered, "Pavel?" Buba clambered out the window barefoot, dressed only in a thin nightgown. I put my coat around her shoulders, and we hurried through the darkness to the rectory. I groped my way up to the priest's apartment and found to my relief that the spare key to the library was hanging on the board next to the wardrobe again.

As I took hold of it, I saw a glint of silver: another small, elaborately decorated key. With a vague idea of what lock it might fit, I put it into my pocket.

Two minutes later I was crawling under the blankets with the shivering Buba on Dimitru's chaise longue. Angela Maria Barbulescu's diary lay closed on our laps.

"I have a bad feeling about this," Buba said, and pressed against me. "For the last few days I've thought of nothing but Miss Barbulescu and what must have happened to her back then in the capital. Then I wished you were with me. But Mother wouldn't let me out of the house. Our teacher must have been a mother, too. She let that creep Stefan get her pregnant. But she came to Baia Luna without a child. I want to know what happened to Barbu's child."

"That's just what I've been wondering the whole time." I put my arm around Buba and with the other hand went to open the green notebook. Then the door flew open.

Susanna Gabor had only to follow our tracks in the snow.

"You slut! You bitch! Crawling in bed with a *gajo*. You whore, you filthy tramp." Susanna stormed toward Buba.

I jumped up to protect her, but I wasn't equal to the raging fury of a Gypsy mother. Susanna pounded me and then her daughter with her fists as if possessed. She grabbed Buba by the hair and pulled out handfuls of curls. While Buba cried out in despair, "He's my friend, my boyfriend. I don't want anybody else, never, never, never," her mother was screeching, "For shame. Be off with you! Get out, you slutty *gaje*-tart!"

She dragged the whimpering Buba out of the rectory and pulled her through the village by the hair. Susanna's hollering cut through the winter night like the howl of a mother wolf. Lights went on in the houses, and the inhabitants of Baia Luna shoved their curtains aside with silent alarm.

I returned to the tavern. Almost blind with worry, I saw two brothers in spirit snoring on the wooden bench next to the stove, drunk on wine and self-satisfaction. Under my coat I had Angela's green diary.

How feverishly I had awaited the moment I could resume reading the missing teacher's journal with Buba. But as I lay alone in bed clutching the green diary with both hands, the precious book had lost something of its value. My worry was not what had happened to Angela Barbulescu but what would happen to my sweetheart. Since I could find no path into the consolation of sleep, I lit the bedside lamp in the certainty that, under the circumstances, Buba would never blame me for leafing through the diary by myself.

I opened to the first pages and read for the second time the sentence Trinka Barbulescu had written into her daughter's autograph book a quarter century ago, Christmas Eve 1931: *Hope for nothing and you won't be disappointed.* Angela had hoped, against the advice of her life-denying mother. And she had been disappointed, disappointed by a man who had awakened her yearning for life. For hidden behind his jovial façade and his smile was nothing but icy coldness. "He'll suck her dry," Buba had said.

*November 3, 1949. Examined by Dr. Bladogan. She says, "Miss Barbulescu, it's time to act if you don't want to show up at the wedding altar with a big belly." I couldn't even cry. I'm in my fifth month. Maybe Alexa told him about it already. Haven't seen S. since the summer. I'll get my child through life by myself. Without him. At least I'll tell it to his face. Going to his office tomorrow!*

A few pages and again I was absorbed in the past of my missing teacher without feeling like an intruder. Angela hadn't hidden her diary in the library with the intention of hiding her thoughts but in the hope that it would be discovered. At least that wish had been fulfilled. As I continued to read, I was disappointed to discover that several pages had been torn out. My dissatisfaction grew when the following pages yielded no information. The handwriting became erratic, almost illegible, and often crossed out with wild, chaotic strokes. I was paging past this part when I saw something that gave me goose bumps and a chill. The right-hand page boasted a brownish cross. The way the color shaded off, you could tell that Angela Barbulescu had smeared it onto the page with her thumb, once up and once across. On the left-hand page were words printed in heavy block letters that looked like a gravestone inscription.

THE MIGHTY FALL FROM THEIR THRONES
THE LOWLY ARE LIFTED UP
HIS HOUR WILL COME
WHEN HE'S REACHED THE TOP
BAIA LUNA, AUGUST 15, 1950

I missed Buba. Having her at my side would have cushioned the blow of seeing the cross and the words whose cryptic significance dismayed me. "He" could be no one else but the party secretary of Kronauburg, Stefan Stephanescu, the man whom I was supposed to destroy and send to hell. I forced myself to think. The date and place revealed that Angela Barbulescu was no longer in the capital but already in Baia Luna when she had written her grim prediction. Three-quarters of a year had passed since she noted down the progress of her pregnancy and her intention to pay a visit to Stephanescu, the father of the baby. I found no answer to the question of what had happened to her in the capital during the intervening months. The most important stones in the mosaic of her life's story were missing.

In August 1950, I was eight years old and had only a vague memory of the teacher's arrival in the village. I was starting the first grade—somewhat late for my age, but back then there was no school in Baia Luna anyway because there was no teacher. The Ministry of Education dispatched Angela Barbulescu as the new teacher for our village. From the beginning, her relations with the villagers were ill fated. The diary entries from the months following her arrival confirmed that. She wrote of the mistrust she encountered as a woman from the big city, mentioned the village gossip about her: rumors, insults, and slurs. The letters *KK* crop up again and again, an abbreviation that could only mean Kora Konstantin. However, the early entries from Baia Luna told me nothing more than what I already knew from my own experience.

In the final part of the diary, Angela Barbulescu had written resolutions in a shaky hand, resolutions that revealed more of a wish than a real resolve to stop drinking. Although undated, they documented the steady downfall of an alcoholic who had no support. From time to time there were moments of clarity. Angela Barbulescu very consciously witnessed the process of her self-destruction without being able to muster the strength to resist it. She knew very well that she was a bad teacher with just enough energy to assign her pupils endless pages to copy. And she also knew that they were more contemptuous than fearful of her. When I read my own name and Fritz Hofmann's in the diary it became painfully clear to me that it had by no means escaped the teacher's notice that Fritz and I were putting down absurdly high solutions to arithmetic problems. She had even found out that Fritz rewrote the stupid party poems to suit himself. *Fritz can be so nasty. Like father, like son, I suppose. But he has a mind of his own. And a poetic imagination. I hope he doesn't turn out like his father, that . . .* I couldn't make out the final word, but I knew enough about the photographer Heinrich Hofmann to make it superfluous.

I paged forward. While I searched for Angela Barbulescu's very last entry, I knew exactly when she had written it: on the morning of my grandfather's fifty-fifth birthday, while he and Dimitru were listening for the Sputnik. I had walked Dimitru home through the fog and through her window had seen her sitting at the kitchen table and writing.

It was a farewell letter, clean and clearly printed. It began with a stiff salutation, like an impersonal letter from some government office:

*Baia Luna, November 6, 1957*

*Dear Comrade Party Secretary Dr. Stephanescu,*

*Yesterday the messenger brought the package from the district administration. I hereby confirm receipt of the photograph. I will follow the instructions to immediately hang your portrait in a prominent place in the Baia Luna school building. Your picture will hang in schools next to the picture of the state president. The children will look up to you. To your smile. Your partner Hofmann has done a good job, as always, although his specialty is another kind of picture.*

*What the two of you did to me during my labor in Dr. Pauker's clinic was bad. The photos that Hofmann made of me with your disgusting friends are repulsive. They kept my mouth closed for a long time. But no longer. As far as I'm concerned, Hofmann can send those pictures to the village priest. Do whatever you want with them. Hang my picture on every lamppost. I'm not afraid anymore.*

*I once told a pupil of mine that you were a sorcerer who turned wine into water. I couldn't tell that good boy the truth: that you turn wine into blood. "Children Are Our Future" it says under your picture. A beautiful sentence, and a true one. My future didn't even make it to nine months. You and your comrades disposed of my future, as a bloody hunk of flesh for the garbage can. Since then, nothing can happen to me that hasn't happened already.*

*Stefan, you're going to make it to the very top. But your last hour has already struck. I'm not praying to any God for that, I'm just making the only sacrifice left to me. And if they bury me in unconsecrated ground for it and if I go to hell, I swear we'll come back to fetch you too someday.*

*Signed,*

*Angela Maria Barbulescu and a child without a name*

As I shuddered in horror at the realization that my teacher had drawn the brown cross in her diary with blood, the door to the bedroom next to mine opened and I heard my mother Kathalina's steps. It must have been about six in the morning. The night was over, although for me the night had just begun. With my not quite sixteen years I didn't want to imagine what they had done to Angela in a doctor's clinic in the capital. I only knew that Dr. Stefan Stephanescu had seen to it that his child in the belly of Angela Maria Barbulescu never saw the light of day. The same must not be allowed to happen to the knowledge of the deed.

With my reading of the green notebook, the days of my childhood were over. My teacher was a different person than the one I thought I knew. And this knowledge entailed an obligation.

*Send this man straight to hell! Exterminate him!*

"Yes," I said, "I will."

Kathalina clapped her hands. "Gentlemen, the night is over." Ilja and Dimitru the Gypsy lay on the tile floor next to the stove. Slowly they regained consciousness and rubbed the sleep out of their eyes. Without complaint they obeyed Kathalina's order to apply the water from the tap in the backyard to their faces, something Dimitru only made a symbolic attempt at. Refreshed by the icy water, Ilja immediately remembered he had indulged in alcoholic beverages the night before. He was pleased to discover that he had neither a headache nor palpitations, while Dimitru reminded him with a raised forefinger: "Lesson One: Reading and Writing. Part One: The Alphabet."

In the weeks of Grandfather's reading lessons, I learned that although not always the most patient of teachers, Dimitru was a good one. Blessed with a wealth of ideas, he wrote his own practice texts for their daily lessons. He began with all the words he could think of that had only two, three, and then four letters. Then he proceeded to compound words and short proverbs, until finally Grandfather was able to read the simple poems Dimitru composed about the beauty of women and the joys of sex. At first he read haltingly, following the letters with his finger, but with growing confidence. Soon Dimitru was bringing slim edifying tracts on the lives of the saints from the library as well as an illustrated children's Bible.

Contrary to all expectations, the fifty-five-year-old Ilja was learning at a breathtaking pace—learning to read but not to write. Grandfather wasn't able to get more than two legible words down on paper without a great deal of trouble. However, after only four weeks of lessons, he was already asking for a "real book."

"What did you have in mind?" asked the delighted Dimitru, who was hell-bent on fulfilling Ilja's wish from the rich holdings of his library.

"I'm thinking of the Old and the New Testament. I only know the Bible from the words of the pastor, and now I'm eager to study the Holy Scripture for myself."

"Wonderful, wonderful! You're on the right path," Dimitru rejoiced, then stopped short and drummed his fingers on the table as he always did when in a state of nervous excitement. "I know the Bible, too; I mean, I think I know it. But I'm like you, in church every Sunday (except when my reliquary business forces me to be on the road), and believe me: every reading of the Scripture, every Gospel, and every sermon of Papa Baptiste still resounds in my ears as if he were right up there in the pulpit this very minute. But to my shame, I must admit that what with all my studying, I never read the Holy Scripture. Why did I need to? I already knew every word of the Lord from the Sermon on the Mount to the Lord's Prayer to his last words on the cross when he finds out his Father has forsaken him. I also know when and where Jesus performed what miracle. He multiplied the loaves, healed poor Lazarus, restored sight to the blind. At his word, demons fled and adulteresses were spared from stoning. Not to mention that he changed water into the finest wine. As for the Old Testament, I can recite the Ten Commandments backward and reel off the descendants of Adam by heart from Abraham and Isaac and wise King Solomon right down to what's-his-name. But only if you insist on it, my friend."

"Some other time." Grandfather waved his hand. "But could you get me a real Bible from the library? Only on loan, of course."

Dimitru sighed. "Ilja, don't be angry. I have to confess there aren't any Bibles in the library. There was one, back when I began my career as librarian. In the winter when your dear wife Agneta and my father Laszlo of blessed memory died, I took the Bible to my people, even though Papa Baptiste had forbidden it. And what did those Gypsies do? They used the paper as tinder in their stoves. The Lord God will forgive them as he does people who know not what they do."

"I see you gentlemen have gotten back to fundamentals," said my mother, emerging from the kitchen.

"Just imagine, Kathalina, among the thousand books in Dimitru's library there's not a single Bible."

"Oh, well, the main thing is you have one yourself now that you can read."

"What do you mean, I have one myself . . . ?"

"I mean the book in your old cigar box. You're really getting forgetful in your old age."

Johannes Baptiste's birthday present! Wrapped in packing paper. When the priest handed him the package on his birthday, Grandfather could feel through the wrapping that it was a book. Now he went to fetch the cigar box and crowed, "The Holy Scripture, Dimitru! What a coincidence!"

"It's no coincidence. Heaven is sending us a sign."

Grandfather decided to wait a few days before beginning the Bible. He wanted to start with the New Testament, and what could be a more appropriate day for that than the imminent Christmas Eve? Joy at the birth of Baby Jesus was overshadowed by the memory of Joseph's fruitless search for an inn for Mary, who was great with child. In his anger at the village for refusing shelter to the tribe of Gypsies, Baptiste had removed the Virgin of Eternal Consolation from the parish church and had her taken to a new chapel on the Mondberg. Amid cold and snow the faithful toiled up the mountain, cursing their own sinfulness and pledging repentance and improvement until Christmas came around again. And had done so for twenty-one years. Last year, Christmas 1956, I had been at the head of the procession and realized for the first time that the pilgrimage against hard-heartedness was no Sunday stroll in the park. Now the twenty-second penitential procession was around the corner.

But Pater Johannes was dead, his body gone without a trace. It hadn't been quite two months since we found the butchered priest in the rectory and the tooth of forgetfulness was already gnawing on many a memory in Baia Luna. The hot-blooded pledges to remain true to the priest's memory were cooling off. In the tavern I was hearing the first tentative mutterings that a six-hour procession up to the Mondberg and back didn't make much sense nowadays. Others stressed their desire to submit to the hardships of the penitential act again this year but hinted they might have to look after an aged father or ailing mother-in-law on Christmas Eve.

In order to ward off the gradual deterioration of the village's sense of community, Hermann Schuster, Istvan Kallay, and Trojan Petrov called an assembly of all men and women in the village for the fourth Sunday in Advent. It turned out to be the most pitiful assembly Grandfather could ever recall. Among the seven men who showed up were five Saxons and the initiators of the meeting, Kallay and Petrov. After less than half an hour they had agreed on three resolutions. First, the procession would take place under any circumstances, however small the flock of pilgrims. Second, everyone present pledged to convince at least two other inhabitants of Baia Luna of the necessity of the penitential pilgrimage. Third—fearing that squabbling about the pros and cons of the procession would grow even greater in years to come—they decided to bring the Virgin of Eternal Consolation back from the Mondberg and reinstall her in the parish church where she had stood before the advent of Johannes Baptiste. When the sacristan Julius Knaup joined the assembly late and opined that once the Madonna was back in the church the Eternal Flame would certainly once again shine in Baia Luna, the assembly was dismissed.

As we gathered shortly before five on the morning of December 24 under a cold, starry sky, Hermann Schuster counted just two dozen Madonna pilgrims. His disappointment was alleviated when a few more willing pilgrims arrived on the village square during the next hour. They excused their tardiness by saying they had lost track of time since the clock in the church tower was no longer striking. At some point during Advent the hands had stopped at twelve fifteen and—rusted and gnawed by the tooth of time—were never to move again.

We had overestimated our strength. Against the advice of our elders, Petre Petrov and I had urged everyone to make up for the late start by increasing our speed. Now it was midday, and we were getting slower and slower. Despite his youth, the Carpati-smoker Petre Petrov was stopping to catch his breath every few steps, and Hermann Schuster Junior was complaining about a stitch in his side that was so bad every stride was torture. He fell farther and farther back. When he finally threw up, he was so weak that his father sent him back to the village. The fact that we weren't cold despite the low temperature was due to the strength of the sun blazing down from a steel-blue sky. Once we reached the tree line, however, the wind would begin whistling mercilessly around our ears. We would reach that point in less than an hour. Another hour up a gentle slope would bring us to the Chapel of the Virgin of Eternal Consolation. It had been decided to stay only long enough for a brief prayer. Then we would pack the statue of Mary in blankets and return to Baia Luna as quickly as possible. Once the sun set behind the mountains it would turn bitterly cold.

Instead of one hour, it took us almost two to reach the tree line. Maybe it was because we were exhausted, possibly also because with each arduous step, the whole point of the pilgrimage was seeping away. Our penitential enthusiasm was replaced by a dull lethargy, so that none of us younger ones at the head of the march screamed in terror. Where the last copper beech raised its black, leafless branches into the ice-blue sky, Andreas Schuster nudged first Petre, then me. In silent horror Andreas stretched out his arm and pointed into the bare, wintry forest. Spellbound, the other pilgrims also halted and looked around, dazed and gasping for breath, until everyone was looking in the same direction.

The corpse hung from a black branch, swinging in the wind. Her hair fell in frozen strands, and on her head was a crown of snow. In that moment of terror, only I knew at once who the woman in the summery dress with yellow-brown sunflowers was.

Karl Koch was the first to react. He took Hermann Schuster and Istvan Kallay aside. They nodded briefly in agreement. Karl went over to the old people and the women who immediately agreed to take the children by the hand and turn back toward Baia Luna. When Karl took Kora Konstantin's arm and gently but firmly tried to steer her back toward the village, she hissed at him and quick as a wink scratched his face with her sharp nails, leaving three bloody welts on his cheek. "I'm not going back," Kora sputtered. "I'm going to the Virgin." Hermann handed his friend Karl a handkerchief, and then we boys and men fought our way through the snow in among the beech trees, followed by the wheezing Konstantin. We stood silently beneath the tree looking up at the corpse whose bare feet swung back and forth before our eyes.

"The dead keep well in the frost," said Karl Koch. "I'm just wondering why Barbu came up here in a summer dress in the dead of winter to do this to herself."

"I'll bet her coat and shoes are under the snow somewhere," said Petre before Schuster shut him up with a stern look. Then the Saxon folded his hands and said, "Our Father, who art in heaven, hallowed be thy name . . ." Everybody chimed in with the murmured prayer and stared down abashedly at the glittering snow long after the amen.

I could not look away. I felt no sadness, only an unending, immense pain tearing at my heart. It was soundless, although it shrilled in my ears. I was too young to give it a name. Only years later would I understand that what I had heard on that Christmas Eve was the death cry of love.

It began to get cold. The procession to the Virgin of Eternal Consolation was over without having reached its goal. But we had to act. Istvan Kallay felt he had enough strength left to continue on to the chapel and fetch the statue of the Madonna. Petre, who just before was threatening to suffocate from shortness of breath, now got a second wind and said he would go with the Hungarian.

"We need you for a trio." Istvan turned to me, referring to our joint trip to Kronauburg and our visit to Captain Patrascu. "Come along!"

Grandfather Ilja backed up Istvan. "Go with them, Pavel. This here is nothing for a boy."

"My place is here."

"My legs still have it in them," said Andreas Schuster, grabbing the wool blankets they planned to wrap the Madonna in. Then he, Istvan, and Petre climbed up toward the chapel, whose pointed steeple rose in silhouette against the sky and the low-lying sun.

I closed my eyes the way I had with Buba and looked up behind closed lids. Second sight was easy. Without trying I saw the image. But I didn't see the girl I missed so much; I saw her uncle. Before my inner eye Dimitru stood in his library, took a running start, and swung up into a handstand, his skinny legs resting against a bookcase. Then I heard the sentence "Things reveal themselves when you stand the world on its head."

I opened my eyes, dropped down, and put my head into the snow. While the men were imagining I couldn't take the sight of the dead woman, the pain I was feeling gave way to a cool clarity of thought. I stood up and turned to the Scherban brothers.

"Can you help me? We have some digging to do."

"You're not going to look for her shoes and coat, are you?" asked Rasim. "That can wait until spring."

I didn't answer but started shoveling into the snow, cutting my hands on the sharp ice crust. Some of the men broke up branches thick as arms that the storm had brought down and used them as digging tools. Soon everyone was helping to clear away the snow. The digging allowed the men to turn away from the half-naked woman in her thin dress. None of them knew what we were looking for except me. When a woman wants to close the store for good, the old commissioner Patrascu had said, then you could bet you'd find the bottle of courage corked up. But what if we found a bottle without a cork, as I feared? In that case, Angela Maria Barbulescu would not have been alone in her final hour. Then she would not have taken her own life. My anxiety proved groundless. We found no uncorked schnapps bottle—and no corked one either.

"Here! There's something here!" Hermann Schuster pulled something out of the snow that had been leaning against the trunk of the beech. Hermann held up his find. A picture in a dull gold wooden frame with a shattered sheet of glass. "Who's this? Anybody know him?"

"Could be one of those party bigwigs from the capital," said Karl Koch, "the way he looks." Koch looked up. "I bet she called it quits because of him. I'm telling you, she was crazy. Somebody hangs herself in a dress like that is nuts. No wonder such a fancy-pants wanted nothing to do with Barbu."

Karl Koch had hold of a corner of the truth, but he was wrong. If only I had grabbed her hand and held it back then, in her parlor. That's what kept going through my head again and again. When she turned away Stephanescu. But she was just Barbu. From the branch hung Angela Maria, and all her pain and suffering lay behind her. And all her hate.

Andreas, Istvan, and Petre returned sooner than expected. Upset, Andreas threw the wool blankets down on the snow and panted, "The Madonna is gone."

"What? Gone?"

"Sh-she's not in the chapel." Petre was gasping for breath. "Just the empty pedestal."

That unleashed a barrage of questions. "Why? How come? What happened?"

"Just gone! Stolen!" Istvan cried. "Get it through your heads: the Madonna is gone."

In his consternation Hermann Schuster couldn't think of anything better to do than start intoning, "Hail Mary, full of grace, the Lord is with thee . . . ," but few of the men joined in. When Schuster got to "Blessed art thou amongst women, and blessed is the fruit of thy womb," all eyes turned to Kora Konstantin.

The whole time she had been sitting over on the side in the snow and giving the impression she was recovering from the strenuous hike. Now everyone could see in her face an enormous tension behind which a slavering spitefulness lay in wait. And it appeared that Kora had only endured this tension in order to let it loose at this moment. Before we had time to realize it, her enormous hate exploded.

"Blessed is the fruit of thy womb! No! No! No! This womb was cursed. Barbu's to blame! The demon! The witch!"

Kora's piercing scream sliced through the silence of the mountains and made the blood freeze in my veins. Like a madwoman she stormed toward the hanging body. "You murderous whore, you damned Satan's bride! To hell with you!" she screeched and leaped at the dangling dead woman. She grabbed a corner of her dress, pulled and tore at the thin material until the sunflower dress ripped into tatters, completely exposing Angela Barbulescu's naked corpse.

This furor had broken over the men like a sudden storm, so that no one made a move to restrain Kora's frenzy. I went up to her calmly and punched her in the face as hard as I could. A fountain of

blood erupted from her nose and sprayed the snow. Kora Konstantin fell instantly silent.

In another half hour the sun would disappear completely behind
the Mondberg.

"Even if she ended up like this, she was a human being, too,"
said the sacristan Julius Knaup.

"That's why we can't leave her to the wolves and bears," said
Hans Schneider while Karl Koch grabbed a limb and hoisted himself into the beech to cut the dead woman's rope.

"The least you can do is catch her!" he called down angrily.
The two Scherbans sprang into action and helped me take the
weight of the stiffened corpse. We wrapped her naked body in the
blankets meant for the Virgin of Eternal Consolation. Then Karl
Koch tied up the bundle with the rope and heaved the dead woman
onto his shoulder. We began the descent into the valley. Each one
of us walked alone, not looking to see if his neighbor was keeping
up or not.

I knew in that hour that the bonds of the village community
were severed, and I wasn't the only one. Grandfather knew it, too.
It didn't matter that the women of Baia Luna had decorated the
parish church in the meantime. In previous years the prayer that
concluded the penitential pilgrimage had always been short and
simple because after arriving back in the village in the evening the
shivering and exhausted pilgrims longed for nothing more than
their warm parlors. Now, however, the women had decked out the
church with yuletide fir sprigs, white candles, and red ribbons to
prepare a proper welcome for the Madonna. But when they discovered it was Barbu being brought down into the valley on Karl
Koch's shoulders, they extinguished the candles.

The sacristan Knaup and the organist Konstantin had already
discussed the destination of Angela Barbulescu's corpse on the way
back from the Mondberg, although Hermann Schuster was not
happy about the solution they hit upon. For in the entire history
of Baia Luna, not a single inhabitant had ever taken his own life.
It was true that in the case of Laszlo Carolea Gabor, an unbaptized
person had for the first time been buried in the cemetery on the
orders of Johannes Baptiste. But in the end it exceeded even Hermann Schuster's capacity for sympathy—and he was by no means

a hard-hearted Catholic—to think that a woman who had been destroyed by alcohol and then killed herself should find a final resting place in sacred ground.

With shovels, pickaxes, and torches, some of the men set off in the direction of Cemetery Hill. Before they reached the entrance gate, they turned off to the left and looked for an appropriate place. At first they thought of under the old oak, but when Julius Knaup objected that from there you could look down on the children playing in the school yard, they chose a spot behind the upper wall of the cemetery. The gravediggers shoveled the place free of snow, hacked a hole in the frozen ground, and placed the dead woman in it. Then they filled in the hole again and stamped the earth down with their boots.

There was nothing for me to do. I was adrift in a sea that knew no shore.

# Chapter Eight

*A STUPID MISTAKE, A LONG FAREWELL,*

*AND THE DELUSION OF A HALF-TRUTH*

Despite his fifty-five years, Grandfather Ilja had never set foot outside the district of Kronauburg. Even if he sometimes dreamed of setting off to see the Virgin of the Torch in faraway America, his intellectual expeditions were never flights of completely unbridled imagination. They never called into question the world of the village, the homeland to which he was attached down to the last fiber of his being. Baia Luna gave roots to his feet and purchase to his life. It was a place where his dreams could return safely back to earth. To be evenhanded to everyone was his sacred rule, and that required a benevolent eye, free from mistrust and suspicion. It allowed my grandfather to put up with sanctimonious Christians like sacristan Knaup as well as party faithful like the Brancusis, both the shrew Kora Konstantin and the snob Vera Raducanu, without ever being consumed by resentment.

Until that ill-fated Christmas of 1957, that is.

While my mother Kathalina slept, Grandfather sat at the kitchen table. His downcast—even bitter—face betrayed that the insidious and corrosive poison of doubt was eating at him.

"Pavel," he said after what seemed an interminable silence, "Baia Luna isn't my Baia Luna anymore. And I'm to blame."

"What are you talking about, Granddad? It's not you. None of this is your fault."

"Yes, it is, Pavel. What that crazy Konstantin woman did to Miss Barbulescu was my fault, although it pains me deeply to say so. If Dimitru ever finds out how stupid I was, he'll stop being my friend."

"But what happened?"

Grandfather poured himself a glass of *zuika* and took a swallow as if to free his tongue from its fetters.

"Forgive me, Pavel, for burdening your heart with tales you're still too young to hear."

"I'm old enough."

"You're right, my boy, you are. As long as I can remember, Pavel, there's been an agreement in Baia Luna not to make one another's lives miserable. And if I do say so myself, I was always a reliable guarantor that we didn't. Honesty is inbred in us Botevs. People always said of my father Borislav that he didn't have an enemy in the world, only friends, and I myself always tried to instill that virtue in your father Nicolai, who died in the war, and in you, his son. But now something has invaded the village that not only sets aside the rules of respectability but throws us all off course. Even though Dimitru and I never heard the Sputnik beeping, looking back it still seems to have been a harbinger of the catastrophe that's now upon us. Too many things have happened, Pavel. The Eternal Flame no longer shines in the church. Johannes Baptiste was murdered, and his Fernanda literally scared to death. The body of our beloved priest has found no rest, his grave is empty, and now even the patron saint of our village, the Virgin of Eternal Consolation, has disappeared. Even in the darkest times, she always kept alive the hope that good would win out in the end. I could always make out the gentleness and affection in her tortured face. Hundreds—no, thousands—of times I've knelt before the Madonna and looked at her. But now she's dissolved into thin air. Since I saw poor Miss Barbulescu swinging from that branch, the Madonna has disappeared. I can't see her anymore, Pavel. She's gone. I can't call her up anymore."

I was surprised and a bit proud that my grandfather was confiding his thoughts to me and no longer talked to my almost-sixteen-year-old self as though I were a child.

"Never, Pavel, never ever was I plagued by doubts. But since Johannes Baptiste's murder, my faith is evaporating like a spring drying up. I wonder who has poisoned the well? Who allowed the tree to wither? At first I thought the State Security was behind everything. But why would they go to the length of slitting an old priest's throat? Despite all the vile things the Securitate is supposed to have done, I can't imagine them doing this. Especially since a priest never stands alone; he has the authority of the whole Catholic church behind him. No state is going to challenge that unless its power is seriously threatened. On the other hand, Pavel, isn't it possible that there is something to what that crazy Konstantin woman is spreading around? What if Miss Barbulescu hanged herself on the Mondberg because she really did have something to do with the murder of Pater Johannes?"

"She didn't," I answered.

"I don't think so either. And Dimitru is also convinced she didn't murder Fernanda and Johannes. And I don't believe the evil rumors Kora spreads about her either. But something bad is still bothering me. Pavel, I did something stupid—really, really stupid, if things turn out badly."

"Wha-what are you talking about?" I stammered. "What did you do?"

"The Konstantin woman claims the teacher Barbulescu paid a visit to the rectory on Wednesday, November sixth, my fifty-fifth birthday. Most people in the village discount it as the gossip of a blabbermouth. But what if that nasty liar was telling the truth for once? The fact is, Barbulescu never visited the rectory otherwise—in fact, during her years in Baia Luna she avoided contact with the pastor as much as she could. I'm surprised that she really was with Johannes on November sixth, but Dimitru confirmed it. Supposedly Angela Barbulescu wanted to borrow the key to the library. So Kora wasn't lying when she kept saying she saw Barbulescu going into the rectory. Dimitru was her witness. And me, I'm such an idiot. I thought I had to tell everyone the truth, so I told anyone who asked—the women shopping in the store and the men drinking in the tavern. Of course people in the village talked about Konstantin's speculations that Barbulescu was behind all the evils being visited upon Baia Luna. At first I kept out of all those discussions. But whenever someone like dear Elena Kiselev was in the store and said Kora was nuts when she claimed to have seen Barbu going into the rectory, I just had to contradict her. Rumors are one thing, but facts are another. If Kora was right, then she was right. But Pavel, now that

I saw that crazy woman tear the dress off Barbulescu's body, I feel like biting out my tongue for saying, 'Dimitru saw Barbu go in there, too.'"

On that Christmas Eve, my grandfather learned the painful lesson that there are times in one's life when craftiness is more important than high-minded principle. You can't always tell everyone the truth. He sensed that his incautious words would have consequences.

On Christmas Day at noon someone knocked at our back door. My mother Kathalina opened it and called up the stairs, "Pavel, a young lady for you!" I rushed down the stairs expecting to see my beloved Buba.

"Oh, it's you."

My disappointment didn't escape Julia Simenov's notice.

"Is this a bad time? Should I come back?" she asked uncertainly. In her hands she held a wreath of fir sprigs and a simple cross made of two wooden laths. When I didn't answer, she explained, "I thought I'd make this for our teacher, since she has no place in the cemetery and no relatives to look after her grave."

"I'll come, too."

I wouldn't have expected it of Julia. She was already sixteen, the oldest student in the class. I'd be lying if I said I liked her. But in this one moment, Julia upended everything I thought I knew about the daughter of the blacksmith after eight years in school together. Everyone thought she was a zealous teacher's pet. She had a quick mind and an even quicker arm, always first to raise her hand. Whether we were using the Rule of Three to solve an equation, regurgitating historic dates, or reciting the homeland poem by Hans Bohn, Julia Simenov always had her hand up before Angela Barbulescu had even finished asking the question. She'd always stayed off to one side when we made cruel jokes about the teacher. Fritz Hofmann guessed she was paving her way to the boarding school in Kronauburg with good grades, something no pupil from Baia Luna, especially no girl, had ever succeeded in doing. No question Julia was ambitious, but now she was standing here in front of me with a simple fir wreath and a cross without a name. I felt ashamed.

I put on my shoes and coat.

"I'm planning to write a letter to Fritz Hofmann, by the way.

My father found out their address in Germany. Someone should tell him where mean words can lead," said Julia.

"Do you think the stuff he wrote about his thing getting hard and out to here drove the teacher to kill herself?"

"Maybe. As the final straw that broke the camel's back. We have to hurry. My parents don't know I'm here, and I'm not sure they would allow us to go to Barbu's grave. When spring comes we can make a proper cross with her name and the year she was born. Do you have any idea how old she was?"

"She was born in Popesti, near the capital, in 1920."

"How do you know that?" Julia exclaimed. "Nineteen twenty? That can't be right. You must be mistaken, Pavel. That would make her only thirty-seven years old. She must have been at least ten years older than that."

"If you say so," I replied shortly. We walked silently along outside the cemetery wall. The tracks the grave diggers had made in the snow the night before led us past the old oak to the grave site above the stone wall.

Suddenly Julia gave a start and elbowed me. "Hey, somebody's lying on the ground!"

Someone was lying, mummylike, next to the mounded dirt beneath which the gravediggers had interred Angela Barbulescu. When I saw the head sticking out of the bundle of wool blankets, I recognized Dimitru's matted hair. Before I had time to fear that the Gypsy himself had gone to his eternal rest next to the grave, the bundle moved.

Dimitru sat up. He was shivering. He rubbed his hands to warm them and squinted, blinded by the snow in the brilliant sunshine. "Is night already over?"

While Julia was so astonished she couldn't utter a syllable, I replied, "The night has begun. What are you doing here?"

"Same thing as you," answered Dimitru when he caught sight of the wooden cross Julia was holding. "I'm paying my last respects to someone. Someone has to keep vigil over this poor soul. But I'm a miserable watchman. I fell asleep like the disciples in the Garden of Gethsemane."

"You can't compare the two things, Dimitru! The disciples fell asleep when their Lord Jesus was still alive," Julia replied as she laid her green wreath on the grave. "You fell asleep during a wake. There's no shame for a watchman in that."

Dimitru thought it over for a moment and then simply said, "My thanks for your wise reply."

I planted the cross in the snow, then stood before the unsanctified grave with my classmate, quietly, with folded hands, while Dimitru tried to drive the frost from his bones with various contortions.

"She was too good for this world," I interrupted the silence.

"No," the Gypsy replied, "this world wasn't good for her."

"It comes down to the same thing!"

"No, it doesn't, Pavel. Not at all." Dimitru gathered his blankets together and shuffled back to his people.

The old year was ending. In the capital, in Kronauburg, and even in Apoldasch, public buildings were bedecked with flags and bunting on the orders of the regime. The walls sported freshly printed posters. On red banners the Communist Party congratulated itself on its progressive achievements and promised the people a national renaissance and a glorious world-class Socialist future. While people all over the country greeted the New Year and hoped for better times, the turn of the year in Baia Luna passed without anyone taking much notice.

On earlier New Year's Eves, young and old alike would gather on the village square in feverish anticipation of the twelve strokes of midnight. But as the year 1958 dawned, the square was deserted, the rusted church tower clock didn't strike, and instead of raising their glasses and wishing one another Happy New Year the residents lay in their beds, sleeping. Only in Vera Raducanu's parlor were there two flickering candles spreading a meager light. With a long-stemmed glass of sparkling wine, Vera drank a toast with herself and stoutly maintained that her hour of triumph was imminent, the hour when her son Lupu would come to fetch her back to the city and reinstate her in the very best circles.

The New Year in Baia Luna began as the old one had ended. People seldom left their houses, and when they did, they exchanged only the minimum words necessary. Mortally offended by the solid punch in the nose I'd given her on the Mondberg, Kora Konstantin stayed out of sight. She stopped coming to our shop for the things she needed because she had sworn never again to enter the house of "that Botev gang." Instead, she put a few coins into the hands of the six half-grown brats the drunken Raswan had left her with when he passed and sent them out into the neighborhood to forage for a cup of sugar or salt or a packet of oatmeal. I'm sure Kora threatened her children with all the tortures of hell should they dare to accept a lollipop or a stick of American chewing gum from Grandfather.

Ilja and my mother Kathalina sat in the shop, longing for an early end to winter and hoping that spring would not only restore life to nature but also a spirit of confidence to the village. Dimitru was often absent from the library, not for lack of interest in his Mariological studies but because his tribe had urgent family matters to negotiate for which they sought his advice. As for me, I was crippled by inaction and yearned for Buba. From morning to night, my thoughts had circled her ever since the hysterical Susanna had dragged her through the village by the hair, threatening to banish her from the clan.

On Saturday, January 18, Mother put a hazelnut cake into the oven. It wasn't until I caught a glimpse of her in the pantry, surreptitiously gift wrapping a warm wool sweater and a dark blue scarf, that I realized why. It was for me. Kathalina was the only one who had remembered that I was going to turn sixteen on Sunday. Even Grandfather Ilja and Aunt Antonia, who always had a little something ready for my birthday, had forgotten the date—which I didn't blame them for, since I had forgotten it myself. Without really being tired, I crawled into bed early on Saturday night, hoping that sleep would free me from my heartache for a while.

It must have been after midnight when I heard a dull thud. Immediately I sat bolt upright and listened. When another snowball hit my window, I knew who was out there in the cold night trying to get my attention. I opened the window and whispered into the darkness, "Come to the back door."

"Have you got wax in your ears? I've been standing out here forever."

I put my finger to my lips, took her silently by the hand, and led her through the dark to my room. The whole house was still.

"I had to see you on your birthday," she said softly and assaulted my face with kisses. I groped for Buba's hair and discovered she was wearing a babushka. Fear of being caught rose within me, but it lost its power as Buba put her arms around my neck and pressed against me. I felt her chilly body beneath her thin little blouse. Buba was shivering. I pulled her close, my hands were on her hips and then slid down over the firm curve of her buttocks to her thighs. I stroked her bare, cold skin while she pressed against me more and more and gently opened my lips with her tongue. She took my hand and led it to the only place on her chilly body that exuded warmth. My heart was hammering with excitement and pumping blood into my swelling penis. Buba slipped out of her blouse and pulled off my nightshirt. I led her to my bed.

"I . . . I don't know exactly . . ." I stammered as Buba stroked my hair. "But I know everything." She nestled against me, skin to skin, and as I shyly responded to her caresses, she lay on top and gently, unimaginably slowly, lowered herself onto me until I was deep inside her and we were united, man and woman. We lay still, trying to prolong the moment into an eternity. I could sense Buba getting warmer and warmer, felt the heat rising to a blaze, smelled her sweat, the aroma of fire, earth, smoke, and the sharp sweetness of her sex. Gently, Buba rocked her hips until I forgot everything around me. All my heartache, all the anguish of the past weeks, dissolved in this moment of pure happiness, while Buba bit her hand to keep from crying out with joy and pleasure. Ever so gradually, we returned from our blissful rapture. We lay in bed, our arms wrapped tightly around each other. And I felt her tears on my chest.

"Buba, what's wrong?" My voice shook with fear and worry. I felt for a pack of matches and lit a candle.

"We won't be together again like this for a long time. A very long time," Buba said in deep sadness.

"But why not? I'll be with you forever, and nothing can keep us apart."

"Yes, it can, Pavel. You're forgetting: I'm a Gypsy and you're a *gajo*."

"I don't care."

To my shock Buba pulled off her babushka: there wasn't a single hair on her head. All the marvelous curls I loved so much were gone.

"They shaved me because Mother claimed I'd been in bed with you. Now at least she's right about that."

My dismay at the loss of Buba's mass of curls turned gradually into anger. "Even if she is your mother, she's a terrible woman."

"Yes," said Buba, "my mother is sick. But only since my father ran off with another woman. She didn't used to be so bad. And you must never forget that we're Gypsies, my mother even more than me. When she caught us together in the library, she wanted to disown me. She really meant to. But they couldn't hold a clan council since no one could notify our relatives because of all the snow. I owe it to Uncle Dimi and him alone that I wasn't cast out. Without him I wouldn't even be here with you. Uncle Dimi knows everything."

"What does he know?"

"About us. I told him I never wanted anyone but you."

"And what did he say to that?"

"He wanted to hear what made me so sure. I told him I loved you and you had sensitive hands."

I blushed. Looking at Buba and her shaved head, I knew no scissors in the world could spoil one iota of her beauty.

"And it's all right with Dimitru that we're together?"

"Yes. He says I could never find a better man than you. He also knows I'm with you tonight. He even made some tea for my mother that made her sleep like a log all night long."

"And Dimitru also saw to it that you wouldn't be cast out from your family just because you want a *gajo*?"

"He threatened them, 'If you expel my Buba, then I'll leave, too. I won't be a Gypsy anymore.' But that's really all he could do for me. Even Uncle Dimi couldn't keep them from punishing me, although everyone in the family listens to what he says."

"And that's why they cut off your hair?"

"Yes, but that isn't so bad. Uncle Dimi says it'll grow back three times as beautiful. But there's something much worse than that," and Buba began to cry again. "This summer we're going to the market in Bistrita, and my mother intends to marry me off to some man I've never seen before."

That took my breath away. "But, but, I don't want some other man to have you! If I even think about you being together with someone else like you are with me, I—"

"Never! It'll never, ever happen. I'm like this only for you, and I never will be for anyone else."

The words were hardly out of her mouth when I saw how her eyes were shining in the light of the candle. She even smiled and gently shook her head.

"What are you thinking?"

"Uncle Dimi's not just a good person, he's sly, too. Very sly. Much much more clever than any of us can imagine."

"What do you mean?"

"I was surprised at first when he allowed me to come to you tonight. But now I know why he did it."

"Why did he?"

"Because for me as a Gypsy, it doesn't matter that there's no other man I want. What's important is that no other man wants me. Uncle Dimi knew I wouldn't be a virgin anymore after this night with you. And no other husband could live with that shame."

"Does that mean we can be together forever?"

Buba smothered me with kisses. "Yes and no. I have to get married. And when the man they choose for me discovers I'm not a virgin, I don't know what will happen. But I have to get married, you understand? It's not about me, it's about my family's honor."

"So what can we do?"

"Uncle Dimi says that day will come when the laws of the heart are stronger than the laws of blood. And he also says it requires patience—a lot of patience. But he promised me on his honor as a Gypsy that the day will come."

"And when will it come?"

"I don't know, Pavel. I really don't know. It can take a very long time. But I will wait. Do you promise to be there when the day comes?"

"I will be there."

"Good." Buba put her blouse back on and wrapped her head in the babushka. "Uncle Dimi said something else: lovers often make a big mistake. In their bliss they forget about everyone else. And when they suddenly discover they have only themselves, their love has died."

I didn't reply. Suddenly the image was there again: Angela Barbulescu swinging in the wind up on the Mondberg.

Buba put her arm around me. "You're thinking of our teacher."

"Yes. I saw her hanging from a branch in her thin sunflower
dress. Everyone thinks she took her own life, but I'm not so sure
because she had a visitor the day before she disappeared. It was
that guy with the wart your uncle Salman gave a ride to when
he brought the television set to the village. He sat in Angela's
parlor and had a drink with her. Maybe it was murder, and he
strung her up. But maybe not. I don't understand what that man
wanted from her. After all, she had said she was going to break her
silence about what happened in the capital. And she told Fritz he
should let his father know she wasn't afraid anymore. I read Angela's diary all the way through, and I know what happened to her
child."

"I must know what you know," said Buba. "I can't leave until
I do."

I reached under my mattress, pulled out the green notebook,
and handed it to Buba. Then I fetched *Das Kapital* by Karl Marx and
got out the photo showing Angela Barbulescu at a happy moment,
pursing her lips for a kiss. Buba took the picture and looked at it.

"I know this picture! That's exactly how I once saw the teacher.
Do you remember? The day we were waiting in the school yard
and she didn't come to school, you asked me as a joke what my
third eye could see. And that's what I was seeing—I saw her with
blond hair tied in a ponytail. But there's a piece missing from this
photo. There was a man, too. Was it that Stefan?"

"Yes. She burned him off with a candle. It's a snapshot Heinrich
Hofmann took on one of their holidays in the capital."

"Where did you get it?"

"Last summer I was alone with her in her house one evening.
She had invited me and I had to go."

"Did you sleep with her, then?"

I shook my head. "I think she was looking for me to be her ally.
But she'd been drinking a lot. She tried to seduce me, but I didn't
want to. No, I didn't want to."

Buba took the green diary. She opened it to the page with the
brown cross and the verse:

THE MIGHTY FALL FROM THEIR THRONES
THE LOWLY ARE LIFTED UP
HIS HOUR WILL COME
WHEN HE'S REACHED THE TOP.

Without a word, Buba leafed forward until she came to the teacher's farewell letter.

When I touched Buba's arm, her skin was again ice cold.

"Stephanescu and his people cut her baby out of her body," she said. "They'll pay for it. Someday Stephanescu will pay this bill. And you and I, Pavel, we'll deliver it to him."

"But Angela predicted that Stephanescu would fall when he'd reached the top. She even said she'd come back to fetch him to hell. Why did she go and whisper to me in her last hour in Baia Luna that I should send him to hell? What did she mean by that? What am I supposed to do?"

"I don't know. All I know is she wants justice. Simple justice, nothing else. I have to go, Pavel." Buba embraced me. "I'll wait for you," she whispered in my ear. Then she disappeared without a sound.

All during the month of January, it seemed that Grandfather's sentence "Dimitru saw Barbu go in there, too" had died away without anyone noticing. Then on February 1, the day before Candlemas, the echo returned. On that day the Gypsy Dimitru Carolea Gabor entered our shop early in the morning, stony faced, and broke off his friendship with Ilja.

"Don't you know that the truth is fragile? No, you serve it on a tray to people who twist everything into a lie. How can you be my ally when you aren't even a match for that crazy woman?"

Then Dimitru turned on his heel and left. Grandfather was not taken by surprise. Dimitru had only put into words what he felt himself. He was a dreamer, incapable of clear calculation and utterly unsuited for the sly stratagems the Gypsy had so urgently recommended. For as long as he'd known Dimitru, Grandfather had thought of his Gypsy friend as a cunning child while he himself was a tavern owner and businessman with adult responsibilities. But it was he who was still a naïve boy despite his fifty-five years. Like a child he had trusted in the innocence of words. "Dimitru saw Barbu go in there, too." When my grandfather realized the consequences of those words, his dreams of America and Noueeyorka died and would stay dead for a long, long time.

It started with Julia Simenov storming into our shop on the afternoon before Candlemas, wailing and distraught.

"What happened, girl?" asked Grandfather just as I came running in from the kitchen.

"Who would do such a horrid thing, Pavel? Who could be so cruel?"

"What are you talking about?"

"They desecrated Barbu's grave. Someone tore the wreath apart and broke our wooden cross, too. And then they relieved themselves on the grave—went to the bathroom right on it."

My blood was boiling. "You mean, they sha . . . Who did it?"

"Maybe it was dogs," Ilja tried to calm himself down.

"No," replied Julia, "it was human animals. Dogs don't break crosses."

Grandfather's suspicion fell immediately on Kora Konstantin. Since she had ripped the dress off of Angela Barbulescu's corpse, she seemed capable of anything. He was unable to imagine anyone else in Baia Luna doing such a despicable thing.

That is, until Vera Raducanu entered the shop, her head held high and her nose in the air as always. But she didn't ask for the soap wrapped in gold foil. Instead she began a conversation in an unusually friendly tone. She let fall a few words about the cold weather, complained briefly about the remoteness of Baia Luna, and finally got to the point: her son Lupu. She was very well aware that in the past few weeks some villagers—without ever mentioning her son by name, of course—had been holding the Securitate major responsible for the murder of the priest. Vera formulated it as "pin it on him." She wasn't going to mention any names, but it was no accident that the ethnic Germans (led by that Karl Koch) were at the forefront of the attempt to smear her Lupu's character. Her son would call those slanderers to account once this awful snow had melted and the roads to Baia Luna were passable again. Especially since the case of Johannes Baptiste was now closed.

"What's that supposed to mean?"

"It was Barbu. Kora's right. Everybody knows it now. Even the Gypsies saw her sneaking into the rectory."

"Get out of my store!" was all my granddad replied to Vera Raducanu. But when Erika Schuster, then Elena Kiselev, and finally Istvan Kallay, Karl Koch, and Hermann Schuster came to see Grandfather in the course of that afternoon, and all said that the crazy Konstantin was now going to break her silence and produce irrefutable evidence that Angela Barbulescu and she alone was behind the murder of Pater Johannes, Grandfather realized he had set off an avalanche with his innocent remark. Only Hermann Schuster kept a cool head and suggested they call a village assembly on Candlemas to put a lid on the overflowing pot of rumors once and for all. To stop the gossip, Kora Konstantin should be given the opportunity to air her view of things, produce her evidence, and also answer the questions of the other village residents. Schuster's idea was immediately accepted, and word quickly spread that on the dot of eleven o'clock on the following day, an extraordinary assembly of citizens would take place in Botev's tavern that all men and women were urgently required to attend. When Kora Konstantin learned of the idea, she declared that she would say what she had to say but never, ever would she say it under the Botevs' roof. Since nothing in the world could change Kora's mind, it was decided to hold the public hearing in the church, which was not a bad decision from a practical point of view, since our taproom would have been bursting at the seams with even a third of the curious who were likely to attend. By ten thirty, a half hour before the announced beginning, new arrivals at the church had to be satisfied with standing room only.

Kora was the last to arrive. Supported by her brother-in-law Marku and the sacristan Knaup, she sashayed down the main aisle at a leisurely pace to the three chairs set up at the front of the sanctuary. Despite the cold, Kora wore only a black suit. Her hair was gathered beneath a fur cap, and a black tulle veil covered her face. She took her place between her two companions as Istvan Kallay, who had been asked to chair the hearing, welcomed those present.

"I give the floor to Kora Konstantin!"

Kora took her own sweet time fingering aside her veil, stuck out her chest, and spoke up. "This is no court, it's the house of the Lord. Praise be to Jesus Christ. Hail Mary, full of grace."

Some of those present crossed themselves and murmured, "Forever and ever, amen."

"Now say what you have to say," Istvan prompted her. All eyes were on Kora when Marku rose, reached into the breast pocket of his coat, and fished out a sheet of paper. "For the sake of accuracy, Mrs. Kora Konstantin has committed her declaration to paper. She would like to read it now. But only if she is not disturbed by uncalled-for heckling. Questions may be asked after she has finished her statement. If anyone objects to this procedure, please say so now."

Istvan Kallay took the murmurs that arose for agreement and sternly warned the audience not to interrupt Kora's speech with expressions of either disapproval or approval. Then he yielded the floor back to Kora. She rose and put on her glasses. I stood at the back, leaning against a pillar and looking in vain for Dimitru. Not a single Gypsy had entered the church.

"With God as my witness, I swear that I, Kora Konstantin, residing at Eleven Liberty Street, Baia Luna, am telling the truth, the whole truth, and nothing but the truth. On Wednesday, November sixth, at about one fifteen in the afternoon, I looked out my kitchen window and saw a woman sneaking through our village. This person was wearing a black babushka, rubber boots, and a dark coat and kept looking right and left like someone who didn't want to be seen. It was a gloomy day, raining, and so at first I couldn't make her out very clearly, but then I saw that it was that teacher Barbulescu. At first I thought she must have forgotten something in the school, but she wasn't going toward the school. She was going toward the rectory. I saw her ring the doorbell for a long time before someone finally opened the door. It's well known in the village that the Barbulescu woman had never set foot in the rectory. Nevertheless, my observation has in the meantime been substantiated by the librarian Dimitru Gabor."

"So what!" cried Grandfather. "What does that prove? Johannes Baptiste was still alive after Miss Barbulescu's visit. Very much alive, in fact. He was a guest at my birthday and in my tavern all afternoon and evening."

A few men clapped. "True, true!" Others were surprised to hear the normally reserved tavern owner take the floor so energetically. Kora, however, had her brother-in-law announce that if she were interrupted again, she would throw a cloak of silence over what she knew, forever. Istvan again called for silence, or he would see himself forced to adjourn the assembly. Kora continued her recitation, repeating what had long since been circulating as a rumor.

"The Barbulescu woman came to the rectory to ask for the holy sacrament of confession. But her misdeeds were mortal sins, unpardonable sins. That's why Pater Johannes refused her absolution. Some mortal sins weigh so heavily that not even the Holy Father in Rome has the authority to forgive them in the name of the Lord. For the Lord God reserves the worst sinners for himself at the final Judgment Day. Before our dear pastor was so foully murdered, he only had time to do one last thing in pursuance of his duties as a priest. He commanded that person to leave our village. We can confidently assume it was on account of the harmful influence the harlot had on our children."

I was furious and called out, "You're nuts, Konstantin. You and your slimy fantasies belong in the loony bin."

There were some muted murmurs of support, but mostly people shushed me, "Quiet, quiet, or she'll never tell the rest." Istvan found it necessary one last time to call for unconditional silence. Whoever broke the rule from then on would be immediately ejected from the church. The Hungarian was applauded for his announcement, and Kora smirked and resumed reading.

"An hour after the Barbulescu woman entered the rectory, she came slinking back out. I saw the hate that glittered in her eyes. Hate for our pastor, hate for our mother the church. And hate for the Lord God himself. At that moment Barbu showed her true face, and I said to my brother-in-law, 'Look at that face, Marku. Barbu's plotting revenge. Something terrible is going to happen.'" Kora looked over at her relative.

Marku nodded and said gravely, "That's more or less what happened."

"Later, under cover of darkness," Kora Konstantin continued, "Barbu crept back to Pater Johannes with a sharp knife under her coat. First she frightened the poor housekeeper to death, and then she assassinated the priest. She silenced him forever so he couldn't peddle the story of her ruthless sinning."

Kora's fantasies were so insane I couldn't even shake my head in consternation. I looked past her, and on the wall to the right of the altar caught sight of the sanctuary lamp with the extinguished Eternal Flame. I thought of Fritz Hofmann. Nothing would happen, he had said as he put out the little lamp. But things were happening. Baia Luna was tumbling into an absurd nightmare.

"Murdering people didn't bother Barbu!" Kora proclaimed in a screech. "I know it! Know it for a fact! Since last summer! Since I was in the capital. 'Everything that's hid away will finally see the light of day.'"

Everyone remembered Kora strutting around for weeks the previous year, boasting about her impending visit to her aunt in the Paris of the East, and in August she had actually gone there. The assembly listened in spellbound silence as she depicted how much she had suffered in the bad air of the capital because of her asthma. Her aunt took her to a pharmacy, where she had been waited on very solicitously by a gentleman with graying hair who gave her the kind of service it was hard to find in Baia Luna. He not only prescribed excellent medicine for her shortness of breath but also kindly inquired about where she was from. There then transpired a long—a very long—conversation about Baia Luna in the course of which it was inevitable that the alcoholic teacher would come up.

"When I mentioned the ill-fated name Angela Barbulescu the pharmacist jumped. 'Do you know the woman?' I asked. 'Yes,' the man said, 'I remember her. But it was years and years ago. A young woman of that name came in almost every day to buy heart medicine. Expensive medicine for her mother, whose name was Trinka.'"

"So what?" Karl Koch called out. Kora maintained her composure.

"Then the pharmacist confided that from one day to the next, this Angela had stopped asking for the heart medicine. Instead, she asked what cheap vitamin pills he had that looked exactly like the medicine her mother needed. The man even remembered that in the following weeks, this customer (whose clothes had always been shabby) started wearing an expensive dress with a sunflower pattern. Exactly the dress she strung herself up in to try to atone for having slipped her mother ineffective medicine from which the poor woman died a miserable death. Presumably."

That gave me a scare. In her diary Angela had in fact hinted that she really ought to have a bad conscience and that her mother hadn't noticed the change in her medication. Moreover, I'd noticed that in the years after exchanging the medicine for vitamin pills, Angela had never again mentioned Trinka's name.

"Anyone who murders their sick mother just because she's getting in the way of their dissolute lifestyle is also perfectly capable of killing a pastor who refuses to give them absolution." Kora sensed that the mood in the church was swinging in her favor. People who were inclined to believe her rumors before saw their suspicions confirmed. Others who had shrugged off her nutty fantasies started to wonder. Kora exploited the situation.

"Once the perpetrator Barbulescu silenced Pater Johannes with her knife, she sees the blood staining her hands. She runs to the watering trough on the village square to wash off the traces of her dastardly deed, but she knows she has lost her soul. Forever. She is the bride of Satan now. And now she commits a crime against God himself. She breaks into the church, dances with the devil on the altar and knocks over the lectern with the Holy Scriptures. Then she climbs onto a chair and puts out the Eternal Flame. On the way out she smears the chancel steps with her menstrual blood. Then she storms into her house, puts on the obscene dress with the sunflowers, grabs her friend the schnapps bottle, and climbs up to the Mondberg. She uses black magic to make the Virgin of Eternal Consolation disappear, and then she hangs herself."

The assembly was silent. I felt the impulse to jump up and wring Konstantin's neck. But I could also sense the mood in the church. An impulsive act, a careless word, and I would become part of her idiotic madness. Of course Angela Barbulescu hadn't murdered the pastor, any more than she had put out the Eternal Flame. But what were my possibilities for action? Should I stand up and bring the truth to light? Who would believe me? To blame the extinguishing of the Eternal Flame on someone who had emigrated a few weeks ago and now lived in far-off Germany—everyone would just think it was a cheap way to shift the blame, especially since they all knew of the feud between the Botevs and the Konstantins. For a moment I considered exposing Kora's lies with a justifiable counterlie by myself taking the blame for putting out the Eternal Flame: I did it! Although it wasn't the truth, it would have taken the wind out of Konstantin's sails. The sick edifice of her delusions would collapse like a house of cards. Then they would drive me from the village in disgrace and shame. Under the circumstances that was all the same to me, but Grandfather Ilja, my mother, and Aunt Antonia would have to live with the dishonor of having raised a boy who desecrates churches. Suddenly I understood how my beloved Buba could see no way to defend herself against her clan's code of honor. I was ready to pay the price of giving up my family. But what good would it do? If I took the act of desecration onto my shoulders, it would clear Angela of putting out the Eternal Flame and explain the blood on the chancel steps, but not the murder of Johannes Baptiste. Some suspicion would linger on forever in Baia Luna. After all, the villagers now believed that Angela Barbulescu was capable of anything—a woman who would give her sick mother the wrong medicine. I was the only one who knew that her mother had been as spiteful as Kora Konstantin.

Karl Koch spoke up. In place of the usual village practice of addressing everybody by their first name, he said quite formally, "Mrs. Konstantin, on November sixth you saw from your kitchen window the teacher Barbulescu entering the rectory and—"

"Slinking, I said slinking!" Kora corrected the Saxon. "Don't twist my words around."

"So you observed Miss Barbulescu on her way into the rectory. And you also saw that the teacher had to ring the doorbell for a long time."

"Exactly so."

"But from where you sit from morning to night in your kitchen you can't even see the door of the rectory."

"Yes, I can!"

"No, you can't!" chimed in Erika Schuster and a few other women. "From Konstantin's kitchen window you can only see the street."

Karl Koch became more energetic. "You are lying, therefore, when you claim to have seen Miss Barbulescu at the door of the rectory from your kitchen window."

"I'm not lying," Konstantin hissed. "And besides, I never claimed that. I definitely observed Barbu ringing for at least ten minutes. But I never said I was in the kitchen at the time."

"So you slunk after Miss Barbulescu as she proceeded to the rectory?"

"I had to, considering what we know about that slut today!"

I abandoned the stone pillar I had been leaning against the whole time and walked slowly to the front of the church. Kora blanched and put her hands up in front of her nose. I looked at Istvan Kallay. "May I ask a question, too?"

Istvan nodded. "That's what we're here for."

"Not him. I won't answer him," Kora cried, but her brother-in-law Marku spoke to her with unaccustomed sharpness: "You definitely will, and make sure it's the kind of answer he deserves!" Kora calmed down.

"Well," I began, "if you followed Angela Barbulescu and saw her coming out of the rectory an hour later, did you speak to her at that point?"

"Me? Speak to that woman? What a stupid question!" Kora was indignant. "Only a Botev would be stupid enough to ask such a thing. 'By their fruits ye shall know them.' Your grandfather can't even read. That idiot can't manage to read a single line."

Grandfather shot up from his seat, hurried up the aisle, and to everyone's astonishment balled his fist. "You lying witch, don't you dare say another word." Ilja grabbed the Gospel Book lying on the altar and held it aloft. "Name a chapter, Kora Konstantin, and I'll show everyone here in the church what a liar you are."

Kora was so dumbfounded she couldn't say a word. The sacristan Julius Knaup came to her aid. He called out in a loud voice, "We'll just see, or rather hear, if you can read. Gospel of John. Chapter three, verse four!"

Ilja leafed awhile until he'd found the passage. Then he read, "'Nicodemus saith unto him, how can a man be born when he is old? Can he enter the second time into his mother's womb, and be born? Jesus answered, Verily, verily, I say unto thee, except a man be born of water, and of the Spirit, he cannot enter into the kingdom of God. That which is born of the flesh is flesh; and that which is born of the Spirit is—' "

"Thank you, Ilja. That's plenty," Karl Koch stopped him and turned to Kora. "It's high time that someone shut your lying mouth for you. What makes you think you can accuse our shopkeeper and tavern owner Ilja of not being able to read?"

Kora turned red as a turkey and was boiling mad. "That Botev deceives us all. He cheats us. I was not lying. He must have secretly learned how to read. Everything I said about the Barbu is right. I swear it! I swear it on the grave of my mother Donata!"

"All right then," I took the floor again. "So you can finally answer my questions instead of slandering my learned grandfather in front of everyone. So what's the answer? Did you speak with Angela Barbulescu when she came out of the rectory or not?"

Kora said no.

"And did you speak to Pater Johannes after the teacher left the rectory?"

Kora said no again.

"Then how do you know that Angela Barbulescu went to the pastor to confess? If you didn't speak to Johannes Baptiste yourself, how do you know that? I've looked into the question. For an ordained priest, the seal of the confessional is still valid even if he refuses to absolve the sinner of guilt. Johannes Baptiste would never, ever have told anyone what was confessed to him in confidence."

The murmuring grew louder, and Kora began to squirm. She stared in turn at Marku and the sacristan Knaup. The veins in her neck swelled, and her chest trembled. Then she screeched so that the assembled crowd shook from the reverberations of her hoarse voice.

"I know it! I know it! I know it! And I swear by the Almighty that I'm telling the truth." Kora threw herself to the ground, all her limbs atwitch and grunting like a stuck pig as she often did when she felt she had to fend off an attack by the devil. A few of the men grabbed her by the arms, stood her up, and shook her. Karl Koch gave her a resounding slap in the face.

Kora collapsed, howling, "But I'm sure!"

"How can you be sure?" asked a dozen voices at once.

"With God as my witness. There was someone who heard what Pater Johannes said to Barbu, a person who wasn't bound by the seal of the confessional."

"And who the devil would that be?" asked Karl Koch in the name of everyone present.

The name Kora Konstantin tossed out into the sanctuary struck the inhabitants of Baia Luna like the blow of a club.

"Fernanda Klein. The housekeeper told me everything."

In an instant, the church was silent. Abashed, everyone looked at one another. No one doubted that Kora Konstantin was speaking the truth at this moment. And no one could imagine that Fernanda, the loyal soul of her pastor, was capable of lying. I, too, was so taken aback that I knocked my fist against my skull to formulate a clear thought. Then I walked over to the Konstantin woman.

"Kora, it's extremely important that you tell everyone exactly what Fernanda said to you."

She nodded vigorously. "I'll tell it all, exactly as it was. After Barbu came out of the rectory, I waited for a while. Then I went to the rectory myself. Not out of curiosity. No, just to keep abreast of what was happening in the village. Fernanda opened the door to me and took me right into the kitchen. She said I should be quiet so as not to disturb Johannes's midday nap again. 'What do you mean, again?' I asked. I had to play dumb. Fernanda told me to guess who had just paid a visit to the worthy old pastor at this unusual hour. I guessed a few names, then Fernanda whispered, 'It was Barbu.' Believe me, I've had many an intimate conversation with Fernanda and I know that trollop was a thorn in her side, too, although Fernanda never made a big deal of it. She assured me she was an accidental witness to the way Barbu greeted the pastor with the words 'Please don't send me away. I need to confess after all these years of hate.' Johannes Baptiste at once ushered Barbu into his study and closed and locked the door."

In view of such an extraordinary statement, Kora explained to her spellbound audience, it was completely understandable that Fernanda wanted to find out more details and therefore listened a bit at the keyhole. Again, not out of curiosity, but so she could come to the pastor's aid in the event of an attack by that unpredictable woman. The housekeeper couldn't provide any details of

Barbu's confession of her sins, since the sly hussy spoke too quietly, but Fernanda heard clearly that Pater Johannes said, "I can't. Please believe me. I cannot do it; it's forbidden." And the Barbu pleaded, "But you have to. You must, Pastor. Absolve me. Please!"

Kora Konstantin looked out at the assembly. Everyone was holding their breath. She raised her right hand and renewed her oath.

"May I be damned in all eternity if I'm lying. Fernanda told me what she heard from the priest's own mouth after Barbulescu's plea for absolution: 'Please leave now, Miss Barbulescu. I shall pray for you. My human sympathy is with you. But in the name of the Lord, I can't do anything for you.' The pastor then called for Fernanda to show the teacher to the door. Pater Johannes even wanted to help the sinner into her overcoat, which Barbu sternly refused. She hadn't even gotten into her coat but only clasped it tightly around her. Fernanda guessed that Barbu was hiding something under it that she desperately wanted to keep others from seeing. But Fernanda wasn't sure. She said only that Barbu asked for the key to the library, supposedly to borrow a book. Pater Johannes gave her the key and reminded her to return it. Knowing how unreliable Barbulescu could be, Fernanda went downstairs with her, opened the library, and waited. For she also wanted to write down the name of the book on an index card for the sake of orderliness, since that Black Dimitru Gabor doesn't fulfill his duties as self-appointed librarian very conscientiously. But that wasn't necessary, since the Barbu didn't borrow a book at all. Fernanda would be able to confirm that if she still was among the living. And here," Kora Konstantin announced, "I draw my own conclusions. Why does Angela Barbulescu want to visit the library on November sixth, of all days, after she has been refused absolution? What's the reason?"

As Kora stared into the abashed faces of those assembled, her lips twitched in a gloating smile. She repeated loudly and clearly, "What was that mother murderer looking for in the library on November sixth? You are silent because you don't know how cold and calculating evil can be. But Barbu knew. When she entered the library she had already decided our priest had to die. By her hand. But how was she going to get into the rectory secretly that night? She didn't go to the library for a book. No, she opened a window on the ground floor through which she planned to climb into the rectory at night, unobserved, with her knife. And why was she by chance able to open the window undisturbed on November sixth? Because no one else was in the library! Because the Black Dimitru Gabor wasn't thinking of his duties but only of the damn schnapps at the birthday party of Botev Ilja, who just led us around by the nose with a passage from the Bible he's learned by heart."

I left the church.

"Everybody in this village is crazy . . . and you, too," Fritz Hofmann had scoffed at me a few minutes before he blew out the Eternal Flame in the church. "What difference does it make if there's a little lamp burning in this Podunk or not?" For Fritz, it no longer made any difference. But my life was divided into the time before it was extinguished and after. For me the darkened church, while not the cause of the chain of ominous and dangerous events, stood in immediate temporal proximity to them. The murder of the priest, Angela Barbulescu's baffling unexplained suicide, the stolen Virgin of Eternal Consolation, and the delusional fantasies of Kora Konstantin had changed Baia Luna. The black of night prevailed even on the sunniest of days. Buba was my only ray of light. But when would I see her again?

I sat in our tavern but resisted the temptation to numb myself with *zuika*. Had Baia Luna really changed, the inhabitants really become different people? Or was it that the dead woman on the Mondberg had forced the village to show its hidden face? I no longer wanted to be one of these people. I wanted out. But where could I go?

I heard voices raised outside. Grandfather entered the taproom, followed by Trojan and Petre Petrov, the Saxons Karl Koch, Hans Schneider, Hermann Schuster, and his son Andreas, along with Karol Kallay, the shepherd Avram Scherban, and to everyone's surprise even old Bogdan, the father of the three Brancusi brothers. The men shoved two tables together and sat down. Ilja asked if they wanted something to drink. They all declined.

"It doesn't surprise me that Barbulescu hanged herself," Avram continued their heated discussion. "You could see it coming. If Fernanda hadn't listened at the door of our pastor, the mess Barbu made of her life would have stayed in the shadows forever. But murdering the priest? I have my doubts about that." No one contradicted him.

"If you had seen Baptiste naked and tied to a chair in the middle of that terrible mess—" Karl Koch added. "No woman could have done that. And I'll bet it wasn't just one person either."

"But did you see the faces in that church? It just goes to show what happens when people cling to their superstitions and resist progress. Most people in the village believe that nutty religious fanatic Konstantin," Bogdan Brancusi said hotly. "But if Barbu didn't murder the priest, who did? Karl, are you saying that something political is behind this dirty business? Even if my sons are in favor of the kolkhoz, they had nothing to do with it. I'd stake my life on that."

"Me, too. Your boys would never do such a thing." Grandfather took the floor. "But we have to ask ourselves, Who had an interest in seeing Baptiste dead?"

"So he couldn't speak anymore," Karl Koch added, and everyone nodded in agreement.

"We have to clear up the sequence of events," I interjected, "to really exclude the possibility that the teacher was responsible for the murder." Since no one protested, I continued, "Konstantin assumes that Pater Johannes was murdered during the night that Angela Barbulescu disappeared. That was the evening and night of Grandfather Ilja's birthday. But I'm sure that Johannes and Fernanda were still alive then. We didn't discover the priest until three days later, after the policeman Patrascu and the security agent Lupu Raducanu had been here."

"But no one saw Pater Johannes alive after he left my birthday party that evening," Grandfather said. Hermann Schuster interrupted him. "Pavel's right. It's true that none of us saw Johannes Baptiste after that. But Fernanda was still alive. I'm sure of that. She turned away everyone who came to the rectory door because Pater Johannes didn't want to be disturbed while he worked on his sermon. I know that from my wife. Erika wanted to talk to Baptiste the day after Ilja's birthday, but Fernanda absolutely refused to let her in because Johannes didn't want to be disturbed under any circumstances. By then the Barbulescu was probably already hanging from her branch."

"I think we won't get anywhere until we know who the devil had an interest in making sure that sermon never got delivered. Everybody knew that Pater Johannes was intending to preach against the damned collectivization." Karl Koch was getting worked up. "The fucking Securitate has people rotting in jail just for making stupid jokes about the party. A sermon against the kolkhoz would have been a huge thorn in the side of the big shots."

"Do you know anyone who had to go to jail?" the old Brancusi challenged him.

"You hear about these things," replied Koch.

"See there. You don't know anyone personally," scoffed Brancusi, "but you act like all Communists have nothing better to do than go around murdering priests."

"I didn't say that." Koch jumped up. "But that repulsive pretty boy Raducanu—he's capable of anything. He better not show his face around here again." The men rapped on the tables in agreement.

"Pavel, bring us a drop." I fetched the bottle of *zuika*. For the first time I got myself a glass, too, and drank with them. Nobody objected. Petre Petrov offered me a Carpati. I ignored my grandfather's disapproving look and took one.

Then Petre spoke up and reminded everyone of his drive to Kronauburg with Istvan and me and our visits with the pathologist Paula Petrin and the retired commissioner with the wiry hair. "Patrascu knows more than he lets on. But he's retired and wants his peace and quiet. He hinted that the authorities were behind the murder of the pastor and the disappearance of his body. They have no patience with anti-Communists and can't afford to make them into martyrs and let their graves become pilgrimage sites. Patrascu told us more than once that the business with Johannes Baptiste would burn us badly unless we kept our flame turned down low."

"And I'm sure that wasn't a threat," added Istvan Kallay. "It was a warning. But Petre is right. On the one hand Patrascu acts like all this Bolshevik terror doesn't get under his skin, and on the other, he's right in the middle of it. He knows all about the murder of Pater Johannes, but he won't say anything."

"He's so afraid he's pissing himself," conjectured Petre.

Hans Schneider shook his head. "For twenty years nobody gave a fart what Pater Johannes preached in church. But now that he's already pretty soft in the head, he's suddenly a threat to the Securitate? Hard to believe. We shouldn't lose sight of the possibility that Barbulescu did have something to do with it. Of course she couldn't have committed the crime by herself. Maybe she had an accomplice, maybe even someone here in the village."

"The murderers came from the city. I'm one hundred percent sure of it!"

"Buy why, Pavel? Since when are you clairvoyant?" Karl Koch asked.

"Funny you should be the one to ask. After all, you were there at the crime scene holding the proof in your hand and then you threw it out the window."

Koch's mind was racing. "Goddamnit! The mouse! The murderers had stuffed a mouse into Baptiste's mouth. Only the tail was hanging out—like a piece of string."

"And they sure didn't catch the mouse in the rectory. They must have brought it along," I said. "That mouse came from town. How often do you think we had to copy out the story of the city mouse and the country mouse in school? Well, there was a point to it after all. City mice are gray. But the mice here in Baia Luna are brown. The murderers didn't think of that."

"The mouse really was gray," Hermann Schuster now recalled. "You got a head on your shoulders, Pavel."

Grandfather nodded. "He sure does."

"But why was he killed? The Security Service got wind that in his old age Pater Johannes was planning to make things hot for the Bolsheviks," guessed Karl Koch. "The Securitate's always sniffing the wind."

"And now it's the other way around: they're making things hot for us. Haven't you noticed that our village is coming unglued?" Grandfather spoke with a passion no one thought was in him. "Since Johannes's death it's been one disaster after another. Don't you see that Baia Luna's going downhill? What's left of our community? One-half backs the crazy Konstantin while the other's groping around in a fog. Securitate! I'm always hearing about the all-powerful Securitate. The evil is right here in the village. We have to ask ourselves who told the Securitate what Baptiste was planning to say from the pulpit and how dangerous it would be for the state. They didn't sniff that out with their own noses. Someone must have told them about the sermon, must have told Raducanu or whoever. Otherwise they wouldn't have sent a death squad up here. Can't you see that among our ranks right here in the village there must be one or more traitors?"

The men swallowed.

"Traitor!" I picked up my glass and drank. Then I stood up and—for the first time right in front of Grandfather—I fetched myself a pack of cigarettes from the shelf behind the cash register. I took a drag on my Carpati and stubbed it out. A monstrous idea occurred to me. Traitor! Yes, I knew someone who wasn't a traitor but would be capable of playing that role, someone I still had a score to settle with.

"Anyone could be the Judas," said the Hungarian Kallay. "Everyone knew that Baptiste had announced that he would preach against Communism."

"How do you know that?" objected Hermann Schuster. "Remember, the idea for the sermon came to Johannes after the Bolshevik blah-blah on TV. After Khrushchev's speech. After the Russians had shot their Sputnik into space. The spaceflight of a dog opened up Pandora's box. That's what our pater claimed, right here in Ilja's taproom. And he intended to preach about it."

"But I'm sure he talked about the kolkhoz, too," Ilja replied. "Late in the evening, after the Brancusis broke that bottle on your head . . ."

"For which my sons have formally asked forgiveness," old Bogdan interrupted. "Why stir that pot up again?"

"Anyway," Grandfather continued, "my birthday party was spoiled, and you had all gone home. Pater Johannes didn't leave until later. He stood here in the door and already had his cane in his hand. I offered to walk him to the rectory, but he refused. He just said he'd see me on Sunday in church. And then he said something about Sputnik being the last straw, and it was high time to confront the collectivists in the spirit of the biblical message."

"Who else was present when Johannes said that?" Karl Koch was feverish with impatience.

Grandfather thought it over. "Me, of course. Pavel. And Dimitru."

"The Gypsy! You think the Black betrayed Johannes to the Securitate?" Hermann Schuster was horrified. "Dimitru of all people . . . No, he's a blowhard but he wouldn't do such a thing."

"I think he would," spoke up Scherban the shepherd. "A Gypsy has neither friend nor foe. Like Judas. A Gypsy would sell his own mother for hard cash. I was always against letting that Gabor clan move into the village. What do they want here, anyway?"

"It wasn't Dimitru," Ilja countered. "He's no traitor. Besides, there was nothing for him to betray. By the end of the evening he didn't know what was going on because he was dead drunk. He fell down the steps outside, and I think he broke a couple ribs. Pavel had to drag him home."

"But who's left as an informant? I'll kill the bastard." Koch was boiling mad.

I knocked my glass over. The *zuika* ran across the table. All eyes turned to me.

"There was somebody else." I hesitated a moment, but it was too late to take it back. "There was somebody else here that evening besides Pater Johannes, Dimitru, Grandfather, and me: Fritz Hofmann!"

For two or three heartbeats the men were frozen and speechless. Not because they lacked the words. I guessed there were too many thoughts pushing forward. A thousand images raced through their heads. The enormous tension of the previous hours, days, even weeks congealed in a single name. Fritz Hofmann! A schoolkid!

Then they all started talking at once. Everyone had a stone to contribute to the mosaic of a family of traitors they were putting together. Was it an accident that only a week after Johannes Baptiste's murder a German truck turned up in the village and the Hofmanns left Baia Luna for good? Hadn't the priest reprimanded the boy in front of all the men in Ilja Botev's tavern as the know-it-all Hofmanns' Fritzy. Couldn't you just see the cold fury in the kid's face after that dressing-down? Of course, a schoolboy scarcely could have access to the means of converting his thirst for revenge into a deed. But what about his father? Heinrich Hofmann, who had nothing but contempt for everything that happened in the village. The art photographer. The divorced art photographer. Who wanted no truck with the Good Lord. And had money. Drove a big

Italian motorcycle. And didn't his wife have an electric stove? The fancy-dancy Herr Hofmann! He never said hello, and Ilja's tavern wasn't good enough for him, and he preferred the high society in the city. He was on intimate terms with that Dr. Stephanescu, the top collectivist in the whole Kronauburg District. Fritz and Heinrich Hofmann were obviously both traitors, two peas in a pod. Along with the party bigwigs. They sent the butchers to our village to make an example of Johannes, the old priest who followed the word of God and not the laws of the temporal authorities.

I had scared myself. I sensed the hidden power I could exercise. With the mere naming of a name I had given the course of things a new direction. My direction. The reaction unleashed by the name Fritz Hofmann had hurled me into adulthood. Now my voice carried weight. Now the men had accepted me into their circle. I wasn't a boy anymore. Many years later I would understand it was guilt that had put out the last spark of my childhood soul. When I said the name of my former schoolmate and friend, I became guilty. Consciously, intentionally, and calculatedly. If Fritz Hofmann wouldn't atone for the deed he had committed, then he would have to atone for a deed he certainly could not have committed.

Fritz had blown out the Eternal Flame. He had defiled the church, and I had been cursed by Johannes Baptiste for the deed. Go to hell, the priest had condemned me. When he was murdered, he died in the mistaken belief that I, Pavel Botev, had sullied myself with the shame of a sacrilegious act, while the imbecilic fans of Kora Konstantin thought Angela Barbulescu was behind all of this madness. Only Fritz could have and should have washed the teacher clean of this infamy, but instead of accepting responsibility for his deed he had scrammed, taken off for Germany. Fritz Hofmann had abandoned me, left me alone with the extinguished lamp in the church, with all the madness in the village, and with the knowledge of his father's swinish activities. Under my mattress was the photo of a naked woman in a sunflower dress, a woman by the name of Alexa, between whose thighs Stefan Stephanescu was squirting a bottle of champagne. Photographed by Heinrich Hofmann. Wasn't it more than just compensation if the men in the taproom blamed Fritz and his overbearing father for a betrayal they certainly hadn't committed?

I reached for my pack of cigarettes and offered the men Carpatis. Petre, old Brancusi, and the shepherd took one. Grandfather neglected to give me a disapproving look. I was grown up. The men had accepted me as one of their own. But I didn't really belong. There was no place left for me in Baia Luna, in this disrupted, divided village. Kora Konstantin's crowd disgusted me; the men in the taproom were as honest as they were clueless. Their anger at the betrayal of Johannes Baptiste was genuine, but it had no outlet. Fritz Hofmann was gone, his father unreachable and protected by his political connections. No one could get at them. Sure, in a burst of fury Karl Koch had sworn to take revenge on the high-class Hofmann, and the impulsive Petre Petrov talked big about going to Kronauburg when the snow melted to throw a couple Molotov cocktails into a certain well-known photography studio. But in the foreseeable future, their anger would dissipate and give way first to bitter resentment and finally to an oppressive feeling of helplessness.

And the real guilty party?

I was lonely and alone and had no other choice but to hang on and wait things out until I could avenge Angela Barbulescu. She was dead and had not taken the party secretary with her to hell. What would happen with that vicious man I was supposed to destroy? The teacher had made me into her instrument, and I was ready for my crusade, ready for a battle, though I didn't know when, where, or with what weapons it would be fought. The only indisputable thing was that I had to go to Kronauburg as soon as the snow had melted.

Chapter Nine

·

*THE LEGACY OF ICARUS, THE DARKROOM,*

*AND HEINRICH HOFMANN'S HOLY OF HOLIES*

Spring kept us waiting. Not until mid-May of '58 did nature con-
cede that its habitual rhythms were reliable. Maple, ash, and beech
finally started bursting with buds, crocus and narcissus broke from
the soil, swifts flitted through the sky, and on the village pastures
the first lambs were bleating, like every year. The farmers went
into the fields with their horses, harrows, and plows to prepare
them for sowing while the Gypsies stood on the banks of the Tirnava for hours on end, staring at the roaring flood and praying the
rising water would spare their dwellings again this year. Dimitru
had barricaded himself in the library. I thought he was probably
still groping in the fog of his speculations, uncertain about the corporeal Assumption of Mary the Mother of God into heaven.

It pained Grandfather Ilja deeply that in his naïveté he had
turned Dimitru into a witness for the frightful Kora Konstantin,
and he made all sorts of attempts to revive their former friendship.
Sometimes he paid penitential visits to the library with a bottle of
schnapps; sometimes he brought the Gypsy a Cuban from Bulgaria
(thereby completely disrupting the rhythm of his own smoking
habits). My aunt Antonia had understood how much her father was
tortured by the loss of his friend and even agreed without complaint when Granddad wanted to take her last box of nougats to
Dimitru. The latter accepted the gifts but uttered not a word and
immediately bent over his books again, which misled Grandfather
into assuming the Gypsy had broken with him forever.

There was one exception to all the character flaws attributed
to the Blacks in our country. Not even the most prejudiced con-
temporaries could accuse the Gypsies of holding a grudge or being
vengeful. Even if Grandfather had disqualified himself from being

Dimitru's ally in his historic mission, the Gypsy had long since silently forgiven Ilja, as he told me in confidence years afterward.

So I'm going to spring forward to April 12, 1961. I remember the date exactly because on that day, Yury Alekseyevich Gagarin became the first man to float weightlessly in space. On that day, Dimitru Carolea Gabor broke the silence that had lasted for years and confided his thoughts to me in a quiet hour. At the time I was sure his audacious, even foolhardy theories were hopelessly off course. Today, in my old age, I no longer presume to judge them.

"Pavel," he said, "there was no one left and I had to shoulder the cross of loneliness by myself. No one else in the village was or is even close to being in a position to grasp *in principio* the world historical threat posed by the Soviet rockets. It was too much even for your good grandfather Ilja. He is incapable of calculating the danger. And it was my own *error fatal* to include my friend on my mission to rescue Mary the Mother of God. Ilja doesn't have the strategies of deceit at his disposal. With all due respect for his honesty—it wasn't what was called for against that idiot Konstantin and her sanctimonious crew. And Ilja talked too much. But it's *mea culpa maxima.* He talked too much because I told him too much. And so I catapitulated. I decided to keep still. And I made a vow. Not one word would pass my lips until the day my search for knowledge was crowned with success, namely, with the answer to the question: What happened to Mary after the Assumption?

"Remember, Pavel, even Papa Baptiste had warned that ascensions are reserved for the risen Christ and his Mother. And now the Soviets have the presumption to imitate them. President Khrushchev has promised a moon landing, and his best rocket builder is supposed to make it happen. That hubristical Korolev is the only one who can do it. He's a cunning master engineer, well read and crafty. A Marxist! That's why I've been combing through the collected works of Karl Marx in the library. I was hoping to find firsthand a clandestine reference to resurrection and ascension. But forget it, Pavel, you won't find anything useful. I intended to interrogate the works of Lenin with the same *intentio,* but then I made a discovery. I stumbled upon a book I urged you to read years ago, but you didn't listen to me. It was lying open at the bottom of one of my many piles. When it looked up at me, I remembered

Papa Baptiste once telling me, 'Forget the Marxists, Dimitru! If you want to fight your way through the storms of religious doubt, read Nietzsches' Friedrich.'

"So I reread the story I'd studied a dozen times before. In the middle of the day a madman runs around with a lamp in his hand seeking God. But he doesn't find him. And then he goes and claims we've killed God. The guy rightly remarks that the deed of killing God was too great for mankind, who ever since (as I can verificize myself) has been stumbling through eternal nothingness in the cold of night. But can we even conceive of nothingness? Who would be able to stand it? Doesn't it have to be overcome? 'Must we not ourselves become gods?' That's the question, Pavel Botev! Keep it in mind. Nietzsche's crazy guy asked the question, but now it's going to be answered. And in the affirmative. By Korolev. Become gods ourselves! Be God! Engineer Number One only has the works of Marx in his bookcase to keep the comrades happy. But believe me, Pavel, Korolev's read Nietzsche. That's why he knew that the madman with the lamp was ahead of his time. His message came too soon. People were not ready for the news of God's death, but now they are. The Russkies' Sputnik verificizes that gravity can be overcome.

"To become gods ourselves! Fly to the stars! Find a home in the sky! Weightlessly! Relieved of the banalities of this vale of tears! That's it, Pavel! Korolev is the heir apparent of Daedalus and Icarus, only much craftier. Those two Greeks were trapped in the labyrinth of the tyrant Minos, a labyrinth Daedalus himself had so cleverly constructed. Unfortunately, in old age the architect had forgotten where the exit was, but he hadn't yet lost his ingenuity. Don't forget, Pavel, when you're stuck and can't move right or left, forward or back, the only direction is up. Daedalus loses no time building wings for himself and his son. So far so good. His only mistake is using wax to hold them together, the idiot. And Icarus is so impetuous he's not satisfied to escape from the labyrinth, he wants to fly up to heaven. Flies higher and higher, too close to the sun. As you can easily imagine the wax melts and wham! The guy falls into the sea like a stone.

"Korolev's not that dense. His flying machines are solid work.

The test Sputniks worked. The goal of the Project is evidential. To become gods ourselves! Korolev is the new Icarus. You understand, Pavel? That big-mustache Nietzsche is the challenge. Papa Baptiste was right as always. But look around the village. People listen to the widow Konstantin, and their memories of Papa Baptiste are fading. No gravestone, no remembrance. And I'll bet you, Pavel, the same causalities are behind the disappearance of his corpse and the disappearance of the Virgin of Eternal Consolation."

With the late spring of '58, life also returned to Baia Luna. The farmers brought out their seeds, the women gossiped by the laundry troughs, and parents hoped the district administration would send a new teacher to Baia Luna soon.

Meanwhile, our family was in poor spirits. Grandfather Ilja was as miserable as a drowned cat. He could hardly get up in the morning, was grouchy all day, and at night tossed restlessly in his bed. In the evening, patrons in the taproom encountered a touchy and grumpy host who slammed the bottles onto the tables and aside from a few mumbled sentence fragments didn't utter a single friendly word. The dispute with Dimitru was harder on him than he liked to admit. Since Kora's big moment in the church, the Gypsy hadn't spoken a word to Ilja. Grandfather consoled himself for the painful loss of his friend by drinking a glass in the morning to meet the day with a certain measure of indifference. Since the effect of the *zuika* wore off in ever-shorter intervals and his foul mood increased conversely, he found it necessary to maintain his false equanimity with further glasses.

Then one morning Vera Raducanu asked for a pound of sugar, and Grandfather said nothing but "Kiss my ass!" Whereupon Vera huffed indignantly and cawed that the level in Baia Luna had sunk to an all-time low when the village peddler greeted his customers smelling like a distillery. That was the last straw for my mother.

"Enough!" she yelled at her father-in-law in a tone that left no doubt she intended to make a clean sweep in the Botev house. She got so wrapped up in her anger that it spilled over onto Aunt Antonia and me. Antonia spent most of her time dozing in bed, and

I had also been completely neglecting my duties in the shop and tavern. We all put our tails between our legs and hung our heads as Mother's storm raged over us.

"Whatever has happened in the village, life must go on. And it's you men's duty to do your jobs, goddamnit! If you don't crawl out of your holes right this minute I'm leaving. I'll move to town, I swear I will. You can go to the dogs in your misery, but count me out!"

Ilja and I had never seen my mother like this. And the shock of her anger was beneficial. We understood at once what we had to do. Just the prospect of going to Kronauburg woke me up from my lethargy and reinvigorated the powers of resistance I so urgently needed for my mission: justice for my former teacher Angela Maria Barbulescu. I got out a notepad and helped Grandfather take inventory of our stock. All our supplies were low. During the long winter months we'd run out of oil, sugar, and malt coffee. We only had enough salt left for the next few days. The last bottles of Sylvaner had been drunk up weeks ago, and the glass candy jar with the American chewing gum was empty, too. A trip to the wholesaler in Kronauburg was long overdue. While Kathalina scrubbed the floorboards and dusted the shelves, Grandfather and I got the wagon ready for the trip to Kronauburg the following morning.

Drowsy and yawning from getting up so early, we clung to the swaying wagon box and restricted our conversation to the minimum. If we spoke at all, it was about our worries that the wholesale prices might have risen again as they did every year. I shared Granddad's concern that our modest family reserves might not be enough to buy all the stock we needed and sensed at the same time as we drove along that the profession of businessman and tavern owner was not a job I intended to spend the rest of my life in. But what else could I do?

At about seven we reached the Schweisch Valley. Its broad fields had once belonged to the richest landowner in Transmontania. The collectivization of the Kronauburg District had already reached this point, and the upland farmers of Baia Luna figured that their own modest parcels of land would soon fall victim to forced expropriation. Beyond Apoldasch we passed the future cattle and hog barns whose dimensions were as formidable as their alignment was monotonous. It followed a plan someone had laid out on a drawing board. Construction cranes loomed everywhere, bulldozers plowed up the heavy soil, and trucks arrived with construction material. Oversize placards proclaimed the official opening of the new People's Agro-Industrial Complex Apoldasch II, scheduled for June 1, an event even the state president Gheorghiu-Dej was expected to attend. When we reached the feedlot for the hogs, we were astonished to see twenty-two brand-new tractors lined up in pairs and glinting orange-red in the morning light. No doubt the vehicles came from the new tractor factory Joy of the Fatherland in Stalinstadt. Grandfather pointed to the tractors. "Our Alexandru put them together screw by screw. I bet he'll get a written commendation for a job well done." For the first time in many weeks, I laughed.

We reached the outskirts of Kronauburg around eleven and drove our wagon to the grocery wholesaler we'd been buying from since the days of Ilja's father Borislav. But instead of the old familiar sign HOSSU BROS. IMPORT-EXPORT AND WHOLESALERS, we found a new one that said STATE-OWNED ENTERPRISE. KRONAUBURG CONSUMER COMPLEX AND TRADING ORGANIZATION. We entered the warehouse to look for the eldest Hossu brother with whom Grandfather usually discussed the list of supplies he needed and calculated their price. It looked like the number of employees had doubled, and everyone had been given identical blue jackets. Most of them were sitting on wooden pallets and smoking. When Grandfather asked for Vasili Hossu one of the warehouse workers uttered "Lunch break" and jerked his thumb toward an office door labeled DIRECTOR. Ilja knocked. Since no one answered, he pushed down the latch, and we entered. A young woman was sitting behind a desk filing her fingernails.

"Lunch break," she said. "Can't you read?"

"The Hossus welcomed us at any time of day," said Grandfather. "Where might I find those gentlemen?"

"Come back at one thirty. No information until then," answered the secretary without looking up from her manicure. We left the warehouse and drove our wagon a bit farther on. The Hearty Appetite was still there, thank God. It wasn't much more than a shabby shed, but there was water and hay for exhausted horses, and the wholesaler's customers could fortify themselves with beer, bread, and meat patties from the grill. There were already half-a-dozen wagons parked in front of the Pofta Buna. Granddad unhitched and fed the nag and then sat down next to me on a wooden bench. We learned from the Pofta Buna's owner that the Hossu brothers had been dispossessed at the beginning of the year and seemed to have disappeared from the face of the earth, but he was reluctant to say anything else. At the next table two men were talking excitedly about the pricing policies of the new trading organization. They didn't seem particularly dissatisfied with them. The other customers had already gone to the adjacent barn and were taking a little nap in the hay to pass the time until the warehouse reopened. At one thirty a siren wailed. Lunch break was over.

The director of the People's Shopping Cooperative was a short, round man in his midfifties wearing a light blue tie and a brown suit that was a bit too small for him. "New customers?" He squinted over the top of his glasses, sat down behind an enormous desk, and began shuffling papers.

"No," answered Grandfather, "we've been customers for decades. The Botev family shop. Baia Luna, Number Seven, Street of Peace. Where are the Hossu brothers?"

The director offered us a chair. "From Baia Luna? Man oh man! No wonder you don't know what's going on in the world. The Hossus have been relieved of their private enterprise. Where are they now? Not a clue. Not here, at any rate. Are you private customers?"

Grandfather nodded.

"The trading organization doesn't sell to private persons anymore. Directive from upstairs. But no problem. How big is your shop?"

Ilja calculated the square footage in his head and stated the result.

"But the greater part of the space is devoted to our taproom," I remarked.

"Aha. You're also running a gastronomic establishment up there. Must do a brisk business. There's nothing much else to do, right? Do you have a concession? Liquor license?"

"Liquor license?" Grandfather's initial wonderment gave way to anger. "Tell me something, do you guys have a screw loose? We've been doing fine without one for a few generations. Don't you have anything better to do than think up this bureaucratic bullshit?"

"Take it easy. I'm not thinking up anything. But there's got to be order, and the law's the law. Otherwise everybody could do his own private wheeling and dealing. And then we'd have capitalism like the Yanks, where everyone does whatever they want. And the Gypsies would have their hands in our pockets."

"But we need fresh stock!" Ilja was getting indignant. "Our shelves are empty, and the villagers are starting to grumble. You can't just stop selling to private enterprises from one day to the next."

"I told you, no problem. All you have to do is join the trading collective. It's just a formality. Then your private shop will be deprivatized. Everything else stays the same. You'll even get your stock under optimal conditions. You'll definitely pay less than you did to those capitalists the Hossus. All you have to do is go to the collectivization office and sign up. And while you're in town, you might as well pick up a state liquor license, too. Without a concession, we're only allowed to sell you soft drinks here at the T.O. You'll find the offices on Square of the Republic. It's a short walk. The offices are open till four o'clock."

With the worst fears and cursing the state, the party, and Socialism in general, we hurried into town and twenty minutes later were sitting on a wooden bench in a deserted hallway. We were waiting outside a door on which hung a piece of cardboard with the hand-lettered directive DO NOT KNOCK. ENTER WHEN CALLED. A small sign was fastened to the wall next to the door: T.O. CONCESSIONS A—D.

We had only waited a few minutes when the door opened and a woman stuck her head out. "Well, why didn't you knock? Please come in." She was wearing a simple suit and radiated an unexpected congeniality. She offered us a seat and even asked if the gentlemen would care for a mocha to pep them up. We declined.

"So you're from Baia Luna? I didn't even know there was a shop there."

Still smiling, the woman explained that in establishing Socialism, the state's and the party's most urgent task was to assure and continually optimize the provisioning of the population country-wide. By no means should even such a remote village as Baia Luna have to lag behind. The State Trade Organization guaranteed progress to their cooperative partners. Then she told us that Western capitalism was headed for a dramatic impoverishment of the masses in the near future while our new republic was close to achieving world-class status.

Grandfather interrupted her explanations. "But I want to know what's going to happen to our business. There's no sugar, salt, or oil in Baia Luna. We're in urgent need of new stock."

"You're going to get it, too," said the woman without losing an iota of her friendliness. Then she went over to a shelf of files.

"Here we are: Botev, Baia Luna."

She opened the file and leafed through it. We realized immediately that it contained the packing lists and invoices the Hossu brothers had filled out for us in past years.

"Well, you've never purchased in large amounts. And as I can see, meat, sausages, and fresh vegetables are completely absent. The farmers in your village probably supply such things themselves. Privately, each for himself?"

Grandfather nodded. "There isn't much money to go around in the village."

"That's going to change. Join the cooperative and you'll see: supplies will improve and become cheaper, too. You say you need oil, salt, and sugar. Since it looks like the planned quotas are going to be exceeded, the government dropped the prices for basic foodstuffs by half last month."

We looked at each other in silence. "And we can continue to sell everything as we have up to now?"

"Yes. But not as a private enterprise anymore. You can't set prices as you see fit to make your profit. You'll be an employee of the T.O., receive a set monthly salary, and take delivery of all stock on the basis of a commission with a monthly statement. And you will have set hours of operation of your T.O. branch: weekdays from eight to twelve and three to six. Saturdays only until noon, of course. But just between you and me, nobody's going to traipse all the way up to Baia Luna to check up on what hours you're open."

The mere thought of no longer being able to operate as an independent businessman and tavern owner was sure to be unbearable for Grandfather. I could tell he was getting stabbing pains in his bowels. He was shifting back and forth on his chair and trying his best to suppress the gas. But when the official mentioned the amount we would be receiving every month from the postman as a salary, he let one fly. It was about twice as much as our usual net profit.

Grandfather thought it over. I asked, "What alternative is there to the cooperative model?"

"None," said the woman, taking a blank contract out of her desk drawer. "You don't have to sign. No one's forcing you. But then you'll have to go back to your village empty-handed. If you don't want to be unemployed, you could of course apply for a job at one of the new state enterprises. From what I know about what's available in your area, you might have some luck at the new agro-complex in Apoldasch. But just between us, do you seriously think anybody who hasn't understood the need to have his private business collectivized is about to be hired by a state enterprise? I ask you, gentlemen." She was still smiling. "Sign this agreement and I guarantee you won't regret it. And let me assure you, up to now there's only been a single self-employed person who didn't sign. And guess what happened? Upset as he was, he slammed the door shut, stormed out into the street, and ran right in front of a truck. The poor man is still in the hospital and will never stand on his own two legs again. How's he going to feed his family now? Wife and five children. If he'd signed the contract two minutes before, he would have been insured by workman's comp from the T.O. cooperative. But as it is? Nothing. Here's the contract. It's all set down in black and white. Take your time and read it all through. Care for a mocha now?"

We read. The contract seemed a pretty straightforward deal with no hidden tricks or pitfalls, as far as I could judge without understanding all the details.

"What about our taproom?" asked Ilja. "They said I needed a liquor license."

"You have a tavern, too?" The young woman was confused.

"I'm a tavern owner and a shopkeeper. That's been the tradition in our house for generations."

"And all that on the same premises! Only in the mountains, is all I can say! Groceries being sold and alcohol dispensed under the same roof? Unbelievable!"

"Where else would you suggest?" I interjected.

"Well, I'll pretend I didn't hear that. Food-handling hygiene isn't part of my job description. You're in the wrong office for a liquor license. You'll find that two floors up, T.O. Division of Alcohol, Tobacco, and Food Services. They'll offer you the same contract we do here in the division of retail food sales. No contract, no sale of alcoholic beverages." The woman paused to think it over. "You know what? I'll take care of it for you. Running around from one office to the next can't be very pleasant. Especially if you're from the mountains and don't know your way around. I just need your papers."

Grandfather fished out his ID. The official looked at his pass and shook her head. "This isn't valid anymore. It must go back to the days of King Carol. And this photo? Is that supposed to be you? No, no, you definitely need to renew your papers. Down on the market square there's a photo studio. Photo Hofmann. You can have a new picture taken there. With the best will in the world I can't get you a liquor license without a current ID. Come back tomorrow morning with the pictures."

As we left the collectivization authority, all I said was "We have no choice." Grandfather nodded.

On the market square across from the police station, the modern Socialist People's Market again caught my eye, the one that had made such a powerful impression on me last November when Istvan and Petre and I unsuccessfully investigated the disappearance of Baptiste's corpse, something people in Baia Luna seldom talked about anymore. Now, in the spring, the villagers had other things to worry about than the empty grave in the churchyard. As I stood on the Kronauburg market square in front of the gigantic glass façade of the T.O. store once again, it seemed much less impressive than I remembered it. The banner with the red lettering THANKS TO THE REPUBLIC! THANKS TO THE PARTY! still hung limply above the entrance, but it had visibly weathered during the winter months.

I asked a passerby, "Photo Hofmann, is it somewhere around here?" My knees were trembling with excitement.

"You're almost standing right in front of it," the man answered. "There, where the government car is parked."

Grandfather was just starting to rant that nothing in the world could get him to let that Securitate informer Hofmann take his picture when I shushed him up. "Be quiet. Take a look at that!" I was staring at the black limousine with chrome bumpers parked in front of the photo studio. A uniformed driver with a peaked cap opened the trunk and put in two valises. I recognized the chauffeur; it was the same guy who had transported Petre, Istvan, and me to Kronauburg after the murders in the rectory, when their bodies were supposedly going to be autopsied. The driver threw open the car doors and raised a hand to his visor. Heinrich Hofmann emerged from his studio. Then I saw the man I probably knew more about than anyone else after reading Angela Barbulescu's diary. Behind Herr Hofmann, Dr. Stefan Stephanescu walked out of the photo shop. Both of them were wearing dark suits. They were joking with each other and clearly in high spirits.

I almost blacked out. My knees threatened to crumble beneath me. I barely made it over to a lamppost and held on tight, unable to believe my eyes: the pretty woman emerging from Hofmann's shop behind Stephanescu couldn't be Angela Barbulescu, but she looked just like her. Like the young Angela in the photo, puckering her lips. The woman coming out onto the sidewalk was in her early twenties. Her blond hair was gathered in a ponytail, and she was laughing. The similarity was frightening. I saw Heinrich Hofmann obviously giving her a few last instructions before he got into the backseat of the limousine. The blond went over to Stephanescu and shook his hand. He casually stroked her cheek, then got into the front passenger seat. The chauffeur closed the doors, wiped off the wing mirrors with his handkerchief, and got into the driver's seat. They waved good-bye.

*Only young women . . . All pretty and all blond.* That's what Fritz had said after snooping in his father's moving crates and finding all those filthy photos.

As the state limousine accelerated off, my gnawing doubts disappeared. Angela Barbulescu had spoken her own death sentence at the very moment she had reached bottom and cast off all fear. She had written in her diary that the pictures Hofmann had made in

Florin's office with all his disgusting friends were repulsive. *They kept my mouth closed for a long time. But no longer. As far as I'm concerned, Hofmann can send those pictures to the village priest. Do whatever you want with them. Hang my picture on every lamppost. I'm not afraid anymore.* I realized that Angela was the victim of a tragic mistake. These two gentlemen would never dirty their hands. The power of Heinrich Hofmann and Stefan Stephanescu consisted in creating fear. Threat was their weapon. Only those who ignored their own fear got eliminated, people like Angela who decided to speak out because she had nothing left to lose. Had Angela Barbulescu really put the noose around her own neck? Or had these two staged her supposed suicide at that tree on the Mondberg?

"Did you see that?" Grandfather asked me breathlessly. "That's the priest betrayer who just left. I'm telling you, that bastard Hofmann is thick as thieves with the bigwigs."

I was thinking and didn't reply. Two valises, two men, one chauffeur. Hofmann and Stephanescu would be gone for several days. *The mighty fall from their thrones,* Angela had written in her green notebook. She was wrong. One impression I definitely didn't have of the Kronauburg party boss was that that prophecy would be fulfilled anytime soon.

"They sure are thick as thieves," I finally replied. "But now Hofmann is gone. Let's take a look at his shop."

I hadn't pictured Heinrich Hofmann's photo studio as so big. Three wide windows on the market square displayed an impressive sampling of the maestro's work. Three huge portraits hung in the middle window, two of which I was already familiar with. I had hung one, in a smaller format, on the wall in Baia Luna next to President Gheorghiu-Dej. Here in the window, the Little Stalin seemed even more imposing and statesmanlike, and the deceptive smile of the Kronauburg party chairman Stephanescu radiated its winning charm even more convincingly. The third photo was a group portrait of the seventy-nine members of the Central Committee of the Communist Party. The other windows were set up to induce ordinary mortals to have their pictures taken, too. On the left, hundreds of small passport photos were arranged like pieces of a large puzzle, which also suggested the volume of the photographer's business. On the right, black-and-white wedding pictures in elaborate gold frames were displayed against a background of wine-red velvet.

A set of brass bells jingled melodiously as we pushed open the door to Hofmann's studio. I was so keyed up I could barely say "good afternoon," and I began looking furtively around the roomy store. I was disappointed that the blond beauty who looked exactly like Angela Barbulescu was nowhere to be seen. There were two other female employees, however, neither of whom had to hide her looks under a bushel either, as far as I was concerned. Both were blond. One was engaged in gift wrapping a small silver frame for an older gentleman. We sat down on a leather sofa next to a green potted plant that was definitely not a specimen of the local flora. To our right, the other employee with the fluffy blond hair of an angel was advising a young couple seated at a kidney-shaped table. The couple was holding hands, nodding incessantly, and exclaiming "Beautiful, very very nice, wonderful!" while she turned the pages of an album for them. Any customer would surely have melted beneath the gaze of her blue eyes.

All in all, the photography studio exuded a cool tidiness that reminded me of the Hofmanns' sparsely furnished living room. The long counter was made of light, polished beech wood and behind it stood glass cases with cameras on display like little artworks of technology. The attractions on the side walls were photographic portraits of uniformly beautiful women.

The young couple stood up. "That's how we'll do it," I heard the young man say. "So we'll see you at Saint Paul's Cathedral at eleven o'clock on Sunday? You won't forget, will you?" The glance of the employee with the angel's hair alone would have been enough to dispel the fears of the bride- and groom-to-be. "You can count on us. I'm sure it's going to be a perfect wedding." The doorbells jingled, and the couple left the store behind the gentleman with the picture frame.

I hadn't noticed the white door behind the cash register until it opened. There she was. The young woman with the blond ponytail surveyed the salesroom briefly and then turned to her colleagues. "Almost four thirty. I'm sure there won't be much more business today. You can go home early if you want to." Then she smiled in our direction. "I can take care of these gentlemen by myself."

A minute later the doorbells jingled again, and the two salesgirls walked off into town, arm in arm and giggling.

"Please forgive us for making you wait," said the blond. She was really beautiful. Although her similarity to the young Angela Barbulescu wasn't quite so striking from close up, it was still there. I tried to imagine this woman twenty years older, standing at the blackboard in the Baia Luna school, wearing rubber boots and a grubby blue dress and with carelessly pinned-up hair, but I couldn't. She gave our clothes a once-over without betraying any reaction. "Would you gentlemen be looking for ID photos?"

We nodded.

"Then please follow me into the smaller studio."

In a back room stood a gigantic photographic apparatus on a tripod, large spotlights, and a portrait stool.

"Don't worry." The woman laughed. "It won't hurt. By the way, I'm Irina Lupescu, Herr Hofmann's right-hand girl."

"Isn't the boss here?" I asked hypocritically.

"No. He's often on the road. He just left for the capital—some party congress or other. Herr Hofmann photographs the highest political officials exclusively. My colleagues and I take care of the small jobs: weddings, anniversaries, ID photos. No offense, of course."

I was genuinely surprised. "But Herr Hofmann . . . doesn't he take all those wedding pictures himself?"

"No, no," laughed Irina. "He hasn't done that for years. My predecessor took care of those. And today it's my job to see that couples have happy reminders of their wedding day. Especially this time of year, in May, we can hardly keep up with the weddings. Just today a dozen couples were in here making appointments."

"Yes, yes," put in Grandfather. "In the spring the sap rises."

Irina gave a mischievous laugh. "I don't think you can blame spring. It's more the fault of the long winters. On cold nights people have to huddle close together, if you know what I mean. And then in May the brides throng to the altar. It doesn't have to be immediately obvious that there's a wee one on the way."

"You said your predecessor took all the wedding pictures? She did a nice job. Even a blind person can see that from your window display. What became of her?" I tried not to show how curious I was.

"I don't know. One morning last November she just didn't show up for work and was never seen again. I didn't even have a chance to meet her, unfortunately."

"Then you haven't been working here very long?"

"Just since January. Before that I did an apprenticeship in a studio in the capital."

I wasn't sure if Irina Lupescu thought I was being too inquisitive, but I forged ahead anyway. "So why didn't you stay in the capital? There's a lot more culture there than in Kronauburg."

Irina laughed unself-consciously. "Let me put it this way: someone I care a lot about wooed me away and introduced me to Herr Hofmann. And your Kronauburg isn't as uncultured as all that. But now we've got to . . . I see you weren't necessarily foreseeing the need for an official photograph. I mean, judging from what you have on."

"If we'd known we would need new passes I'd have brought my suit along," Grandfather apologized.

"We are prepared for such cases. Afterward you can take a look at the pass photos in the window. There's more than a thousand of them. And I'll bet every fourth . . . probably every third man is wearing the same sport coat, the same shirt, and the same striped tie." The salesgirl opened a wardrobe and took out some clothing. "Pick something that more or less fits. In the next room there's a brush and comb by the mirror. I have to go down to the lab in the basement for five minutes. I'll be back here to help by the time you've changed."

"Who would have thought Hofmann had such a nice colleague?" asked Grandfather.

"That scumbag doesn't deserve her."

I pulled off my sweater, put on a white shirt and a dark blue jacket that fit me fine. Instead of the striped tie I chose a dark one but had no idea how to tie the damn thing. Although Grandfather had worn a tie a time or two in his youth, he wasn't making any progress with the unfamiliar item either.

Irina Lupescu's high heels clattered up the stairs from the basement. With a "May I help you with that?" she knotted my tie quick as a wink.

"What a difference! Clothes make the man," she joked. "May I ask where you're from?"

"Baia Luna."

"Are you kidding? Then you must know the boss personally? He lived up there in the mountains with his family for years. It must be beautiful, especially in the summer. Although to be honest, Herr Hofmann isn't the man for village life. I wonder how he ended up there. Don't you hear wolves howling at night?"

"Yes, and even more during the day."

"You don't say." The joke went over Irina's head. "No, that's not for me. Too bad you missed Herr Hofmann by just a few minutes."

"Really a shame. Our bad luck." I realized that Heinrich Hofmann's assistant had no feel for irony. She was gullible in every bone of her body. With a gentle hand Irina positioned me on the stool. Chest out, chin tilted a little forward. Then she adjusted the camera and reached for the cable release.

As the flash popped I felt bad for Irina because at that moment, I knew I was going to play a dirty trick on her. I had a daring plan that was going to make this trip to Kronauburg mean more than just carting sugar and oil back to Baia Luna. All winter long, crippled by enforced inactivity, I'd been deep in depression. But today I could take an important step forward in my campaign against the machinations of Heinrich Hofmann and Dr. Stefan Stephanescu. I just had to exploit the pleasure and care Irina Lupescu took in her work and her guileless nature for my own purposes. I took off the borrowed clothes, and Grandfather struggled into the very same ones (except that he chose the striped tie) and submitted himself to the photographic procedure.

"A camera like that is a magic machine. It pops and flashes, and before you know it, you're immortalized in a picture," I said in feigned naïveté.

Irina smiled. "Oh no, there's a lot more to it than that. First you have to develop the film, then fix it and wash it in water. Once the negative is dry you can print the image on paper."

"The negative? What's that?"

"You mean you've never seen a negative?"

"We don't have anything like that in Baia Luna. But it'd be interesting . . . I mean, very interesting to see how the trick is done, how you get the picture onto the paper. Or is it a trade secret?"

"Oh heavens!" Irina was amused. "You can learn about it in school. Chemistry and physical science. Well, I was planning to develop your pictures after I closed the shop, but there aren't any more customers anyway. If you want, I can show you how everything works in the lab. I mean, if you're really interested. Would you like to see?"

"Yes, it would be great to see the lab." I was enjoying playing the inquisitive boy.

"Then follow me!"

"I don't understand that technical stuff anyway," Grandfather interrupted. "I'll take a look at the People's Shopping Cooperative in the meantime."

Ilja left the studio.

Irina took the film cassette out of the camera, and I followed her down the steps. In the basement things weren't anywhere near as orderly. Innumerable cardboard boxes of photographs were stacked to the ceiling on uneven shelves. Canisters of developing chemicals stood around everywhere. Dusty picture frames and old optical equipment were piled in a corner. Irina opened a heavy iron door to the darkroom and turned on the red light. It took my eyes a while to get used to the half darkness, but gradually I could make out enlargers, pans containing various liquids, glass beakers, tongs, and clotheslines from which hung drying strips of film and enlargements. Although I was seeing all these things for the first time, I already had an idea what they were and how they were used. Fritz Hofmann had explained to me how the photographic development process worked. Irina took a black cloth and shut out the light from a basement window onto an airshaft.

"That seals it off. Not a sliver of light can get through. You have to understand: film can only be developed in absolute darkness. The smallest ray of light and it's spoiled."

"Why not just brick up the window instead of having to hang the cloth in front of it every time?"

"Because of the fumes from the chemicals. If you had to breathe them for hours at a time, they'd make you sick. You have to air out the darkroom from time to time. Are you ready? It's going to get completely dark now." The pretty lab assistant picked up the film cassette and turned out the light. "I need a few minutes to bathe the film in developer. When it's done, it has to be fixed and washed, then we'll put the light back on, and you'll see your first negative."

I listened to the sounds of Irina working; obviously, she could find her way around blind. After about five minutes, she turned the light back on and opened up the tap. "You can do the washing yourself," she said with a laugh and handed me the developed film. "But only hold it by the edge, or there'll be fingerprints on your photo when it's done. Hold the film up to the light, and you'll see why a negative is called a negative. Your light skin is dark and the pupils of your eyes are little white specks. On a negative, every-thing is reversed. You see? By the way, customers usually have to wait three days to pick up their finished ID photos. I'm making an exception in your case. But in case you run into Herr Hofmann, not a word about being here. Nobody from outside is allowed down here. Even my colleagues aren't. Herr Hofmann is afraid someone could turn on the light by accident when we're working in here. That's why the switch is way up here above the lintel. But Herr Hofmann is funny about some things. I'm the only one he trusts to do the lab work. He only takes care of the most important jobs himself. Okay, now I'll show you how we make a positive from a negative. You'll see how the image gets transferred to paper."

In other circumstances I would have found Irina's explanations extremely interesting, but in this situation I had to force myself to listen attentively. My mind was on something else entirely, but I needed patience and a good deal of luck. In the dull glow of the red light Irina took a piece of printing paper out of a cardboard box and placed it in a frame under the enlarger. She laid a strip of film on top of it with four negatives the size of an ID photo, then a glass sheet. "If a customer wants a bigger print, I put the negative up here in the enlarger. That isn't necessary for small ID pictures. For them the negative is directly in contact with the paper. Do you understand what I mean? Here, I'll show you."

Irina turned on the enlarger, counted "twenty-one, twenty-two," and turned it off again. Then she took the photographic paper and slid it into a pan of developing solution. "Now the magic begins," she whispered as she swished the sheet back and forth with some tongs. I watched the edge of the paper get gradually darker, and then the suit jacket and the dark tie and finally the contours of my face emerged. The girl waited awhile longer, lifted the sheet out, and put it in the pan with fixer. She handed me a pair of tongs and told me, "Keep it moving around. Count to sixty slowly, then you can turn on a regular light, let the paper drip off, and rinse it under running water for a few minutes. When that's done, I'll name you honorary first assistant to the assistant. And you can decide which print you want for your ID."

Then I got the lucky break I was hoping for. From the first floor came the faint sound of the doorbells.

"Darn. I should have closed up the shop. I've got to go upstairs, but you know what to do." Irina pushed open the iron door and disappeared.

"Fifty-eight, fifty-nine, sixty." I had counted fast, but not too fast. I put the sheet into the water bath and turned on the faucet. Then I hurried to the blacked-out window and pushed aside the black cloth. Behind it, a grill separated the lab from an airshaft that very probably led up to a back courtyard. The window was locked. I thought of Kora Konstantin. The old woman was good for something after all. Now I set about actually doing what Kora in her twisted fantasy had accused the teacher of doing. Barbu was supposed to have secretly opened the window to the library and then used it to gain entry to the rectory at night. I turned the latch ninety degrees. I was able to open and close it easily. Then I left the window open a crack, hung the black cloth in front of it again, and went back to rinsing my portraits.

Irina Lupescu returned. "Your grandfather's back. It was too boring for him in town. He's waiting upstairs. So, have you decided which picture you want for your ID?"

I hadn't. "Why did you take four pictures? One would have been enough."

Irina took the contact print from me and examined the little portraits. "Here's why I took four! Look here! This one is blurry. And here you blinked just as the flash went off. The other two turned out all right. I would choose this one. You look friendly and determined and not so terribly stiff and serious."

I decided I could depend on Irina's judgment.

"I'll cut out your picture, and then it will take a few more minutes to have your grandfather's ready."

"What'll you do with the pictures that didn't turn out?"

"I throw them away, but you're welcome to take them with you. We don't have any use for them."

"What about the negatives?"

"Oh, I can't give you those. We have strict orders from Herr Hofmann. They are the most valuable thing any photographer has, and for my boss they're close to sacred. That way, we can make as many prints as you want whenever you need them. Even though hardly any customers take advantage of the opportunity."

"And what do you do with the negatives if nobody needs more prints?"

"We collect and file them. The archives are in the next room. As a joke we call it the tabernacle, Herr Hofmann's holy of holies. There are thousands of negatives stored in there. All in file boxes, neatly labeled and filed alphabetically. If we didn't do that, we'd never find anything again. In twenty years you may have grandchildren of your own and want to give them a photograph of yourself when you were young. As a stylish young gentleman in jacket and tie."

Irina gave another hearty laugh. I had to force myself not to be too attracted to her.

"Here I've been talking away and I don't even know your name. What is it, anyway?"

"Pavel. Pavel Botev. My grandfather's name is Ilja. My father's no longer alive, unfortunately."

"It's a nice name, Pavel Botev. I like it."

"And you, are you married already? Do you have any kids?"

Irina gave me a serious look. "No, I just got engaged. But I'd like to have children. A lot, in fact. But first comes the wedding."

I summoned all my courage and asked, "May I ask who the lucky groom will be?"

"Of course you can ask. But I don't want to give it away yet. As my mother always says, blow the trumpet when the wedding bells ring, not when the dress is still hanging in the closet. But I'll tell you this much: he often works with my boss, Herr Hofmann."

I bit my tongue. I wanted to take her in my arms and say, Don't do it! Go back to the capital. Forget about that man. Forget him for the rest of your life. Instead, I let the name slip out.

"It's Dr. Stephanescu, isn't it?"

Irina stared at me in astonishment and shook her head. Then she broke out in a peal of laughter that really annoyed me.

"Are you completely nuts? Why in the world would you guess our party boss? He's much too old for me. He could be my father. But my fiancé does know Mr. Stephanescu. Quite well, in fact. They often go out to eat with my boss, in the Golden Star. If you promise to keep it a secret . . ."

"I promise. Word of honor."

"His name is Lupu. Lupu Raducanu."

Up in the shop Grandfather sat dozing on the sofa for customers. I shook him. "Granddad, we're finished. You've got to pay."

"Keep your money," said Irina. "I had fun with the two of you. I know for a fact that Herr Hofmann makes almost nothing from ID photos anyway. We only offer the service because we earn plenty on the orders from the party. But don't tell anyone I said so."

"But we insist on paying, just like anyone else." Tortured by my bad conscience, I tried to get my feelings for Irina back onto the commercial level.

"Are you trying to insult me? You just mustn't say anything to Herr Hofmann if you run across him in town."

Once back on the market square, I felt dirty. Irina Lupescu's credulity pained me. And I had exploited her with cold-blooded calculation. But what should I have done? Stephanescu was not going to fall on his own as Angela Barbulescu had prophesied. He would have to be brought down. And if anything could bring that man down, it was what was located in the basement archives of Hofmann, the master photographer.

Since we wouldn't be able to get our new ID cards and sign the contract with the State Trade Organization until the next morning, there was no getting around having to spend the night in the district capital. We returned to the grounds of the trade organization's Kronauburg wholesale market, but found the gate locked with a heavy chain and padlock. Two attack dogs leaped furiously at the chain-link fence, trying to get at us.

"The Hossu brothers stayed open in the evening and never had dogs," grumbled Ilja. We moved on to the Pofta Buna, where we gave the owner a few small bills to keep an eye on our horse and wagon overnight.

"I've never stayed in a hotel. You haven't either, have you?" I said.

Grandfather pretended to try to recall. "I can't remember at the moment. But do you have any idea what a hotel costs? It's not for the likes of us."

"I saw a place called the Golden Star on the market square. Why don't we ask the price of an overnight there? Without any commitment, of course. And besides, we can eat there, too. They've got a real restaurant and my stomach's starting to growl. And we saved money. We got our pictures for free and when the postman comes with your first paycheck from the T.O., we'll be in the clear."

Granddad thought it over. Of course, the relatives of his deceased wife, my grandmother Agneta, would have put us up as they always did when we had to spend the night in Kronauburg. But Grandfather wanted peace and quiet, not to have to talk to his in-laws. And besides, he was hungry, too. "Okay. Let's go back into town. It won't hurt to ask."

The prices at the Golden Star had been high even back in the days of the monarchy, when King Carol had stayed there. But they were much lower than Grandfather had feared. Although they were still exploiting its royal past to promote the hotel after it had been nationalized, the prices for rooms categorized as standard had been drastically reduced. At the hotel desk where his old ID was accepted without question, Grandfather paid for a double room.

It was a small but spotlessly clean room with colorful flowered wallpaper. The bed was freshly made up and had a scent unfamiliar to me. "Lavender," Ilja said appreciatively and pointed to the pillows where two tiny chocolate bars lay. In the bath there was a white enamel tub with two faucets that Granddad immediately tried out. Hot and cold. They worked perfectly. Two bath towels hung from a polished brass rod, and there was a pile of neatly folded hand towels on a shelf.

"Take a look at this!" Grandfather was beaming like a child. In each hand he held a bar of soap wrapped in gold foil. "Genuine

Luxor. We'll use one and take the other one home. That old Raducanu woman's going to be flabbergasted next time she asks for her
fancy soap."

We freshened up and, wary of the elevator, descended the stairs
to the second floor. We pushed open the double door labeled RES-
TAURANTUL, not suspecting what a powerful assault on our senses
awaited us within. The walls were painted a jarring orange that
clashed harshly with the blue carpeting.

"Would the gentlemen care for a table by the window?" A
waiter had materialized out of nowhere. He was wearing tails and
had a white towel draped casually over his left arm. I thought at
once of what my teacher used to tell us about the Paris of the East.
As far as the achievements of civilized culture were concerned,
Kronauburg certainly couldn't hold a candle to the capital, but at
least it could provide a foretaste.

"The window wouldn't be bad," I answered and saw myself
straightening my shoulders and jutting my chin out a bit. Like on
my new ID picture.

"If the gentlemen would please follow me."

Grandfather had already seated himself, but I allowed the waiter
to pull out a chair for me. While we contemplated the table with
its starched white tablecloth on which an impressive array of plates,
glasses, and small bowls already awaited us, I tried not to show how
impressed I was. As a barroom gofer, of course, I was not unfamiliar with the gastronomic profession, but the painstaking accuracy
with which these knives, forks, and spoons large and small had
been placed next to napkins folded into towering pyramids was
something else entirely. There was even a vase of red roses in the
middle of the table.

Ilja raised no objection when I took out a pack of cigarettes.
The waiter immediately stepped forward and gave me a light.

"What've you got to eat?" asked Grandfather.

"The gentlemen would like to see the menu? At your service!"

"Yes, please," I replied before Granddad could say something
else embarrassing and betray our humble origins. In a flash the
waiter was back at our table. He opened the menus and handed
them to us. Then he stood there waiting for our order. The guy
made me nervous.

"We need a little time." I again assumed the energetic expression and jutting chin Irina had taught me. It worked. The waiter silently withdrew across the blue carpet. In elaborate typefaces, the menu itemized suspicious-sounding dishes and dinners of several courses. In this establishment, there were culinary curiosities that apparently occupied the plate not *with* but *à la* something else, like "artichokes à la vinaigrette," which Grandfather was unable to imagine as something to eat. In addition, the prices were positively astronomical. But on the last page, under "Rustic Treasures from Our Folk Cuisine," we discovered the kind of thing our taste buds were longing for. Although the prices were still lordly, they weren't dizzyingly high. We motioned the waiter over, and Granddad ordered stuffed cabbage, pork chops, boiled potatoes, and sour tripe soup as an appetizer. "Same for him, and don't be stingy with the portions." The waiter suggested a draft beer with our order, which delighted Grandfather, since in our tavern we as good as never had any beer. I ordered a mineral water. I feared alcohol would make me sleepy, and I needed a clear head for the night to come.

Although Ilja was licking his lips after the meal and ordered another beer, he was still griping that Kathalina cooked better, but for a town meal it was not bad at all. I, on the other hand, insisted I had never dined so well in my life. As the waiter was removing our empty plates, he asked if the gentlemen would care for a digestif or an espresso, and now at last I could see how heavy and coarse and rude life in Baia Luna—where there was only one kind of glass for whatever you drank—must appear to someone from the city. Grandfather, who was acquiring a taste for beer, ordered another pilsner. "You won't find better service than here anytime soon, Granddad. Let me treat you to something good," I said patronizingly and ordered him a double *konjaki* Napoleon. He hadn't the foggiest what my real motivation was. A tipsy Grandfather falling fast asleep would be useful to me. I could slip out of our hotel room unnoticed.

The *konjaki* was served in a large snifter. I was familiar with such glasses: Stefan Stephanescu had been holding one at the birthday party of young Dr. Florian Pauker while he flirted with the hopelessly love-struck Angela Barbulescu. That was the very moment Heinrich Hofmann had pressed the shutter release. The proof of whom the woman in the sunflower dress was about to kiss had gone up in smoke in the teacher's living room. But that didn't mean the possibility of proving it was lost forever. From Irina Lupescu I had learned a bit more about Heinrich Hofmann. If anything in the world was sacred to the photographer, it was the negatives in his archive.

Grandfather yawned. The effects of the alcohol were showing. When the waiter called for last orders shortly before nine, Grandfather handed me his wallet and mumbled that I should pay up. Since I had no idea it was customary to leave a tip, all I got from the waiter was a surly "Good night," and he didn't bother to escort us to the door.

We climbed the stairs to our room on the sixth floor. To take advantage of the lovely opportunity, Granddad decided to have a short tub bath before going to bed. I lay down on my bed, resigned to wait.

As the clock in Saint Paul's Cathedral struck twelve, I was tying my shoes. Grandfather's breathing was even and deep. He was sound asleep. I put the room key into my pocket and pulled the door shut behind me. There was a night-light glowing in the hallway, and the carpeting on the stairs swallowed the sound of my steps. The night doorman was asleep on a chair by the entrance, his chin on his chest. I pushed the door, but it was locked. I shook the night porter awake.

"What's wrong?" The man jumped to his feet. "Nothing's going on out there. Everything's closed."

"I can't sleep," I answered and gave a little cough. "It's my damn asthma. When you're from the mountains, town air always bothers you. I need to take a walk to make myself tired."

"I know what you mean," the night porter replied sleepily. "I'm from the Schweisch Valley. The air's better there." He unlocked the door. "I'll leave the door open and the key in the lock. When you come back, turn it twice in the lock. Just don't make any noise and wake me up again with a lot of banging around."

The streetlights on the market square had been turned off, but I could orient myself well enough by the moon shining in a cloudless sky. I looked around. No light on in any of the buildings. Even what I guessed were the windows of the police station were all dark. I strolled leisurely past Hofmann's photography studio. I was worried that the airshaft in the back courtyard could be reached only from a street above the market. To my relief, however, I discovered a narrow alley a few yards to the right of Hofmann's display windows. I struck a few matches, went down it, and stopped before a door with a dozen doorbells and nameplates. The door wasn't latched tight, and I entered a foyer from which a passageway led out to the dark rear courtyard. I listened for a moment, but everything was still. Then I felt my way forward. On my left was the side of the building in which I guessed were the rooms of Hofmann's photo shop. I stepped on a metal grate. Beneath it there was an airshaft going down to the basement. I bent down to remove the grate. I could move it a little but couldn't lift it off. The brief flicker of one of my matches revealed that it would be impossible to get in that way. The grate was secured from below with a chain and padlock. I continued along the side of the building for two or three yards, then I was brought up short when my right foot found nothing to support it. It was a second airshaft. I lay on the ground, reached down into it, and felt a window. I pushed against it, and it swung open into the room. I guessed the depth of the shaft to be about a yard at most. I carefully lowered myself into it, pushed aside the black curtain, and found myself in Hofmann's darkroom. Slowly I groped my way to the door, felt for the switch above the lintel, and turned on the light. On the cutting table lay a pair of scissors and the remains of the photo paper on which Irina had printed our pass pictures. I opened the darkroom door, stepped into the basement hallway, and turned on the ceiling light. Heinrich Hofmann's holy of holies, the archive of negatives, was in the next room, Irina had said. I spied the iron door right away, pushed down the latch, and pulled. Nothing happened. I threw all my weight against the door, jiggled and tugged at the heavy latch until there could be no doubt: I would never get into the archive without a key. I was enormously frustrated. I should have thought of this before. If the negatives and pictures I hoped to find were in fact concealed behind this door, then Heinrich Hofmann alone would have access to it. I was certain he wouldn't leave the key hanging from a hook somewhere in plain sight.

I had rushed blindly into my crusade. What made me think

my opponents would fail to observe the elementary rules of their evil game: secrecy and caution? The only thing left for me to do was rummage through the innumerable cardboard boxes stacked to the basement ceiling on the uneven shelves that lined the corridor. I pulled out a carton at random: CODARCEA WEDD., KRONAUBURG 17.05.56 was written on the lid with a thick black crayon. I opened the box. Inside were wedding pictures. Another wedded couple emerged from GHERGHEL WEDD., KRONAUBURG 29.05.56, a pimply-faced groom and a bride you could have taken for his mother. In the carton ILIESCU WEDD. ANN., KRONAUBURG 04.10.55, an elderly couple had obviously posed for the camera on the occasion of their fiftieth anniversary. Under GEORGESCU-BUZAU WEDD., SCHWEISCH VALLEY, 28.04.57, the viewer could not help noticing that the betrothed of the very young groom with a tortured smile on his face had a big belly under her wedding dress.

I cleared away entire piles of cartons in order to at least spot-check the boxes at the bottom that had probably not been opened since the forties. But I didn't find anything but grooms staring straight into the camera while the brides were usually in profile, gazing up at their betrothed. Otherwise just parents of the bride, bridesmaids holding bouquets, children with baskets of flowers, large and small wedding parties with now and then a reception banquet or brides dancing with their fathers. And scattered everywhere among the wedding pictures, photos of party comrades and Heroes of Labor having medals pinned on them.

At the end of two hours all I had to show was the knowledge that Heinrich Hofmann demanded strict orderliness from his female employees. They were required to enter names, places, and dates on every cardboard box. I could have kept looking until the following evening; here in this corridor I was not going to find any evidence that the partners in crime Hofmann and Stephanescu used pornographic photos to silence people. Or make them talk. Or make them do whatever.

*"I let him take pictures of me." For a fee.* Angela Barbulescu had recorded Alexa's sentence in her diary. Back in those days, in the capital, her former friend had hinted that some men were ready to pay a lot of money to see such pictures. And some were willing to pay even more so that no one would see them. Alexa *spread her legs*

and let them take pictures, as Stephanescu had put it. Somewhere there were some photos like that of Angela. All those years in Baia Luna she had been terrified someone would slip them to the priest Johannes Baptiste. All those years, fear had kept her lips sealed. Heinrich Hofmann had shot the photos in the office of a doctor who had aborted the baby in her womb. Whatever they were like, my former teacher had not allowed them to be taken voluntarily. They had done something to her she didn't want done.

I sat down on a canister full of used lab chemicals. I had left traces in this corridor. Too many traces. Tomorrow morning at the latest, Irina Lupescu would discover that someone had broken in. Dejectedly, I lit up a Carpati. I imagined the doorbells jingling at this moment, and Irina descending the basement stairs in her clattering heels. My dear friend Pavel, she would say with a smile, here's the key to the negatives. Now Hofmann is finally going to get what he deserves. And that swine Stephanescu, too. I've canceled my engagement. I can't stand the sight of that Lupu guy. You and I will take care of these crooks.

I thought of Buba. What would she say now? What would her third eye see? I felt only that she was far away. I closed my eyes and saw Fritz Hofmann, but not in Germany. He was somewhere out in the world, on the go, harried and haunted, always searching. Fritz was always looking through a camera, like his father. When I opened my eyes again, I saw the carton.

Among broken picture frames carelessly jumbled in a corner, I could see the brown cardboard. I ground out the cigarette with my shoe and cleared away the frames. It was clearly one of the cartons Heinrich Hofmann had transported on his motorcycle when he moved from Baia Luna to Kronauburg. I pulled it out of the corner. It was heavy.

Well concealed among old wedding pictures, Fritz Hofmann had discovered the picture from the Christmas party in 1948, the one in which Alexa, wearing her friend Angela's sunflower dress, was spreading her thighs and Stephanescu was spraying a bottle of champagne. I tipped over the carton and stood before a disordered pile of black-and-white photographs. Among them lay a dozen yellowed paper envelopes. I pawed my way through weddings, weddings, and more weddings, all presumably from the early postwar era. Then I picked up the envelopes. Some bore the date 1946 or 1947. The photos had probably all been taken in the capital. Innocuous pictures of young people, shot in the summer. I guessed they were university students. They were strolling through town with their girlfriends, holding hands on park benches or in sidewalk cafés, flirting and making funny faces in front of the statue of the poet Mihail Eminescu. In some of the envelopes were photos Heinrich Hofmann had taken in the evening at parties. There was much laughter and more drinking. With only a few exceptions, the men had combed their hair straight back with pomade, had their arms around their girls, and were grinning into the camera. Angela Barbulescu was not in any of the pictures, which was logical, since she hadn't met Stephanescu until later. I recognized him in some of them right away. He was always in the center, with a cigarette in the corner of his mouth and usually surrounded by two or three attractive women. He clearly preferred blonds even then. I couldn't find anything lewd in any of the snapshots, however. But one of the pictures gave me a start. Stephanescu was lolling on a sofa with his arm around a smiling young woman. It wasn't the fact that his hand was clearly in her décolletage that surprised me, however. It was the woman's dress. It had a striped pattern. Angela Barbulescu had exchanged her sunflower dress for her friend's striped one for the Christmas party in 1948. But this picture was from the envelope labeled 1947. The pretty brunette with the full lips at Stephanescu's side could only be Alexa. The small glass in her hand was another proof of her identity. I knew from Angela's diary that Alexa stuck to liqueurs. I had always imagined Alexa as a wild and dissolute woman. It was hard for me to correct that image. The girl so breezily allowing Stephanescu to grope her breast seemed more like a pretty, somewhat-overexcited schoolgirl with the physical endowments of a woman.

My hands began to shake when I picked up the envelope dated December 24, 1948. That was the day of the Oh Unholy Night party at a certain Koka's house, the day that ended so disastrously for Angela. Hastily I tore it open. From the first photo a man looked out at me. He was just putting a cigarette to his lips and had a prominent wart on his right cheek. That had to be Albin, the stranger who paid Angela Barbulescu a visit on her last day in

Baia Luna. Dimitru's cousin Salman had picked up a man along the road with a wart on his cheek the day he brought the television to Baia Luna for Grandfather's birthday. The next photo was of a table spread with an expensive buffet. Koka had prepared his guests a huge grilled ham in which an oversize carving knife and fork were stuck. I didn't know what the curious things were piled in a pyramid on a silver platter next to the ham, but I guessed they must be the ominous oysters the host would pee on later that evening. The wager! Angela had mentioned a stupid bet between Koka and Albin about who could guzzle the most "Russian piss" in a minute. It had ended in a fight between the two contestants. Hofmann had captured the two with his camera, tilting vodka bottles into their mouths. Albin was the one with the wart, so the other must be Koka, the Communist Party functionary. He was the man who had insulted Angela Barbulescu so coarsely when she said the stupid drinking contest was a tie. He'd called her a cheap Catholic cunt, and her Stefan hadn't made a move to shut the creep up. Two other pictures showed Koka dancing while the onlookers applauded. The guy with glasses was probably the doctor, Florin Pauker. Alexa had taken his arm and was laughing. Her left hand was holding a glass of liqueur. She was wearing her friend's sunflower dress. There was only one picture from that evening in which Angela appeared, and she was in the background and out of focus.

Fritz Hofmann was the first to discover these photographs while snooping around in his father's moving cartons. What he told me just before leaving Baia Luna was true: when Alexa had lain down on the cleared-off buffet table and spread her legs, Heinrich Hofmann had snapped a few pictures. There were five snapshots of that scene. I put four of them next to one another and had no difficulty arranging them in chronological order. The only picture in which Stefan Stephanescu appeared was missing. It was in Baia Luna, under my mattress. Stephanescu must have removed himself from the dicey situation after the first flashbulb went off. Koka was also nowhere to be seen. I guessed that the hand holding a bottle and entering the picture on the right side belonged to the host. In the other photos, Alexa lolled on the table while Albin, the man with the glasses, and two others beat off.

As I put the photos from Christmas Eve 1948 back into their

envelope, my fingers felt another, smaller envelope taped inside the big one. I tore it open, clenched my fists, and gave a short whoop of triumph. Heinrich Hofmann had ignored the rule of caution. He had not protected his holy of holies. What I was holding against the ceiling light were the negatives. Although you couldn't identify much on them with the naked eye, I could make out a pair of female thighs on a deep black background. I knew that would turn into a white tablecloth on the positive. And the dark spots around Alexa's private parts were the light traces from the champagne foam spurting from the shaken-up bottle.

*Do whatever you want with my pictures.*

Heinrich Hofmann had taken some despicable pictures of Angela Barbulescu as well. Against her will. Whatever they showed, they now had no more role to play in the game of threats, blackmail, and murder, an evil game whose murky rules I could only guess at. Wherever those pictures were now—probably behind the locked iron door to Hofmann's archives—they had lost all their power over Angela. But the photo under my mattress whose negative I now carried beneath my sweater still had power.

*Hang my picture on every lamppost. I'm not afraid anymore.*

All I had to do was turn the threat around. Having his picture on every lamppost would not please the champagne squirter and party boss of Kronauburg, Dr. Stefan Stephanescu.

The muffled tolling of the bells of Saint Paul's Cathedral reached the cellar. I wasn't sure if I had counted four or five strokes. Whichever it was, time was short. Quickly I tossed the pile of wedding pictures back into their carton. Just when I didn't expect to find anything else, I did. I caught sight of an inconspicuous pack of photos held together with a single rubber band. They were the pictures for which the only words Fritz had at his disposal were "hard core," the ones that showed everything in the raw. They must have been taken more recently. I recognized one of Hofmann's salesgirls, the one who had been advising the young couple yesterday up in the shop. She had that unmistakable, glorious blond hairdo. I felt an unsettling mixture of repulsion, fascination, and powerful arousal. There were two or three different women, all of the same type, whom I had not seen before. Same for the men. For some of the pictures, Herr Hofmann had almost crept right into the woman's crotch with his camera; others were taken from a greater distance. I rushed my way through them. The beauty with the fluffy blond hair of an angel recurred. She was undressed and leaning over an older gentleman lying on a bed with his fly open. She was using her mouth. I knew the man. I was a hundred percent sure I had seen him before. But where? The harder I tried to remember, the more the image retreated into the furthest chambers of my memory. But the present was all the more vivid. When I looked at the background of the indiscreet photograph, I knew where the picture had been taken. The wallpaper in the rooms of the Golden Star had the same flowered pattern.

I had to go. I stowed the cardboard box back behind the picture frames, straightened up the cellar corridor a bit, knowing that my secret visit would not go unnoticed. I was about to climb out the lab window and back up the light shaft when I noticed I still had a big erection. I felt the need to relieve myself.

I opened my pants and thought about Irina Lupescu, whom I hadn't seen among all the women who'd let themselves be photographed. But then I realized I had put Heinrich Hofmann's assistant and Security Agent Lupu Raducanu's fiancée into an unpleasant if not dire situation. She was responsible for the darkroom in the basement. I stopped, buttoned up my pants again, and crawled out the window.

Five minutes later I opened the door to the hotel. The doorman was asleep. The clock above the desk said a quarter past five. I reached our room without encountering anyone else. Grandfather was asleep. I needed a cigarette. When I reached for them in my pocket, I discovered I had made a mistake. My matches and a pack of Carpatis lay on a canister of chemicals in Hofmann's cellar corridor.

After two hours of restless sleep, I was awakened by Ilja. He was groaning and complaining about a headache. "It was that *konjaki* Napoleon."

We did without breakfast, and on the dot of eight we were walking down the corridor of the state registration office with our ID pictures. The often-criticized bloated bureaucracy of the new republic and its sluggish and unqualified personnel were nowhere in evidence that morning. By eight thirty a clerk was handing me my new ID while remarking how stiff and serious I looked in the picture. Then she gave Grandfather his new ID to sign.

"I can read, but I can't write," he said. The clerk reached for an ink pad. "Happens more often that you'd think. You can sign it with your thumb."

Shortly thereafter we were sitting in the collectivization office in the room for State Trade Organization concessions A–D and drinking a Turkish coffee. An hour later, Grandfather had signed a contract for the concession of the Baia Luna branch of the Kronauburg regional grocers' cooperative. Moreover, he was no longer a private tavern owner but the possessor of a state liquor license to dispense spirits up to eighty proof. To be sure, only until 10:30 p.m. on weekdays and 9:00 p.m. on Sundays.

"How come the bureaucracy is finally getting its butt in gear?" Grandfather inquired as we were leaving.

The lady cleared her throat. "Let me put it this way: official efficiency has improved enormously since Comrade Dr. Stephanescu became first party secretary of Kronauburg. If you ask me, that man is a blessing for everyone."

I didn't ask her anything. How wrong that was suddenly came home to me just as we were entering the central warehouse of the T.O. to pick up our supplies at last.

"I wonder what the new prices are going to be," said Ilja. "The Hossus were always fair, at least."

The Hossus! Exactly! A few times I had caught a glimpse of the Hossu brothers when I accompanied Grandfather on his trips to the wholesalers. I didn't know their first names, but I knew their faces. I had seen one of them last night, but I hadn't been able to place him exactly. An older gentleman enjoying himself with a blond angel in a hotel room—certainly that could occur from time to time. But that he would voluntarily allow himself to be photographed in the act—probably not.

# Chapter Ten

●

## A FILTER CIGARETTE, A FLASH OF INSIGHT,

## AND MARY AND THE OCEANS

As our overloaded wagon crossed the bridge over the Tirnava in Baia Luna toward evening, the news that Botevs' shop had not just fresh but extraordinary wares for sale spread like wildfire. We hadn't even completely unloaded the wagon, and women were already lining up to replenish their household stocks of sunflower oil, salt, sugar, and flour. There was even—for the first time and especially for the ladies, as grandfather pitched it—lemon-scented dish detergent, tins of cream for delicate hands, and two vials of Rêves de la Nuit perfume, one of which Vera Raducanu purchased immediately, while the second bottle would remain on our shelves for years to come, until Dimitru the Gypsy and I finally found a use for it. But most sought-after were the bittersweet exotic fruits only the oldest residents could recall having seen (but never tasted) during the monarchy.

Ilja explained that the low but curiously unrounded prices, pre-scribed by state decree down to the last decimal, were the result of a national subvention policy he himself did not understand. His new status as an associate of the state cooperative provoked Hermann Schuster to make the malicious remark, "Now you're in league with the Communists, too."

Erika Schuster defended Grandfather from her husband's attack and told him to forget that awful political stuff and judge things by the bottom line. The village women agreed with Erika. But the children were deeply disappointed when Granddad explained that from then on there would be just fruit drops with raspberry flavor but no more genuine chewing gum. Since their sad juvenile eyes continued to weigh on his mind, however, he invented the fairy tale that a raging storm in the Atlantic had prevented the resupply ship from America from dropping anchor punctually in the Black Sea port of Constanta, but that it would arrive soon. He didn't tell them that the director of the Kronauburg trade organization had declared American chewing gum to be a decadent excrescence of capitalist consumer behavior, and as such it had been completely eliminated from their product line. From then on, the children still reached into Ilja's candy jar but despaired of getting at the raspberry drops melted together in a sugary clump.

All in all, people in Baia Luna were coming to the conclusion that times might not be exactly rosy, but they weren't black either. As long as the regime in the capital was lowering prices and the collectivists from Kronauburg hadn't shown up yet, although village life might not settle back into its old routines, at least there was an acceptable orderliness even without a priest, a Madonna, and an Eternal Flame. Of course, parents were not pleased that there was still no teacher for the school, but that too would certainly get straightened out in a year or two.

The cooperative model seemed to be paying off for our shop. Grandfather had paid with cash from our family savings for half the first batch of wholesale stock and gotten the other half on consignment, according to which he would pay for the rest once he'd sold it. If we subtracted the expenses of staying overnight at the Golden Star and eating in the restaurant, there was still some money left over. At my urging, before we left Kronauburg to return to Baia Luna Grandfather made a down payment on a piece of equipment that would enable us to bring some "cultural enrichment" to the monotony of life in the village: an antenna for the TV. Ilja's guess was correct that a functioning apparatus would considerably increase the attraction of our taproom, which had been flagging of late. As soon as the postman brought the first month's salary and it was time for another buying trip to Kronauburg, he would pay the balance for the antenna. And when Grandfather served the men fresh Sylvaner and a few cases of Kronenbräu to boot, even the most dyed-in-the-wool anti-Bolshevist had to admit that although Socialism in general was an instrument of the devil, it undoubtedly also had its good side. From then on, instead of playing cards in the tavern and rolling dice for the check, the men stared at the TV screen.

While the television noticeably bolstered Grandfather's reputation in the village, another matter was weighing heavily on my mind for a few days after we returned from Kronauburg. I avoided contact with my mother and hardly dared look her in the eye. In a quiet moment Kathalina had pulled me aside and with an angry glare made it clear that she never again wanted to find any filth under her roof. While airing out the bed in my room she had stumbled upon a photograph. She didn't even want to know where it came from. I turned red as a beet and wanted to sink into the ground for shame. Mother said that, of course, she had torn up the cheap piece of pornography then and there and thrown it into the woodstove. As far as she was concerned, that was the end of the matter, and she would never mention it again. Obviously she hadn't recognized the champagne squirter, Dr. Stephanescu, or any other man in the objectionable picture.

After a few days of shame, my relationship with my mother was restored to its normal footing. I could get over the loss of the picture. The negative, after all, was in my possession. However, that piece of film by itself did me no good. I didn't have the technical means at my disposal to print a positive from the negative. I was imagining eye-catching prints the size of the ones hanging in the windows of Hofmann's shop. But I had no plan for gaining access to the necessary lab equipment. The clock was ticking, however, against Dr. Stephanescu. I needed to be patient. I had to wait.

The first thing was to find a safe place for the negative, for Angela's diary (which I had temporarily hidden among the out-of-service schoolbooks in my backpack), and for the half-burned photo of the kiss that was still between the pages of Marx's *Das Kapital*. I took the picture out and looked at Angela with her ponytail. There was unquestionably a resemblance between her and Heinrich Hofmann's assistant Irina Lupescu, although Irina was certainly prettier in a conventional sense. But a beauty shone through from beneath the surface of the photo of young Angela Maria Barbulescu, blossoming only at the moment of recognition, beyond all desire. As I discovered for myself the precious beauty of the teacher's picture, I realized where it could be kept safe. If Pater Johannes's little silver key that I had taken from the board next to his wardrobe fit the lock I thought it did, then that place was the most secret and safe place for the photo and the revealing negative.

Once Baia Luna was asleep, I crept into the church and felt my way in the darkness up to the chancel and the wall beneath the extinguished Eternal Flame. In the flare of a match I saw the silvery metal plate with the images of bread and wine. It was the door to the niche for the tabernacle where Johannes Baptiste had kept the communion wafers. The key fit. Inside there was an empty goblet covered with a white cloth. I put the negative and the photo of Angela into the goblet, covered it with the green diary, and locked the niche.

The four-wheel-drive vehicle showed up in Baia Luna again at a moment when probably no one except me and Karl Koch was still thinking about Lupu Raducanu. Irina Lupescu's fiancé arrived with the policeman Cartarescu and three heavily armed militiamen. Cartarescu was wearing a new uniform with stripes and little gold stars on his epaulettes. They stopped on the village square, got out, and headed directly for our T.O. concession. I watched through the window as Cartarescu told the men with the Kalashnikovs to wait on the steps.

Grandfather hadn't even had time to ask, What do they want? and I knew the answer already. They'd come because of me. At the moment Lupu Raducanu ground his cigarette out with his shoe before entering, I knew the major of the Securitate was following the trail of the things I had forgotten on that night in Heinrich Hofmann's studio. It was a mistake to leave my cigarettes in the basement.

Raducanu and Cartarescu entered and greeted us.

"It's really nice to get out of the city in the summer," said the security agent. "Wonderful up here where you people live. We really appreciate the good air." He looked at me. "Especially if you stay in a hotel and can't get to sleep because of your asthma."

"What are you looking for?" asked Grandfather while Kathalina disappeared into the kitchen.

"Just a routine visit," said Cartarescu, who had been promoted to captain in the meantime. "General supervision of personnel. Your IDs?"

Grandfather took the new pass out of his billfold.

"You, too!" Cartarescu barked at me.

"Got to go up to my room and get it."

"Make it snappy!"

I ran up to my room, sat down on the bed, and took a few deep breaths. "It'll be okay, it'll be okay," I murmured as I heard in my head once more the voice of Buba's uncle Dimitru: You've got to stand the world on its head. I placed my pass on the counter next to Grandfather's. Raducanu reached for Ilja's ID first, regarded it impassively, then said only, "Yes, yes, the good old striped tie. Never out of fashion."

Then he took my pass. He turned his gaze from my face to the pass and back again. I stayed calm.

"Anything wrong?"

"All in order," answered Raducanu. "New photo, what? Why are you looking so serious in it? Photo Hofmann, right?"

I looked Raducanu right in the eye.

"Exactly. You're very well informed. My compliments. We just recently had our pictures taken there. It's my first real ID, the first time I've been photographed. Hofmann's studio, a fancy place, I'm telling you. They know something about photography. Even a blind person can see that."

I noticed that Raducanu's eyes were twitching, and his mind was turning over at a furious pace.

"Have you got an ashtray?" he suddenly asked, although there was one on the counter to his left. Grandfather pushed it over to the security agent. Raducanu fished a white Kent from his pack. "Want to try a good one? Filtered. From America."

I stuck out my chin. "Thanks, but I don't smoke."

"You should give it a try. They're really good. Don't scratch your throat like those Carpatis."

"Sorry, but I never smoke."

"Very admirable." Lupu Raducanu's smile looked forced. I sensed a growing threat. Everything depended on Grandfather Ilja. He knew I smoked.

"But to be completely honest"—I was risking my neck—"'never' is an exaggeration. Once I did smoke half a pack behind the school building with my old classmate Hofmanns' Fritz. You wouldn't believe how much I threw up. That cured me."

Ilja was silent, and I thought what a smart man my grandfather was. Lupu took another tack. He groped around in his pocket as if looking for his lighter.

"Got any matches?"

"Sure," I said. Instead of taking the pack out of my pocket I went to the shelf, tore open a fresh box of matches, and handed the Securitate major a pack stamped PEOPLE'S COOPERATIVE, KRONAU-BURG TRADE ORGANIZATION.

"You can keep them. Right, Grandfather?" I looked at Ilja.

"Sure, no need for him to pay. Of course not."

Raducanu changed color. He wasn't in control of the situation anymore. His pale face flushed, and his small eyes flickered. Then he started screaming so that his voice cracked. "You were down in Hofmann's basement! What were you doing there? I know you were down there! I'm absolutely sure!" Raducanu dropped his voice again. "You're young. But I guarantee that when they let you out of Aiud or Pitesti in five years you're going to look old. Admit it and I promise you we can work something out between the two of us."

I closed my eyes and held my hands in front of my face in a gesture that one could interpret as an admission of guilt. I felt Raducanu put his arm around my shoulder. "Everybody does stupid things when they're young." The security agent's voice had nothing threatening about it. "Believe me, I used to do a lot of crazy things myself."

I sobbed. "I admit it. I was down in the lab. But I promise I never touched her. Absolutely not."

Vexed, the security agent looked over at Cartarescu, who was so confused himself he didn't know where to look.

Raducanu took his arm away and snapped at me, "Who do you mean?"

"The lady, I mean, the pretty blond with the ponytail. She was so nice. And so I asked her if she would show me the lab, even though that photography stuff doesn't interest me. But I don't have a girlfriend, and since she was so beautiful . . . I had no idea she was already spoken for. If I'd known you were Irina's fiancé I never would have gone down to the basement. But word of honor: I only looked at her but didn't do a thing. Even though it was dark."

I had the impression that a mocking grin flitted across Raducanu's face.

"Their IDs are in order," Cartarescu announced and turned to the major. "I think we've accomplished what we came for. Let's go."

"Just one more thing. That television over there. Whose is it?"

"Mine," answered Grandfather brusquely.

"And presumably you can prove that?"

Granddad reached into his billfold again. "Here! The first payment on the antenna. And . . . just a second . . . the receipt for the TV, where'd I put it?" Then he opened the cash register and took out the receipt Dimitru had given him. "Here it is! All in order!"

Raducanu glanced at the receipt.

"Your shop seems to be prospering. Where did you come by so much money?"

Grandfather squirmed a bit, looking for an answer.

"If you don't reveal the source of the money immediately, we're going to confiscate the TV and take you along, too," Cartarescu threatened.

When Grandfather finally answered, I had to work hard not to show my astonishment. Grandfather was not just a smart man, he was a very smart man.

"Business," said Ilja softly. "Private deals." His billfold proved to be a real treasure trove. "Here's the new contract with the People's Shopping Cooperative. The supply situation is tip-top now. But the last few years, before Socialism, how was I supposed to pour a decent *zuika* for folks? You know yourselves that the supply chain is poor in the mountains. Everything comes to a standstill in the winter. You've got to wheel and deal a bit here and there. I had to do business with the moonshiners and, of course, I always made a bit on the deal. Over the years I put the money aside. For a TV. If I had to make a list of everyone who has a still in his barn, you'd have to arrest every man in the village. And if you absolutely have to confiscate the television, what are we going to do here? We hear nothing about the world up here in the mountains. Go ahead and ask around. When they broadcast Khrushchev's Sputnik speech about overcoming gravity and the victory of Socialism, my place here was full to bursting."

Cartarescu ticked off the violations: "Illegal production of alcohol, tax evasion, illegal sales. We're gonna confiscate the TV set!"

"Leave their set alone!" Lupu barked in annoyance at the new captain. "Do you think I've come all the way up here to catch moonshiners and confiscate televisions? You can kiss my ass with all this insignificant shit. By the way, where's that Saxon, that Karl Koch?"

Without saying good-bye, Raducanu stomped out of the shop. Outside, the three militiamen with their submachine guns fell in behind him.

Since the arrival of the four-wheel-drive vehicle, the farmers in the fields had laid aside their hoes and hurried into the village, Karl Koch among them. He was holding a list with the names of all the grown men of Baia Luna. The security agent walked up to him.

"Here's your damn list, you . . ."

"'Pretty boy'! 'Pretty boy,' that's the phrase you want, right, Herr Koch?"

Hermann Schuster elbowed his Saxon friend and hissed, "Just keep quiet."

Karl Koch shut up. Lupu Raducanu took the list and laughed. Then he ripped it up in front of everybody and threw the scraps over his shoulder.

"You son of a bitch!" Karl Koch exploded but was held back at the last minute by Schuster and Istvan Kallay.

"You're a real warrior." Raducanu grinned. "Even back in the day. Russia, right? You volunteered for the great campaign against the Bolsheviks. Were you as brave back in the old days as you are now, back then with the women and children in the villages by the Don, you Hitlerist?"

Karl Koch spat in Raducanu's face.

The security agent took out his handkerchief, nodded curtly to the militiamen, and said only, "Bring him along."

Hermann Schuster came running. "You can't just arrest people without cause. Even in this country you still need an arrest warrant."

"Show this man that everything's in order," said the security agent to Cartarescu. When the Kronauburg chief of police pulled out an arrest warrant, the men of Baia Luna knew that Karl Koch's fate had already been decided. Cartarescu took care of the formalities: "Herr Koch, you are accused of resisting an organ of the state, anti-Socialist propaganda, and disturbance of the peace. We hereby take you into investigative custody."

Koch tore himself free from Hermann Schuster and Istvan Kallay, but before he could go for Raducanu's throat, the militiamen trained their rifles at his chest.

"You can shoot me on the spot, but you're not taking me to Pitesti!"

"But who said any such thing, Herr Koch?" Raducanu stepped right up to him. "Wait until you've had your hearing. Maybe you're innocent and you'll be back with your family before you know it."

As the representatives of state authority drove off with Karl Koch, Grandfather was in the shop complaining of sweats and nausea. Kathalina went to prepare cold compresses; then she saw her father-in-law lying on the floor. He had tipped sideways and fallen off his chair. After a while he opened his eyes again, and I had to tell him everything that had happened in Baia Luna in the past hour. There was a gap in his memory.

At noon on a Saturday in the middle of the summer, the Gypsies set out for the big horse market in Bistrita; just as I was locking up the shop and starting to sweep the steps to the front door I spotted their covered carts crossing the bridge over the Tirnava. I dropped the broom and took off running. I caught up with the caravan in a few minutes. Gasping for breath, I ran to the middle of the column where Buba and her mother Susanna sat in the open rear part of their wagon. From a distance Buba looked like a boy with her short black hair. She waved madly as if she had been longing for this moment. When her mother spotted me she started pummeling Buba with her fists. I was just able to press something into Buba's hand. I had no breath left to say anything but her name, but Buba cried out, "I'll wait for you!" before her mother pulled her back into the wagon. I stood there until the Gypsy caravan was lost in the distance. In Buba's closed fist was a little ID picture showing an earnest young man in a jacket and tie.

Desperately sad, I dragged myself back to the village. I would not feel such pain again until decades later, when I became aware that my love for her was drowning in a swamp of hopeless misfortune.

Dimitru Carolea Gabor had remained behind in Baia Luna with Ion Vadura and his family. He was the man who kept an eye on the Gypsies' settlement while they were traveling. Dimitru had tried to explain his reluctance to travel by the urgency of his researches, but since he could use only his hands and feet but not his voice, he had met with incomprehension among his tribe. His self-imposed silence necessarily precluded talking to his own people as well as to Grandpa. Dimitru was hardly ever to be seen in the village. Sometimes he shuffled to the watering trough to get himself a jug of fresh water. The sight of him aroused the sympathy of Erika Schuster and my mother, so the two of them took turns cooking an extra midday meal and setting it on the doorstep of the library to keep Dimitru from starving to death.

Grandfather was also undergoing a disconcerting change in those months. Although the times of economic hardship seemed to be coming to an end, his health was not good. The silence of his friend Dimitru weighed heavily on him. He could hardly get up in the morning and went to bed so early in the evening that I was forced to take over his duties in the shop and tavern if our business was to stay afloat. He was sunk in a slough of depression, and even my encouraging words or Kathalina's tirades of scolding would only briefly lift him out of his lethargy. We gradually began to be seriously concerned.

Working in the business was so demanding that the summer and fall flew by in a flash, even though I grieved for weeks when the Gypsies returned in late summer without Buba. Though I had hoped that her mother would change her mind, I'd never really expected her to.

Our inventory needed restocking for the winter. Since I didn't want to subject Grandfather to the strain of a long trip in the wagon, I asked Petre Petrov to come with me to buy supplies in Kronauburg. When we reached the compound of the Kronauburg trading organization there was a long line of concessionaires waiting to pay for their purchases. It turned out that because of their restricted hours of operation we would have to wait until the following morning to get our supplies. We decided to spend the night on the hay of the Pofta Buna and have a few beers in town with the money we would save. As a precaution I avoided the immediate vicinity of Hofmann's photo studio but not of the Kronauburg market square. I had no intention of risking running into the lab assistant Irina. On the lookout for a cheap pub, Petre and I strolled up the medieval Castle Hill. Below the clock tower Petre discovered a shop that appeared to be still in private hands. A sign hung there that said GHEORGHE GHERGHEL. ANTIQUES BOUGHT AND SOLD. ON COMMISSION. In the shopwindow, which hadn't been cleaned in years, there were various optical instruments on display: antique monocles, old army-issue field glasses and rifle scopes, spyglasses, and even a big telescope on a tripod. Petre was fascinated by the old scopes. Although I was his friend, I'd had no idea he and his father sometimes went out hunting at night with a carbine.

"Let's go in here."

I expected an aged gentleman with snow-white hair, but instead a young fellow just a little older than myself asked if he could help us. While Petre had the clerk show him the rifle scopes from the window, only to be disappointed that even the used instruments far exceeded his financial resources, I took a look around.

I discovered what I wouldn't have expected in my wildest dreams. Among piles of radios with tubes, a gramophone, and used typewriters stood an enlarger.

"How much for that?"

"I'll have to ask my uncle," said the clerk. "He's sick. But I know he won't sell that separately. Only the complete darkroom set. The whole thing belonged to a retired judge who spent all his free time crouching in the underbrush to take pictures of reclusive forest animals. He died last spring."

"When can you find out the price from your uncle?"

"Right now. He lives one flight up and he's in bed. He's . . . ah, how shall I put it . . . sick in his head. I have to tell you that we don't own the building. The owner has sold it to a big shot in the party. And since Uncle Gheorghe found out he'll have to move out of here and won't be able to find any other place because he's a private dealer, he's been brokenhearted." The young man disappeared and was back in a few minutes. "Gheorghe is sleeping, and I don't want to wake him. But I'd guess the whole thing, with a camera, would be about three thousand."

I swallowed hard. That was half a year's salary for my grandfather.

"But Uncle Gheorghe's not a highway robber. If he likes you he'll sometimes sell you something for less than he paid for it himself. But I'm sure he wouldn't sell it for less than two thousand. Come by again when he's awake and ask him."

I didn't fool myself into thinking I'd ever be able to come up with the money.

Around six o'clock Petre and I went into a bar. It was a rundown dive whose interior was just as shabby as its exterior led us to expect. The grimy gorilla of a bartender had dandruff in what was left of his sparse hair. But since our thirst and weariness were greater than our desire to look for another place, we sat down at a table near the window.

"Is there beer?" asked Petre.

"But of course, gentlemen."

The bartender opened two bottles, wiped off the lips on his apron, and put them on the table. Then I saw the two women. One of them was slumped over the bar and dozing; the other was looking at us. It was only a matter of time before she came over.

I hadn't even set the bottle down after my first swallow and there she was in front of me. She wore a cheap dress that was much too tight around her buttocks and breasts.

"I'm Luca. Mind if me and my colleague join you? Just for a little. For somebody to talk to. She's from the capital and doesn't know anybody here."

We looked at each other, and since we didn't say no right away, Luca called, "Come on, Ana. These guys are okay."

The other woman almost fell down as she slid off the bar stool. She tried to walk straight, but she swayed right and left and had to steady herself on the chairs.

"Actually, we don't want—"

I cut Petre off: "Have a seat." It was like a punch in my gut: the woman who could hardly walk straight wasn't named Ana. She looked like someone with nothing more to live for. Her right eye was black and blue, and when she forced herself to smile you could see past her cracked lips that she was missing two upper teeth. There was nothing left of the child-woman who once let Dr. Stephanescu squirt champagne between her legs. Petre slid over, and the drunk woman collapsed on a chair while Luca squeezed in next to me.

"I'll have a beer, too," she said boldly. "And a liqueur for my friend if you guys are paying."

I ignored the request. "Hello, Alexa."

"Her name's Ana." Both Luca and Petre corrected me at the same time.

I'd expected a surprised reaction, but the woman just looked at me wearily. "Ana, Marina, Elena, Alexa—whichever you want, boy."

The bartender brought over another beer and a water glass half full of liqueur.

"Ana's only been here since November," Luca explained. "She had her best years in the capital, right, Ana? Isn't that what you said?"

Alexa nodded weakly and sipped her liqueur. Then she put her trembling index and middle finger up to her mouth, and I offered her a Carpati. She inhaled eagerly and gazed off in a dream.

"She's had too much," Luca whispered to me as if it were a secret.

"I gotta take a piss." Petre stood up, and the bartender pointed to a door with peeling paint. Alexa reached for her glass again, and I got up and put my arm around her. There was only one way for me to get through to this woman. I whispered something into her ear that I would regret only a second later: "Angela's sunflower dress looked good on you."

In a flash, the woman beside me was gripped by fear. Her glass fell to the floor and shattered. She jumped up and stumbled out the door. Luca rushed at me, but I ducked her slap. "What'd you say to her, you fucking pervert?" Then she ran out after her.

"What happened to the ladies?" asked Petre as he noticed the glass shards and sticky mess under his feet.

"They left."

"Thank God. Shall we have another beer?"

"I've had enough." I wished Luca's slap hadn't missed.

. . . . . . . . . . . . . . .

$A$s the fall progressed, it became clear that it had been a mistake for Grandfather to stop following the advice of Dr. Bogdan, who had passed away in the meantime. The country doctor had warned Ilja over the years that because of his childhood poisoning in the vat of mash, his delicate constitution couldn't stand even small amounts of alcohol. Dr. Bogdan had been right. Although he very seldom got the shakes, his memory was beginning to fail him.

It started with him taking an order from one of the housewives and then standing blankly in front of the shelves, not recalling what he had meant to get. Kathalina noticed that her father-in-law, who used to be able to find his way around the world of numbers blindfolded, now often made mistakes to his own disadvantage when adding up the accounts receivable. Women began asking for me when they wanted quick service, while Grandfather retreated more and more into an imaginary world because he couldn't cope with the real one.

For the men, too, Ilja wasn't the same old tavern keeper anymore. They often had to ask him three or four times to refill their glasses, and although he did so politely at first, he began to get more and more cranky. He even started losing his temper and cursing like a trooper if anyone dared to speak to him when he was sitting in front of the TV. At first he only watched the news and Soviet movies, but gradually he started watching everything that flickered across the screen, even the test pattern at the end of the day. Another of Grandfather's quirks was that the television could never be turned on before six o'clock, the official closing time for his T.O. concession. My mother and I could live with that, especially since Grandfather also had days of mental clarity now and then, days on which he was his usual, congenial self.

However, Kathalina's patience ran out in 1960 when a powerful autumn storm snapped off the antenna. Granddad wouldn't leave his seat in front of the idiot box and kept pulling his chair closer and closer. Every time the black bar slid down the screen he clapped like a child and cried, "There it is again! There it is again!"

In our despair at the change in Ilja's character and his increasing senility, mother and I went to talk to Hermann Schuster. The only thing he could think to do was to pack Grandfather into the wagon and drive him to the hospital in Kronauburg to be examined. I insisted on going along with Grandfather and the Saxon, partly from real concern but also partly because I wanted to take the opportunity to visit someone in the hospital: Dr. Paula Petrin.

In the presence of the specialists in the department of neurology Ilja was fortunately granted one of his rare moments of clarity. He understood that something was wrong with him and he would need to be admitted to the hospital for a period of observation and examination. It was agreed that we could pick him up again in six weeks.

As Hermann Schuster was heading for the exit from the People's Hospital, Health of the Fatherland, I asked him to give me five minutes. Without waiting for his reply, I scooted down the steps and followed the sign for the Institute of Pathology until I reached the yellowish door that said DR. MED. PAULA PETRIN, SPECIALIST FOR INTERNAL MEDICINE. I knocked.

"Yes?"

I entered. The doctor looked up from a desk piled high with files.

"What is it?" she asked. I sensed none of her former congeniality.

"Pavel Botev. From Baia Luna. Three years ago three of us were here looking for the corpse of our dead pastor, Johannes Baptiste."

Paula's face brightened.

"Yes, of course. I remember you very well. I sent you to old Patrascu."

"We went to see him. But he didn't know anything about the body either."

"Nice of you to come by again. Unfortunately I'm under a lot of pressure at the moment. In a half hour I have to be putting an important report onto our director's desk. Your pastor was Catholic, not Reformed, right?"

"Exactly."

"As far as I know, Catholic priests are not buried in their parishes but in the episcopal cemetery. I haven't been in Saint Paul's in a long time, but there's a cathedral treasury, a kind of museum, in there, and from the treasury there's a passageway that leads to an interior courtyard with the graves of priests and bishops. Maybe that's where your pastor is. Sorry, but I've got to get back to work."

"Many thanks for the tip." I turned toward the door. "How's the old police commissioner, by the way?"

"Didn't you hear? He's dead. Good old Patrascu was only able to enjoy his retirement for two or three weeks."

"What did he die of?"

"His heart gave out. He probably smoked too many Carpatis."

"Did you examine the body?"

"No, why should I?"

Hermann Schuster agreed at once to take a detour past Saint Paul's, and we found the cemetery just as Paula Petrin had described it. The oldest gravestones went back to the eighteenth century. The most recent grave was relatively new. The dirt had settled, and it was bordered with irregular stones. Chiseled onto the simple gravestone was JOSEPH AUGUSTIN METZLER, 16/3/1872–12/11/1957.

"Strange," I said. "Almost all the stones have the birthplace and the place of death. Pastor Metzler's doesn't even say what parish he served."

"Curious," agreed Schuster. "This Metzler died about the same time as our Baptiste."

As we left the cemetery, any hope that we could clear up the disappearance of Pater Johannes's body disappeared.

Fourteen days later, a white ambulance drove into Baia Luna. It wasn't the fact that Ilja Botev had been released from the hospital earlier than expected that raised a stir in the village, but the splendid way the State Trade Organization apparently looked after its members and even provided them with transportation free of charge.

Grandfather got out smiling and waving. "I'm cured!" he called.

Kathalina, who seldom expressed her joy in a physical way, threw her arms around her father-in-law and began kissing him. Ilja was bursting with praise for the skill of the doctors in Kronauburg, especially a neurologist whose name he couldn't remember. Grandfather said he had felt completely healthy for the first three or four days after his arrival at the hospital, and none of the doctors could find anything abnormal. He even overheard one of them use the word "malingerer" as they were talking out in the hallway. But then he had a strange attack he had no memory of. The doctors later kept referring to it as "gran moll." Granddad said that one morning after tea with white bread and marmalade, he'd had a kind of flash in his head. Afterward he must have uttered a piercing scream, gone into spasms, and fallen to the floor. He'd turned blue and bitten his tongue without feeling any pain. When he woke up his tongue had hurt terribly, but that wasn't as bad as his embarrassment at not having controlled his bowels during the seizure. But that was normal with this illness, the doctors had told him after they saved him from choking to death.

"I had to put on an oxygen mask and they gave me shots. When I could talk again, they told me I was lucky not to be living in the Middle Ages or even earlier."

"Why?" I asked.

"Back then they thought epileptics were possessed by the devil, and they drilled holes in their heads to let the evil spirits escape. Today they have medicine for it. If I take my tablets regularly—they have this stuff in 'em, something like 'fennyteen' and 'mazypeen'— the attacks may not stop completely, but they'll be under control. That's what the nerve doc with the glasses said. He was real educated and knew everything about my illness. They used to call it Saint John's disease because people prayed to that apostle to make the seizures stop. But today they know that something doesn't flow right in the brain when you have epilepsy. People used to think it was caused by the moon. Lunacy. Even the Romans talked about *morbus lunaticus*. It's right there in the Bible, the doctor told me. Gospel of Matthew, chapter seventeen."

Kathalina didn't hesitate. She dug the Holy Bible out of the corner and handed it to Ilja. He leafed through it awhile, then he read without stumbling, "Lord, have mercy on my son: for he is lunatic, and sore vexed: for ofttimes he falleth into the fire, and oft into the water. And I brought him to thy disciples, and they could not cure him. Then Jesus answered and said, O faithless and perverse generation, how long shall I be with you? How long shall I suffer you? Bring him hither to me. And Jesus rebuked the devil; and he departed out of him: and the child was cured from that very hour. Then came the disciples to Jesus apart, and said, Why could not we cast him out? And Jesus said unto them, Because of your unbelief: for verily I say unto you, If ye have faith as a grain of mustard seed, ye shall say unto this mountain, Remove hence to yonder place; and it shall remove; and nothing shall be impossible unto you."

In the following days it often happened that even I wanted to read the Bible, but Ilja always said, "Me first." Reading the word of God became his new obsession. It burned almost as strongly as his yearning to redeem his friend at last from his night of silence.

The key to that feat was provided by an event on April 12 of the year 1961, only ten days after the Feast of the Resurrection. My mother had turned on the TV early in the midday break prescribed for family-run concessions. Just like every Wednesday, the state television network in the capital was broadcasting the half-hour show *The Homemaker: Simple Meals in a Jiffy!* In the studio kitchen the head chef of the Athenee Palace Hotel would demonstrate how to conjure up delicious and economical meals from just a few ingredients with a modicum of culinary skill. Kathalina liked the show less because she was trying to put some variety into her cuisine than because she liked the chef, who made her laugh. He had a strange brand of humor and way of expressing himself. Every so often he would put his little finger into the pot, lick it off with closed eyes, and groan in pretended perplexity, "There's still still still something missing." Of course, he would suddenly discover the missing ingredient on the kitchen table and exclaim with contrived astonishment, "It's here here here after all!"

While Mother laughed at the chef, Grandfather sat on the bench next to the potbellied stove, groaning. He'd begun reading the Old Testament, had finished the books of Moses, and moved on through Joshua, Samuel, and the books of Kings to First Chronicles. When at last in the sixth chapter, after endless genealogies listing when who begat whom with whom, he got hung up at the sons of Manasseh and became so furious he hurled the sacred book across the room.

"Who in God's name came up with all this boring shit? Who can keep it all straight?"

Kathalina turned away from her TV chef only long enough to remark casually, "When Pater Johannes preached, he always made the Bible interesting. Why not read what his patron saint put down on paper back then?"

Grandfather followed her advice, retrieved the Bible, and

turned to the last book of the New Testament, the Revelation of Saint John the Divine. For some unfathomable reason that Dimitru would later call intuition, he didn't begin to read the Apocalypse at the first chapter but at chapter 12. At the precise moment that Grandfather realized what was written there in the first two verses, the midday break ended.

As I was turning the sign on the door to OPEN, Ilja jumped up as if stung by a thousand wasps and staggered around in euphoric intoxication. He rejoiced and raised his fists in triumph as if he had won a hard-fought battle. At first I thought the lunatic madness had seized Grandfather again. Just as when he'd been fascinated by the black bar on the television screen, Granddad shouted again and again, "That's it. That's it," his index finger playing a staccato rhythm on Revelation, chapter 12. "The proof! That's the proof!"

"Shush! Quiet, dammit!" Kathalina turned up the TV.

"We interrupt our popular program *Simple Meals in a Jiffy!* for an important announcement. Following the successful flight of the Sputnik in 1957, the Union of Soviet Socialist Republics has reached another milestone in the history of mankind. Air Force Major Yury Alekseyevich Gagarin has today become the first human being to fly into outer space. Today, April twelfth, 1961, the cosmonaut spent one hundred eight minutes in weightlessness aboard the spaceship Vostok 1. In the meantime, Gagarin has returned safely to earth. We congratulate our Soviet friends on this epoch-making accomplishment and announce the broadcast of a special program at eight fifteen this evening: *Yury Gagarin—Man Conquers Space.*"

Grandfather's high spirits at his discovery in the Revelation of Saint John suddenly changed to pure horror. "Come with me," he said, took his Bible, and ran to the rectory. Without knocking he stormed into the library where Dimitru was staring at an impenetrable pile of books with disheveled hair and bloodshot eyes. He'd lived in hermitlike silence for three years and five months without saying a word.

"Here! Read this! Revelation of Saint John. Chapter twelve, verse one!"

Dimitru obeyed like someone without the strength to contradict.

"'And there appeared a great wonder in heaven, a woman

clothed with the sun, and the moon under her feet, and upon her head a crown of twelve stars: And she being with child cried . . .'"

Dimitru wept. He wept in the arms of his friend Ilja.

"Papa Johannes knew it," said Dimitru softly. "And now we know it, too. The woman clothed with the sun. If she has the moon under her feet, that means . . ."

". . . that she must be standing on the moon," Ilja finished the sentence.

"That's it. That's the proof. Now my heart is light. That's why the Virgin of Eternal Consolation had to disappear."

"What do you mean?"

"My dear friend Ilja, I rememorate the Madonna's face exactly. The puny Baby Jesus! Oh, and those great big breasts of hers, but her delicate feet, too. Those feet! That's it! The Madonna is standing on a crescent, a crescent moon! The tale about how Baia Luna came to be is a mistake. An *error fatal* everybody fell for. The crescent moon doesn't stand for the victory of the Christians over the Mussulmen. It's a symbol of Mary's Assumption! That old sculptor knew that. You see? That's why the Bolsheviks swiped the Virgin from the Mondberg. So their propaganda for converting mankind to atheism could run smoothly. There should be nothing left to remind us that the Mother of God is on the moon. Mary is the sovereign of the moon."

"Incredible," said Ilja. "Why didn't we think of this before?"

"Because we hadn't studied the Holy Scripture. It's the source of all knowledge, the source Papa Baptiste always drank from. What more proof do we need than the word of God in person?"

Grandfather shook his head. Dimitru looked toward the ceiling, illuminated to the furthest corner of his soul by the light of understanding. Then he threw his arms around Ilja, who returned his friend's joyous, noisy kisses with equal delight.

"I talked! I said something!" cried the Gypsy suddenly, realizing that his spell of silence was finally broken. In graceful, almost weightless hops he danced across the books that lay scattered on the floor. I interrupted.

"Soon there will be more to say, Dimitru. The situation's critical. Korolev's project is entering its final phase. He's not sending up dogs anymore. Gagarin was in space. They're going to show the proof on TV soon."

"Well, what are we waiting for, then? *Tempus fugus!* We're just wasting time here." Dimitru locked the library and marched over to our house, arm in arm with Ilja. Kathalina was overjoyed when she heard "Greetings, my dear" coming from the Gypsy's mouth, and I squeezed in a "You're finally back among the living again!" amid the general rejoicing

"Right"—Kathalina laughed, wrinkling her nose—"but before the living accept you there's some urgent hygiene that needs attending to, Dimitru. You smell awful." Mother turned on the boiler to heat water for the tub. Then she sent me to Hermann Schuster to announce Dimitru's rebirth and ask if he could lend us some hand-me-down pants, a shirt, and a jacket from the wardrobe of their oldest son Andreas. After his bath, she jockeyed Dimitru onto a chair on the porch, grabbed her scissors, and gave him a haircut amid howls of laughter from the village children.

"But the beard stays!"

When Kathalina joked that without a beard he'd be even more irresistible to the ladies, Dimitru replied, "Do you think the Children of Israel would have followed Moses through the Red Sea if he hadn't had such a magnificent beard? Never! It was on account of his beard, not despite his beard, that the old guy never went to bed alone."

Grandfather chimed in with "Read your Bible, Kathalina, and you'll see what a clan Moses begat." It was obvious that Dimitru Carolea Gabor was his old self again and his friendship with Grandfather Ilja was as strong as ever.

By seven o'clock, the best seats were taken in front of the television. By seven thirty the taproom was full to bursting. The sensational announcement promised for eight fifteen was preceded by a lengthy introduction. Even people who could see through its propagandistic purpose had to admit that it had been put together in a fiendishly clever way.

A slow, leaden funeral march introduced the report. By the end of three measures it gave you the foreboding sense that something truly important was about to be buried forever. On the darkened screen there suddenly appeared an oversize image of an American dollar bill. A solemn voice intoned, "This money wants to rule the world," followed by a dramatically beating kettledrum and then a drumroll. "But who is behind the money?" At that question, the sorrowful music became even more sorrowful, and short film clips followed one another in seemingly random order: dark-skinned chauffeurs held limousine doors open for cigar-puffing capitalists, unemployed workers with hangdog expressions waited in line at locked factory gates. One was even barefoot. We gaped in amazement as a stout movie producer in knickers pinched a starlet with swelling breasts in the behind, followed by dozens of police nightsticks raining blows onto an unarmed black man. The high point of tastelessness was when a peroxided blond positioned herself on purpose over a ventilation grate and it blew her skirt up above her bottom so everyone could see her panties. Then came a smooth operator who beamed while being kissed by a pack of half-naked women wearing silly rabbit ears. All of a sudden the music got so loud and shrill that some people in the tavern held their ears. To wild guitar chords some crazy screamer jerked his hips back and forth. Then he yowled something unintelligible into the microphone while young girls screamed ecstatically and stretched out their arms, straining to get to the animalistic guy. Dimitru sat with one leg over the other, swinging his foot to the rhythm, but then the music stopped abruptly. We saw American students lounging on a university campus and chewing gum.

"Are these young people supposed to inspire the human spirit and advance progress?" asked the voice of the announcer as whispering and then exclamations broke out in the tavern. A rocket stood on a launchpad, and someone began to count in English—five, four, three, two, one—and then some more words we didn't understand. A gigantic ball of smoke and flames shrouded everything. A title appeared on the screen: "Launch of the Vanguard TV3 satellite, USA, December 6, 1957." The rocket slowly lifted off, then it fell sideways and exploded. "America's dream is a nightmare," said the voice. Cut.

Then came Tchaikovsky. The beaming Yury Alekseyevich Gagarin waved for the cameras. A lot of cameras. Then another picture of a rocket on a launching pad, tall as a castle tower. The name of the space capsule, Vostok, means "the East." The name alone would annoy the Americans. Countdown in Russian, 9:05 a.m., Moscow time. Again, smoke and flames. Fantastic launch. A perfect dream of a vapor trail. Higher and higher. Gagarin's voice: "Looking at the earth. Good view. Everything normal. Everything functioning excellently. Still flying. Mood optimistic. Everything running well. Machine working normally. Looking into space."

Cut and flashback. Scenes from his career: Gagarin, from a poor farmworker's family, son of the people, diligent, ambitious, looking ahead. The pupil Gagarin, the student of mathematics, the party comrade. Gagarin the scholar, Marx and Lenin under his arm. The air force major, always the best, always with distinction, everything maximal. Cosmonaut, Hero of the USSR, first man in space, weightless, immortal. Enough Gagarin.

Khrushchev appeared on the screen. Superior, self-assured, jovial. Waved a telegram from the American president. Kennedy sent congratulations, spoke of noble aspirations of mankind and even offered the Soviets his cooperation. Explore the heavens together? Khrushchev smiled and shook his head. Who wanted to make a deal with losers? The viewers already knew the Americans couldn't cut it. Then Khrushchev shaking hands, patting backs. He took Gagarin's hand, raised it into the air. "Well done, Yury!" Storm of flashbulbs. A historic event.

Then the crucial question: "Tell me, Comrade Yury, did you see God up there in space?"

"No," Gagarin replied.

"Good question from Nikita," remarked Nico Brancusi.

"Good answer by Yury," added his older brother Liviu.

Nobody from Baia Luna contradicted them. The special broadcast was over. Ilja turned off the TV. His guests went home as though nothing earthshaking had happened. Only Grandfather, Dimitru, and I remained in the tavern.

"Don't you agree it's time for a little glass again after my epoch of abstinence?"

I got up. But unlike past years when I served Dimitru as the taproom gofer, now I put the Gypsy's bottle of *zuika* onto the table in my capacity as barkeeper. "On the house."

"Man, Pavel." He looked up at me. "You've turned into a real man."

To my astonishment and Ilja's, too, the Gypsy drank just one glass.

"It's not looking good for America," said Grandfather. "Their rockets are no good. But I think Khrushchev made a mistake."

Dimitru nodded slowly. "Oh yes, my friend, that he did. A *grande error fatal.*"

"If the Yanks are smart," Grandfather continued, "they know by now why the Russians are sticking cosmonauts into rockets."

"But the Americans aren't smart. They're just lucky that Nikita is dumber than they are. He's so stupid he broadcasts every fart of progress on his project to the whole world instead of waiting until the final blow can be struck. The Russkies aren't on the moon yet. They haven't got the Madonna yet. The question about God came too soon."

"Much too soon," said Grandfather. "The Yanks already smell a rat. How many billions you think they're going to fork over now to prove there's a God in heaven after all? They're not about to get caught with their pants down and then have to burn all their dollars."

"Absolutely exact," Dimitru confirmed. "Khrushchev blabbed too soon. A cardinal sin. He fell into the trap of vanity. *Superbia* is well-known *causaliter causalis* as the essential source of human stupidity. I bet Korolev knows his president is pretty much of an idiot. But that's politics: some people have the knowledge; others have the power. That's what happens when proletarians instead of intellectuals rule the world."

Grandfather scratched his head. "To summarize: the pope's dogma certifies that Mary the Mother of God was transported bodily to heaven. And she's on the moon; God himself guarantees it in the Revelation he revealed to Saint John the Apostle. Now the decisive question is, What will the Bolsheviks do when they find the Madonna?"

"That, Ilja, my friend, is the question of questions. And I can only think of one answer if I stick to the laws of logic."

"And that would be?"

"The Soviets will reverse the Assumption. They'll return the Madonna to earth."

"And then? They won't do anything to her, will they? They wouldn't kill her? Or would the Bolsheviks not even draw the line at killing the Mother of God?"

"They wouldn't kill her, for sure. Korolev's no stupid Marxist; he's a clever Nietzscheist, if you know what I mean."

Grandfather shook his head.

"Doesn't matter. Listen: if they bring Jesus's mother back to earth, then Korolev will draw the logical conclusion that God exists even if Gagarin didn't see him out the window of his rocket. But if God exists, then Engineer Number One can forget his project to become God himself. And he will not touch a hair on the head of the Mother of God, much less have her snuffed out by the Securitate. 'Cause then he'd have to kiss good-bye to the eternal life Jesus promises after death. There's no point at all for a Madonna killer to even think about detouring past God's throne on Judgment Day. He can save himself the trouble and go straight to hell."

"Makes sense to me," said Ilja. "But what does Number One do with Mary here on earth?"

"He lets her go. With his good wishes. She's free to run through the streets in broad daylight claiming to be the Mother of God. If she's lucky, people will laugh at her. If she's not, she'll end up in one of those psychiatrical nuthouses for the rest of her days. And Korolev can claim he meant well and wash his hands in innocence like that Roman Pontius Pilate."

I yawned and remarked that it was well beyond official closing time. Dimitru handed me the opened bottle and asked me to put it away until tomorrow evening. Meanwhile, Grandfather fetched a glass of water to take his epilepsy tablets.

Although I went up to my bedroom without having untangled the nonsense Dimitru and my grandfather had discussed, I did have an idea. The longer I thought about it, the more I saw a way I could put the wild notions of those two to my own uses.

When Dimitru arrived at the tavern the following afternoon, ambitious to get going, I steered him and Grandfather into the kitchen and asked them to have a seat. Then I hung the CLOSED sign on the door, took out Dimitru's bottle of *zuika,* and sat myself down at the kitchen table. I got right to the point.

"Do you have any idea how big the moon is? One thing we learned in school, in physical science, was that it's about two thousand one hundred fifty miles in diameter. That's about a quarter of the earth's diameter."

"Really?" Grandfather was surprised. "That's pretty big."

"Voluminous, in other words," observed Dimitru. "You wouldn't think so from here."

"Exactly," I said portentously. "And that's going to be a problem for the Soviets."

"What kind of problem?"

"If I understood you yesterday, you're both convinced that the Madonna has been living on the moon since the Assumption and the Soviets intend to bring her back to earth."

"That's right." The Gypsy nodded. "And that rocket scientist Korolev is behind it all. A cunning materialist. Earth to earth. And since you're so well informed, Pavel, promise you won't tell anyone."

"Word of honor."

"Good. Our mission is to warn the Americans. They have to get to the moon first—in anticipation of the Russians—and protect the Madonna, see?"

"I understand. But that's where the difficulty lies, as I see it. In the size of the moon. Russian or American, it makes no difference, they'd both have to spend years looking for the Mother of God. Like finding a needle in a haystack. And maybe they'd never find her, if she goes into hiding."

The two of them looked at each other. You could tell from their expressions that they were following me.

"From that I conclude," Grandfather submitted, "that we have to more or less know where the Mother of God is located before we can write a letter to the American president or set off across the Atlantic."

"Exactly how I see it," I said.

"Man oh man." The Gypsy groaned. "The stuff you have to

keep in your head. But how are we supposed to find out where the Mother of God is? From down here you can't see a thing with the naked eye."

"I think I know a way to make the distance sort of shrink and bring the moon closer."

Four eyes stared eagerly at me as I let the cat out of the bag: "You need a telescope."

The recommendation had the intended effect. I mentioned that just such an optical instrument was on display in an antiques-shop window in Kronauburg. Dimitru and Ilja were itching to get going. I continued that in addition to the telescope, the mentally ill antiques dealer by the name of Gheorghe Gherghel also had photographic equipment—including a camera with lenses. At first the pair of them didn't see the use of such an apparatus, but they went completely nuts when I explained that although you could find the Madonna with the telescope, you needed a camera with film in it to have visible and lasting proof in the form of a picture.

Dimitru started performing one of his dances of joy again until Grandfather brought him back to earth.

"If you've been to this shop already, Pavel, did you ask what the whole shebang would cost?"

"It's fairly inexpensive, considering the quality. Fifteen hundred or two thousand at most. For everything. Complete."

Grandfather stroked his chin and nodded. "Sorry, but I don't have that kind of money. I'd have to save for at least a year."

Dimitru swore. "What a dope I am. Why did I have to keep silent all those years? That meant I couldn't hawk those relics. You really can't unload stuff like that without talking, you know."

Then Ilja snapped his fingers. "I have an idea how to get some money. But I don't know if you'll get mad and stop talking to me again, Dimitru."

"Never again in my life will I be angry at you for anything."

"Your birthday present to me—we could sell it. You know, the TV."

"You'd do that? Sell my present to you? You'd really do without the set so we can foil Korolev together?"

"It'd be worth it to me."

As the sun rose the next morning, I was sitting on the wagon box. Grandfather and Dimitru were sitting back in the wagon, their arms resting on a crate covered with a blanket.

We reached Kronauburg early that afternoon. I drove the wagon to a square at the foot of Castle Hill, not far from the clock tower. After I'd made sure that Gherghel's Antiques Bought and Sold still existed and the telescope was still in the window, I hauled the heavy TV into the shop.

"Hang on, gentlemen," called out a man in his seventies with snow-white hair. "I'm not buying anything more."

Dimitru pulled the blanket off the set, and Mr. Gherghel put on his glasses. He gave it an expert, appraising look.

"Whew, you don't see something like this very often. A wonderful set. A dream. Top-notch quality. Loewe Optalux, from Germany. The Germany in the West, mind you . . . but you're too late. I'm really not buying anymore. By the end of next week I have to move out of this place. I've got a clearance sale on right now."

"What would you have paid for it if you were still in business?" I persisted.

"A set like that would have just about brought me to the limit of my financial capacity. Sixteen, maybe eighteen hundred. If that's not too low for you. And, of course, only if you can prove where you got it. I never took anything from customers without a receipt of sale. At least, nothing expensive. If I'd received stolen goods, I'd have one foot in Pitesti already. But as I said, I'm not buying anymore. I'll be happy if I can get rid of the rest of this stuff."

I looked around to make sure all the objects of my desire were still present. Then I ticked them off: "That telescope in the window, the camera with the lenses, and the darkroom equipment with everything included—trays, paper, chemicals—what would all that come to?"

"All together? Do you have that much?" Mr. Gherghel thought it over. "Around two thousand. That's really more than fair."

Grandfather jumped in. "Let's make a deal: we'll trade. The TV for all that stuff. Is that fair, too?" And he put the sales receipt onto the counter.

Gheorghe Gherghel was speechless. He went to the stairs leading to his private rooms and called for someone named Matei. His nephew came right down and recognized me from my first visit.

"Hello! Are you still interested in the enlarger?"

Before I could answer, Matei's uncle said, "Take a look at this TV. We can have it in exchange for this optical stuff. What do you think?"

The only thing Matei said was "Then you wouldn't have to be bored to death staring out the window all evening long."

A quarter hour later, none of us had the slightest doubt that Gheorghe Gherghel was not just an honest but also a happy man. When we mentioned that we lived in the mountains, he threw in a somewhat-battered but still-functional radio set with a green dial. Matei asked if my friend from the last visit was still hot for one of his rifle scopes. When I answered, "Absolutely," he added one of his army-surplus ones to our pile. "No private party's going to buy these anyway, since they've made hunting illegal." While I was imagining Petre Petrov's shouts of joy, Gheorghe Gherghel took the telescope out of the window and explained that it had an achromatic lens according to Kepler's principle with an impressive magnification factor.

Dimitru asked, "Will an unchromed lens work for the moon, too?"

Gherghel was momentarily at a loss, but then he assured him that the instrument was positively designed to see even the smallest details on distant celestial bodies. "You're in luck. Along with the telescope I'll give you an old map of the moon by an astronomer named Giovanni Battista Riccioli, a learned Jesuit from Italy. The map's from the middle of the seventeenth century. It's not the original, of course—that would be priceless—but it's a good modern reproduction. It will help you get oriented in your lunar studies."

As the friendly antiques dealer unrolled the 1651 map *Maria et Monti Lunae,* Dimitru froze in astonishment. Then he shouted for joy. "Maria and the mountains! That scholar, that Jesuit monk, already saw Mary three hundred years ago. On the moon! And with a simple telescope!"

"Who? Who did Riccioli see?" Gheorghe Gherghel shook his head.

"The Virgin Mary. The Mother of God in person. That astronomer found her."

"How in heaven's name did you come up with that?"

"Right there!" Dimitru tapped his finger on the map. "It's right there in black and white: *Maria et Monti Lunae.* According to my modest knowledge of Latin (thanks to Papa Baptiste, God rest his soul), that means 'Mary and the mountains of the moon.'"

Gheorghe Gherghel slapped his thighs and held his tummy, he was laughing so hard. "You folks up in the mountains are really loony. God in heaven, what a bunch of linguists. Maria! Maria! I couldn't figure out what you meant! *Maria* is the plural of *mare.* And *mare* means 'sea.' The first astronomers took the dark spots on the moon for seas. That's where they got the names Mare Australe, Mare Imbrium, Mare Vaporum: Southern Sea, Sea of Showers, Sea of Vapors. Now we know those seas are really giant deserts of stone, but we kept the names. And all the seas together are the *maria,* with the stress on the first *a: mária,* not *maría.* It's the language of science, but how would you know that?"

Piqued, Dimitru cleared his throat, but he and Grandfather were still completely convinced that what was behind the identity of the Latin names for "seas" and the Mother of God was anything but a coincidence.

## Chapter Eleven

### MARE SERENITATIS, TWELVE WHITE DOTS,

### AND A LITTLE PLAYACTING

So as not to attract any attention, I hauled the optical equipment into Baia Luna under cover of darkness and stowed it away in our storeroom. Ilja and Dimitru were burning with impatience to set up their telescope, and what place was better suited to look for Mary on the moon than the peak of the Mondberg, Moon Mountain? They would have liked to set out on their expedition immediately, but for days clouds came up every afternoon and obscured the stars at night. Nevertheless, the two of them didn't sit idle. To familiarize themselves with the terrain of earth's satellite, they bent over the map *Maria et Monti Lunae*. Using pencils, rulers, and compasses, they made various calculations in order to be ready to identify potential locations for Mary even before looking through their telescope. Once Dimitru had translated all the entries on the moon map with the help of a Latin dictionary, he came to a conclusion.

"Mary is enthroned in the Mare Serenitatis."

"Where?" asked Grandfather.

"In the Sea of Serenity. We can exclude all the other seas."

"How can you be so sure? The moon is a big place," Ilja objected. "Mare Imbrium, Mare Humorum, Mare Nubium. The blessed Mary could have landed anywhere after her Assumption. That means we have to look everywhere except for Mare Moscoviense. She would go out of her way to avoid the Russian Sea."

"I agree." But then the Gypsy definitively excluded other locations as well. "Do you really think she would be celebrating in the company of the twelve apostles in a place as inhospitable as the Oceanus Procellarum, the Ocean of Storms? Or would the teeth of the Mother of Our Lord be chattering in the frosty Mare Frigoris? Or worst of all"—and Dimitru held his nose—"in the miasma of the Mare Vaporum or in the Palus Putredinis, the Swamp of Decay?"

"You're both crazy!" Kathalina was amused at first. But gradually she became really concerned about the mental health of the two friends and, finally, completely irritated. "The both of you are hopeless cases. Since Johannes Baptiste left us, your heads are full of nonsense. Mary on the moon! I pray the village gets a new priest soon who can bring you back to earth from your delusions of heavenly flights."

To their objection that they had the highest authority behind them: a papal dogma and the biblical word of God in Revelation, Kathalina replied she had no doubts about the truth of the Bible and the church, but she did about the influence of the Holy Ghost. Instead of illuminating the minds of her fellow men, it obviously was befogging their brains. "Only boneheads would come up with the idea of swapping a wonderful television set for an old radio and all this other useless junk."

Despite my mother's annoyance, the radio became Ilja's and Dimitru's connection to the world. It delivered the latest news directly into our taproom. To be sure, only such reports as had been filtered through the state censorship office and embellished by the rank imagination of the propagandists. In addition, the information suffered some diminution in transmission by the outdated technology. After tinkering with it for a while, I discovered that the radio set had no difficulty in receiving broadcast signals, just problems in reproducing the tone. Dimitru conjectured that the plus and minus poles of the speaker magnets had possibly exchanged places while being transported on the jolting horse-drawn wagon. The defect was evident in the fact that the radio would sometimes deliver the very best quality sound for hours on end before suddenly starting to chatter again or fall completely silent for brief but decisive moments. The irritated Gypsy would snap the fingers of his right hand while continuously turning the dial with his left, which got on Kathalina's nerves so much that she regularly pulled the plug from its socket.

Shortly after the triumph of Gagarin's spaceflight for the Soviet Union, we heard the news that Grandfather's beloved America not only built inferior rockets but also was a bad actor on the world political stage. Ilja cocked his ears as soon as he heard the name Fidel Castro. Dimitru turned up the volume as high as it would go. America had obviously tried to topple a revolutionary revered in the circles of the Transmontanian Workers' Party. Because Castro had chased all the capitalists out of Cuba, was proceeding apace to proletarianize the island, and now also had a pact with the Soviet Union, the USA was gearing up for a counteroffensive. If the newsman was to be believed, counterrevolutionary Cubans had been lured to the USA with a few lousy dollars, there to be armed to the teeth and sent back to Cuba to fight against their own compatriots. In the end, what exactly was happening in Cuba remained a mystery, since the radio started acting up again. But at least Grandfather and Dimitru had repeatedly heard the name of the American president who had already sent Khrushchev a congratulatory telegram after Gagarin's spaceflight. Apparently, this John Eff Kennedy had also ordered the storming of Cuba to bring its citizens American liberty, which, however, was not appreciated on the island of revolutionaries. As far as Dimitru could determine, Fidel's rebel guard had thrown all the invaders into a bay with pigs, whereupon my grandfather, who knew his Bible inside and out, merely remarked that Jesus had also once exorcized demons and commanded them to enter some swine that proceeded to throw themselves into the sea and drown. For me, the news contained a kernel of truth: Kennedy's people had botched the overthrow of Castro. Logically enough, Ilja and Dimitru wondered if the Americans were not just smart enough to see through Korolev's secret plan but also had a strategy to defeat it.

"It's high time," Grandfather postulated, "for America to respond."

And it did respond. On May 25, 1961, the president of the United States gave a speech to Congress of utmost urgency for the nation. He spoke of the coming battle between freedom and tyranny from which, no matter how it ended, America would emerge victorious. As it would in the struggle to conquer space. Kennedy proclaimed, "This nation should commit itself to achieving the goal, before this decade is out, of landing a man on the moon and returning him safely to the earth."

Before Ilja and Dimitru could comprehend their good fortune, a radio commentator demanded their full attention. The chairman of the Transmontanian State Council Gheorghiu-Dej, a staunch supporter of Moscow, was going to speak in person. In a disquisition on the international political situation, he declared that the USA's delusions of grandeur with respect to the conquest of space were in inverse proportion to its terrestrial failures. Kennedy had only announced his utopian plan to fly to the moon in order to create a stir nationally and internationally and distract attention from his Cuban disaster and his private sex scandals. When Dimitru heard that Kennedy's compulsive infidelities with a constantly inebriated starlet who also took drugs had weakened him politically, he clapped his hands in joy.

"The Bolsheviks are getting cold feet. They're getting nervous. Now their bloodhounds are sniffing around in the president's bedroom. When the Russkies have no other ideas, they always go for the balls. But a man who's determined to get to the moon won't get tripped up by peccadilloes with women. Believe me, Ilja, if anyone can stop Korolev, our John Eff can." Dimitru suddenly stopped and slapped his forehead. "Man, Ilja! This story about the president's girlfriend! It's a divine coincidence! On Radio London they're always talking about some Marilyn. You know what that means in translation? Marialein, Little Mary! Mary and John Eff! 'John' is short for 'Johannes.' Eff: Evangelist! John the Evangelist was the only person to whom the woman on the moon appeared. Understand, Ilja?"

"The Yank gets it!" Grandfather was ecstatic. "Kennedy's started his counterproject. He wants to go to the moon. And he knows that time is short."

"I'm guessing John Eff is going to throw the on switch for presses to start printing money. A moon flight costs a lot of dollars. If I understood the news from London, America's even hired a German to build its rockets. Wörner Brown or something like that. I'm telling you, when a German has a hand in something, it's going to work."

"If America's got a German on their side," my grandfather summed up, "Korolev's holding a bad hand."

"You can take that to the bank. Pavel, *zuika*!"

As always, the evening news closed with the weather forecast.

For Friday, May 26, and the following days summer temperatures and clear blue skies were predicted for the Carpathians. At once, Ilja and Dimitru ran to the door. The stars twinkled in a clear night sky. There would be a full moon in two days. What could be more perfect for their telescopic observations than the last days of the Mary month of May?

Next day the two of them had me explain how to set up the telescope and use the camera, film, and flashbulbs. They asked my mother to pack them supplies for a few days. After Dimitru suggested that peering through the telescope's eyepiece for long stretches could cause eye strain and necessitate concentration-enhancing beverages, I added a couple bottles of schnapps, although I felt the stirrings of a bad conscience. After all, I was the one who had enabled the two Mariologists in the first place by taking them to Gheorghe Gherghel's shop.

"Don't forget your loony pills," Kathalina razzed them.

In the evening, the pair set off.

At about midnight they reached the chapel where the Virgin of Eternal Consolation had once stood. In a clearing between the rocks they set up camp, rammed the tripod into the ground, and mounted the telescope on it. They thanked the powers of heaven for their clear view of the bright, almost full moon and followed up with a supplication that the Mother of God not shrink from the telescope's glassy eye. When it came to deciding who should look through the telescope first, the two started quarreling. Each wanted to let the other go first. Finally Ilja aimed the instrument in the direction of the moon.

The moment Ilja pressed his own orb against the eyepiece of the Keplerian telescope, he departed this earth. His mouth agape in astonishment, he entered the space between times. Studying the lunar map had been worth the effort. The Jesuit Giovanni Battista Riccioli had done his work well. What Ilja was now seeing conformed in every detail to the astronomer's cartographic record. As if his spirit were bridging heaven and earth, he floated between the chasms and ravines of monumental mountain chains, flew over wrinkled ridges and corroded crests, and glided above endless desert wastes. Gray-shadowed plains opened before him, punctuated by jagged walls and piles of reddish-brown rocks. In between

emerged what looked like the branchings of dry riverbeds, towering crater walls, round or oval, some like gigantic maws, others
without number as tiny as the head of a pin. Ilja recognized the
crater named after the Roman historian Pliny. It lay in the north of
the Mare Tranquillitatis, the Sea of Tranquility, where it bordered
on the southern edge of the Mare Serenitatis.

"I've got it!" Ilja cried.

"What?"

"The Sea of Serenity."

"What's there?" Dimitru stopped shivering with cold and
started trembling with excitement. "Can you see her?"

"No. Take a look yourself!"

"That's really it. The Mare Serenitatis. But all I see is stones."

The question "What do you see?" and the answer "Nothing"
would be repeated often in the course of the next four nights, but
with longer and longer pauses in between. Since their eyes were
smarting, they would spell each other every half hour. To no avail.
When the moon sank below the dark horizon, they would talk
awhile to confirm there was nothing to talk about. Otherwise,
they encouraged each other not to grow impatient—anything but
that. With the first rays of the rising sun, Ilja would walk down
to a little spring to quench his thirst and take his epilepsy pills
while Dimitru permitted himself a few glasses of *zuika* so he could
sleep through until evening. On the last day of May, a Wednesday
(they had long since run out of bread, sausage, and bacon), they
decided to stick it out for one more night, until Thursday, the first
of June, despite their growling stomachs, aching backs, and bleary
eyes. When at last night fell and the moon rose, Dimitru uncorked
the last bottle of plum brandy. Because Ilja complained that looking through the telescope was making him dizzy and he was getting black spots in front of his eyes, Dimitru—his speech already a
little slurred—called him a stubborn mule who should go to bed.
Whereupon Grandfather crawled into their tent.

Dimitru kept watch. His eye was glued to the ocular, watching the Mare Serenitatis even though his dry throat was tortured
by thirst. From time to time he would nod off for a few seconds
and tip over to one side, then start awake again and force himself to
keep looking until at last he was overcome with the impression that

the moon was beginning to gently rotate. Dimitru spun along with it, dipping into the cascading colors of the rainbow bay Sinus Iridum, growing intoxicated by the purple of the Palus Somni, ecstatic at the geometric purity of the Taruntius crater's concentric circles. From the Mare Humorum he roamed westward, passing the Sea of Clouds and reaching the Mare Nectaris, turned north until his eye crossed the Plinius crater and returned at last to its starting place, the Sea of Serenity. He took a last swallow of *zuika* and mustered what strength he had left to keep his eye to the telescope.

And just as twelve faint strokes from the distant Apoldasch church reached his ear, he saw her. In the middle of an unprepossessing crater on the southwestern edge of the Mare Serenitatis, she flared up, her shining face turned toward the earth. And surrounding her on the edge of the crater, arranged like the numbers on a clock face, stood the twelve apostles. From their open mouths issued the angelic *Salve Regina, Mater misericordiae.*

Dimitru was weeping with happiness when he suddenly remembered his mission. He mounted the camera onto the telescope, fired the flashbulbs to light up the night sky, and took one picture after another. Then he collapsed, drunk on *zuika* and even drunker on bliss, embracing the telescope in his arms like a lover after a night of love.

Grandfather woke him as the sun was almost at noon.

"Well?" he asked.

Dimitru said only, "Ilja my friend, our expedition is a triumph."

While Grandfather packed up the telescope and the camera with its precious film, Dimitru fetched the grazing Percheron and hitched it to the wagon. Then they headed for home.

I saw her. *Sine dubio.* She appeared to me just as she did to Saint John the Evangelist," said Dimitru, handing me the camera. "It's all in there, Pavel. Now we need your services. Are you sure you can turn the film in this thing into a real picture on paper?"

"No problem." Although my curiosity was roused about Dimitru's photographic results, I was feverish to finally develop the picture whose negative was hidden safe and sound in the tabernacle of the Baia Luna church. "I'll get right to work on it tonight," I said.

Since Grandfather and the Gypsy were completely ignorant of technical matters, they left setting up the darkroom to me. When I said I would need running water for the lab, Dimitru had the idea that I could refit what had been Fernanda Klein's laundry room in the rectory for my purposes. It had been standing empty for years.

Setting up the darkroom didn't cause me any significant difficulties. The previous owner had kept his enlarger in good working order and also saved all the instructions. I had conscientiously studied the explanations in them. Under cover of night, I carried the equipment into the laundry room in the cellar of the rectory, hung the windows with dark cloth, set up the enlarger on an old ironing table, and made sure the timer and the light source were working. Then I followed the instructions for mixing soda, sodium sulfide, Metol, and fixing salts with water and poured the developer and the fixer into their respective trays. Then I turned on the darkroom light and opened the packages of photographic paper.

To my disappointment, most of the packs had already been opened. They contained exposed photographs of no interest to me, although they revealed a lot about the passions of their former owner. Brown bears and stags in rut fighting over territory were clearly some of his favorite subjects. Unfortunately, however, very few unexposed sheets remained for my own enlargements.

I took out my most precious possession, the negative, which I had previously retrieved from the church. I clamped the strip of film into the film carrier and turned on the enlarger light. I turned a crank that raised the enlarger head high enough that the cone of light spread out to poster size. I focused the image, turned off the light, and put an experimental piece of paper into the easel. Since I had no idea how long to expose the image, it took me a few tries to find the right value.

Two hours later I was looking at the fruits of my labor: five photographic posters hung from a wash line in the rectory basement. Two of them got spoiled during the drying process. That left three. The enlargements showed Dr. Stephanescu with pomaded hair, spraying champagne between the naked thighs of a woman in a sunflower dress while a man I assumed to be Florin Pauker was masturbating in the background. These three enlargements would be a bombshell. Their explosive power would topple the party chief

Stephanescu from his pedestal. *Hang my picture on every lamppost,* Angela had written in her diary. I knew an even better place to present the Kronauburg party boss to the public. Intoxicated by the thought of my successful crusade, I made a mistake.

Dimitru's pictures of the Madonna still needed to be developed. As I was taking the film out of the camera, the sudden memory of what the lab assistant Irina Lupescu had told me hit me like a club: even the smallest bit of light would spoil the film. I was holding Dimitru's film in my hands and realized with horror that the lamp was still on. The last glimmer of hope that a bit of detail might still be recognizable blinked out as I pulled the film from the developer. The strip was as transparent as glass, which meant that the positive would be nothing but a black surface. But there was no way I could show my face to Dimitru and my grandfather with such a thing. I considered what to do. Their belief that they had captured the Mother of God on film was nothing but the cuckoo idea of two crazy but harmless old men whose notions were arcane but not dangerous. Should I disappoint them? Or should I make them happy with a bit of photographic sleight of hand? Dimitru had claimed he saw what Saint John had described in Revelation. As well as I could recall, a sign had appeared in the heavens—a shining woman with the moon beneath her feet and a crown of twelve stars on her head. I had to get something like that onto paper.

I searched my pockets for all the change I had: a big ten-cent piece and about a dozen smaller aluminum coins. There were only four photo papers left in the pack, all the size of a postcard. I put an unexposed piece under the enlarger and placed the big coin right in the middle, then I scattered the other coins around it. I snapped on the enlarger light for just a second or two and then put the paper into the bath of developer. After just a few seconds, it turned black with a round white spot in the center, surrounded by smaller white dots. I repeated the procedure with the other papers, washed them in water, and waved them in the air until they dried.

Grandfather and Dimitru were still sitting at the kitchen table. They had waited all night. Dimitru was panting with impatience. "Well? And so? Did they turn out?"

"Depends," I answered. Then I put the four black photos with white dots on the table.

Dimitru froze. "What's that supposed to be?"

"I don't know what you shot up there on the Mondberg," I replied coolly, "but it does look remarkable, somehow. Could be the moon and stars. But maybe the flashes were too bright and overwhelmed everything else."

"But that's not the Madonna." Grandfather was also deeply disappointed. "What'd you go and photograph, Dimitru? You said you saw her."

"I did see her, I swear I did. I really saw her."

"And what did your Madonna look like?" Dimitru didn't detect the sarcasm in my tone.

"Beautiful! She looked just beautiful. Madonnas always look beautiful."

Dimitru stood up. Disappointed, disconsolate, and dog tired, he shuffled back to the Gypsy settlement and went to bed. For seven days and seven nights he buried himself beneath the covers and exuded such an air of bitterness that even his own people didn't dare speak to him.

When he finally emerged from his lair on a Saturday morning, he frightened the Gypsy children and not just them. Dimitru's lush black beard had turned gray. He set off for the library where he hadn't set foot since the end of his vow of silence. Books still lay scattered about, and the air was still pregnant with the stale odors of rumination. Dimitru pushed back the curtains, threw open the windows, and started airing it out. Then he set about putting all the books back on the shelves. Once he had transformed the chaotic mess into a model of order, he returned to his tribe, sat down on a chair in the warm June sunshine, and called for the women. He asked them to remove on the spot anything about him that reminded them of the biblical Moses, and the women obeyed. Fifteen minutes later, he was rid of his magnificent beard. When that was done, he climbed into the bathtub and had them scrub his back and towel it dry. Then he doused himself with Tabac Oriental, slipped into a white shirt, put on the black suit he usually wore only on business trips, put a wide-brimmed hat on his head, and strolled over to his friend Ilja's house.

Kathalina, Grandfather, Aunt Antonia, and I were sitting in the kitchen, and we all did a double take when Dimitru walked in.

"Unbelievable!" said Antonia. "What a fine handsome fellow you are!"

Kathalina too was mightily impressed. "It looks like you've finally gotten some sense in your golden years. Sit down and have a bite."

When the women had cleared the table, Dimitru said, "Ilja, I was an idiot. I thought the Blessed Virgin would conform to the laws of optical instruments. Can there be a worse error? How can an intelligent person even assume the Madonna would allow herself to be conjured onto a piece of paper in some chemical brew in a laboratory?"

Grandfather fetched the pictures with the white dots. "Just look, Dimitru! Look at this! It doesn't look so bad. When you saw the Madonna, was she very bright?"

"Like a shining sun."

"And the apostles—were they there, too?"

"Like the stars on her shining crown."

Ilja tapped the photos excitedly with his finger. "Man, Dimitru, that's it. In the middle, the white circle—that's her. Right in the middle of the black darkness, you see? But she's so bright she just outshines everything else. All around her, those little dots, those are the apostles. The pictures are proof for those who can read the language of signs."

Dimitru pricked up his ears. "Interesting. What you're saying has some merit." Then he counted—to eleven. "There's a dot missing. There ought to be twelve. Twelve apostles, twelve white dots. But I only count eleven."

"Exactly, I noticed that, too." You could read the excitement in Grandfather's face. "Since I started reading the Bible, I've been thinking logically. You should, too, Dimitru. There should be eleven apostles, not twelve, and you know why?"

"Tell me!"

"At the Last Supper Jesus had twelve gathered around him. But we have to assume his Mother up there on the moon doesn't want her son's betrayer anywhere near her. Judas is number twelve, and logically, he's not there."

"*Sic est!* I agree. I bet the traitor is sitting up there in the Mare Moscoviense cursing his thirty pieces of silver." Dimitru went to stroke his beard but realized he was grasping at thin air. "You're a smart fellow, Ilja. Nevertheless, we have to be reasonable. To people with the eyes to see, this photographic paper only proves what they already know. But the blind remain blind."

"You're probably right," admitted Grandfather. "So what should we do with the pictures now?"

"Forget the photos," I broke in on their feckless conversation. "I found a new station on the radio. It's the best insider tip so far: shortwave, 3564 kilohertz, Radio Free Europe from Munich. You don't need to save the world anymore 'cause the Yanks are building a monster of a spaceflight center in Huntsville, Alabama. And they've named a man to be director of all the other engineers who's supposed to be better than your archenemy Korolev. And you know who the new American rocket director is?"

"Wörner von Braun," said Dimitru, "a German."

"Wow, you're really up-to-date! Wernher von Braun's his name, all right. Do you know anything else about him?"

"How could I? The announcer on Radio London always yaks too fast."

"I told you, Radio Free Europe is better. Anyway, this von Braun understands something about rockets. He was Reich Engineer Number One under the Führer. Now he's an American citizen and believes in God like every good American. His wife confirms it, and by the way, her name's Maria."

Grandfather and Dimitru were fidgeting. I took out a piece of paper. "Here, I wrote it down so I wouldn't forget what von Braun said on the radio: 'Above all, we must honor God who created the entire universe. Day by day, in deep reverence, man continues to explore and tries to understand it with his science.'"

"The German really said that?"

"Guaranteed, although a few years back, he built fairly nasty rockets for the Hitlerists. He seems to have cleaned up his act. Maybe he has something to atone for?"

Dimitru moved his head to and fro. "Cleaned up his act, you think? Could be. But Germans are sly and never forget. Wörner von Braun still has an account to settle with the Bolsheviks now that he's been forced to resign from the Thousand-Year Reich. Wörner won't forget that he was liberated and had to scrap his lovely rockets. I bet Wörner von Braun would stop at nothing to keep the Soviets from raising their hammer-and-sickle banner on the moon just like they raised it on the Reichstag. That must still rankle."

Grandfather's commentary: "And that's why the Americans know they won't find anyone else in the whole world to build them better rockets than this von Brown German."

"Right. On the radio they also said that Kennedy had pressed a few billion dollars on von Braun to build a gigantic Saturn rocket that will overshadow all the rockets the Soviets have managed to construct up to now."

"I'll draw the *conclusio*," said Dimitru, reaching out his hand to Grandfather. "Congratulations, Ilja. America doesn't need us anymore. We've carried out our mission."

"What a shame," sighed Grandfather. "I wanted so much to go to Noueeyorka."

"You may still, someday," I comforted him. "But for now you can be sure you're on the right side. America will win."

From the kitchen I heard some patrons entering the tavern. "How come you're closed? How about some service?" Liviu Brancusi's voice reminded me that it was Saturday. The three Brancusis, who had gotten jobs fattening hogs in the new Apoldasch agro-complex, were in the best of moods and wanted to celebrate the weekend, i.e., they wanted to drink. The Transmontanian Workers' Party, boasted the Brancusi spokesman, had signed up its millionth member just a few days ago.

As I brought a bottle of *zuika* to their table, Liviu sang, "Socialism wins the day, whatever the pope and the church may say." Then he started trying to recruit me again. He pointed out that as a member of the Kronauburg State Trade Organization, it wasn't just my commercial but also my patriotic duty to declare my allegiance to the party of the people. If not as an active member, then at least as an observer at the big Party Day on the market square in Kronauburg. I could pay my respects and show solidarity with the accomplishments of the comrades.

"I'll think about it," I said. "When's the shindig getting under way?"

"Two weeks from today, on Saturday," Liviu replied. "There'll be thousands of people there. All you can eat and drink for free, courtesy of the party. Everyone who is anyone will be there. Gonna be an unforgettable event. By the way, you can't miss me in the crowd. Because of the exemplary way I met the quota, I was chosen to carry the banner of the AAC Two in the procession."

"The what?"

"The banner of the Apoldasch Agro-Industrial Complex Two."

I promised to think it over, since I needed to make another trip to Kronauburg soon anyway to purchase more stock for the store. I could do that on a Friday afternoon. And that evening I could personally see to it that the Party Day would be really unforgettable for the Kronauburg secretary Stephanescu.

Supply and demand, that's what sets the price." I had to put up with the owner of the Pofta Buna instructing me about why he had summarily tripled the fee for spending the night on his straw. I paid without complaint. I wasn't the only one wanting to spend the night in Kronauburg before the big party spectacular. Two dozen loaded wagons belonging to trade organization concessionaires were parked in front of the cheap inn. They'd all used Friday to buy their stock from the central warehouse so they could party the next day at the expense and in honor of the party. I sat down with my fellow shopkeepers and ordered beer, bread, and *mititei*—spicy patties of grilled meat. I gathered from the conversation that no one had any complaints about doing business in the cooperative. On the contrary, they had good things to say about the improvements in the supply chain as well as state price supports. The only people in the country who were always groaning and complaining were the farmers. When I commented that the party wasn't exactly using kid gloves to introduce collectivization, all I got in reply was the stale old adage about breaking eggs to make an omelet. My question if anyone knew what had become of the former wholesalers the Hossu brothers was met with shrugs and sullen scowls. One of the older concessionaires did allow that in times like these, you were well advised to keep some questions to yourself.

Early in the evening, I strolled over to the Kronauburg market square to reconnoiter the situation. I was struck by the pompous

show of red bunting and gigantic national flags with which the orga-
nizers had transformed the façades of the buildings into a setting for
their propaganda. If you believed what the twenty-five-yard-long
banners said, then our nation was the most progressive, most
peaceful, and most productive of all nations, perpetually poised for
above-average achievements. The slogans were filled with awaken-
ing, buckling down to work, and constructing. Solidarities were
proclaimed, friendships between peoples invoked, alliances recon-
firmed, revolutions promoted, and much gratitude expressed: the
fatherland was thanked, fraternal Socialist states were thanked, the
proletarians of all nations were thanked, and so was the International against capitalism, imperialism, and fascism. But above all,
the party thanked itself in the name of the people.

Hosts of underlings were busily putting the finishing touches
on the market square. Radio and TV personnel were setting up
their broadcasting equipment. Marshals were running here and
there. Soldiers from the National Guard were lounging around
in their fatigues, and on every corner was a civilian in a black leather
jacket, scanning the crowd and speaking into a walkie-talkie. In
front of the Socialist People's Market, carpenters were nailing the
final boards onto the gigantic rostrum where the dignitaries would
sit. I was pleased to discover that from the speaker's platform, one
looked straight across to the police station and Hofmann's photo
studio. I had seen enough and uttered a quick prayer that the market square would empty out that night.

As I lay on my straw pallet in the Pofta Buna, time flowed as
sluggishly as the glue I'd mixed up in Baia Luna and poured into
a marmalade jar. Beside me some concessionaires were snoring,
and now and then a horse would snort. Otherwise, all was quiet.
At some point the clock in the tower of Saint Paul's Cathedral
struck four short strokes and three long ones. Time for me to get
moving. Despite the warm night I put on my coat and crept under
my wagon. The rolled-up photos were in a cardboard tube I had
attached to the front axle. I hid the pictures under my coat and
put the jar of glue in one coat pocket. Out of the other peeked a
half-full bottle of *zuika*. Just in case.

A quarter hour later I entered the market square behind the

speaker's platform. The streetlights were turned off. Some soldiers were standing near the entrance to the Golden Star Hotel. Their laughter echoed dully across the square, and the bluish smoke from their cigarettes drifted in the light from a lantern. I listened, but except for the muted voices of the soldiers, nothing could be heard. When I had crept silently over to the three plateglass windows of the photo studio, I could see the soldiers quite clearly in front of the hotel. Sometimes their gaze wandered across the square, but I was sure I was invisible in the darkness of the night. I unrolled the photos, smeared glue onto their backs, and pasted one onto each of the three windows. The cathedral clock struck three thirty. The soldiers had disappeared.

The sound of heavy boots on cobblestones echoed across the square without my being able to locate exactly where it was coming from. The steps came nearer. They were heading my way. I closed my eyes and took a deep breath. An image flared up in my head: Buba, carrying a jug of water. She handed it to her uncle Dimi, who said, Your Pavel, my dear, can stand the world on its head.

I pulled out my schnapps bottle and quickly moved away from the window.

"Hey! You bitch!" I bellowed into the dark at the top of my lungs. "You filthy whore, you c'n, you c'n, you c'n kiss my ass. Thassit, you c'n jus' kiss my ass, you cheap slu—"

Immediately, two flashlights sprang to life. I heard someone give the order, "Safeties off!" The metallic clatter of submachine guns rang through the night. Then the soldiers had me in their sights.

"Halt!"

I ignored the command, held up the bottle of *zuika,* and staggered a few steps to the left and then to the right. "Fuck'n women, goddamn buncha whores," I babbled to myself. Then I came to an abrupt stop, rolled my eyes, and gaped at the soldiers. I gave a clumsy salute and held out the bottle to the boys in uniform. "Here's t' th' sake . . . sake . . . sacred fatherland. Fuck'n fascists! Long live Fidel! Viflah revoloosh'n. Havva drink, comrades!"

The commanding officer walked up and grabbed me by the collar. "Piss off. This is a restricted area," he snarled at me and grabbed away my bottle. "Beat it!" I staggered off slowly. "Another drunken idiot," I heard one of them say. I slipped onto a side street and ran.

It was just starting to get light as I hitched up the horse, and the sleepy patron of the Pofta Buna came out. "Where are you off to so early? I thought you were going to fill your belly at the party's expense."

"I'm all set." I swung up onto the wagon box.

"Wait! I need your signature. Every overnight guest has to confirm his arrival and departure. It's a new law."

"I wasn't here last night, understand? I wasn't here. I ate here yesterday and then drove right back into the mountains. Got it?"

"No," he said, rubbing the sleep out of his eyes, "not when you're right here in front of me."

I bet on the power of a threat. "If you tell anyone at all that I was in Kronauburg last night, I'll set the Securitate on you. You can imagine what they do with capitalist price gougers who rent out straw pallets at triple the price. Remember the Hossus."

Immediately the guy offered to refund the whole price of an overnight.

"Keep the money!"

"Thanks. I don't know you. Beat it."

I gave the horse the whip and was back in Baia Luna before noon on Saturday.

I stayed by the radio all afternoon, from which issued one report after another about the grand success of the party rally in Kronauburg. About four o'clock they announced the imminent speech by President Gheorghiu-Dej, who had flown in from the capital especially for the occasion, to be preceded by an official welcome for the head of state delivered by the first secretary of the regional party, Dr. Stephanescu.

I had lost. The Kronauburg party boss had not been overthrown. Instead, the usual big words boomed from the radio. I had overestimated the power of the pictures and my own power, too.

On Monday morning I asked my mother to look after the shop for me and walked to Apoldasch where you could buy the *Kronauburg Courier*. Spread across three double pages were reports of the spectacular weekend rally. Nothing but paeans for the party. Many

photos showed the aged president Gheorghiu-Dej. And Stephanescu: laughing, patting flag-wavers on the shoulder, shaking hands,
holding babies. Stefan Stephanescu obviously was more firmly in
the saddle than ever before. Then I did a double take. Under the last
article was the notice "All photographs: Irina Raducanu." It wasn't
the fact that Irina Lupescu had married her fiancé Raducanu, major
in the Securitate, that surprised me. What troubled me was that it
didn't say "All photographs: Heinrich Hofmann." A week later I
had a good idea why.


A young man showed up in Baia Luna asking after a talkative
Gypsy and an elderly gentleman with his grandson, about twenty
years old. They sent him to our shop, and I recognized him immediately. It was Matei, the nephew of the antiques dealer Gheorghe
Gherghel.

"Man, what are you doing here?"

"I came to warn you," said Matei. "Scary things are happening in Kronauburg these days, things I don't understand. Last night
they arrested my uncle for illegal business deals and support of the
counterrevolution. What a load of crap! Politics is the last thing my
uncle cares about."

"Who arrested him?" I was chewing my lips nervously.

"Cartarescu, the police chief of Kronauburg. And another guy
from the State Security, a slimy guy who smiles all the time. Name
of Raducanu."

"And what did they want from you? Why did you come here?"

"They interrogated Uncle Gheorghe for hours. Raducanu kept
asking him who had bought the photo-lab equipment. He wasn't
interested in the telescope and the camera, just the darkroom stuff.
Cartarescu said you had to register darkroom equipment to prevent
unauthorized pictures of potential danger to the state from getting
into circulation."

I was really rattled. "Wha-what kind of photos do they mean?"

"No idea. That smiler was going on about the Cold War
and plots by Western secret services paid by the USA to weaken
Socialism and the party. Apparently some politcadres are being
blackmailed with photos showing them in—let's say very delicate

situations. That's why Raducanu's putting all his effort into finding everyone who has a darkroom. But that seems like just a pretext to me. How would you guys way up here in the mountains have a chance to photograph officials in compromising situations? It's laughable. But they're after you all the same."

"Did you tell them anything about us?"

"Not me," said Matei. "Believe me, I didn't. They let me go because I said I hadn't even been in the shop when the equipment was being sold. All my uncle said—over and over again—was that a Gypsy with a beard and an older man and a young guy, meaning you, were in the store. He didn't know your names. He also couldn't recall where you were from—just somewhere in the mountains. Then they searched my uncle's private rooms. They found the television and confiscated it on the spot. They'll show up here pretty soon; that TV set put them on the scent."

I could feel the fear rising inside me. "Are you sure?"

"Yes. Raducanu smiled when he saw the TV. My uncle got out your receipt to prove that everything about the trade had been legal and he hadn't received any stolen goods. As soon as the security agent took a look at it, he smiled even more, as if he recognized the piece of paper. But that can't be so, can it?"

"Yes, it can. Raducanu was up here once. They wanted to take the TV from us then, too, but my grandfather showed them the receipt to prove he was the legal owner of the set."

"I don't get the whole thing. But tell me the truth: why do you need a darkroom in Baia Luna?"

"Village festivals, weddings, ID photos, portraits," I said. "I wanted to photograph life in the village and then sell the pictures. It's too far to Kronauburg and, anyway, Photo Hofmann does good work, but they're expensive."

"I can't imagine earning any money taking photos here in this hole, but I'll take your word for it. Especially now that you have no more competition from Hofmann the photographer."

"What do you mean?"

"You really are in the dark up here. Motorcycle accident down by Campina."

The color drained from my face. "Was Herr Hofmann killed?"

"It was all over the papers: 'Master Photographer Dead.' He was doing seventy-five on a straightaway. Went right under an army truck, without a helmet. Took them hours to find his head—it was thirty yards out in a cornfield, sliced clean off. That's what it said in the *Courier,* anyway."

"But how could it have happened? What time of day was it?"

"I only know what I read in the paper: going too fast and lost control. When was it, now? Sunday before last, I think, the day after that big party shindig in town."

I felt dizzy. "Matei, did you know that Herr Hofmann was from Baia Luna? His son Fritz and I were in school together."

"No, that's news to me. I only knew Hofmann from the newspaper. He ran around with the fancy crowd. I saw him a time or two in town on his way to the Star of the Carpathians. Not my scene. Too slick. They say Hofmann was thick as thieves with our party boss Stephanescu. But wait . . . now that I think about it . . . At the party rally I was on the market square—free food and drink, you know—so me and my friends were really helping ourselves. We even stayed when they started their stupid speeches. Stephanescu was standing on the podium next to the president. But Hofmann wasn't there. I would have noticed, because he was always hovering around the big shots. But on that Saturday he wasn't onstage. There was a pretty girl, a blond, taking all the pictures."

When I was silent, Matei continued, "No wonder you were so surprised by Hofmann's death if his son was a friend of yours. The newspaper was full of eulogies, pages and pages of them. The longest was by Stephanescu."

"What'd it say?"

"Something about eternal friendship lasting beyond the grave. If you ask me, he was laying it on a bit thick for my taste, if you know what I mean."

"No, not really."

"How should I put it? The expression of sympathy seemed a bit overdone, phony somehow. The magical gaze of the master, a life for photography, the unerring eye of a great artist, and so on and so forth. And that Hofmann would live forever in his pictures and stuff like that—when it was common knowledge that his assistants took the photos. He was an ass kisser who took portraits of the party cadres that looked just like they wanted to see themselves. Well done technically, sure, but where's the art in it?"

"It's not something I can judge. But what made you come up here from Kronauburg just to warn us?"

Matei looked surprised. "But that's obvious. Maybe I'll need help someday, too. Anyway, think of something before that Raducanu gets here. He's a nasty guy and capable of anything."

As Matei was taking his leave to get back to Apoldasch in time to catch the evening bus to Kronauburg, I regretted being suspicious of Gheorghe Gherghel's nephew instead of thanking him and accepting his offer of friendship.

I was alone. I had poured oil onto a fire, and now it was flaring up and threatening to consume me. *Keep your flame turned down, or you'll have a fire on your hands that will burn you badly.* That's what Commissar Patrascu told us after Johannes Baptiste's murder. The captain with wiry hair hadn't had time to enjoy his retirement. Had it really been all that cigarette smoke that killed him? And now, Heinrich Hofmann. I had a fearful foreboding. My photographs glued to the windowpanes had been aimed at Stefan Stephanescu. But had they hit Heinrich Hofmann instead? Whoever had discovered the pictures had prevented them from causing any trouble for the Kronauburg party chief. But if Stephanescu had heard about the photo posters, which I assumed he did, then he would order his people to find the perpetrator, the person with the negatives. And wouldn't he also be furious with Heinrich Hofmann? Shouldn't the photographer have kept the revealing negative so well protected that there was no possibility of anyone stealing it? Did the friendship between the two of them end when Hofmann became a security threat to the party chief? Why wasn't Heinrich at the party rally? And the motorcycle accident just a day later? Without a helmet, when I'd never seen Fritz's father get on his Italian bike without a helmet?

I needed someone to share the unbearable burden of these questions with. And my fear, too. They were after me. I was a monkey wrench in the works of the powerful. I'd lost control of the tiller. But there was no one to relieve me of my fear. Fritz lived in Germany. Did he know of his father's death? I thought it unlikely he and his mother had come to Kronauburg for the funeral of his hated old man. I longed for Buba, would have liked to take her hand and flee, get out of there, go somewhere, farther into the mountains. Would we have made it through, like the rebels down in Walachia? Or to Germany, like Fritz? But I hadn't the slightest idea where Buba was or who she was living with. I had asked her uncle repeatedly, but Dimitru had sworn a thousand oaths that he didn't know where his niece had ended up.

Stephanescu was going to send his henchmen to Baia Luna, if they weren't already on their way. Raducanu would be showing up soon. Very soon, and certainly not alone. I wouldn't get away with playing a cheap trick on him a second time. I had to act, and right now. All traces that led from the display windows of Hofmann's photo studio to Baia Luna had to be removed. I couldn't deny the trade of the TV for the darkroom equipment and the telescope, not after Raducanu's visit to Gheorghe Gherghel. But there couldn't be any evidence that a darkroom had actually been set up in the village. Only Ilja, Kathalina, and Dimitru knew of its existence. Now I'd see whether my family could not just stick together but also be smart. I called Grandfather, my mother, and Dimitru together for an urgent conversation. I had to show them some of my cards without letting them know about my failed attempt to topple the Kronauburg party chief from his pedestal. Once I gathered them together, we all sat down, and I turned to my mother without beating around the bush.

"Do you remember that disgusting photograph you found under my mattress?"

Kathalina blushed. "Oh yes, very well."

"And do you remember the guy who was squirting champagne?"

Embarrassed, Mother nodded. "Why are you bringing up that horrible thing again?"

Dimitru interrupted, "What kind of filth are you talking about, Pavel? And can you tell me why I have to sit and listen to this?"

"That photograph showed a naked woman and some half-naked men, among them the Kronauburg party secretary," I explained. "Fritz Hofmann found the picture in one of his father's moving crates and gave it to me. And Dr. Stephanescu has a powerful interest in never allowing that picture to be copied and distributed. And that's why he's having the Securitate search for the negative."

"I don't understand," said Grandfather. "Why don't they search in Hofmann's studio? What's it got to do with us?"

"Heinrich Hofmann had a motorcycle accident ten days ago. He's dead."

"How awful!" Kathalina said and covered her face with her hands. "You say he's dead?"

"Yes. The trouble is the Securitate thinks I've got the negative. They're after me."

"But how did they get that idea?" Ilja wondered.

I lied. "I don't know. Probably because I was a good friend of Fritz's. Or maybe because of the telescope and the photo stuff. After all, it looks suspicious to have the lab equipment if you don't have any negatives. How am I going to explain to the Securitate that we needed the darkroom for your Madonna photos? They'll put me right into the nuthouse. They already grabbed Gheorghe Gherghel. His nephew Matei was just here. He says they arrested his uncle yesterday because he let us have the darkroom setup. It's against the law now."

"The basic question is," Dimitru interjected, "do you have the negative? Yes or no?"

I lied again. "No. But the Securitate's going to turn this place upside down. We have to hide everything: the darkroom, your telescope, the camera!"

"Including Dimitru's Madonna photos?" asked Grandfather.

"Everything's got to go." I thought for a moment. "Except the radio."

"Okay," said Dimitru. "Do you have a plan?"

"Yes, more or less."

Kathalina was trembling with fear, and suddenly it was all too much for her. "I knew it!" she cried out. "All this craziness of yours brings nothing but trouble. Now the security agents are coming to get all of us. You'll all end up in prison, and so will I. Just because of that dirty picture!"

"Calm down, Mother." I put my arm around her shoulders. "You burned that picture."

Kathalina was sobbing. Finally she wiped her tears away with her apron. "I . . . I . . . I . . . ," she stammered in embarrassment, "didn't burn it. I wanted to, but then . . . I hid it." Mother left us sitting at the table, went upstairs, and returned, blushing bright red. She opened the door to the stove.

"Are you crazy?" cried Dimitru. "You can't burn that!" The Gypsy jumped up in a flash and grabbed the photo out of her hand. He stared at the picture and winced. He didn't seem surprised so much as unable to trust his eyes. He held the photo up to the light and then looked at it up close again, as if seeking something hidden in it. Then he tapped his finger on the man with the champagne bottle.

"This one, Pavel, he's Stephanescu?"

"Yes."

"I see," murmured the Gypsy. "And he wants to get his hands on this photo and the film. For evidential reasons. Should we prevent that? Yes, we should. Which makes the situation serious—very serious."

"Give it back," wailed Kathalina. "We've got to burn it."

"Of course, of course, my dear! Ashes to ashes. But all in good time. It's still too early to burn it. You're afraid this photo is a threat to us. No, no, it isn't. It's a threat to this Stephanescu. It's giving him a giant headache. But Pavel's going to protect this picture, protect it like a holy relic, not like those fakes the Gypsies try to sell you. It'd be a mistake to throw it into the fire, believe me. An *error fatal*. But it would be an even bigger mistake to let this precious photo fall into the hands of the Securitate. Pavel, do you know of a safe hiding place that would never occur to those chuckleheads in the Security Service?"

"I think so."

"Good." Dimitru handed me the photo. "Can we hide the lab equipment there, too?"

"No. There's not enough room. But your Madonna pictures will fit."

Dimitru closed his eyes and raised his face to the ceiling.

"What are you doing?" asked Grandfather, who was fidgeting as if sitting on hot coals.

"Shhh. I'm thinking of a hiding place and asking Papa Baptiste for heavenly succor."

"Johannes Baptiste," I cried, "that's it! I know a place the Securitate will never look for all that lab junk."

Dimitru opened his eyes. "Me, too." And then, without pausing for breath, "Are you all ready to do a little playacting? We should rehearse a little."

"What do you mean 'rehearse'? What kind of playacting?"

"It's simple. When that Lupu fellow shows up here, we'll all be onstage and ready to raise the curtain. Then we'll give a performance inspired by our phantasmagorical rationality. A dog only barks when you're afraid of it. We're going to turn the world upside down and throw that cur Raducanu a bone that'll give him plenty to gnaw on."

Two hours later we'd worked out our strategy and practiced our parts for the performance. Mother had calmed down, felt reassured, and knew exactly what she was supposed to do and say. I, too, had put aside my fear, and Dimitru was rubbing his hands together as if looking forward to the encounter with Lupu Raducanu with malicious glee.

Since we expected Raducanu and his men to turn the whole village upside down looking for the darkroom, I went over to the Petrovs' to warn Petre and his father Trojan that their house would probably be searched. The carbine and scope the Petrovs occasionally used to go poaching could cause them some problems. It turned out my warning was superfluous. "They can search all through the mountains till they're blue in the face." Petre laughed.

When I was sure Baia Luna was asleep, I stole into the church, opened the tabernacle, and put in the Madonna pictures and the photo. Then I pinched a couple votive candles and met Dimitru in the laundry room of the rectory.

The lab was just as I had left it two weeks ago. As expected, it smelled strongly of chemicals, and as planned, Dimitru had brought along the little bottle of Rêves de la Nuit perfume that had been gathering dust in our shop for years. Dimitru lit the candles while I opened the cellar window. Then I disposed of the cloudy brown developer liquid, rinsed the sink clean, and disassembled the enlarger. A half hour later all evidence of the presence of a darkroom had been removed. The Gypsy dragged in a few worn-out mattresses that had been stacked in the basement hallway and sprayed everything with Rêves de la Nuit to drive out the lab odors. There was an overwhelming scent of roses, and I felt a twinge in my heart: it was the same perfume Angela Barbulescu had used. I saw her again in her sunflower dress, hanging from a black beech on the Mondberg. *Your last hour has already struck,* Angela had written in her farewell letter to Stephanescu. She was mistaken. Angela Barbulescu had not found justice before she died or since then either. And my attempt to destroy Stephanescu with the compromising photo had been a miserable failure.

After midnight we gathered up the lab equipment and snuck across the village square to the churchyard. We stood before the grave that had been dug years ago for the body of our priest Johannes Baptiste. In a short while, the enlarger, trays for the developer and fixer, and bottles of chemicals, as well as the camera, telescope, and the key to the laundry room, had disappeared into the hole, which was now filled in and topped with rotted wreaths, bouquets of plastic flowers, and tattered silk bows. I hung on to a cardboard box with photos of stags in rut. It was part of our plan. Then we went to bed. Let Lupu Raducanu come if he was going to.

And he did, next morning at eight. And as expected, he wasn't alone.

A dozen militiamen jumped out of three olive-green SUVs and formed into groups of three.

"Search all the empty houses first!" ordered Captain Cartarescu.

The men fanned out. Then Cartarescu and Major Raducanu headed straight for our concession. That was the cue for Kathalina's first scene.

She opened the door and came out to meet them.

"About time you show your faces around here again. Are you going to return our things or pay us compensation?"

Raducanu and Cartarescu slowed their steps. Now Grandfather, Dimitru, and I came out of the shop as well. "I don't want compensation, I want my lab and my camera back!" I shouted at my mother.

"And I want my telescope! Are you going to give it back to me or not?" Granddad was really into his part. He seemed genuinely outraged.

"You crooks!" raged Dimitru. "First you confiscate all our

beautiful equipment and then you're not even going to compensate us for it. That's what we call robbery, you outlaws!"

Raducanu lost his temper. "Shut up!" he screamed, several times. "Shut up!" His voice cracked. His downy cheeks were flushed.

Dimitru was uncowed. "You steal like magpies and then blame it all on the Gypsies." He clenched his fists and spat on the ground.

Captain Cartarescu struggled to get hold of himself and finally drew his pistol.

"Everybody into the store! Into the store for questioning!"

"But you already questioned us two weeks ago! Do we have to go through this again? It's getting to be a drag." I could feel that our play was working according to plan.

Major Raducanu asked for an ashtray and lit up a Kent. He inhaled deeply, trying hard to keep his cool. "You purchased a darkroom kit and optical instruments in a shop in Kronauburg. Where are they?"

"We didn't purchase them, we traded for them," shouted Ilja. "Traded a good TV, a German Loewe Optalux. You got any idea what something like that is worth?"

"Where the hell is that darkroom, goddamnit?" Raducanu was steaming.

"Are you serious?" I replied calmly. "Your colleagues were here two weeks ago and confiscated everything. They promised to bring it back if it was all legit. We've been waiting ever since."

"What? What colleagues?" Cartarescu spluttered.

"Your left hand doesn't know what your right hand is doing, apparently," I said. "Two majors from the Security Service."

"And Heinrich Hofmann," Ilja added, "but he didn't have anything to do with the confiscation."

Totally perplexed, Lupu Raducanu massaged his temples. He obviously had no idea where to begin asking all the questions he had. "So tell me once more: two majors were here from the Security Service? That's impossible because I would have known about it."

I assumed an expression of bewildered innocence. "But they were here and Heinrich Hofmann was with them."

"He must have had something to take care of in his old house since—"

Raducanu cut Grandfather off. "We'll get to Hofmann later. These two men: when were they here and what did they want, exactly?"

"That's just what we'd like to know," I replied. "At first we had no idea they were from the Securitate. We thought they were here to collectivize us, that it had something to do with expropriation."

"They sat right here!" Ilja pointed to one of the tables in the taproom. "My daughter-in-law even served them coffee."

"Couldn't be bothered to thank me," hissed Kathalina.

I continued, "They asked me if I knew Heinrich Hofmann's son Fritz. What a stupid question! I spent eight years at the desk next to his at school! Did I still have contact with him? How would I? He's been living in Germany for years and I'm sure he thanks his lucky stars for every day he doesn't have to spend in this boring Podunk. Suddenly those guys wanted to know if I was also a photography enthusiast. Yes, of course, ever since Herr Hofmann's assistant showed me how a darkroom worked. I even took the two security people into our storeroom to show them all the equipment I'm so proud of, the things we traded the TV for in Gheorghe Gherghel's shop. And you know what one of them told me?"

"I'm all ears," said Raducanu.

"'You can be arrested for having these things in your possession!' These guys are crazy, I thought. I hadn't even unpacked all the stuff yet. But they explained that it had been obtained illegally."

"But it was all *legalamente*. Or do the rules of Socialism forbid trades?" Raducanu ignored Dimitru's remark and turned to Kathalina.

"These two men supposedly from a state agency—what did they look like?"

"My God, what did they look like? Let's see—like men from the city. One was wearing a nice sport coat, salt and pepper, very good material. The bigger of the two had on a brown leather coat, even though it was very warm. He was a least a head taller than his partner with the glasses. If you ask me, the man in glasses looked educated, somehow. Not like those ruffians from the state militia."

"The one with glasses looked like a politician," I interjected, "or maybe a doctor."

"A doctor with glasses?" Raducanu pricked up his ears, took out a pad of paper, and made some notes. On his right ring finger was a gold wedding ring.

"Did the men tell you their names?"

"No, but the tall one was very striking," continued Kathalina. "With a mustache. Early forties, I'd say."

"And he had a wart on his cheek," I added. "On the right side . . . no, the left . . . to my left, so it was on his right cheek."

"A big one," said Dimitru.

Kathalina shook her head. "That wasn't a wart, it was a birthmark. But it was very noticeable."

The major continued to take notes. He seemed to be calming down.

"What was Hofmann the photographer doing here?" Raducanu addressed the question directly to Grandfather.

"I don't know. He hasn't been in the village in years, not since he moved to Kronauburg. They say he can't get his house here sold. Who's going to move to Baia Luna in times like these? Anyway, while they were questioning us, he went to his old house. Maybe he left something there by accident when he moved away. All I know is that he roared away with the other two in one of those green jeeps. And they took my telescope and my grandson's photo equipment with them."

Raducanu gave me a sharp look. "Why do you need a darkroom?"

"Hang on!" I ran upstairs and returned with the box of photographs. I spread the rutting stags out on the table. "Impressive, aren't they? When I saw these pictures at Mr. Gherghel's it struck me like a bolt of lightning: that's what I want to do, too! Hunting with a camera. That would be fun. There's nothing going on here in Baia Luna. And besides, the stags in our mountains are even more impressive than these in the photos. I should be able to make some money with pictures like these or better."

Raducanu thought it over. "What about the telescope?"

It was the question Kathalina had been waiting for, and she jumped right in. "Idiots! They went and traded my beautiful TV for that telescope, these two loonies right here!" She was pointing at Dimitru and Grandfather. "I told you that thing would cause us trouble, didn't I? But nobody listens to me."

Dimitru played the wounded party. "You don't know the first thing about scientific precision or about *morbus lunaticus.*"

"Feel free to call your disease by its proper name: lunacy—moon sickness. My father-in-law's moon sick and epileptic," Mother stormed on, "and this Gypsy persuaded him to get the telescope—to observe the moon."

Ilja went to the cash register where all our important family documents were kept and handed Cartarescu the medical certificate without uttering a word.

"She's right," the captain conceded. "The Kronauburg hospital diagnosed epilepsy."

Raducanu didn't even glance at the paper. He demanded another glass of water, opened a pill bottle, and swallowed a handful of headache tablets.

"That's what I said," repeated Dimitru. "My friend Ilja suffers from *lunaticus morbus.* And so it's logical for him to observe the moon minutely through a telescope. Determine the causes! That's what he's doing. But it looks like there are certain people in this country who have a powerful interest in preventing our research. Pinched our telescope without further ado in the name of state security. Are we going to get compensated for it or not?"

Raducanu grabbed the water glass and hurled it at the Gypsy. It missed Dimitru's head and shattered against the wall. The security agent jumped up screaming "Shit, shit, shit!" and stormed out of the shop.

Vera Raducanu was waiting patiently among the curiosity seekers gathered at a respectful distance around the jeeps on the village square. She hurried toward her son, bemoaning his neglect and ingratitude.

He pushed his mother roughly aside. "This is where you belong!" he said.

One by one, the search parties trickled in with nothing unusual to report. Only the head of the commando that had searched the rectory spoke of a strange room in the cellar with mattresses, candles, and a powerful odor of perfume. It had to be a secret love nest.

They had asked around and determined that only the sexton Julius Knaup possessed a key to the cellar. When the militiaman asked if Major Raducanu wanted to inspect the room and interrogate the sexton, Lupu Raducanu's response was to get into a car, slam the door, and roar off toward town.

Captain Cartarescu put his hand to his cap in salute and apologized for the inconvenience. He mumbled something about a misunderstanding and assured us that the Botev family wouldn't be bothered again in the future.

By the time the vehicles of the militia were crossing the Tirnava, Erika Schuster and a few other women were already bustling into the rectory and down to the cellar. "That's how it smelled in Barbu's wardrobe, too," Erika declared. And everybody knew that the only person who used Rêves de la Nuit nowadays was Vera Raducanu.

While the sexton's hidden love nest was restocking the village with rumors, sneers, and derision, Dimitru and I were dancing for joy in the taproom. I uncorked a bottle on the house while Grandfather gasped for breath on the bench next to the stove, he was laughing so hard. And then Kathalina had to let off some steam.

"Never, never again," she screamed, "never again will I be pulled into one of your schemes. I thought my heart was going to stop. I almost died of fear." She was trembling all over and wept bitterly.

Mother didn't calm down until that evening, when she wrung the promise from Dimitru, her father-in-law, and me that we would act reasonably from now on and for all eternity. Ilja and Dimitru had to swear their oath with hand on heart in the name of the Holy Trinity. Kathalina forbade them even to mention the name of the Mother of God.

# Chapter Twelve

●

## THE AGE OF GOLD, THE FOURTH POWER,

## AND ILJA BOTEV'S MISSION

"They've forgotten us," said Hermann Schuster, "plain and simple forgotten us." Like the Saxon, his sons Andreas and Hermann Junior, as well as Hans Schneider, the Hungarian Istvan Kallay, and the two Petrovs, were all uncertain whether Schuster's assessment of the situation was good news or bad. I, too, had at first paid little attention to the announcement that issued from our taproom radio on a spring evening in the year '62, but then we all pricked up our ears.

The National Congress was no longer predicting the triumphant victory of Socialism in the future but instead proclaiming its arrival in the present. By official decree, the utopian ideal had mutated into a fait accompli.

"Ten thousand farmers streamed into the capital today to cheer the Central Committee and express their gratitude to the party for its extraordinary achievements. Amid euphoric ovations, President Gheorghiu-Dej announced the successful completion of the collectivization of Transmontanian agriculture. All private agricultural enterprises the length and breadth of the country have been transformed into productive state cooperatives. Sources close to the State Council report that on the occasion of the celebrations, forty thousand former counterrevolutionaries have been pardoned and released from prison, thereby gaining the chance to fulfill their patriotic duty to help build the New Nation."

"Socialism's been achieved? I'd like to know where," Trojan Petrov grumbled. "We've been waiting for those fucking expropriators for years. No sign of them. They really have forgotten us. The world must end for the Communists just this side of Apoldasch."

On the first of May, the Day of the International Proletariat,

Karl Koch walked through the gate into his yard. His wife Klara and the children had been waiting for his return for three years. Every few months the mailman had handed her a postcard with the identical message: "I'm well. The food is good."

When Koch knocked on his own front door and Klara opened, she froze in shock for a second, then she threw her arms around him and wept for joy. She had feared he would return in an emaciated state, but outwardly Karl was surprisingly unchanged since the day when Raducanu and Cartarescu had arrested him.

"You must be hungry," said Klara, who put black beans on the kitchen table and sat down across from him. He pushed the plate away and looked at the linen sampler that hung above the stove: FROM NOTHING COMES NOTHING.

"I'm getting a late start. I have to till my field. If you don't sow, you won't reap." He sighed and went out into the barnyard. But then he turned around. "Tomorrow," he said, "tomorrow. I'm too tired today."

But the next morning, although the Saxon had Klara pack him a lunch to eat out in the fields, he couldn't pull himself together. And as this procedure kept repeating itself over the following weeks, Klara realized that for the rest of their life together there would be nothing left for her except the painful memory of what Karl Koch used to be.

Working in our shop and tavern over the years, I had developed a fine feel for changes in the mood of our customers. I sensed that the country was undergoing a sea change. Every two months Alexandru Kiselev would come back for a week of regular home leave from the tractor factory in Stalinstadt, bringing with him not just a nice pile of money but also the latest news, which the young men of the village eagerly lapped up, especially Hermann Schuster Junior. Despite his father's disappointment, he was quite frank about not seeing any future in agriculture and preferring a job in industry. But Alexandru kept telling him that new hires were restricted to members of the party. Hermann knew that, beyond a doubt, a membership card in his pocket would mean his father would never speak to him again. But he still asked Alexandru the same question every time: "How do things look in Stalinstadt?"

"Good. But Stalinstadt isn't called Stalinstadt anymore. It's called Brasov again, like it was before."

While Hermann didn't see much significance in the change, I concluded that the once-mighty pillars of our relationship with the Union of Soviet Socialist Republics were getting wobbly.

My suspicions were confirmed the evening I heard Liviu Brancusi saying openly that people in the agro-complex in Apoldasch were starting to grumble because, at Moscow's urging, the value-producing comrades were being compelled to constantly exceed their quotas. As an oft-decorated collectivist, of course, he was always ready to put his labor at the service of the proletarian cause and exceed production targets when it was a question of improving the nation's nutrition, but not just so the fattened hogs from AAC 2 could be exported to the Soviet Union. Liviu made a point of saying he was representing the official party line by calling not for the severing of the bonds of friendship with our great Socialist brother, just a gradual relaxation. Before advancing the cause of the international proletariat, a comrade's first duty was to keep his own doorstep swept. "We need full independent sovereignty," he said, "or the Russians are going to bleed us dry."

There was method behind the retro naming of Stalinstadt to Brasov. Street signs all over the country were being switched once again. In the case of all the Stalin Squares, Stalin Avenues, and Stalin Boulevards, the name of the dictator was replaced by the name Gheorghiu-Dej, which would later fade in the radiance of his successor. Although the Central Committee continued to swear allegiance to the inviolable bonds of solidarity with the Soviet Union, the troops of the Red Army were obliged, given the principle of national sovereignty, to depart from Transmontania. In the capital, the Soviet monument to the unknown soldier was dismantled, and someone hung a sign on the Russian Museum saying CLOSED FOR RENOVATIONS. In the schools, Russian was no longer required, and, little by little, anything that even vaguely alluded to the Slavic roots of the New Nation was removed from the history books. The reason was presumably that a great nation needed a great history of independence, and moreover, they wanted to put a stick in the Hungarians' eye. The Socialist neighbor kept raising territorial claims to its old ancestral homeland in Transmontania, while the Transmontanians insisted they had been there first—since the pre-Christian era—that is, their ancestors the Dacians and the Romans had.

And to substantiate these claims, the new first secretary of the Central Committee and Conducator-to-be dispatched squads of archaeologists into the countryside to dig for Roman potsherds. If their discoveries were indeed Roman, they found their way into the vitrines of the countless local history museums being opened in every provincial town. But if the potsherds were of Slavic origin—which in Kronauburg was almost always the case—the digs had to be filled in again at once. And people whispered to one another that to steer the historic facts in his direction, the first secretary had had a secret pottery constructed near the Schweisch Valley where brick makers were sworn to secrecy and hired to produce pots in the antique style, smash them, and bury the shards in formerly Hungarian settlements. How else to explain that even in Baia Luna they were coming upon traces of the Romans by chance, especially at construction sites.

Just when no one in the village expected change to happen anymore, a construction crew with heavy equipment appeared without any warning. The workmen distributed the party brochure *Children Are the Future* to all households, then they proceeded to tear down the empty school building. Within weeks the portraits of the future Conducator and the Kronauburg regional secretary Stephanescu were hanging in three brand-new classrooms.

Right on time for the new school year 1967–68, a truck with desks and textbooks drove into town, followed by a dilapidated Lada from which emerged Adrian Popescu, the new teacher, a man in his midforties. He moved into the former house of the Hofmann family and proved to be an unsociable loner who avoided the male camaraderie of evenings in the taproom. But since he got along with the children, was acceptably strict, and didn't bother anyone in the village, people got used to his presence. A sort of friendship even developed between him and Istvan the Hungarian based on their shared view that the faking of Roman potsherds deserved the adjective "clumsy," if not worse.

When the successor of the Little Stalin proclaimed in the mid-sixties that—the Socialist phase having been completed—the New Nation was now proudly and with head held high setting out on the path to Communism, people in the village at first judged it to be politicians' twaddle. Socialism? Communism? What did they mean, anyway? Except for the new school, low prices for groceries, and the propaganda harangues on the radio, no one in Baia Luna knew exactly what the newness of the New Nation actually consisted of. However, when the transmission assembler Alexandru Kiselev brought home an electric sewing machine, an automatic spin dryer, a hood dryer, and a television with antenna right under the envious gaze of his neighbors, we had to admit that the party's promises of progress were more than just hot air.

It was thanks to the Conductor that the capitalist class enemy provided a generous source of credit for the construction of the New Nation. At the beginning of his rule he had portrayed himself as a tireless worker and modest servant of the people. But then some poor poet had decided there was something to be gained by celebrating him as the guarantor of prosperity and proud scion of his native earth. And since the verses pleased him and his spouse Elena even more, she had all the poets in the country called together and ordered even more poems. They praised the shining Evening Star, celebrated the Guardian of Wisdom, and hailed the Universal Genius and the Titan of Titans. All this persuaded Elena to take a plane to Persia, where for practically a song she purchased a golden scepter from the shah. Then Elena sewed with her own hands fantastic sashes of watered silk that her husband donned whenever he made a public appearance, brandishing his new scepter.

After assuming the post of general secretary in 1965, the Conducator laid the cornerstone for his meteoric rise with a decision not to follow in the footsteps of his deceased predecessor Gheorghiu-Dej. Instead of constantly flying off to Moscow like the Little Stalin, he preferred to pay visits to China and America, thus muddling up the fronts in the Cold War. Although he was by confession a Marxist, they rolled out the red carpet for him in the USA, calculating that in return he would drive a wedge into the Communist bloc. And indeed, when Soviet tanks rolled into Prague in 1968, the Conducator turned a cold shoulder on Leonid Brezhnev and his other Socialist allies and kept his troops at home instead of sending them to war against the rebellious Czechs. In Transmontania this refusal earned him the reputation of a national hero, to the delight of the poets. Other countries also paid him the highest diplomatic respect, not least because he was constantly inviting high-level guests whom he wined and dined like princes and showered with presents. In return he accumulated medals for himself and gifts for his wife. The queen of England even went so far as to knight him. But the crowning glory of the Conductor's international connections was his close relationship with Richard Nixon. Even before becoming president, the American had added a crimson Cadillac to the Conductor's private fleet, which the latter never used, however, because it hadn't been bulletproofed.

In the sixties, there were only two inhabitants of Baia Luna besides the Saxon Karl Koch who didn't care whether the country was flourishing or not—namely the two friends Ilja and Dimitru.

At eight every morning, Grandfather rose, ate breakfast, and took his epilepsy pills. When he was having a good day he helped me in the shop or swept out the storeroom. On bad days he moped around, argued with his daughter, my heavyweight aunt Antonia, and made a general nuisance of himself. On very good days he would take a long walk beside the Tirnava. Sometimes Dimitru went with him. They didn't talk much because there was hardly anything to talk about.

Kathalina thought their gradual loss of vitality might have something to do with the pair's pledge to act reasonably from now on. Mother was secretly plagued by a bad conscience because she sensed that the promise she had extracted from her father-in-law and the Gypsy had clipped the wings of the two friends' spirits. But her nerves simply couldn't take having to playact for Lupu Raducanu again. Grandfather and Dimitru did feel constrained to keep their promise, but the reason they were downcast was something else.

The calamity began on August 5 of the year 1962. Dimitru was listening to Radio London.

"Quiet! No! Oh no! It can't be true. She's dead!"

"Who's dead?" I asked.

"Marilyn! Little Marilein. John Eff's mistress! Suicide! They say it was pills, too many pills and whiskey. That's supposedly what killed her. She was only in her midthirties!"

"But why would she commit suicide?" Kathalina chimed in. "They say she was beautiful and famous. She had money and could have any man she wanted. Why on earth would she go and kill herself with pills!"

"I ask myself the same question," Dimitru agreed. "It isn't reasonable. There's something behind it! A Black like me can smell it a mile away."

Mother's sour look and the sentence "Don't start in again!" were enough to shut Dimitru up.

Although Dimitru and Grandfather avoided any speculation about the death of the blond actress, their suspicion received new nourishment the following year. In both America and the Soviet Union dark forces were at work. Their vague fear turned into depressing certainty on the day when even the Transmontanian Broadcasting System was full of nothing but the news that the American president John Fitzgerald Kennedy had been assassinated. A respectful eulogy spoke not only of his visionary leadership but also his ambitious plans for space exploration. There was no mention of his love affairs. Instead we learned that as one of his last official acts, he had received the director of the National Space Flight Center in Huntsville at the White House. Wernher von Braun had filled in the president on the details of the Saturn rocket and the Apollo program to land a man on the moon.

When Dimitru and Grandfather learned that the assassin, a certain Lee Harvey Oswald, had lived in the Soviet Union, the two friends were sure they knew who was behind the murder plot. I'm certain the only reason they didn't mention the name Korolev was their fear of getting Kathalina all riled up.

All Dimitru said was, "Oswald won't talk. The CIA can torture him all they want. If Oswald's working for the Russians, he'd sooner bite off his tongue."

Two days later any lingering doubts Dimitru might have had about the plot to kill the American president were dispelled. On his way to prison, Oswald was silenced forever—gunned down by a shady nightclub owner. In retrospect, for Grandfather and the Gypsy it was the initial spark for a fateful chain reaction.

The Soviets would stop at nothing, and neither would the Americans. The two dominant world powers might be engaged in only a Cold War, but they were obviously rubbing out each other's leading minds. At least, that's the conclusion Dimitru and Grandfather drew from the radio news, and years later they would believe they had confirmation of it.

"Moscow, January 5, 1966. The Soviet rocket scientist Korolev is to be hospitalized for a few days to have a growth removed. After his recovery, the date for the first Soviet lunar flight will be announced. The cosmonaut Yury Gagarin has let it be known that he is ready for the mission even if they never bring him back."

"Moscow, January 14, 1966. The Soviet rocket engineer Sergei Pavlovich Korolev has unexpectedly died of cancer. He passed away two days after his fifty-ninth birthday, following an unsuccessful operation in a Moscow hospital. His death is expected to set the Russian lunar landing program back by several years."

"Washington, January 1, 1967. The American vice president Richard Nixon named February 21 as the launch date for the first American Apollo manned spaceflight."

"Moscow, January 2, 1967. The Union of Soviet Socialist Republics is confident of sending cosmonauts to the moon by the fiftieth anniversary of the October Revolution."

"Cape Kennedy, January 27, 1967. Huge setback for the Apollo lunar flight project of the United States of America. During a test involving a simulated countdown, fire broke out in the space capsule. The astronauts Gus Grissom, Ed White, and Roger Chaffee died from smoke inhalation. The son of Commander Grissom told the press after the accident that his father had received death threats and was fearful of becoming the victim of a plot. Possible sabotage has not been ruled out."

"Moscow, March 27, 1968. Yury Gagarin, the Russian cosmonaut who seven years ago set a milestone in world history by becoming the first human in space, is dead. He died at the age of thirty-four in the crash of a plane he was test piloting. It is considered possible that the crash was the result of an act of sabotage."

"June 6, 1968. Robert Francis Kennedy killed at the age of forty-two. Kennedy, who was following in the footsteps of his brother John Fitzgerald Kennedy as a leading contender for the Democratic nomination for president, died of gunshot wounds inflicted by an assassin."

The evil is stronger than we are," said Dimitru resignedly. "It's all over. Our mission has definitely failed. Marilein, John Eff, his brother Robert, Korolev, Gagarin, three American astronauts. To say nothing of the many unsung cosmonauts who went before and got blown up in test flights—they all had to die: burned, poisoned, shot, crashed. Some may even be buzzing around in the cold vastness of space, unable to return. And no one hears their calls. And you don't hear a peep out of Khrushchev either. Do they have to execute each other like this? What do you think, Ilja, is it worth it?"

Grandfather said nothing. Kathalina could have seen the defeat of the two friends as a triumph of reason, but instead the Gypsy made her sad when she saw his distress and despair. I was also plagued by a bad conscience. After all, the two of them had no idea how much I had manipulated them for my own purposes. The telescope, the white dots on Dimitru's photos of the Madonna, the playacting for Lupu Raducanu—all that drama, now already several years in the past, had left me indebted to them both. I had some reparations to make. Like my mother, my dearest wish was that Dimitru and Ilja could be their old selves again.

And our wish came true on a warm summer day in 1969 when Grandfather and Dimitru had gone on one of their walks. Panting, I raced to catch up with them with some exciting news. I found them at the roadside cross marking the spot where Laszlo Gabor had died trying to keep Grandfather's young family from falling into the Tirnava. The two friends were sitting on the bank, chewing blades of grass and staring silently into the river.

"Haven't you heard?" I asked. "The whole world is talking about it!"

"What do you mean?"

"Apollo Eleven is about to take off. In a few hours a rocket with Americans on board will fly to the moon. The general secretary has announced that he'll be on the line continuously from launch to landing—on television, no less, round the clock. If you hurry, you can make it back before they start counting backward."

"That, my dear Pavel, is known as the countdown!"

Ilja looked at Dimitru and shook his head. "A moon flight! I don't believe it. Murders, accidents, assassinations. Everyone who's important to the moon project is dead, on both sides, Russians and Americans. They're in a war."

"Almighty God." Dimitru groaned. "You're mistaken, Ilja. You're right that they're at war, but not everybody's been killed off yet. There's one guy left, one rocket builder! The German! Wörner von Braun! Didn't I say so? The Germans never forget."

Although Grandfather was sixty-six, and Dimitru wasn't the youngest either anymore, they ran like rabbits to the house of the Kiselev family. The only television in Baia Luna stood in their parlor on a veneered corner chest.

Petre Petrov greeted them with the words "You're too late." Like many others, he'd invited himself over to the Kiselevs'. "The countdown just finished, and Apollo is airborne."

When Dimitru and Ilja looked at the TV, the only thing still to be seen in the middle of the black screen was a bright, fiery trail getting smaller and smaller until it was no bigger than an aluminum coin, an image that reminded me of Dimitru's Madonna photos. When the tiny, pinhead-sized dot had finally winked out in the night of outer space, the Gypsy asked, "Everything went smoothly?"

"Perfect liftoff," Petre answered. "The best. Too bad you missed it."

"And how many men on board?"

"Only three. Collins is going to stay in the command module while Armstrong and Aldrin go down in the lunar module. Two hundred thirty-nine thousand miles, just imagine! They'll be up there in four days if all goes well. The announcer just said Nixon's speechwriters have already slipped their eulogies into his pocket, just in case."

"Did they say where the two astronauts are going to land?" Dimitru was almost bursting with curiosity.

"Man, Dimitru, don't bother us with such stupid questions,"

grumbled Petre's father Trojan. "They're landing on the moon, where else? Haven't you got that through your skull yet?"

"But where? Where exactly? In which *mare*?"

"Haven't a clue." Trojan shrugged. "Some dusty place. There's plenty of room up there for the *Igel*."

"For what?"

"That's what they called the lunar module," explained Petre. "We've been wondering why the Americans couldn't come up with a better name."

As in days of yore, Petre's remark was a welcome excuse for Dimitru to launch into a sermon about human ignorance. He explained patronizingly that *Igel* in American doesn't mean hedgehog. It's the name of a gigantic bird of prey.

While the other men left Elena's parlor one after the other because the pictures of Mission Control in Houston bored them, Grandfather and Dimitru stayed on for four days, staring at the screen in such concentration that the Gypsy didn't even need any attention-enhancing liquid refreshment.

July 20, 1969: the Kiselevs' parlor was full to bursting. Elena passed around canapés and good salted crackers from the capital, but no one was having any. All eyes were glued to the TV screen. At 4:18 p.m., a hundred two hours and forty-five minutes after launch, the lunar module landed. No one noticed that sixty seconds later, Dimitru put both hands to his head in horror. The others watched the screen impatiently. Any moment now a man would step onto the moon for the first time. The Gypsy didn't care. He sensed—no, he knew—that it was all for nothing. At 7:34 p.m. the spokesman announced that Armstrong and Aldrin were donning their space suits. It took a while. At 10:39 p.m. Neil Armstrong stood on the steps of the lunar module in his padded overalls but didn't hurry down. Ten fifty: "Come on, already," Petre Petrov shouted. Six minutes later Armstrong stuck out his left foot and became the first man to touch the moon. Then the astronaut said something in American, which nobody in Baia Luna except Dimitru understood. Thank the Lord the TV announcer translated the sentence in such a proud voice you'd think he was standing up there himself. Everyone cheered and hugged. Dimitru stayed seated. He was weeping. Everyone thought he was very moved. But the small step of a man and the giant step for mankind didn't move Dimitru. He plucked at Grandfather's sleeve, took him aside, and whispered something in his ear. He motioned me over, too. We left the Kiselevs' living room and sat down outside on the bench next to the watering trough where Karl Koch usually sat, staring at his hands.

The Americans' Marian mission had failed. That was already clear to Dimitru the minute the lunar module landed. Commander Armstrong had called Mission Control in Houston. Houston responded, asking how things looked, and Armstrong spoke into his mike, "Tranquility Base here. The Eagle has landed." But where? "Tranquility Base!"

"The Yanks have messed up again," groaned Dimitru. "They'll never find Mary, not even with the help of Wörner von Braun."

"How can you be so sure?" asked Grandfather. "The astronauts only just arrived up there, didn't they?"

"Armstrong is clambering around in the Mare Tranquillitatis, not in the Mare Serenitatis. Mary's enthroned in the Sea of Serenity, not in the Sea of Tranquility."

"Oh shit" was all Ilja replied.

I had to react, say something, anything. The two friends were utterly deflated: clueless, speechless, helpless. It all made no sense, had no point, no goal. And no hope. With the purest of intentions, I wanted to fan a spark of reassurance and give them the courage to go on living. But I had underestimated Grandfather and Dimitru. I had seen their Madonna madness as a crazy obsession but hadn't realized the genuine earnestness of their despair. And so with a foolishly clever argument, I provided the impetus for the next act of a tragedy whose course I would be unable to control.

"Dimitru," I said, "that German, that Wernher von Braun—you always said the Germans were cunning. What if this von Braun didn't miss the Sea of Serenity at all? What if he meant to miss it? On purpose! What if he intended to send Armstrong and his colleagues to the wrong *mare*?"

"What did you say, Pavel? It was planned? An act of sabotage! Do you think Wörner wants to keep the Americans from finding the Madonna?"

"I don't know, but could be."

"But it isn't evidentical! The Americans pay Wörner von Braun a lavish salary. Is the German plotting in secret with the Soviets, against the Yanks?"

"Never, Dimitru," Grandfather objected. "The Germans—I'm talking about the Germans in the West—would never revolt against the Americans. That would be the end of the airlift over the Wall into Berlin. And that can't be what the Germans want. But still, I don't trust that von Braun. Did he really repent having built rocket bombs for the Führer's Thousand-Year Reich? Is he really a new person? An ally? The savior of the Mother of God? Or is he secretly pursuing different ends? His own shadowy goals?"

"My, oh my, oh my! Ilja, I get you! To recapitulate: the Soviets want to fetch the Madonna from the moon to undo the Assumption, so they can continue to believe in their atheism. The Americans have to prove that God exists. They have to find the Mother of God because they don't want to have to pulp all their dollars. But the German is in the middle. He doesn't want either the one thing or the other. He wants Mary not to be found. And that's why Wörner von Braun is sending Armstrong and Aldrin to the wrong *mare*. And that's why they all had to die: the Kennedys, Korolev, Gagarin, and all those astronauts and cosmonauts. Wörner's outlived them all. He's behind everything. I just wonder why. I mean, what does the German get out of it?"

"What did you just say?" Grandfather interjected. "What sea did the lunar module land in?"

"Mare Tranquillitatis."

"That's no accident. The German wants to finally have some peace and quiet, some relief," Grandfather explained.

"Relief from what?"

"Man, Dimitru, you as a Gypsy ought to know the answer to that. They wanted to rub out all you Blacks, too, back then. Don't you see? Since the Thousand-Year Reich didn't work out, the German wants some relief from all those murdered Jews. And Mary is a Jew! The Mother of God is from the Children of Israel! Mary is the only one of her people who has corporeally risen from the dead. That's what the papal dogma says, too. Now imagine that this von Braun finds her. Mary would certainly have a few unpleasant things to say to him about how her people were treated and would constantly keep the Germans from forgetting. The best thing for the German would be if Mary stayed up there in the lunar dust. She can party with the apostles and not disturb the progress of the world with her memories."

"Sounds logical, Ilja," Dimitru said without a trace of enthusiasm. "Or better: it sounds too logical. But Papa Baptiste taught me to test every theory by collecting contradictatorial theories."

"Explain what you mean."

"Perhaps Wörner is really nothing but a clueless rocket builder, a curious scientist who just wants to know what's happening up there on the moon. Perhaps he's really not a German anymore but a true American who regrets having built rockets for the Thousand-Year Reich. After all, he was a friend of Kennedy's! John Eff forgave the Germans, didn't he? He didn't constantly remind them of dark times in the past. He even converted to being a Berliner."

"Your theory's not without interest, Dimitru," I jumped in, conscious of the risibility of these speculations. "But that would mean that some entirely different power is pulling the strings. Neither the Soviets nor the Yanks, and not Wernher von Braun. Someone hidden. Someone who wants to prevent the Madonna at all costs from being discovered. Someone who really has something to fear from the Jewish Mary."

"*Sic est!*" Dimitru was bowled over by the force of his insight. "I draw the *conclusio:* a power—we'll call it *x*, hypothetically—has used Wörner von Braun for its own ends. Perhaps lured him into the wrong *mare*. Neither the Americans nor the Soviets nor the Germans—none of them is pulling the strings for the conquest of the heavens. It's the Fourth Power, Ilja. I'm telling you, it's the Fourth Power that's behind everything. And I'll tell you something else: Papa Baptiste knew it. That power raised Mary onto her heavenly throne, declared an incarnate Jewish woman to be the *Regina coelestis* of heaven in 1950, after the world had left her people so shamefully in the lurch here on earth."

"And who do you think that Fourth Power is?"

"Well, the Vatican, of course."

Like everywhere else in the world, in Baia Luna the first lunar landing was the topic of much conversation. But only for two days.

The three American astronauts hadn't even started on their return voyage when the village was consumed by excitement about something else entirely.

A gray, factory-fresh limousine rolled into Baia Luna. The Conducator's grandiloquent prophecy that under his leadership the agrarian state of Transmontania would blossom into an industrial nation was not just empty rhetoric. The First Man of the State had kept his word: the New Nation possessed its own automobile factory. The name "Dacia" was proudly spelled out in silver letters across the trunk of the car from which two gentlemen in black were emerging. They greeted everyone in a measured way, raising their right hands and bowing their heads first in one direction and then in the other. Primly conscious of his own dignity, the older of the two introduced himself as the vicar-general of the diocese of Kronauburg.

"The parish of Baia Luna," he said, "will soon have a new shepherd to lead it."

At first the bystanders didn't know how to react to the news, but then the Saxons started shaking one another's hands in congratulation, first shouts of joy were heard, hats began flying into the air, and finally a torrent of joy burst forth to which the shrieks of the Gypsy children made a significant contribution. The representatives of the bishop in Kronauburg found this reaction very gratifying and asked that the young priest, whose name was Antonius Wachenwerther, be received with due respect, since his calling had led him from his native Austria into the diaspora. His installation would be celebrated little more than a week from that day, on the last day of July. The men and women promised to have the rectory and the church dusted out by then and to decorate the village.

"If I might be allowed to make a comment to your honored excellencies." The sacristan Julius Knaup unctuously sidled up to the visitors. "Our Virgin of Eternal Consolation was stolen years ago, and the Eternal Flame over the tabernacle is out as well. And if you ask my opinion, satanic powers were at work in the person of a sinful female by the name of Bar—"

"You still stink of rosewater," called out Petre Petrov, and the other men who were standing around laughed so hard they had to hold their bellies. The representatives of the clergy looked uncomfortable and then laughed a little themselves.

Then the vicar-general explained that at the installation of Father Wachenwerther, the extinguished light would burn again as in pious bygone days, reignited by an altar candle lit from the consecrated light in Saint Paul's Cathedral in Kronauburg. As for the theft of the Madonna, the diocese noted with burning concern the growing number of thefts of sacred objects and saints' statues. The vicar-general would venture no opinion as to the identity of the perpetrators but could not help mentioning that members of a certain national minority well known for habitual thievery were smuggling precious cultural artifacts and icons into the capitalist art market via an international Mafia based in Moscow. He would therefore caution Pastor Wachenwerther to leave the church door locked except for services.

A new priest! For me that meant the tabernacle in the church would be needed for clerical purposes again. I realized in dismay how long it had been since I had thought about the teacher Angela Barbulescu and her diary. The fire in my heart was still glimmering, but it wasn't blazing anymore. It was painful to look myself in the eye. The youthful fighter who had run risks and met dangers without a second thought had become a tavern keeper and trade organization concessionaire, a congenial and respected but lukewarm man pushing thirty, doing his best to deal honestly with everyone and not alienate anyone.

I had only myself to blame for my lack of passion, although maybe I blamed time a little, too, blamed it for creeping along in Baia Luna in uneventful monotony. I did my work, sold my wares, waited on my guests, and drove to Kronauburg once a month to replenish my stock. Sure, I saw the signs of change but had long ago been infected by the virus of lassitude. My will to life would only flare up from time to time, usually when I felt a sexual urge. When that happened, I would seek relief with the women who sold their favors in the district capital, although they supposedly didn't exist in Socialism. By the time they were whispering into the ear of their next john that he really knew how to put it to them, I was already thinking wistfully of the promise I had given Buba Gabor on the wondrous night of my sixteenth birthday and of the promise

she had given me. After my visits to those women, that night Buba
and I had become man and wife stuck in my conscious mind as a
mere thorn in the flesh of memory, no longer able to make me cry
out in pain. Whenever I recalled in my loneliness Buba's promise
to wait for me, I was overcome by a rush of tearful sentimentality.
I would get drunk, feel strong and full of fight, but I awoke the
next morning with a throbbing head and unable to act on the brave
resolutions I had made the night before. What could I do? Buba
was gone—somewhere. Angela had been wrong. Stephanescu had
not been toppled, much less destroyed. Instead, the news was filled
with stories of his successes in the district capital. Heinrich Hofmann was long dead, and no court in Transmontania in those days
was about to rule on whether he died by accident or at the hand
of Stephanescu's goons. There was no justice in this world. Would
there be at the end of days? What was one to think about the Last
Judgment in which my grandfather still put all his trust? Could be
that there was something to it, but could be there wasn't.

I entered the church in broad daylight, took the steps to the
chancel two at a time, and unlocked the tabernacle. Everything was
there as I had left it. The photo of Angela puckering for a kiss, the
one of her former friend Alexa with the sunflower dress hitched up
and the negative that went with it, and the four black postcard-sized
pictures with one large and eleven small white dots all lay between
the pages of the green notebook. I opened the diary, and for one
heartbeat the smell of fire, smoke, and damp earth rose from its
pages. *Hope for nothing and you won't be disappointed.* I was dismayed
as Buba's image came to my mind. "That's not right, Pavel," she
had said to me as I held her in my arms. "Whoever hopes for nothing is not a flesh-and-blood human being."

I took the diary and the pictures, locked the tabernacle, and left
the little silver key in the lock for Antonius Wachenwerther. Then
I went straight to the Gypsies, to Susanna Gabor.

"Where's Buba?"

Buba's mother shivered in the icy coldness I was giving off.
She'd become old. Her hair was disheveled and her back bent. The
large eyes she had passed on to her daughter had shrunken to narrow slits from which she peered suspiciously at me.

"I know nothing. Get lost, *gajo*! I don't know where she is."

I was in a cold fury. I grabbed Susanna and locked my hands around her throat. "I'll wring your neck," I said so fiercely that Susanna went white with fear.

"I-I-Italy."

I let her go. "What did you say?"

The Gypsy woman dropped onto a chair and sobbed, "Buba's in Italy. It's not what I wanted, believe me. The men said she would send home a lot of money every month, so I let those fellows take her. They were heading for Italy by way of Yugoslavia. But no money ever came. I haven't heard from Buba since." Susanna sobbed tearlessly. "It's not what I meant to happen. It was all because of how you shamed us. But I don't care about the money anymore, if only Buba would come back. You can have her as far as I'm concerned. Go to Italy and bring her back."

As I walked back into the village, my old schoolmate Hermann called to me, "Come over and lend a hand!" I ignored the invitation and went home to bed. A trip to Italy was an utter impossibility for me.

Meanwhile, the inhabitants of Baia Luna were busy getting ready for the festive installment of the new priest Antonius Wachenwerther. The schoolchildren were learning poems by heart. The men were currying their horses and polishing their wagons to a high shine. And the women sat at their sewing machines late into the night, making white and yellow parade banners and costumes in the old Kronauburg peasant style. It was high time for me to make another trip to the T.O. in Kronauburg, but I had so little motivation that I postponed the restocking until after the priest's arrival. Which would have consequences for my grandfather Ilja, since his epilepsy medicine was running low.

The installation ceremony for Antonius Wachenwerther went off to everyone's satisfaction. That is, it did until the High Mass. The procession took place in such an orderly, disciplined way it led the vicar-general of Kronauburg to smile approvingly upon the inhabitants of Baia Luna. The young pastor himself seemed not at all dissatisfied, although he still avoided direct eye contact with members of his flock. The procession was led by a splendid white horse with braided mane and colored ribbons on his tail. Andreas Schuster sat astride him with a straight back, carrying the flag of our patron saint. After Antonius Wachenwerther came the vicar-general and other priests from the diocese. The schoolchildren followed with their teacher, the women with the small children, the young men, the older men, and the Gypsies. Bringing up the rear—although actually not part of the procession—was Karl Koch, who had somehow lost his place and was being barked at by two stray dogs.

The scandal came during the closing service in the church. But first it has to be mentioned that during the procession, somebody suddenly realized that the Kronauburg clergy had forgotten to bring consecrated fire for the Eternal Flame. The vicar-general, a thoroughly practical churchman, had thereupon hurried over to a group of men and asked for some matches. When I produced a pack of matches from my pocket, the priest whispered that I should go light the Eternal Flame, but to hurry. I agreed and so the little red lamp was burning once more when I sat, as in the days of my youth, with my grandfather and the Gypsy in one of the front pews to listen to the new pastor's first sermon.

Without any words of greeting, Antonius Wachenwerther launched right into an explanation of why he was not allowed to preach from the pulpit. The Second Vatican Council (no one in the congregation had any idea what that was) forbade God's word being promulgated from on high, which he personally very much regretted for the sake of the honor of the divine word. Then he intimated that there was at least one good thing about the reforms of those modernizing intellectuals in Rome, since they were finally declaring war on the superstitions rampant among the common folk. In only two weeks, on August 15, the Feast of the Assumption, he intended to make it clear that the corporeal Assumption of Mary into heaven was not to be understood literally, since according to the Bible this was reserved for the Son of God exclusively. Besides which, the veneration of Woman, as clearly evidenced by the naked breasts of Eve, only distracted Man from devoting himself completely to the mystery of the virginity of the Mother of God. I cast a glance at Dimitru, but the Gypsy had fallen asleep.

After the credo, litany, and Lord's Prayer, Father Wachenwerther prepared to celebrate Holy Communion. Just as the new priest was about to transform the profane bread and wine into the sacred body and blood of Jesus Christ through the Eucharistic words, Grandfather Ilja started to get dizzy.

At first I assumed it was the cloud of incense.

But then Ilja stood up with staring eyes, pointed to the empty pedestal where the Virgin of Eternal Consolation used to stand so many years ago, and cried out to everyone's horror, "The priest is lying! He's lying to us. Mary lives! In the flesh! Enthroned in the Sea of Serenity. Down with the church! Down with the pope! Down with the Fourth Power!"

Grandfather uttered a piercing scream, flailed his arms, and dashed forward into the chancel. Dimitru, torn from his slumbers and still half asleep, jumped up and ran after him, but one of his friend's uncontrolled fists struck him so hard on the temple that he fell against the communion rail and didn't get up again. In an instant, the powerful arms of some of the men were grabbing for my grandfather, but it wasn't easy to subdue him until he suddenly went as limp as an empty sack and collapsed.

At that moment, the golden communion goblet fell from the hands of the priest. The consecrated hosts went spinning in all directions, and the blood-red wine spilled out onto the altar cloth. In horrified embarrassment, the young priest disappeared into the sacristy while the vicar-general kept his composure and picked up the hosts.

Hermann Schuster, Hans Schneider, and I firmly ushered my dazed grandfather out of the church.

The priest was so demoralized at his disastrous installation in office that he remained embittered for years. But instead of giving vent to his anger at Grandfather's irreverent behavior, Antonius Wachenwerther took refuge in silent rancor which, in the course of his time in office, took root as a profound antipathy to anyone who even mentioned the name Botev in his presence.

As you would expect of an epileptic, Ilja had no memory of his seizure and, despite the tireless pleading of Hermann Schuster, was unwilling to utter an apology to Antonius Wachenwerther. Instead, Grandfather kept babbling about a Fourth Power that was now active in Baia Luna in the person of the new priest. Which was why it was urgent that he get to the capital, since everyone knew that in two days the American president Richard M. Nixon would be honoring the Conducator with a visit. Hermann thought Grandfather's announcement was just crazy talk, but he humored Ilja by asking him who this ominous Fourth Power was.

"It's in the Vatican. The pope and his people are betting everything on the Mother of God not ever being found. That's why Wachenwerther is turning the dogma of Mary's corporeal Assumption upside down. He's making a redeemed woman and mother into a disembodied virgin. He wants to distract us from the fact that she's alive. The crescent beneath her feet proves she reigns on the moon, and that's why Khrushchev asked Gagarin about God."

"Man, Ilja, what's gotten into you? Since you've had this moon sickness you've been getting weirder by the day." Hermann Schuster grabbed Grandfather by the collar and was giving him a good shaking, trying to bring him back to reality, when he was brought up short by Grandfather asking, "Hermann, you were in the war. Tell me the truth: did you know that the Germans killed all the Jews?"

The Saxon let Grandfather go. "Yes, Ilja, I knew it. But I didn't want to believe it. I was young and at the front. What could I have done about it?"

"Probably nothing, but the pope in Rome could have. He should have cried out, Hermann. But he didn't. And so he promulgated the dogma of the corporeal Assumption of the Mother of God in 1950. You want to know why? Because his bad conscience about the Jews was torturing him. He left the Chosen People in the lurch during the Third Reich. Just like Johannes Baptiste used to say, never in history did the Church ever lift a finger for the Jews, even though they had to bear the heavy burden of crucifying their fellow Jew Jesus so we could be redeemed. The pope wanted to do Mary a favor with his dogma certifying that she had not returned to dust. By announcing her Assumption, Rome managed to save at least one Jew, if only posthumously."

Hermann Schuster was speechless.

Grandfather continued undeterred: "Then things got complicated for the Vatican. It all started with Sputnik. When he promulgated the dogma, the pope couldn't have known that one day man would overcome gravity and land on the moon. If the dogma was true, then someone would eventually find Mary, the Russians or the Americans or whoever. But that was definitely not something the Vatican wanted to happen. And so the clergy is putting all their efforts into the Madonna remaining undiscovered. The best thing would be if nobody ever again got the idea to look for her. That's why Wachenwerther announces that the dogma is not meant literally—so that anybody who keeps on searching will look like an idiot."

After trying for two hours to follow what Ilja was saying, Hermann Schuster felt like his skull was going to explode. Weighed down by the sad certainty that the *morbus lunaticus* had befuddled the brain of the formerly commonsensical tavern keeper, Hermann shuffled back to his Erika, while for the first time in his life Grandfather set about the difficult task of composing a letter in his clumsy hand, addressed to the last man on earth who had the power to challenge the Fourth Power.

As I learned later, Grandfather asked his daughter, my aunt Antonia, to take needle and thread and carefully sew that document into the lining of his wool jacket—with triple stitches, just in case.

It was the last day of July 1969, and Richard M. Nixon's visit to the capital had been announced for August 1. That an American president was about to visit a Socialist country for the first time just a few days after a successful landing on the moon was due to the influence of the Conducator, who was said by the poets to outshine even the sun. A parade from the airport to the Palace of the Republic was planned with stops along the route for handshaking with the crowd. It was a once-in-a-lifetime chance for Ilja.

Dimitru would have liked to accompany his friend but couldn't. He lay in bed with a concussion, so shaken he even forgot to ask for morphine. Ilja explained his plan to the Gypsy in a few words and kissed him farewell on the forehead. Dimitru nodded weakly and said only, "My friend, I'm with you. Be careful for both of us."

"Are you out of your mind? Where are you going?" Kathalina shouted at her father-in-law when she saw him bringing the horse out of the barn.

"To America!" he called, not because that was his destination but because he mistrusted even his nearest and dearest when it came to this mission.

I didn't even try to stop Grandfather from leaving. There was no point, and he was sure to show up again in a few days. But I was starting to realize that instead of protecting Grandfather from his Madonna madness, I was letting him get deeper and deeper into trouble.

With Grandfather's disappearance, Dimitru's time in Baia Luna was also running out. At first he had wanted to await Ilja's return in the library, but then he decided to leave Baia Luna immediately. It was the day on which he cursed Antonius Wachenwerther and prayed to God that there really was a hell.

A few days after taking office, the new priest had set about putting things in order in his parish. First he had all Catholics in the community register and set up church records; Johannes Baptiste had never kept any. Then he set his sights on the parish library. At Wachenwerther's instructions Dimitru, who had retired to his red chaise longue, had to remove that piece of furniture to the basement and surrender the key to the library. The priest spent one day in there alone, sorting through everything. He had all the books he deemed inappropriate for the parishioners stacked up in the laundry room where, in the course of the coming years, the musty smell of moldering paper would gradually drive out the scent of roses.

Then he inspected the cemetery. With the comment that the half-empty and useless hole next to the grave of Fernanda Klein was a testimony to the neglect of the churchyard, he had it filled in. Based on the names on the crosses, he then had the sacristan Julius Knaup give him an introduction to the history of the families of Baia Luna. The priest halted before a grave covered with elaborate decorations and cast a skeptical eye on the pile of plastic flowers that engulfed its cross.

"Who's buried here?"

"Laszlo Gabor, the father of that unspeakable Gypsy from the library. He died in 1935 under mysterious circumstances on the banks of the Tirnava right where a mother and daughter from our village were in the middle of the icy stream crying for help. And if I may be permitted to say so, Gabor died unbaptized."

In his militant determination to defend the Catholic faith against the forces of disintegration, the priest had the mortal remains of Laszlo Gabor exhumed and his bones stacked in a wooden crate.

Dimitru didn't utter a sound as the sacristan delivered his father's bones to him with the remark that there was still room on the slope above the cemetery wall next to Barbulescu.

Within the hour, Dimitru had loaded a covered wagon with the wooden crate and his other possessions and hitched up his horse. He drove over to our house to say good-bye.

"Kathalina and Pavel, my dears, thank you for everything."

Mother turned away in tears.

"Where are you going, Dimi?" asked Antonia, who had heaved herself out of bed.

"I'm going to join my father. But first I'm going to look for your father, my friend Ilja, and keep looking until I find him."

"Then I'm going with you. That is, if it's all right with you to have such a large woman along."

"It's fine with me, Antonia."

"Take this as a keepsake." Kathalina handed Dimitru the Bible the priest Johannes Baptiste had given Grandfather on his fifty-fifth birthday. "I hope Ilja gets some sense in his head and comes back soon. He won't miss the Bible, and if he does, at least he'll know the word of God is in good hands."

"Thank you for this gift. I'm accepting it, Kathalina, but you understand that I won't read it again until I've found Ilja."

I decided to wait a few more days for Grandfather and then begin looking for him myself. I gave Dimitru a farewell embrace and asked him to please send me a message if he heard any news about the whereabouts of his niece Buba.

His only reply was "Remember the foolish virgins, Pavel. When they got to the wedding, the oil in their lamps was all burned up." Then he squeezed onto the box next to Antonia and drove his wagon with the wooden crate over the Tirnava bridge for the last time in his life.

It remains to be mentioned that the catastrophic floods of the following year carried away more than the iron bridge. When the river overran its banks, the clay-brick dwellings of the Gypsies dissolved in the floodwaters. The homeless Gabor clan thereupon moved with their horses and wagons to the outskirts of Apoldasch, where the men were recruited as assistants to the workers constructing a dam on the upper reaches of the Tirnava. From then on, a giant power plant controlled the waters of the river in the spring and provided the Kronauburg District, including Baia Luna, with round-the-clock current until the time when the great shortages began, money and materials dried up, and the country went dark. But by that time, in Baia Luna, there was nothing left to remind people that Gypsies had once lived there.

When Grandfather had not returned to Baia Luna two weeks after his departure for America (of course, no one believed that was where he was going), I set off to find him. I guessed that Ilja had taken the train from Kronauburg to the capital to be at the state visit of Richard M. Nixon after leaving his wagon in the care of the owner of the Pofta Buna. But the latter denied knowing anything about an Ilja Botev from Baia Luna.

I weighed the possibilities: an accident, a crime, or the likelihood that he had suffered an epileptic attack and been found lying in a ditch somewhere along the road. I paid a visit to every hospital and police station between Kronauburg and the capital and finally ended up in the central Securitate office on the Calea Rahovei. There they listened to my story, but in that labyrinth of secrecy, no information about the whereabouts of my grandfather was forthcoming. I drove home, fervently hoping that Ilja had returned to Baia Luna in the meantime.

He had not.

To be sure of getting a good place, Ilja Botev was already on the Boulevard of Victory on the afternoon of July 31, 1969, leaning against one of the police barriers. The American president and the Conducator would surely pass by here on the next day. The colorful forest of flags already lining the streets promised a fancy parade.

Two men in black leather jackets came up to Ilja and asked to see his papers.

"Don't have them with me."

"Who are you? What are you doing here?"

"Ilja Botev from Baia Luna. I'm waiting."

"We can see that. Baia Luna? Where's that?"

"Kronauburg District, Apoldasch Township."

"You're telling us you came all the way down from the mountains just to see the American president?"

"I didn't say that!"

"Then what are you doing here without an ID?"

"None of your business, big shot!"

Quick as a flash, one of the men grabbed Ilja by the wrist and twisted his arm behind his back. His partner patted him down around his waist, from his crotch down his legs to his shoes, then his shirt, belly, and back.

"Nothing. No weapons, no pamphlets. So what are you doing here?"

"That's my own business."

The security agent who was holding Ilja's arm gave it a sharp jerk. The old man grimaced at the pain in his shoulder but gritted his teeth.

"I'm an old man," groaned Ilja. "Why are you doing this?"

They didn't answer. The security agents pushed him along and bundled him into the rear of a green car, then drove to the Calea Rahovei. In his entire sixty-seven years of life, Ilja Botev had never before entered a building as huge as the headquarters of the Security Service. The men led him through side wings, corridors, and hallways and finally into a room with two chairs and a battered metal table on which stood a black Bakelite telephone. Although it was summer, the interrogation room was as cold as a refrigerator. The security agents pulled off Ilja's jacket and pants and left the room, locking the door behind them.

Ilja's entire body was shivering and his right shoulder hurt like the devil by the time a Securitate major entered the room. He was wearing a fur coat. He began questioning Ilja about the sense and purpose of his long journey and after an hour was convinced that the prisoner was harmless. There were many crazy people in the country, but in all his interrogations, he had never met another nut like this man who insisted he had come all the way from the mountains to the capital to ask President Nixon to send another shipload of chewing gum to Transmontania.

The major handed Ilja his pants and helped him into his jacket.

Then he felt something. He tore out the lining of the woolen garment and removed a letter and a black photograph with a dozen white dots. He read the letter, shook his head, and left the room.

After a while, he returned with his superior. Ilja Botev knew the man with the pudgy face who looked him fiercely in the eye.

Colonel Lupu Raducanu picked up Ilja's letter. It was addressed to the first chairman of the State Council and began with the words "Most honored Comrade General Secretary, Titan and Conducator, we need your help." Lupu read the letter to the end and grinned. "Well, what do you know. Ilja Botev from Baia Luna. What are we going to do with you, Mr. Botev?"

Ilja said nothing.

"You have total confidence in our country, and you would like our head of state to have some rockets built? Our nation's very own lunar landing program, financed by the American president! Sounds good."

Raducanu put a wool blanket over Ilja's shoulders. "But you must be cold. I think your ideas have a future. We can certainly do something about this."

Ilja's eyes were shining confidently.

"I would think," said Raducanu, "that the Conducator can take care of the Fourth Power. Who else, if not him?"

Ilja nodded.

"If I read this rightly, your client is a certain Jewess by the name of Mary who lives in the Sea of Serenity on the moon, surrounded by shining lights, as proved by the white dots on this photograph."

"Correct."

"Do you know what I suggest, Mr. Botev? I'll hang on to this letter and give it to the Conducator myself. That way, you don't need to push your way forward through thousands of people at the parade. The head of state will then confer with President Nixon about the matter. Agreed?"

Ilja nodded again. Raducanu put the letter and the photograph into his pocket, then picked up the telephone. Shortly thereafter, two men in plainclothes entered the room. Before Ilja had time to grasp what Lupu Raducanu meant with the order "Bring him to Dr. Pauker," the men had given him a shot.

Ilja woke up in a remote area, a side valley of the Alt River, three hours by car from the capital. Behind the façade of a former military barracks was a psychiatric hospital that the locals talked about in hushed voices. They said anyone sent in there never cast a shadow again.

In days gone by, Dimitru had always made great claims about the power of his loins, but if anyone thought that my aunt Antonia, sitting beside him, would become his lover, the sight of the unequal couple would soon change their mind. While even in hard times, Antonia Botev's already generous proportions continued to increase, the Gypsy became skinnier and skinnier. He was actually shrinking, getting smaller and smaller until he was so insubstantial that you hardly noticed him next to the ample body of his companion. No matter what village they were passing through, they seldom stayed longer than a few hours and always asked after a certain Ilja Botev from Baia Luna. But no one knew of a man with that name. Only once—it must have been in the seventh or eighth year of their search—a coffin maker in the Maramuresch Mountains told them about a burial that had recently taken place in the cemetery in Viseu de Jos. If he remembered right, the deceased was over seventy and his name was Botev.

Dimitru purchased one of the ready-made white lacquered children's coffins the carpenter had stocked up on in anticipation of the coming winter, transferred his father's bones into it, and headed for the cemetery the man had named. And there was in fact a freshly dug grave with a cross on which, to Antonia's and Dimitru's horror, was written the name Ilja Botev.

They quickly found the relatives of the deceased, friendly people who offered them hospitality for several days, although they turned out not to be even remotely related to the Botevs of Baia Luna. Dimitru and Antonia were relieved to discover that the deceased could not possibly have been their friend and father.

The Gypsy and his companion stayed one night and then continued their journey in the knowledge that in a respected family in the far north of Transmontania, there had been a second Ilja Botev.

Although Antonia and Dimitru were not a couple in the conventional sense, their relationship was nevertheless much more than that of a homeless man and his voluntary companion. For one thing, Antonia liked being on the move. She even found the constant change of location to be a sort of liberation. For another, she had developed a fondness for Dimitru that sprang neither from the fleeting excitement of desire nor the established love between husband and wife. Instead, in their relationship she adopted the role of an attentive mother, a role that proved so congenial and satisfying to Antonia that, for the first time, she realized she had simply slept through her years in Baia Luna.

Although the Gypsy's physical self was shrinking, he had lost none of his intellectual alertness, but he did develop a state of mind that complemented Antonia's maternal role. Not that Dimitru's behavior was childish. He didn't complain and whine or make any sort of infantile impression during the day. But at night, when even in the summer he was chilly and shivering, nothing made him happier than to roll up in a ball and snuggle in the security of her ample body, not like a man but like a sad, hurt little boy.

Aside from the child's coffin in which Dimitru carried the bones of his father, their most precious possession proved to be Ilja's Bible. Since for a Black it was an awful thing to make a firm promise but, once made, an even worse thing to break it, he kept his oath not to open the sacred Scripture again until he had found his friend Ilja. But even in the darkest of dark times, Dimitru never completely lost his craftiness, and that being so, he waited patiently for Antonia to draw the correct *conclusio* from the two "facticities," namely, that he owned a Bible but was not allowed to read it.

"Dimi dear," said Antonia one August evening as they were lying in the grass next to their wagon, bathed in the last rays of the setting sun, "your oath wouldn't prevent me from reading to you from the Scripture, would it?"

"I'm delighted by your wisdom, my love. You recite and I'll memorize. Once I've got the word of God *completamente* by heart, my oath can go to hell. Let's get started right away. From chapter one to chapter . . . say, how many chapters did the Lord God dictate to his chroniclers back then, anyway?"

"Many, I'd say. Very many, even."

From then on, Antonia read aloud, and the next morning she quizzed him on the verses from the night before. Dimitru always had them letter perfect—with book, chapter, and verse—unless he had indulged in concentration-enhancing beverages. But after a demanding day of driving the wagon his capacity to absorb the text was very limited, and so Antonia's evening readings were often restricted to two or three verses.

And so it was that disaster didn't strike Dimitru Carolea Gabor until the beginning of the eighties, in the twelfth year of his search for his friend Ilja. They had reached the Gospel According to John, and Dimitru was feverish with excited anticipation, since many passages in it were familiar to him from Papa Baptiste's sermons. He was especially eager to get to the end, where the risen Christ descends to earth once more to display his wounds and let doubting Thomas put his fingers in them while the Savior tells him that blessed are they that have not seen and yet have believed. That sentence was one of Dimitru's favorites, since the word of God confirmed it was only the timid soul who needed some visible proof but not the trusting soul able to see the reality of ideas. Thus, of all the sentences the Gypsy's receptive ear had ever heard, he loved the beginning of the Gospel of Saint John, just like Papa Baptiste in bygone days.

"In the beginning was the Word, and the Word was with God, and the Word was God," read Antonia. As she continued with "And the Word was made flesh, and dwelt among us," her Dimi shone like a comet in the heavens.

"That, my dear, is the most beautiful message ever bestowed on the world." As Dimitru said that sentence, he had no idea that it would be burned to ashes a few chapters later.

Antonia read on. In the years of reading the Bible aloud, she had always refrained from any commentary so as not to confuse Dimitru in his reception of the sacred word. But then she got to chapter 3, verse 5, of the Gospel of Saint John: "'Verily, verily, I say unto thee, except a man be born of water, and of the spirit, he cannot enter into the kingdom of God. That which is born of the flesh is flesh; and that which is born of the Spirit is spirit.'" Antonia cried, "I know that! My father Ilja recited that in the Baia Luna church to prove to Kora Konstantin how well he had mastered the art of reading."

"That's right," said Dimitru. "Keep reading."

And then he heard from Antonia's lips the words of Jesus, "'If I have told you earthly things, and ye believe not, how shall ye believe, if I tell you of heavenly things? And no man hath ascended up to heaven, but he that came down from heaven, even the Son of Man.'"

"What was that you just said?"

Antonia repeated the last sentence.

In horror, Dimitru grabbed the Bible out of her hands and broke his promise. He said softly, "'And no man hath ascended up to heaven, but he that came down from heaven, even the Son of Man.'"

"What's wrong, Dimitru?" asked Antonia, who was as bewildered as she was anxious about the expression on her companion's face.

"It was all for nothing. Mary never went up to heaven in the flesh. It says so right here. God himself says in his very own words that only one person ever ascended to heaven. Only Jesus, the Son of Man. No one else. Why didn't anyone tell us? If only I had known this earlier! I would never have let Ilja leave Baia Luna. It's my fault and no one else's. I pulled my friend into the biggest mistake of my life. Mary was mortal and stayed mortal. She's not on the moon. She returned to the dust of earth. Ilja will never forgive me, never."

"But Mary is in heaven! You told me yourself you saw her that time on the Mondberg, looking through the telescope."

"Antonia, Antonia," Dimitru wept. "I did see her! For sure! But I can't remember anymore. I was so drunk because your nephew Pavel gave us all that schnapps to take along!"

"And what about the pope's dogma? The Assumption of God's mother into heaven was an infallible promulgation!"

"A lie! I don't know why, but it was a lie. How should a Gypsy like me know why the pope puts his own word above the divine word in the Gospel?"

Since Antonia had no answer, she could feel her Dimitru shrivel in her arms to a pitiful little old man.

Chapter Thirteen

THE ABYSS BEHIND THE WORDS, UNEXPECTED ENCOUNTERS,

AND THE MOST DANGEROUS FOE OF ALL

Today, as I look back over my life, the Age of Gold seems like the rise and fall of a distant star, a sun that gives light and warmth for a while, expands into a huge red giant, and finally collapses under the weight of its own mass. In the end, all that remained of the New Nation was a greedy black hole that had devoured years of my life and turned the ardent dreams of my youth to ice.

We couldn't see colors any longer. Although the meadows of Baia Luna were green in spring, the sky blue in summer, and the snow white in winter, all we could see was gray. We were blind. And we were mute. There was a time when we were silent for fear of the Security Service. But my fear of Colonel Raducanu and his henchmen had never crippled me. It just kept me on my guard. We were mute because of the emptiness behind the words. There was nothing there but an abyss. Of course we still spoke, but things dissolved and disappeared in their names. Time was so used up that names had no more need of things. You could no longer point to something and say, That's what that is called.

The church was no longer the house of God but just dead stone walls. The steeple clock was no longer a clock. The priest was no longer a shepherd of his flock, and the cemetery no longer a final resting place, just somewhere to stow corpses. Even the Eternal Flame was nothing but a wick glimmering in oil. Nothing was what it was called anymore.

Our family-run co-op market with its empty shelves was a store in name only. There was no sugar, no milk, no oil, only rationed cornmeal and canned tomatoes. We had plenty of those, but nothing else. To have at least a few drops of fat floating in their soup on holidays, the village women trekked to the district capital—on foot, since the buses couldn't run without diesel fuel. I remember vividly my mother coming back with a pig's foot and two chicken feet. As furious as Kathalina was, she vented her anger on the priest. "Go to hell, you gravedigger!" she told him to his face. Every morning Antonius Wachenwerther ate eggs, sausages, and the bacon parishioners brought him, while the village children went for weeks without so much as a swallow of milk.

As for me, I stopped going to church when the priest had the bones of the unbaptized Gypsy Laszlo Gabor disinterred. That act met with the approval of some people in the village, but not everyone. The Kallays, the Petrovs, and the Scherban brothers weren't seen at Mass thereafter, or Hermann Schuster either. The Saxon was unable to say the Lord's Prayer anymore. He couldn't force himself to say "Give us this day our daily bread" along with Wachenwerther. Sadly, Schusters' Hermann died shortly after the revolution, and Istvan Kallay as well. I wish the two of them could have experienced the era of freedom.

The red giant imploded, but not with a powerful bang. It winked out so quietly and gradually that, at first, people in Baia Luna didn't even notice that the Age of Gold had collapsed. The man whose glory outshone the sun had cooled to a dead star. His final rays still glimmered here and there, long after people began whispering that they had been extinguished forever by a firing squad against a wall in the courtyard of a military barracks.

Something's happening. I'm sure something's going on." Excitedly, Petre Petrov turned to Istvan Kallay's son Imre and me. "You try it."

We'd been hunched in front of the radio for hours turning the knob, but reception of Radio Free Europe kept getting interrupted.

"They're jamming it," Imre guessed. "They don't want us to know what's happening in our own country."

All we'd been able to find out was that there was fighting in the city of Timisoara. There'd been an insurrection. Finally, Imre found a Hungarian station. According to their news broadcast, the army and armored units of the Securitate from the capital had been sent to the Banat region in the western part of the country to put down the revolt with tear gas, water cannons, shields, and riot sticks. The Protestant pastor Laszlo Tokes had started the ball rolling with his courageous sermons. His audience grew by the day and took away a single message: the Conductor had to go. Obviously, Tokes's own bishop had stabbed him in the back. The Securitate had pressured him to discipline the pastor by transferring him to a village so far out in the sticks it wasn't to be found on any map of Transmontania.

But the people didn't cooperate. They shielded their pastor, and their demonstrations grew larger and larger. Workers in the state-owned enterprises refused to lift a finger and called for a strike. They streamed out of the factories chanting "Freedom! Freedom! Down with the tyrant! Death to Communism" and waving Transmontanian flags with holes cut in the middle where the red star used to be.

Then the first shots, the first blood, the first fatalities among the demonstrators.

We went over to the Kiselev twins' place—Petre Petrov, Imre Kallay, Andreas Schuster, and I—and sat ourselves down in front of their TV. Drina apologized for not having any cookies to offer us. The Conductor stepped in front of the cameras of the state network. His wife Elena straightened his tie. If the subsequent testimony of one of his bodyguards is to be believed, she hissed at him, "Don't start babbling again!" The Conductor spoke, and the people still listened. It was the evening of December 20, 1989.

"Hooligans," he said. "Hooligans are to blame! They throw stones at shopwindows, torch nice cars, and want to destroy our Age of Gold."

"'Huligens'? What's that?" said Petre. I had no idea what kind of people our head of state was talking about either. Then we learned about all the other people who were to blame for threatening law and order in our country: reactionary rioters in the pay of capitalist imperialism were to blame, notorious disturbers of the peace financed by counterfeit money from the wallets of Western intelligence agencies were to blame. They were being paid by spies from England, France, America, even from Russia. The only world leaders we could still count on were the Chinese. They were holding the banner aloft. Shirkers were to blame, too, that pack of lazy good-for-nothings. And the Gypsies were the worst of the lot, an ungrateful people despite the lovely homes they had been given. They slunk along behind the huligens, waiting until the terrorists threw stones through the windows and then plundering the people's jewelry stores. And who had incited them? Who was stirring all this up? Budapest! The Hungarians were behind it, directing the uprising after betraying their own Socialism. Now they wanted to snatch half of Transmontania for themselves. And the Democratic Germans were traitors, too, the ones who had just awarded him the golden Karl Marx Medal and sworn that neither ox nor ass could keep them from achieving world-class status. We'd been betrayed by the Poles as well, paying more attention to the pope and their Black Madonna than to Lenin. And the Czechoslovaks weren't a bit better, not to mention the Bulgarians. Fraternal republics my eye! Judas states in thrall to international capital was more like it. Sure, there were some things in our country that needed improvement. But the expensive oil we had to buy from the Soviets was to blame, and the missing hogs we needed to fatten so we could pay the Russians for their oil. And what about Gorbachev? It was his idiotic glasnost that was plunging the world into chaos. Of course, freedom would continue to be guaranteed in our country. Everyone was welcome—Cubans, Chinese, and North Koreans. But basically (so declared the Conducator afterward in the back room), his incompetent cabinet ministers were to blame.

"M-m-make these hooligans shut up!" he bellowed at his generals. "Or I'll put you all up against the wall!"

Elena intervened to calm him down and soothe his feelings. "First we'll declare a state of emergency: organize a lovely rally, distribute flags, produce red banners. Everything's going to be okay."

The functionaries had to watch videos from Tiananmen Square in Peking so they'd get it through their heads how a resolute state brought rebellious demonstrators to their senses. The president set up a hotline for an emergency conference with every regional secretary in the country. They all agreed to organize gasoline, assemble any buses that were still operational, and send seasoned collectivists to the capital to cheer on the regime.

All except one.

In Kronauburg, Dr. Stefan Stephanescu's telephone was permanently busy. Later, the chroniclers would write that those were the hours when he was mustering up important people to form a Front for National Salvation and Rebirth.

December 21, 1989: Red flags, red banners, eternal gratitude as far as the eye could see. In the Paris of the East, ten thousand people held aloft placards with pictures of the royal couple—although at a considerably younger age—and the masses pledged their loyalty to the nation, the party, and eternal loyalty to the Conducator.

Imre, Petre, and I were still sitting in front of Drina's TV. We couldn't believe our eyes. What had Radio Free Europe been talking about? Rebellion? Uprising? Revolution? Where were they?

December 22, 1989: More and more people kept streaming into the capital. Without flags, without banners, without placards. A boundless sea of dark faces, determined to do something, but still waiting. The TV cameras showed the first fists hammering on the gates to the Central Committee's building. Then the camera panned to the balcony. The Conducator appeared and stepped to the microphone, minus his scepter. Black sport coat, white shirt, dark tie with a pattern of dots that looked like tiny suns. When he opened his mouth, people's anger broke out. Excited yells, shrill whistles. Helpless and intimidated, the head of state raised both hands: Double wages, triple wages! They're yours! Higher pensions, more child support, too. Enough to eat, warmer apartments—it would all be ordered. The Conducator mutated into an ancient little boy, promising to make up for everything without even knowing what he'd done wrong. No one heard him. The loudspeakers were loud, but the people were louder. They raged, booed, bellowed, a roaring hurricane of fury. Crucify him! Crucify him! Responsible parties at the TV station were still ruled by fear. Were they allowed to show that? The final beam of light from the dying star was still on its way, still capable of burning someone. Then we heard nothing more. The TV guys had turned off the audio.

When a helicopter took off at noon from the roof of the building where the Central Committee held its meetings, the screens remained dark.

We turned on Drina Kiselev's radio and found Radio Free Europe. The station announced that the dictator and his wife had fled. But Petre and I were doubting Thomases. We wanted to see, not just hear. We waited until afternoon, when images again flitted across the picture tube.

At a long table in the old Royal Palace sat the leaders of the revolution: Voiculescu, Roman, Brucan, Mazilu. There were also a couple of generals, officers who had gone over to the people's side. Except for Iliescu, recipient of the Hammer and Sickle Medal, I'd never heard their names before. And how would I have? They were all second- and third-tier party comrades now emerging from the shadows. Each of them had a go at the microphone. Then it was Mircea Dinescu's turn, a dissident writer under permanent house arrest. He announced the flight of the dictator couple. But I had no eyes for the poet, only for the man sitting to his left: graying hair carefully combed back, serious demeanor. They handed him the microphone.

"Dear Comra—." Dr. Stefan Stephanescu stopped short, grinned. Everyone laughed except for the poet. "Honored ladies and gentlemen. In this revolutionary hour I appeal to everyone in our country, and announce the formation of a Front for National Salvation. The Conductor and his wife, who have plunged our nation into the abyss, are about to be apprehended. They will have to answer for their crimes before the law, and I promise you, our courageous and long-suffering people . . ."

I saw the cameramen crowding around Stephanescu, shoving and pushing one another aside. Someone was forging his way to the podium through the pack of journalists, moving ahead easily and without using his elbows, as if unaware of the tumult around him. It seemed they were voluntarily opening up a path for him. He approached Stephanescu without haste, almost sedately. You could only see him from behind. His light clothing identified him as a foreigner, a Westerner. American, perhaps? He raised a camera to his eye. There were a few flashes, and Stephanescu smiled.

Suddenly there were shots, the TV images wobbled, rifle fire rattled and grenades detonated. The cameras cut to the square in front of the former Royal Palace: running figures, burning barricades, wailing sirens. And repeatedly: shots, blood, the wounded, and the dead. The remaining stalwarts of the Conductor brought death until the very end. In the midst of it all moved the man in light-colored clothing. Calmly and without the slightest fear, he shot his pictures. I knew that walk, got a fleeting glimpse of his face. It had been more than thirty years since I'd last seen him. Petre Petrov didn't recognize him, but I was absolutely sure: Fritz Hofmann had returned, treading in his father's footsteps, a photographer documenting the end of the Age of Gold.

I stood up to leave Drina Kiselev's living room.

"You're leaving at such a historic moment?" Petre was indignant.

But in ten minutes I was back with a green diary and two photographs in my pocket. I looked at Petre and said only, "Wachenwerther has a German Volkswagen."

"Count me in."

Once Petre's army carbine was stowed in the trunk, we roared off and reached the capital early the next morning. It was two days before Christmas, and the night had not ended, the day hadn't begun, and the acrid smell of tear gas hung in the cold December air.

Petre joined a group of rebellious miners from Lupeni who didn't quite know whom to shoot at in the confusion of the revolt, and I sat myself down on a greasy sofa in the foyer of the Hotel Intercontinental. That's where the press people stayed. I waited for the man who had once extinguished the Eternal Flame in Baia Luna and on whom I had pinned the blame for betraying the priest Johannes Baptiste.

Then he came ambling down the stairs. Despite the heavy bag of photo equipment hanging from one shoulder, his step had something light-footed about it, as if no one and nothing could surprise him. No doubt at all that it was Fritz Hofmann. My heart was pounding. This man was a stranger. "You aren't really one of us," I had told him once. Now he was back, back from another world.

I walked up to my old school friend. Fritz blinked and stopped short. Then he let the bag slide off his shoulder.

"Pavel Botev," he cried and spread his arms, but then immediately let them fall again. For a split second I had the impression that Fritz wasn't looking at me but through me. We shook hands like two people who don't trust their own joy.

"How could you stand to stay in this country, Pavel?"

"I ask myself the same question. And that's why I'm here."

While shots echoed through the capital, Fritz Hofmann's cameras stayed in his bag. We sat in his hotel room until the morning of Christmas Eve. Fritz listened, talked, and surprised me with a frank openness I had not expected.

"So now you're a photographer, like your father."

"Yes. Like my father, but with one difference. He photographed the powerful because he wanted to belong. I make pictures because I know that I'll never belong anywhere."

"How do you mean?"

"A long time ago you said something I never thought at the time would turn out to be true for me. Remember the night before I blew out the Eternal Flame? You said I'd have to pay a price for leaving Baia Luna, and you were right."

"Did I really say that? It was such a long time ago."

"Not for me, although this is the first time I've been back in the country in more than thirty years. When I moved to Germany with my mother I was sure I would soon forget Baia Luna, and I probably would have if I hadn't gotten a letter from Julia the spring after we moved."

"From Julia Simenov in our class?"

"Yes. She told me they'd found the teacher Barbulescu up on the Mondberg during the Christmas procession. Julia really reproached me. She wrote that my impertinence had driven the Barbu to take her own life, when I wrote the sentence on the blackboard about my thing getting hard. The worst thing was that Barbu didn't take the switch to me. I wish she had thrashed me. Blows never bothered me very much. But when she just stood there at the board and cried, I had to get out of there. I couldn't bear to look at her. Do you still remember how we took the drunk Gypsy home that night, on your grandfather's birthday? I noticed right away that there weren't any lights on in Barbu's house and it didn't take a genius to figure out she had done something to herself. Doesn't matter, I told myself again and again, doesn't matter. She was only a broken-down drunk. And I blew out the light in the church to prove that nothing mattered. I was just stupid. Then Julia writes me that it was my fault that the teacher resorted to the rope. I didn't mean to hurt Barbu, Pavel. It was a game, just like the imaginary numbers we wrote in our notebooks during class. I wanted to see how much I could get away with, but I never meant for her to do something to herself because of me."

I was silent, as a sign that I understood.

"Believe me, as a photographer I've seen half the world in the last twenty years, and always the dirty side of it, really bad, bad things. If there's a conflagration somewhere, I have to go there. It's like a compulsion. That's the price I pay. I can't stand staying anywhere too long. But I wanted my photographs to show what people can do to other people. Not because I'm so noble. For me, all beauty is boring, empty. Only war is real—war, catastrophe, famine, suffering, and pain. When I see the pain of others, I feel alive."

"That's a dangerous life," I said in embarrassment.

Fritz hesitated before answering. "Maybe so, seen from out-side. But for me, peace and quiet are unbearable. Homelessness has become my home. But I'm tired, Pavel. Always on the go and never really getting anywhere. Photographing the world's atrocities so I won't have to see that one image from Baia Luna. As if I could shove aside a terrible picture with even more terrible pictures. But I don't succeed. Barbu keeps reappearing, as if emerging from black waters. I often go for months without seeing it, but then I see her again, alone and dragging herself up the Mondberg. And before she puts the noose around her neck, she says, Fritz, you're just like your father. Pavel, when you came up to me today in the lobby I was really happy, until Barbu suddenly appeared behind you. She was standing by the back wall of the classroom, and I was sitting beside you again on the bench, rewriting party poems by that guy . . ."

"Margul-Sperber!"

"Exactly! Alfred Margul-Sperber. 'Hymn to the Party'!" Fritz smiled and then he had to grin. "Be honest, Pavel, weren't my verses poetic masterpieces compared to that rhymed nonsense in the schoolbooks?"

"Now look about. Where'er you bend your gaze, / Another party idiot is born, / And our Miss Barbu's daily drunken daze, / Shall be in progress long before the morn," I quoted from mem-ory. I reached for Fritz Hofmann's cigarettes and lit myself a Marl-boro. "By the way, Angela Barbulescu was totally aware of all your rewrites. And of our fantastic solutions in math, too. She really did think you had talent as a poet, Fritz. Everything was different than we thought. Her death may not have been a suicide. What Julia wrote you isn't right. It's possible that Angela's death was only rigged to look like a suicide, that she was really hanged by someone else. On the day she was last seen in Baia Luna she was visited by a certain Albin, a big strong guy with a wart on his cheek. This Albin was a buddy of Stefan Stephanescu's and your father's. Fritz, I know Angela Barbulescu's death had nothing to do with your dumb scribbling. It had to do with those filthy photos you found in your father's moving crate."

"What? What are you saying?"

I got out Angela's diary and took out of it the lewd photo Fritz had left with me. Fritz started reading without another word. Occasionally he would narrow his eyes as if he couldn't believe what was in the green notebook. Not until he got to Angela's entries about the Christmas Eve party at the apartment of the party boss Koka did Fritz make a comment.

"But what about this photo from my father's moving crate? Before I left for Germany, you claimed the naked woman was the teacher Barbulescu, but it was her friend Alexa."

"Right. But when I told you that, I hadn't read the diary yet. How was I supposed to know that the two women had exchanged dresses?"

"I can't believe this," Fritz read aloud from Angela's farewell letter to Stephanescu: "*The photos that Hofmann made of me with your disgusting friends are repulsive. They kept my mouth closed for a long time. But no longer. As far as I'm concerned, Hofmann can send those pictures to the village priest. Do whatever you want with them. Hang my picture on every lamppost. I'm not afraid anymore.*"

Fritz was pale. I showed him the half-burned photo of the young Angela puckering for a kiss. "That's what she looked like before she took up with the wrong crowd."

Fritz looked at the woman with the blond ponytail for several minutes, closed his eyes, and balled his fists. Then he took a deep breath. "Pavel, I'm starting to understand what must have happened. On the day you were supposed to hang up Stephanescu's portrait in our classroom, the teacher said you had to see the smiling doctor from Kronauburg in the right light. Not everything that glittered was gold, she said, or something like that. I had no idea what she meant, but I told my father about it because I was so angry. My father was a pig. I can say that today without hate, but he really was a filthy swine. As he was about to whip me with his belt again, I threatened that the Barbu was going to expose his friend Stephanescu, without really knowing what there was to expose. I remember just how I grinned at my father and threatened him. 'If Stephanescu falls, you're done for. Without the secretary and the party bosses, you're all washed up.' But I didn't have a clue what I was saying."

"What about your father? How did he react?"

"For one thing, he didn't whip me black and blue. He let me be. For another, the next day he had me put a sealed envelope into Father Baptiste's mailbox."

I was burning with curiosity. My white-hot excitement made the last thirty-two years shrink to a single yesterday.

"These disgusting photographs of Angela must have been in that envelope!"

"That's what we have to assume. But how could I have known? Of course, I asked what kind of letter it was, because my old man had never had anything to do with the priest. Now I know my father lied to me. He said he was going to leave the church. His baptismal and marriage certificates were in there—his parish records. I just thought to myself, This chicken is making me see to his affairs. But I left the envelope at home because you unexpectedly came over that afternoon to say that your grandfather had gotten a television for his birthday. I didn't remember the envelope until we were sitting in the tavern with Johannes Baptiste and the priest was telling those strange stories about Sputnik and the spaceflight project of that Korolev guy. Remember? Before my idiotic attack on the Eternal Flame I said to you and Buba, the Gypsy girl, I had to take care of something. And I really did. I had to mail the envelope. But in the meantime, my father had obviously taken it to the rectory himself. I hadn't the faintest idea that he had taken such evil pictures of Angela Barbulescu. Now I see clearly that my father assumed that those pictures would be the end of the Barbu in Baia Luna. All that remained was for her to hang herself."

"But the pictures disappeared. They were never made public! Johannes Baptiste was murdered and the rectory turned upside down. After which, that idiot Kora Konstantin spread the rumor that Angela Barbulescu had slit the pastor's throat to silence him and then had condemned herself to death for the deed. Most men in Baia Luna, however, assumed that the Securitate had the pastor on its conscience. They wanted to prevent him from preaching against the kolkhoz. What do you think?"

"I think the perpetrators were looking for the photographs. That's why they killed the priest. But I can't believe that my father would have gone that far. He was a mediocre photographer, a mediocre person, a parasite on the powerful who fantasized about Nietzsche's Superman. Perhaps he was useful for a while, until he made a mistake in the eyes of some functionary or other. Johannes Baptiste may have been a senile crank, or maybe a wise man. I can't judge that. But he was certainly not stupid. Once he held the photos of Angela in his hands, he must have wondered, Who are the men in these pictures? Who takes such pictures? And why are they putting these shameful objects into my mailbox all of a sudden? I wonder why my father gave the priest those photos. Did it make sense to ruin a woman who was already at the end of her tether? Dirty pictures don't just sully the person in them. Most of the dirt remains invisible, sticking to the person who took the pictures and distributed them. My father would only have used the photos as a threat but would never have really published them. And if you ask me who could have had an interest in seeing these blackmail pictures disappear again, then I can only think of Stephanescu. If what the diary says is right, he saw to it that Angela never had her child. In the hands of the priest, those photos could possibly have brought the entire truth about Stephanescu's machinations to light. And the good doctor wanted to prevent that from happening."

I confirmed Fritz Hofmann's suspicion and told him about visiting the photo lab assistant Irina Lupescu, stealing the negative, and my failed attempt to bring down Stephanescu by pasting the photographs onto the windows of his father Heinrich's studio.

"And you say my father had the accident one day after the big party spectacular? By the time we got the news in Germany, he'd been dead for a week. My mother and I have never visited his grave.

The Kronauburg regional administration wrote us that Father had gotten caught under a truck on his motorcycle."

"Without a helmet," I added. "That's what it said in the paper."

Fritz Hofmann bit his lip. "There was nothing about that in the letter we got. But that's impossible. He always wore his helmet. As a child, I never saw him get onto his motorcycle without a crash helmet. Never. Now I don't know what to think. I always thought Father was a swine. But maybe he was just a coward, a little cog in malevolent machine."

"Maybe they were blackmailing him, too?"

"I don't know." Fritz was silent while he studied the photo he had last held in his hand thirty-two years ago. "Who are these horny guys next to Stephanescu the champagne squirter, our new champion of national salvation?"

"The one nearest Stephanescu must be the doctor, Florin Pauker. He was the go-to guy for unwanted pregnancies. I don't know the next one, but this one here, the big hulk with the mustache and the wart, is Albin. He's the one who was in Baia Luna the afternoon Angela disappeared. And the hand holding the bottle, on the right edge, could be the one they called Koka. The party was at his place, and he was in a drinking contest with Albin."

"You didn't happen to come across a photo of Koka?" Fritz asked.

"No. Why do you ask?"

"Pavel, don't tell me you really didn't know how potentially explosive these pictures are—or, rather, used to be?"

"Sure, of course. Stephanescu didn't send the security agent Raducanu to find the darkroom in Baia Luna just for fun."

"But on whose orders? It may be that even Stephanescu was only a middleman. If the Kronauburg District secretary kowtowed to anyone, it was this Koka from the capital. That's why he didn't say a word when Koka insulted his Angela at the Christmas party. But he doesn't have to fear the cobbler anymore. The man who peed on the oysters way back then fled in a helicopter two days ago."

"What? The Conductor? But what does the head of state have to do with Koka in Angela's diary?"

"Man, Pavel! I thought you knew. They're one and the same. Koka is the Conductor."

"How do you know?"

"It's obvious. Besides, everything's there in the diary. At Christmastime in '48, Stephanescu made fun of the uneducated shoemaker in the party, but he put his tail between his legs when Koka called Angela a cheap Catholic cu— Well, you know what he called her."

"But the Conducator met with the most powerful men in the world! He was no shoemaker!"

"Yes, he was. Koka was an early nickname. His onetime buddies called him that before they learned to fear him. Everyone in other countries knew that the Conducator insisted on mixing his drinks with American Coca-Cola, even at state receptions. You wouldn't believe how many jokes people made about it. The best Bordeaux and Coca-Cola! Champagne with Coke! All the big-shot politicians would drop their jaws at state banquets. Of course, no statesman made jokes about it in public. But we journalists did. The Conducator is a total laughingstock, and so is his wife. Angela wrote in her diary that he married somebody called Lenutza, the hot number who swallowed down the pissy oysters on Christmas Eve. Her maiden name was Petrescu. Lenutza was a real slut. Later, they made her out to be a revolutionary heroine of the working class. As the woman at the side of the Conducator, of course, she couldn't be called Lenutza anymore, and Lenny was too cutesy for her. After the wedding she adopted the name Elena, probably to divert attention from her background. With only three years of elementary school, you're not likely to be a chemist with multiple Ph.D.'s, the state's leading scientist, and the most powerful woman in the country—except maybe in this particular country."

"It's unbelievable. In Baia Luna we didn't have the faintest idea what was going on in the rest of the country."

"Angela's friend Alexa," Fritz continued, "told her that Koka had loaned my father the money to buy a motorcycle and had given him the use of his apartment for those special photo sessions. Apparently, some of the pictures were taken without the subjects' knowledge. That can only mean that my father, Stephanescu, and Koka were in it together, until my father made a mistake and showed the pictures of Barbu to Johannes Baptiste."

I recalled the warning of the wiry-haired police commissioner:

*Keep your flame turned down, or you'll have a fire on your hands that will burn you badly.*

"So you figure that Stephanescu and your father were only the Conducator's accomplices?"

"I have no idea, but it's possible. They all profited, at least financially. My father gained access to the highest social circles even though he could hardly make a decent wedding portrait. It doesn't matter. But in any event, Stephanescu must have had a huge stake in keeping the champagne photo under lock and key. The picture couldn't do any damage to Koka, since he wasn't in the picture. By now it's all ancient history and doesn't matter anymore. At this point, the Conducator and his Lenutza won't have a shot at a normal trial. If I read the situation right, they've only got a few hours left to live. And I'll bet that as soon as that threat is gone, our party secretary from Kronauburg is going to be the man of the hour."

"What? That scumbag?"

"Sure. At the moment, Stephanescu is still holding back, but his people are already constructing a legend about him. They'll say he was always a man of the people and an opponent of the Conducator. Of course no one noticed anything of the kind. It's known as 'inner opposition.' Besides, Dr. Stephanescu is supposed to have been pulling the strings that brought down the Conducator. That's how they're clearing the path for his political future."

"It's . . . it's not right" were the only words I could get out. Without thinking, I opened Angela Barbulescu's diary: " '*His hour will come when he's reached the top.*' What does this mean, Fritz? Angela has been dead for more than thirty years."

"It's very mysterious. Oh, by the way, there's someone else who's displaying a remarkable interest in our Dr. Stephanescu, a woman to be exact. It was yesterday at the press conference, as they were introducing the Front for National Salvation. There was a woman sitting among the journalists, and when all my other colleagues were holding up their microphones and taking notes, she just sat there without moving. And she reminded me of Buba Gabor."

"Buba? How come? What did she look like?"

"She looked good. I mean very good for her age. But not like people around here, and not like a Gypsy either. She was dressed in

Western clothes, from southern Europe, I'd say. She looked like a Spanish woman, or an Italian."

"And what was she doing at the press conference?"

"No idea. She just caught my attention. Maybe because she was shivering even though the room was heated. She didn't notice me, just kept looking at Stephanescu with a really strange expression. How can I describe it? Not obtrusive, more detached, as if she was waiting for something to happen. Most of the time her eyes were closed. She was in sort of a trance, if you see what I'm trying to say."

"I understand perfectly. It was Buba! And Buba knows that Stephanescu will fall when he's reached the top. She knows our teacher's prophecy. Buba and I read the diary together. But we should help the Savior of the Nation along in his fall. It's high time to roll a couple stones into the path of the good doctor. How do you get near these big shots, Fritz?"

"With a press pass."

"Have you got one?"

"Of course. Several, in fact, and even a couple from American press agencies. In America they aren't worth the paper they're printed on, but around here they can open a lot of doors. Your Salvation Front people are drooling for any reporter who can lend them even a hint of international publicity. The Conductor is like that, too. But what do you have in mind?"

"I'll think of something."

Fritz laughed and handed me a stick of American chewing gum. "Okay. Whatever you think up—if you're sawing at Stephanescu's throne, I'll saw with you."

It was the afternoon of Christmas Eve, and Petre Petrov had been waiting in the foyer of the Interconti for hours. It was crawling with people: rebelling students, injured demonstrators, military personnel, party cadres, undercover security agents, members of the National Front, black-market currency traders, photographers. Nobody knew who belonged to whom or what side they were on, least of all the Western journalists for whom the uncertain fate of the Conducator had much higher news value than the confusion and struggle for spoils surrounding the political future of the country.

When Petre finally discovered me in the crowd, he barked at me, "Where've you been all this time? I thought we wanted to make a revolution."

Before I could answer, Petre did a double take. He stared at the man beside me and searched the farthest corners of his memory. Then he came at the photographer with his fists clenched. "Hofmann, you asshole, you priest murderer! What the fuck are you doing here?"

It was all I could do to restrain Petre. "No, Petre. Stop! It wasn't like that. Fritz had nothing to do with betraying Baptiste. I guarantee it one hundred percent. It was Stephanescu."

Petre broke off his attack.

"What am I supposed to have done? Betrayed Baptiste?" Fritz was dumbfounded. "Are you guys out of your minds?"

"Pavel used to claim that you and your father turned the pastor over to the Securitate because he was going to preach against fucking Socialism and collectivization. Then you took off for Germany."

"Bullshit," I said and blushed. "Petre, you got it all wrong."

Fritz put on the impudent grin I remembered from our school days together. "So now the score is one to one. You had all the trouble because of the Eternal Flame, and the betrayal was chalked up to me. Still tied, okay?"

"Okay," I said. Then someone tapped me on the shoulder.

I turned around.

"You still get just as red as you used to."

"Buba? No! Yes, it's you! You're here?"

I stood amazed, looking Buba up and down. Fritz had been right. She was different. She no longer fit the pale image I still clung to, the sad remains of my youthful memories, and yet I recognized in her the Buba who had once been so dear to me. She was beautiful. She had a wool shawl thrown over her shoulders to protect them from the wintry cold, and it made her seem light, almost weightless. The wrinkles around her eyes magnified their shine, and she emanated a warmth that made me afraid instead of joyful. When Buba unconsciously brushed the black locks from her eyes and pulled at a gold earring with her slender fingers, I stuck my hands in my pockets in embarrassment.

I was abashed. My threadbare jacket, faded pants, and run-down shoes were much more than just cheap clothes. They testified to a shabbiness that over the years had worked its way from outside to inside and taken possession of me. I wanted to hide. I was facing a woman who knew she was a woman. But I was not a man who considered himself worthy of her. I desperately tried to remind myself that it was Buba Gabor who had given herself to me in the most wonderful hour of my life. She was here, but I had vanished.

"Ah . . . ah . . . are you here because of Stephanescu?" I stammered, trying to hide my shame.

"No . . . that is, not really. I just flew in from Milan two days ago. Your aunt Antonia sent me a message about Uncle Dimitru. This is going to be his last Christmas. Uncle Dimi is dying. But Antonia wrote me that he can't go yet. Something's still missing. I don't know what it is, but I had to come back from Italy so he can look forward to his end. That's why I'm here. What about you?"

Someone knocked me to the ground. A commotion had started in the foyer, and in a few moments it turned into a panic. Outside, shots crackled through the streets again, at first only scattered, but then machine guns opened up in front of the Interconti, cross fire shattered the front windows, sirens wailed, and people screamed and ran for their lives into the hotel lobby.

Fritz put a stick of gum in his mouth and hung his cameras around his neck. "I'll see you later."

When I got back to my feet, rebels were carrying in a badly wounded man. They laid him gently onto the floor. The bystanders turned away in distress. There was nothing to be done for the victim. His upper body was almost completely separated from his lower extremities, but his eyes were still flickering. The man was about my age, and when I looked into his face, I had to suppress a scream of horror. I owed this man a debt. I knelt down and took his limp hand from which the warmth was ebbing.

"Thank you, Matei," I whispered to the nephew of the Kronauburg antiques dealer Gheorghe Gherghel. Matei showed no sign of recognition. I crossed myself and closed the eyes of the faithful ally who had once warned me about the security agent Raducanu.

"I want to see Dimitru," I said to Buba.

"You'll see him. I'll take you to him and your aunt. You'll be shocked, like me. But first we have something to take care of. That is"—Buba hesitated before finishing her sentence—"I don't really know if I can still talk about 'we' in our case."

Unsure of myself, I started to babble, "I saw Fritz on TV and recognized him. I had to come here. We weren't getting any news about the revolution in Baia Luna."

"So you're here on account of your friend from school. Well, why should you be looking for me just now, when you haven't looked for me in thirty years? I guess that means I—"

"But you . . . you didn't send any word either," I interrupted her. "You only came back on account of your uncle, too!"

"Are you going to argue with me? Think it over. What do you know about my life? Don't you know that a man looks for a woman, but the woman finds the man? Don't fight with me about it. I can fight better than you. I learned that in Italy. I'll tell you, any guy who groped me without paying got a slap in return that made him run home crying to Mama."

I was speechless, unable to utter a word in reply.

"But what do you know about life in Italy? I've been sitting in this miserable hotel for two days hoping you would come looking for me. Uncle Dimi said, 'Buba, dreaming doesn't pay, not in times like this, anyway. Forget your Pavel. He's stuck in Baia Luna.' Do you actually know how much faith Dimi set in you? He loved you like a son. Much, much more, in fact. I was still a girl when he said to me, 'Pavel's the right one for you. Pavel Botev can do something that no other *gajo* has ever succeeded at. He can turn the world upside down.' Yes indeed, that's exactly what my uncle said. But you, you—"

"Shut up," I shouted at her. "You don't know anything, either. Locked up in a goddamn Age of Gold for three decades. Do you have any idea what that means? How was I supposed to see colors when everything was gray? How was I supposed to turn the world upside down when it'd already been turned on its head by all the insanity? How was I supposed to know what was up and what was down when everything was turned around and inside out?" I reached into my jacket and took out the green notebook. "Here's why I'm here! Not to turn the world upside down, but to put it back on its feet. I saw Stephanescu on TV as he was announcing the Front for National Salvation. Everyone needs to be saved in this country, Buba, but not by that man."

Buba dropped her eyes. "Uncle Dimi said something like that to me yesterday." She reached hesitantly for my hand like a shy girl. "The diary—so you haven't forgotten Angela?"

"Yes, I did, Buba. I haven't thought about her for years. Everything that was once precious to me evaporated, finally even the strength to fight. All that was left was a memory that things had been alive once, I had been alive once. Sometimes I tried to call you to me. But there was no image there. The memory was there, but it was dead. What's wrong with me? Why did it take that creep Stephanescu on the screen to shake me awake?"

She looked at me. I felt a fleeting stab of happiness when Buba stroked my cheek.

"You're a good man," she said softly. "You didn't forget that you forgot. Come with me! This isn't a good place."

She took me by the arm and led me outside, far away, where there were no people wandering around with fear, hope, and uncertainty written on their faces. It was already dark and bitterly cold. We walked hand in hand through canyonlike streets between rows of apartment buildings, with the final rifle shots of the next-to-last day of the revolution fading away, the night of December 24, 1989. We told each other about ourselves by remaining silent.

When our feet began to ache, we discovered a church whose doors were open. Inside a few women in black murmured *Doamne miluieste, doamne miluieste*, Lord have mercy. Around midnight we sat alone on one of the rear pews, our hungry arms around each other and warmed by Buba's wool wrap. We slept. Next to the altar, a small red light flickered.

When Buba awoke in the early-morning hours, she kissed me on the lips.

"Pavel, there's a strange thing I can't get out of my head, something I don't understand. When I landed in the capital I got right on a bus to Titan II, the neighborhood where my people have lived since the Conductor forbade us to travel around or risk serious punishment. I wanted to go straight to Uncle Dimi, but it took forever because the streets were blocked on account of the revolution. Men kept jumping into the bus and crying 'Freedom, freedom, down with the Conducator!' and passing out leaflets. Everything they were demanding seemed to make sense to me until I read the name 'Dr. Stefan Stephanescu' at the bottom of the manifesto. I felt like I was falling down a hole. But not because of that malevolent man and not because of Angela and her child, whose lives he destroyed. It wasn't my pain at the suffering of others. It was my own pain. I no longer knew why I was there and what I wanted. Even Uncle Dimi didn't matter, suddenly. I thought of you, Pavel, of our night together. And it broke my heart that there was nothing left. I felt ancient. When I was forced to leave Baia Luna so long ago I was so terribly sad, but I was young and full of the certain knowledge that everything would be all right some distant day. Because life was just. But it isn't just. Not in Baia Luna and not in Milan or anywhere else. This thought is unbearable for a Gypsy. That's why we trust in heaven and believe in hell. But what's left if heaven is dead? Dust to dust! And that's why Uncle Dimi scared me so much when I saw him. I love him, Pavel. And that love hurts so much. He's not a Gypsy anymore, he's like me."

Buba knelt down and folded her hands in prayer. She ended with the *Ave Maria,* "Pray for us sinners now and in the hour of our death." Then she began talking again. "The strange thing I wanted to tell you happened the morning after I arrived. I told my uncle about the manifesto of the Democratic Front for National Salvation, which had scheduled a press conference for that afternoon in the old Royal Palace. When I mentioned the name Stefan Stephanescu, Dimi jumped up from his bed and cried, 'Dear God in heaven, please do a Black a favor just this once and bring him down!' Isn't that strange?"

"Yes, it is," I said. "It means Dimitru must have known Stephanescu, but how?"

"That's why I attended the press conference in the city. I had to see what kind of man he was. And I'll tell you, when you look at him, he seems friendly, even charming, and when he smiles he wins everyone's sympathy. But when you listen to him with your eyes closed, it makes you shiver. He's addressing you but he's not thinking of you. He's hollow. He fills people up with a bunch of words and sucks them dry at the same time. That evening, I asked Uncle Dimi if he thought Stephanescu was evil."

"And what did he say?"

"Something else I didn't really understand. Dimi said that was beyond his ability to decide and was a matter between Stephanescu and the Lord God at the Last Judgment. All he knew was that the man carried a demon within, a demon who would kill anyone who interfered with his progress. But then my uncle said something else: he gave me a warning. He forbade me to undertake anything against Stephanescu, much less try to fight him. He was cunning, he said, the most dangerous enemy you could imagine. Then Dimi prayed. Your aunt told me that the last time he had done that was when they were still traveling around in the wagon searching for your lost grandfather. Dimi prayed for a long time. He was speaking in a strange tongue that sometimes sounded like Italian: 'Papa Baptiste, Papa Baptiste,' was all I could understand. My uncle was appealing to the soul of the murdered pastor. When he was done, he lay down and went to sleep. When he woke up again, he told me there was only one chance to overcome the doctor."

"I'd like to hear what it is," I said, with steely determination.

"We have to wait for his moment of triumph and then use his own weapons against him. Dimi says that when the demon is backed into the farthest corner, he will show his face. And then the person who carries the demon within him is either redeemed or burned up."

"Okay," I said, "we'll have to turn the world upside down a bit."

"Yes, we will, with a little bit of playacting."


The date was December 25, 1989. When I returned to the Hotel Intercontinental with Buba Gabor in the wee hours, we were hatching a desperate plan and didn't yet know that we would be putting it into operation that very night.

At two minutes to three on the afternoon of Christmas Day, a telephone rang on the reception desk of the Athenee Palace Hotel, the best address in the capital. The caller, an army doctor at the Targoviste barracks who had just filled out two death certificates, asked to be connected to the presidential suite where Richard Nixon had once stayed. Stefan Stephanescu picked up the receiver and heard the words from the lips of Dr. Florin Pauker: "It's over."

One hour later, the main masterminds of the coup d'état (poets and dissidents excepted) met in secret in the hotel's conference room. For the present, they agreed to keep their deliberations in strictest confidence. At the same time, unconfirmed reports began to circulate among the journalists in the Intercontinental that the president had been found guilty by a drumhead court-martial and had sung "The Internationale" shortly before being shot.

The news of the execution of the Conductor and his wife spread like wildfire. But since absurd rumors that seldom turned out to be true were an hourly occurrence in recent days, the reaction was muted at first. When people close to the National Guard announced that Studio Four of the state television network, now under revolutionary control, intended to broadcast original footage showing the execution of the dictatorial couple, the streets and squares of the capital emptied in a flash. While everyone waited spellbound in front of their TVs and network spokespersons kept postponing the broadcast of the videotape because they wanted to ensure that they hadn't fallen for a clever falsification by counter-revolutionaries, the handpicked members of the Front for National Salvation took their seats around a conference table.

In less than two hours, under the direction of Stephanescu, the members of an interim government had been sorted out. During the negotiations, the faction of the Kronauburg District secretary had quashed any doubts about who had the strongest claim to lead the country as future prime minister. Stephanescu extended their vow of confidentiality until that evening and adjourned the meeting. A public proclamation was scheduled for 8:00 p.m. in the former Royal Palace of the Republic. It would fall to Stephanescu as the designated head of state to announce the death of the Conductor and the victory of freedom over Socialism.

When Fritz Hofmann, Buba Gabor, and I learned who was going to lead the country out of the darkness and into the light of a democratic future, I told Fritz, "The time has come for us to start sawing."

Fifteen minutes later, the three of us were sitting in Fritz's hotel room. "The best protection against bugs," Fritz said as he opened the tap in the tub as far as it would go. "Believe me, a waterfall like that drives every secret service guy listening totally crazy. Although I doubt that at this point there's a security agent left with any desire to listen in. But better safe than sorry."

I sketched out the plan Buba and I had hatched, and Fritz listened closely. He rubbed his hands. "Okay," he said. "Very good. I'm in. But you'll never pass as my colleague wearing clothes like that. At least not for an interview with a foxy politician." Fritz pointed to the closet. "My things will fit you. Pick something out."

"And as long as you're about to transform your appearance," added Buba, "a bath and a shave wouldn't do you any harm either. But I have to get going, too. Nobody will take me for a passionate Italian looking like this. But just wait till you see the chic things I have in my suitcase."

"How long will it take you to get to your uncle's, change, and get back here?" asked Fritz.

"At least two or three hours by bus."

"There's a revolution going on today," I said, "and besides, it's Christmas. The buses won't be running."

Fritz reached into his camera bag and pulled out a wad of green bills. "There are taxis in front of the hotel." He gave Buba a fifty-dollar bill. "That should do the trick. But wait—what if the Securitate check you and want to see a press pass?"

"You doubt my skills?" Buba replied in mock annoyance. "You can bet I've learned how to persuade men to do anything I want. See you at nine. We'll meet at the Atheneum, by the monument to . . . what's that poet's name?"

"Mihail Eminescu!"

●

# Chapter Fourteen

### A CLEVER PLAN, THE STUPIDITY OF THE CUNNING,

### AND THE FALL OF THE REAL CONDUCATOR

Buba didn't get back until ten, worn out and complaining. "The taxi driver messed me up. He wouldn't drive me into Titan II for all the dollars in the world. He promised to wait for me just outside the neighborhood, but he left while I was changing. It was stupid to give him his money before he brought me back. I never would have done that in Italy. I had to walk back, and in these shoes! Is he in the hotel already?"

"Man, I'm just happy nothing happened to you." A weight fell from my heart. Fritz was relieved, too. "No, they're all still at the Royal Palace. I would guess there are a few thousand people crowded into the ballroom. There was lots of activity in town just now. Everybody wants to hear the head revolutionary Stephanescu. Our time line has been moved back. The new government clique won't show up at the hotel before midnight. Let's only hope our doctor delivers a brilliant speech. That'll increase his desire to celebrate his triumph in the bar."

"What if he doesn't drink as much as he used to when he partied with Angela?" Buba seemed nervous. "If he stays sober and wants to keep a clear head, what'll we do then? What'll I do then?"

"He still drinks," Fritz assured her. "People like that can't stand themselves otherwise."

"Let's go to his hotel and wait for him inside." I was shivering. I was wearing nothing but an anthracite-colored jacket, a white dress shirt, and clean blue jeans. My clean-shaven cheeks exuded the scent of fresh cedar and Italian lemon ice. "You smell good, Pavel," Buba remarked, "and you look good, too."

A porter in a sequined jacket, flanked by two National Guard soldiers in camouflage uniforms, threw open the door of the Athenee Palace Hotel. The almost-deserted reception hall was pregnant with an atmosphere outside of time. The oppressive burden of past history was as much in evidence as the exciting confusion of the present and the uncertainty of the future, all mixed together with the sticky sweet taste of the Christmas message of Christ's birth. Silver tinsel glittered from the ceiling. Colorful lights twinkled in a Christmas tree whose tip had been clipped off so it would fit under the staircase next to the elevator. Teenage soldiers dozed in the corners, arms around their assault rifles. They raised their heads, looked the three of us over, their eyelids drooped, and they nodded off again.

Buba plopped down onto one of the heavy leather easy chairs across from the reception desk. I hardly dared look at her. I had expected another Buba and, as I admitted to myself, I had feared another Buba, a woman who attracted rapacious stares. Brash, provocative, louche. But a quick glance at Buba revealed her to be almost inconspicuous. She seemed to sink and almost disappear into the black easy chair. She laid her dark cape over its arm and I saw that beneath it, she was dressed entirely in black. To my surprise, with her expensive shoes, silk stockings, long skirt, and soft wool sweater with a modest neckline, Buba revealed much less of herself than I had feared in my suspicious anxiety. Although she by no means hid her cleavage, a delicate cross hanging between the curves of her breasts gave them a hint of girlish charm and chaste innocence. She had put on just a bit of lipstick and otherwise dispensed with cosmetics or flashy jewelry. Her locks were hidden by a black head scarf. A widow, the thought flashed through my mind. She was married and she's a widow. But when Buba slipped off her pumps, stretched her aching feet, and gave me an impish sideways wink I knew she was playing a sophisticated game. She didn't reveal herself, she concealed herself instead. She made known her feminine attraction by keeping it hidden. For the first time since rediscovering her, I felt I didn't just love this woman, I desired her with a yearning that almost consumed me. She stroked my cheek. "Trust me, dearest. I know what I'm doing."

"Okay, time to throw the fish some chum." Fritz Hofmann shouldered his camera bag. Buba and I watched as he strolled calmly over to the reception desk and exchanged a few words with an employee behind the counter. She smiled, disappeared for a moment, and returned with the head reception clerk. Hofmann shook his hand, wrote a few lines on a piece of paper, and handed it to the man along with a banknote he had discreetly slid beneath it. Fritz garnered an eagerly subservient nod, and the man placed the message into the mail slot of the presidential suite.

The elevator boy took us to the hotel bar on the second floor. There was no one at the semicircular bar except three women in tight leatherette miniskirts, sucking on slim filtered cigarettes. They gave Buba a dismissive once-over, giggled among themselves, and then went back to sipping their cocktails.

Fritz gave Buba a gentle pinch in the side. "You've got some hot competition there," he smirked.

She replied, "Don't talk about those girls like that. The bodyguards will be kicking them out of their beds before the night is over."

Buba ordered orange juice, Fritz and I mineral water. Around eleven thirty the first leather jackets showed up with scowling faces and beeping intercoms to reconnoiter the bar. The noise level started to rise. In a few minutes there was hardly any room left to stand at the bar. Then he arrived. The people at the bar cleared a path for him and applauded—just a few at first, then the applause became a rhythmic clapping punctuated by frenetic cheers.

Stefan Stephanescu sat down at a reserved table with blue plush benches along with some other Salvation Front people. A waiter brought Rémy Martin and Dom Pérignon. After an hour, the sleepless nights of revolution began to have their effect on most of the guests. The first sleep-deprived ones had already started dragging themselves off to bed when the head of the reception desk entered the bar. Although he hadn't heard it, he congratulated Stephanescu on his magnificent speech and handed him a note, then pointed in Fritz Hofmann's direction.

Stephanescu rose and buttoned his sport coat. Then he lit a Carpati, cradled his brandy snifter between index and middle finger, and approached our table.

"Allow me to introduce myself. Stefan Stephanescu." As he held out his hand to Fritz, Buba took off her head scarf and tossed back her locks with a gentle sweep of her hand. "Oh, please pardon me. A cavalier greets the lady first." The soon-to-be head of state offered her his hand. "May I join you?"

Buba shifted her behind to one side. "It would be a pleasure."

"And you are the American journalist from *Time* magazine?" Stephanescu turned to Fritz. "I must say, it's a prestigious publication. It'll be available again here in our country as soon as we clear the bookstores of the Conducator's unspeakable magazines. But I think we know each other, don't we? Not personally, of course. But you took my picture day before yesterday at the press conference of the Front for National Salvation, Mr. . . ."

"Fritz Hawfmen," Fritz introduced himself in the broadest possible American accent.

"Hoffman? Like the famous actor? Dustin? The legendary Marathon Man?"

"Exactly. And as things look now, you're going to achieve not inconsiderable fame yourself. I must have had a good nose. As of today, my photos of you have historic significance. I've already sold two dozen of them. And your train has hardly left the station yet. The swan song of the Conducator has ushered in a new era. Your face will appear on the cover of the next edition of *Time* magazine, just in time for New Year's. Not bad, right? The title story is already in the pipeline. Headline: 'Light in the Realm of Shadows' or something like that. My colleagues have already faxed the first copy to Washington. Perhaps I should introduce you to my Italian colleague. Angelique Gabo from Milan. Next to her is the indispensable and indefatigable Herr Paul, our interpreter."

I twirled my finger at my forehead and gave a bored yawn. "Indefatigable, always on call, and all for a handful of dollars. But in view of the late hour, we don't want to take up too much of your time. In a word, we hope to interview you, Dr. Stephanes—how soon may we address you as Mr. Prime Minister?"

"You'll have to be patient a little longer." Stephanescu could hardly contain his pride and vanity. "The appointment won't be official until tomorrow afternoon. But when did you want to do the interview? Not right now, I hope?"

"No, not now. But it should be soon—tomorrow noon at the latest," answered Fritz. "With a seven-hour time lag, the editors will have it on their desks at breakfast time. Three days later your picture will be on display on every newsstand. And other magazines and newspapers will follow suit. All over the world. But we need an exclusive interview for the American market. The boys from *Newsweek* are buzzing around here somewhere, too. You mustn't grant them access until the day after tomorrow—I hope I can count on your cooperation? Would two thousand dollars be acceptable as a fee for your time and trouble?"

"You Yanks are really smooth operators. Slick, really slick!" Stephanescu unbuttoned his sport jacket. He was back in a jovial mood. He emptied his brandy snifter in one swallow and called for another bottle of Rémy. "You must forgive me—it's the strain of the past few days. A revolution like this is also a war of nerves. Brutal, I'm telling you. Lots of stress. At some point, you have to wash it all down. But about that exclusive interview—of course, that can be arranged. For you: anytime. The new cabinet is meeting tomorrow at noon. Shall we say ten thirty? Here in the hotel? In my suite, so no one will disturb us."

"Okay, at ten thirty then. And just one little tip while we're on the subject. You don't need to tell the *Newsweek* reporters about our little Q-and-A, 'cause if you do, they'll leave their dollars in their wallets. I suggest a down payment of five hundred." Hofmann turned to Buba. "Angelique, take it out of the account for special expenses if you don't mind."

Buba looked right and left and fidgeted uneasily with the gold cross between her breasts. "Too many men here," she whispered to Stephanescu in feigned modesty. Then she discreetly lifted the hem of her dress, reached slowly under her garter, and made a great show of coaxing out a few bills. Stephanescu stared at her thighs. When he didn't take the money right away and instead turned to yell at the dumbfounded waiter that he'd ordered champagne for the lady, not just Rémy, Buba Gabor knew that the fish had taken the bait. It was obvious that the hook had also been set when Fritz and I rose from our seats and Buba gave the impression she was leaving as well.

"Must you leave so soon? I insist on treating you—treating you all, that is. Today, on this historic day. Besides, who doesn't like to be among friends on Christmas?"

"To be honest, dear colleagues"—Buba played her role with amazing credibility—"I don't really feel ready for bed yet. A glass of champagne after all that excitement today—well, why not? And anyway, it's nice and warm here. You need to know, Mr. Stephanescu, that there's no heat in my room at the Interconti. It's freezing cold, atrociously cold. Meanwhile, my two colleagues can't fall asleep because their rooms are so hot." Buba was so convincing that she really had goose bumps on her arms. As the intimidated waiter was uncorking the Dom Pérignon, Fritz and I took the opportunity to take our leave. We wished them good night, and Buba promised to catch a cab in an hour or two.

"Are you still cold, my dear? I hope you will permit me to address you as such?" Stephanescu stroked Buba's arm almost paternally. She indicated she was feeling more comfortable. Then he poured her a glass of champagne while he stuck with cognac. "A drop of the good stuff will warm you up. From France! I must tell you, I won't stand for any criticism of France. A perfect dream of a country—the cuisine, the wine, the culture. Montmartre, Sacré-Coeur, Pigalle. *Fantastique!* Paris! *Mon Dieu!* That's what the French say. But the women, they stick up their noses a bit too much, don't you think, Angelique? Angelique—that sounds more French than Italian, doesn't it?"

"My mother gave me that name. My friends call me Angie. It sounds more American. My father was Italian, but my mother's from Paris. And I was born in that wonderful city but have never lived there long. I've traveled all over Europe, always on the go. Madrid, London, Munich, sometimes here, sometimes there. Like a Gypsy."

"I knew it! I could see it right away. You have some mysterious fire, a glow. Your husband must consider himself a lucky man."

"Please! Let's talk about something else." Buba's hoarse voice sank to a deep sigh. "Believe me, Mr. Stephanescu, that man was no . . . Let's forget it. It was a long time ago. He died a few years ago in a motorcycle accident." Buba hurriedly crossed herself.

Stephanescu took her hand. She smelled his alcoholic breath. The acrid smoke from his cigarette made her tear up.

"After the shadows comes the light. Your American colleague

said something like that. That's absolutely right! But please, call me Stefan! *Mon Dieu!* A native *Parisienne*! Right here in the Paris of the East. I'll tell you what, Angie: in all honesty"—Stephanescu refilled his snifter—"our Paris is dead. You should have seen what it used to be like. But today is the day our people emerge from the shadow of the past. I will resurrect this city. I promise you, my dear, on the ruins the Conducator left us the new Paris of the East will blossom. We're going to live again!"

His tongue loosened by the cognac, Stephanescu had spoken so loudly that the men at neighboring tables started clapping and cheering at the words "Paris of the East." A drunken officer had the idea to strike up "The Internationale," whereupon some took aim with their index fingers and yelled "Pow, pow, pow" while others thrust their right fists into the air and bellowed, "So comrades, come rally, and the last fight let us fa-a-ace." Stephanescu drank.

"Getting a little wild here. Maybe not a good place for a woman."

Buba brushed her hair back and reached behind her with both hands to undo the chain and take off the golden cross. "It does bother me a little." She smiled at him, picked up her glass, and toasted him before drinking. Immediately he slid nearer to Buba, put his arm around her, and stared unabashedly at her cleavage. "It's too loud in here for me, Stefan. And too many eyes." Beneath the table she ran her hand slowly up his leg and gently massaged his crotch. She felt his reaction and whispered, "Right now I need a real man who knows what he wants." By this time the man was staggering drunk but trembling with lust, and it took less than five minutes for them to reach the Presidential Suite of the Athenee Palace.

A quarter hour later he was sprawled naked and snoring on his bed with his underpants around his knees. Two long-stemmed glasses and an open champagne bottle from the minibar stood on the night table. Buba hadn't drunk any more. Stephanescu had emptied about half his glass, which was more than enough. Buba poured what was left into the toilet. Then she concealed the little bottle with drops for fending off unwelcome advances in her bra again, picked up the house telephone, and dialed the reception desk.

Fritz and I were waiting in the black armchairs in the hotel lobby. Sooner than expected, the woman behind the desk announced, "Herr Hofmann, a call for you from the Presidential Suite. I'm supposed to let you know that the photo session can take place as scheduled."

The red illuminated numbers of the alarm clock built into the headboard of Stephanescu's bed showed 1:28 a.m. as Fritz set about arranging the scene. I provided the props. I put a portrait of the Conducator on the nightstand and shook up the bottle of champagne. Buba exposed her feminine charms to just the extent necessary and without a trace of shame. Knowing how interchangeable reality and illusion were, she mounted Stephanescu's prone form and leaned back with an expression of voluptuous ecstasy. With the remark, "Okay, that's perfect," Fritz pressed his shutter release a half-dozen times. The flash caused Stephanescu's closed eyes to twitch almost imperceptibly, but that was all.

While Buba and I lay wide awake with exhaustion in Fritz Hofmann's room in the Interconti, the night staff of the newspaper *Voice of Truth* considered it their duty to help out the international photojournalist. Although the technical capacities of their in-house photo lab were limited, Hofmann was able to develop the film, get usable negatives, and produce some prints he found very satisfactory. Then he had them ring up the editor in chief out of a sound sleep—a man who had published a courageous editorial in which he didn't conceal his preference for the engineer Ion Iliescu as head of state instead of Stephanescu, whom he labeled an opportunist. The widely respected editor was a man of few words. He took a look at the photos and said only, "Professional job. He won't survive this. We'll drop this bombshell day after tomorrow on page one."

On Monday, December 26, shortly after 10:30 a.m., Buba was already on her way to her uncle Dimitru when armed militiamen accompanied Fritz and me into the elevator leading to the suite on the top floor of the Athenee Palace. Dr. Stefan Stephanescu opened the door. He was alone and looked hungover. He offered us seats in a grouchy voice, making no attempt to hide his foul mood. "Where's your Italian colleague?"

I shrugged my shoulders.

"A woman, Italy, and punctuality . . . Forget it," Fritz said. "Angelique must have gotten to bed pretty late last night."

"She didn't show up for breakfast anyway," I added. "I guess we can take care of the interview without her."

"Then shoot. But keep it short. I don't have as much time as I thought."

Fritz Hofmann spared Stephanescu any more wasted time. "Dr. Stephanescu, your opponents have attacked your past politics. Let's take a look back. During the developmental phase of Socialism you were in charge of collectivization in Walachia. You are said to have put down rebellious farmers with a heavy hand. Today, you're leading the people's revolution. Aren't those two things incompatible?"

"I'm glad you asked. It gives me the chance to clear up a few things. Yes, I was a genuine believer in the idea of collectivization. No question about it. I'd never deny it. But do you have any idea how dirt-poor the smallholders were after the war? Did you see the appalling lot of the mothers? Did you look into the eyes of the starving children? We had an obligation to do something about it. Socialism! Wealth for everyone! Yes, indeed, that's what we in the party believed. I parroted Marx myself. But in Walachia, I always trusted in the power of the word. Persuading the people to accept the inevitable, ideological education—call it what you will, even propaganda for all I care. But the work was important, and it was the right thing to do. The problem was President Gheorghiu-Dej. He yielded to Soviet pressure from Moscow—too much for my taste. The Little Stalin they used to call him—just so you know. And it's true, there were some unpleasant cleanup operations. You have to break eggs to make an omelet. I never liked that proverb, by the way. But what was I supposed to do? I was young, an idealist if you will. Fresh from the university with a degree in economics, but still a political greenhorn. Worst of all, I didn't have any influential friends who thought the same way. And as you know, there's strength in numbers."

"I don't quite understand. You seem to have had no lack of political cover; otherwise how could you have had such an impressively rapid rise? If our information is correct, as party chief in Kro-

nauburg you were the youngest district secretary in the country.
You had that post for more than thirty years. And this afternoon
you're going to be named prime minister."

"Correct. I got a lot done during my time in Kronauburg.
Cleared away a lot of sleazy bureaucracy. Administrative efficiency,
new jobs in the agro-industrial complex in Apoldasch, optimiza-
tion of the food supply and nutrition, etc., etc., etc. The town of
Kronauburg was flourishing. So was the entire district. Let's not
forget the new schools either, even in the remotest mountain ham-
let. Children are our future. I came up with that slogan myself, if I
may be a little immodest. Feel free to confirm it. All of which is to
say, without meaning to boast, that I was popular with the people.
That's one of the reasons why the leadership was hesitant to cut me
out. They kept my flame turned low, but they couldn't extinguish
it completely."

As Fritz Hofmann nodded in agreement, and I also showed
that I understood his plight, Stephanescu's initial grumpy hangover
gave way to a verbosity on autopilot. He stood up, walked over to
the minibar, and got out a glass and an already open bottle. We
declined the proffered drink. As Stephanescu took his first swallow,
I knew we had our enemy where we wanted him. Dr. Stephanescu
smiled. He thought he was on solid ground.

"*Konjaki* Napoleon. Not the best brand, but it drives out the
ghosts of the past. Ghosts I admit to being haunted by as well. But
let's keep going. The central role I played in the development of the
Kronauburg District was talked about in the capital, especially after
the catastrophic floods. The Tirnava River destroyed wide swaths
of the countryside. When I was able to get a dam and hydroelectric plant built in record time, thus securing electric power even in
the remotest regions of the mountains, I gained more influence in
the party. I was even mentioned as a candidate for the post of minister of the interior. But with the rise of the Conducator, the atmosphere changed. He took all the credit for the hydroelectric project
and arrived by helicopter for the dedication. Cheering crowds surrounded him. From then on, he put nothing but stumbling blocks
in my path. New roads, bridges, construction projects—nothing
got approved by the Central Committee. The taps were gradually turned off. And you know why? You can't have missed seeing

the Conductor's gigantic palace, all covered in gingerbread. He had half the center of our wonderful Paris of the East torn down to make room for it. You can imagine how much of the people's money was thrown away on that. I was always against that pompous pile. But take it from me: the voice of reason counted for nothing in our delusionary dictatorship. The individual was powerless. All opposition was quashed. The Conductor and his unspeakable wife couldn't stand having anyone beside them."

"That means that you and the Conductor were enemies?"

"Frankly, that would be giving myself too much credit." Stephanescu poured himself a second glass. "To be honest, I knew the Conductor well. Not during the Golden Age, of course. His delusions of grandeur had caused a break long before that. I met him during my student days. His—how shall I put it?—uncivilized lack of taste had already begun to manifest itself. His bad character didn't escape my notice, but it wasn't that prominent yet. If you ask me, it was his wife Elena who really awakened the evil in him. By the way, here's an intimate detail especially for the readers of *Time* magazine: at that time, when the Conductor was just a simple party official, his nickname was Koka. He was literally addicted to American Coca-Cola. He put it into whatever he was drinking: red wine, bubbly, whatever. An awful person. Basically always was. But I don't mean to whitewash my part. And to my shame I have to admit that I went into politics to do good and in the end merely averted the worst. I must say it's a sense of guilt felt by many of us in my country. And you can quote me on that."

"As long as we're talking about guilt, Dr. Stephanescu, are you a religious man?"

"Oh yes, I believe. Otherwise we wouldn't be sitting here. In the depths of our being, our entire people never lost their faith. Even though the Conductor once declared us the first atheistic nation, we remained believers in our souls. Not everyone, of course. Some had no respect for life. But I invite you to go to Kronauburg. When the recent rebellion spread from Timisoara to my city, we were prepared for the worst. Ask people how many deaths the Securitate in my district has on its conscience after the rebels stormed the State Security headquarters. Not a single one, guaranteed. On my orders, no one fired a shot. Here's another piece of confidential information: you should know that there were forces in the country who wanted to take God from the people, turn churches into halls of culture with party slogans in place of prayers. When religion dies, the community dies. I always resisted. Let the people have their churches, that was my motto. I wish I could have prevailed. There was an influential security agent in Kronauburg who had the churches cleared out of their treasuries, icons, statues of saints, Madonnas. I'm no coward, but I'll tell you I was always afraid of that man. Please keep this confidential, but his name is General Raducanu, and I don't know whether at this very hour he's on the side of the revolution or its betrayers. My advice is watch out for him. At any rate, Raducanu acquired Western currency by diverting the most valuable antiquities via Polish channels into the capitalist art market. The stuff that couldn't be sold is gathering dust in the cellars of the Securitate. It was a mistake to violate the pious soul of the people. But I guarantee that the people will get back their Madonnas and their saints. And the churches will be full again."

Fritz and I were silent.

"What else would you like to know? Oh yes, before I forget: let's handle the interview fee in a different way. If it became public knowledge, people might misunderstand it as a false signal. I think I'll donate the remaining fifteen hundred to an orphanage or to widows of the revolution. What do you think, Mr. Hofmann?" When he uttered Fritz's name, Stephanescu suddenly stopped short and then started to stammer, "You . . . you . . . could take a picture of me handing over the money . . . What . . . Why aren't you taking any notes on the interview? Where's your tape recorder?"

I wiped my sweaty palms on my pants. Fritz stayed calm.

"Excellent idea. A photo in an orphanage. I promise you'll look just as splendid as you did in that portrait of yourself in the window of the Kronauburg photo studio. Heinrich Hofmann took quite decent pictures, didn't he? At least they served their purpose."

Stephanescu's face froze. He distractedly stubbed out the Carpati he had just lit in an ashtray. "You're not from *Time* magazine! Who are you? Show me your papers."

Fritz Hofmann tossed a green passport onto the table. "You're a German!" Stephanescu opened the passport. "Born Baia Luna.

You . . . you're Heinrich's son. Fritz Hofmann! What do you want from me?"

"Why did my father Heinrich have to die?"

Stephanescu struggled to control the situation. "You've been lying to me the whole time! Pretending to be a journalist. I'll tell you this much: your father was my friend. But you, you're a big disappointment to me. You know what? We'll make this short and sweet. This interview is over. You two get out of here, or I'll have you arrested by the militia."

"No, you're not going to do that." I spoke up for the first time. "We're going to speak about the dead now. Why did the Baia Luna priest Johannes Baptiste have to die?"

Stephanescu pushed his cognac glass away. "A pastor had to die? Someone named Johannes Baptiste? Sorry, I don't know that name."

"Okay." Fritz smiled. "If that name means nothing to you, then you're not going to find out why our nice colleague Angelique wasn't lying next to you in bed this morning and why you're not going to be named prime minister this afternoon. It's all over, Herr Doctor, you just don't know it yet. But we have faith in your curiosity."

When Stephanescu coughed and suppressed a nauseated belch, I knew that by now the demon was wide awake. But he wasn't showing his face yet.

"Who sent you?"

I didn't need the quick glance from Fritz to know that I was the one to answer that question.

"I come at the behest of a child."

"What? What's that supposed to mean?"

"And I come at the behest of its mother. At the behest of Angela."

"What do you want from me? What goddamn devil sent you here? I don't know any Angela!"

"Oh, but you do, Herr Doctor. You knew Angela Barbulescu very well. And you liked her best in her dress with the sunflowers."

"No, no, no! I swear I don't know her. I never knew such a person."

"Then let me help you recall a day more than forty years ago, October seventh, 1947, to be precise. Right here in the Paris of the

East." I took out the first photo. "You see, Herr Doctor, that was Angela Barbulescu. Her supposed friend Heinrich Hofmann took this picture at a birthday party for your buddy Florin Pauker. Go ahead and take a look at Angela."

"You're crazy! Psychotic! You belong in Vadului with the loonies!" Stephanescu was working himself into a rage. The door to the suite flew open.

"Everything okay?" asked one of his bodyguards.

"Get out! Out!" bellowed his boss, then he collapsed into his chair. He lit up a Carpati and looked at the photo. The demon was stirring and made Stephanescu grin.

"I see a blond with a ponytail. Quite pretty, I have to admit. Right. I was indeed as a young man at a birthday party for Florin Pauker. And if this woman had crossed my path back then, I think I would have been tempted. But my God, that was four decades ago. I'll be seventy in three years. How am I supposed to remember a woman I met as a young man?"

"This photo was taken at the moment that Angela Barbulescu was about to give her dear Stefan a kiss."

Stephanescu stared at me. For a split second, time seemed to stand still, then Stephanescu burst into laughter. He sneered at me from the heights of an illusory superiority. "You're an idiot. I can see very well that this blond Angela, or whoever she is, is about to kiss somebody. But what makes you think that I'm the man? What's this stupid snapshot supposed to prove? I see a woman who's a total stranger to me. What are you trying to do, blackmail me? What a joke! With a picture I'm not even in." He laughed again. Then he drank.

"But there's another photo of Angela Barbulescu, one in which you're clearly recognizable. She's wearing the sunflower dress and you, Herr Doctor, are spraying champagne between her legs."

Stephanescu went chalk white, as if all the blood had drained from his arteries in a single second. My blood, meanwhile, ran cold. I was staring into his dead eyes. The demon showed its face and betrayed itself. As I placed the photo with the half-naked woman on the table, it was already too late. Stephanescu knew that he would never be able to take back the words "That wasn't Angela. It was Alexa." Now the demon had to report for duty in the final struggle. Stephanescu clapped his hands over his mouth to keep himself from vomiting. Then he put all his chips on the last card he held.

"It was the Christmas of 1948. Koka had invited us to an Oh Unholy Night party. I went with Angela and Alexa. The two of them were always together, and they'd exchanged dresses for the party. We'd all been drinking. Koka had tanked up on vodka. Everyone was in a great mood. And then Alexa lay down on the buffet table, spontaneously, on the spur of the moment—one too many liqueurs. My God, was she hot. Florin, Albin, and half the others had already jerked off over her. It was a game. Angela made a scene afterward. She had no idea how to have a good time. I was the one who showed her everything. I even took her to the seaside. First she pretended to be chaste, but then it turned out she was a girl who couldn't get enough. She wanted to stay in bed all day long. She was really great. But she was also moralistic, insufferable, bourgeois. Always talking about marriage, children, a house. She wanted me all to herself. If I had a little something on the side, she locked herself in her room for days and cried. She got on my nerves. She was just an episode.

"Of course, the high life cost a pile of money in those days. Eating out every night, and only in the best places. Trips to the Black Sea. I needed a car, Heinrich a motorcycle. Angela was really too dumb to get how we paid for everything. Naïve, is what she was. It was Koka's idea how we could make money. When Koka saw the photos Heinrich had taken of Alexa on Christmas Eve, he got really excited. Of Lenutza, too. Florin Pauker was the only one who almost wet his pants. He said we should burn the pictures then and there. If they got into the wrong hands, it could ruin his career as a doctor. And that's why he refused to hit on any more girls and recruit them for our art portraits, as we called them. And Albin had such an ugly wart on his cheek he only could make it with the sluts at the bottom of the barrel. So it was my job to haul in more women. Heinrich took the pictures. If the girls didn't want to cooperate, we put a few drops into their champagne. It was all done in Koka's apartment. The work was fun for Alexa until the day she announced she was pregnant. Florin had some scruples. He didn't want to get rid of the child for her, but Koka made it clear to him that if he didn't, an obscene photo of Florin might accidentally be made public. After that, Florin was our go-to man for workplace accidents. He treated Angela, too. She showed up one day in my office with a big belly and claimed it was my child. It's likely she really hadn't slept with anyone else. Maybe it would have been better if we'd let her keep the brat. But Florin had already done the deed, and we had to make sure she kept her mouth shut.

"Later, we moved the business to Kronauburg. Heinrich had hired two or three blonds to work in his studio. One was a photographer by the name of Irina. The security agent Raducanu had his eye on her, and we kept our hands off. But the other one, with the hair of an angel, she was great. You could put her onto any man who still had anything at all left between his legs. She could make it even with the most decrepit old geezers. We usually set up shop in the Golden Star. Heinrich shot the pictures without the subjects' knowledge. It all ran smoothly until one day things threatened to get out of hand, and just when I was about to leave the business.

"I'd just become party chief and district secretary in Kronauburg when Heinrich said that Barbulescu was planning to expose me. That was her mistake, but she'd always been naïve. We had to silence her for good. But Heinrich was too soft. Too weak. He could quote Nietzsche, but when push came to shove he had scruples. That's how all the shit started to hit the fan. Heinrich was counting on her killing herself. That's why he took the dirty photos of Barbulescu to that priest in Baia Luna, 'cause he thought that would put an end to her. And he wasn't completely off base. In the end she really did string herself up. But how could I be sure she would? I had to see to it that the job got done. Albin was supposed to take care of it. He went to Baia Luna, but he had scruples, too, as he later admitted to Alexa, the idiot. Instead of liquidating Barbulescu, he warned her about us. Of course, he pronounced his own death sentence by betraying us. But that wasn't the end of it. The real problem was that priest Johannes Baptiste. Until then the Securitate had always avoided crossing swords with the Catholic clergy. Raducanu's people got a bit overenthusiastic. But they would have left the pastor in peace if he'd just coughed up the photos. Heinrich's first mistake was to get a priest involved in the affair. His second mistake was when some cretin pasted giant photos of me with Alexa and the champagne bottle onto the windows of his photo shop. The pictures were immediately removed. Someone had obviously broken into Heinrich's studio. Negatives had disappeared that no one ever should have found. Your father"—for the first time Stephanescu turned directly to Fritz Hofmann—"had become a liability."

Fritz Hofmann had stopped listening long before. He had seen and photographed—and endured—the filth of the world. But not the words coming from the mouth of Stefan Stephanescu. The man without his mask, holding back nothing, awakened neither fury nor hatred in Fritz. Nor any need for revenge. Stephanescu didn't matter to him. Fritz had lowered his eyelids and was looking into himself. He saw himself as a fifteen-year-old, standing on a chair in a church and blowing out a small red light. Fritz never prayed. But now, in the Presidential Suite of the Athenee Palace, he asked God for forgiveness, while the only words I could produce from the depths of my dismay were "You are a devil."

"How would you know? You know nothing! How many years of your life have been wasted by the history of this country? How much dead time do you owe to the Conducator? Tell me. How many days, months, years? I, I would have given them to you. You don't realize that only I could have saved this country. I and I alone! I knew about the key to power. And if Heinrich Hofmann hadn't given that key away, no foolish Titan would have plunged this country into the realm of shadows. Terror, extortion, fear—those were the Conducator's tools. Only I had the courage to turn those weapons against him. What does the life of an old priest matter? A lunatic ignored by his own fellow priests. When Lupu's men brought him to Kronauburg for disposal, his own clergy had dug him a grave in the cathedral graveyard with a fake name. What's the life of a man worth when even his own church doesn't stand behind him? What's it worth compared to the prospect of leading an entire people into a truly Golden Age? That was always the difference between me and Heinrich Hofmann. He was never inspired by the will to power. He had no burning ambition. He was even afraid of a drunken village schoolteacher, a human wreck, a meaningless nothing. Otherwise he wouldn't have taken those photos, the key to the doors of power, into a rectory. I had to find the pictures of Angela that we made in Florin Pauker's office, no matter what the cost. Not because of Angela Barbulescu. It could have been any of the girls. The pictures were irreplaceable because Koka was in them. Don't you see? Koka, naked, in an obscene, perverse setting. That's why I needed the photos. They would have ruined Koka. He was a devil, but he would have been powerless. With those photographs in my hands he never would have been able to rise to become a caricature of a president. I was the better of the two of us. The course of history would have been different with me. And this would have been a better country. And now it will be better. In a few hours I'm going to become the prime minister. And you're not going to stop me. I've sold you the truth as truth, but it won't do you any good. You'll only be able to peddle it as falsehood. No one will believe you. The people are tired of insanity. You have no witnesses, no proof. And if I give my people an order, you won't even be able to prove that you were sitting at this table this morning with Stefan Stephanescu."

He picked up the photo of himself with the champagne bottle, took his lighter, and set it on fire. We didn't try to stop him. Black ash drifted through the Presidential Suite and settled onto the carpet like black snow in which Stephanescu's shoes left tracks on their way from his chair to the bar. He opened a cabinet door.

"But I'll give you one more chance, your last chance to beat me. I bet fifteen hundred dollars you won't take advantage of it." Stephanescu took a pistol from the cabinet and put it down on the table. "Go ahead. You can kill me. But you won't. You're too weak. What's your morality worth? I'll tell you. You can't even kill a devil. Shoot, Hofmann! Shoot me. But I say you can't do it. You're like your father. He could bring filthy pictures to an old priest, but that's as far as his courage went. You're just like him."

"I was wrong," said Fritz quietly. "I thought it would be a pleasure to experience your downfall. But it isn't." Then Fritz spoke in a clear voice: "Yes, I'm like my father. I'm bringing filthy pictures to an old man, too." He opened his camera bag and took out a brown envelope. "For you, Herr Doctor, a memento of last night. And greetings from Angelique, Angie, and Angela. Sorry about your portrait on the cover of *Time* magazine—it's not going to happen. You'll have to be satisfied with the *Voice of Truth,* page one of tomorrow's edition."

As the door to the Presidential Suite closed behind us, Stefan Stephanescu ripped open the envelope and held a black-and-white photograph in his hand. He saw himself. Naked. Then he started throwing up and couldn't stop.

Out in the streets new skirmishes were erupting. To judge from the rifle fire and detonations from the direction of the university library, they were more serious than they'd been in the last few days. Roaring tanks made the asphalt shake as they rolled south past the Athenee Palace. Sharpshooters were holed up on the rooftops, and no one had any idea who they were aiming at. Although Studio Four had broadcast a video of the execution of the head of state and his wife, there was no assurance that the tape was not a fake. The fear that the Conducator and his henchmen could reemerge from the shadows still hung in the air, despite scenes of rejoicing and fraternal reconciliation. And the dictator's most loyal minions, who had to fear that his downfall would suck them into its vortex and take them down as well, were still counting on the power of their weapons to turn back the tide of history. The revolution was not yet certain of its victory.

Dozens of taxi drivers in their rattletrap Dacias were waiting in front of the Athenee Palace, but no one wanted to be chauffeured through the city in these hours of uncertainty. I approached a few drivers, but when I said we were going to Titan II, they all shook their heads and demurred. The fifth or sixth one I asked said he would rather drive through the cross fire than into the quarter where the Blacks lived.

Fritz Hofmann was just about to solve the transportation problem with a generous contribution when three jeeps suddenly roared up and squealed to a stop in front of the hotel. A dozen men with submachine guns jumped out and pulled black ski masks over their heads. Some of them secured the entrance while the others stormed into the Palace. As a first brief burst of firing rattled in the lobby, the taxi driver cried, "Hop in!" Then he put the pedal to the floor and brought Fritz and me to within a quarter mile of where the Gypsies lived.

As I entered that other world on the outskirts of the capital, I thought the settlement was the saddest place I had ever seen, an impression that I would revise by the following day. The houses the Conducator had once promised our Gypsy compatriots turned out to be dreary shells, high-rise buildings without heat or electricity that looked like stacked-up, burned-out caves. They had no doors, and the windows were dead black eyes from which all one saw was the dead eyes in the dirty gray façades across the way. Garbage was piled in the unpaved streets. Only the freeze of the last days of December kept foul bubbles from rising out of the sewers. Men with caps pulled down over their eyes warmed their hands on the street corners, huddled around oil drums whose fires they fed with plastic trash that smoldered rather than burned. Children, half naked and barefoot, were jumping up and down on a tattered mattress. The acrid fumes made them cough from unhealthy lungs. Fritz had to suppress his nausea at the sight of some teenagers using dull knives to cut hunks of meat from a cadaver that was once either a horse or a cow—it was impossible to tell which.

When the arrival of us *gaje* was noticed, it stirred up half the neighborhood. The children ran up, frolicking and laughing. Fritz was their main object of interest, not me. They yelled, "Photo! Photo! America! America!" and Fritz made the mistake of fishing a pack of gum out of his jacket pocket. In an instant there was a horde of kids around him, its size doubling every few seconds. The upshot was that the ones who got no "gummas" cried bitter tears. Their initial joy turned into a wild, howling clamor, supplemented by their mothers yelling rude insults from the windows. The men had to knock some heads together to get the children to back off enough so we could ask where the Gypsy Dimitru Carolea Gabor lived.

At first the men just shrugged, but then someone asked, "You looking for Papa Dimi?" and Fritz and I were overwhelmed with directions and explanations and people pointing in all directions.

Finally a certain Jozsef offered to show us the way. His boast was that Dimitru's cousin Salman was a half brother of his cousin Carol Costea Gabor. Fifteen minutes later we were standing with our guide before a half-demolished building. Without his help we never would have found it in that desolate sea of neglect.

Jozsef pointed to the tangle of wires hanging out of a bank of doorbells that didn't work for lack of electricity. "Dimi and his fat white wife live at the very top." Then he asked Fritz for another cigarette. With the words "Be careful, he's not right in the head," he twirled his finger next to his temple and left us.

At our repeated knocking, Antonia finally opened the door. She rubbed her eyes, took a deep breath, and exhaled. "Pavel!" She called at the top of her voice, "Dimi! Dimi! He's here! Pavel is here!" Then she pressed me to her considerable bosom and almost suffocated me.

Fritz and I entered the spotlessly clean apartment. Buba greeted us with a quick peck on the cheek, turned on the bottled-gas stove, and put up water for coffee. Her lips were pale, and she looked exhausted.

Only then did I spy the Gypsy. Dimitru was sitting in a corner and rose painfully, leaning on a cane. I wasn't sure this old man was indeed Dimitru Carolea Gabor, and to my surprise I noticed he had been sitting on a battered white crate that looked like a child's coffin. Dimitru was wearing the same black suit he had worn decades ago on special occasions in Baia Luna. It used to lend him a great deal of dignity, but now he seemed lost inside it. I was horrified at Dimitru's diminution. I hardly recognized him. Looking into the eyes of this fragile old man, I could find none of the sly intelligence that had once made Dimitru so unique. But it was he. His voice was unchanged.

"You're late, my boy."

Then he turned around and shuffled back, the cuffs of his oversize pants dragging along the floor, and sat down on his crate again.

"He doesn't talk much anymore," Antonia whispered, "but he hears everything."

Buba put coffee cups on the table. Her hand trembled as she poured, and she said quietly, "We must never repeat what we did last night, Pavel. Never, ever again."

As though it had taken these words to make me realize it, I suddenly felt how much the encounter with Stephanescu had exhausted all my strength and left me burned out. Fritz, too, was suddenly overcome by oppressive weariness and could hardly keep sitting upright.

"I'm done in," he groaned and crossed his arms on the edge of the table. Just as he lowered his leaden head onto them, a crystal-clear voice cut into our unfathomed weariness of soul.

"Whoever compels the demon to show his face is in great danger. For the sight of the demon makes a person empty. It sucks a person out, and once he is hollow, the demon enters him. Whoever sees the demon becomes a different person."

Buba was trembling all over and cried out, "You're scaring me, Uncle Dimi!"

"We're all scared, Buba," Dimitru continued, "because we destroyed something. Today we destroyed a person. It doesn't matter if he deserved what he got or not. Judge not, that ye be not judged. But we did. You, Buba, you, Pavel, and me. I have sinned. I as chief justice. I pronounced his sentence long, long ago. But I had to, and I would do it again, even if it cost me my peace of mind in all eternity."

"What are you saying, Dimitru," I pleaded with the old man. "I don't understand! Are you talking about Stefan Stephanescu? Yes, we destroyed him. We did him in and it was terrible. But I would do it again. I had to! The man was unbearable! What else could we have done? But what about you? What kind of sentence did you pronounce? I don't get it, Dimitru."

Without answering, the old Gypsy in his corner continued, "The demon is stupid. Very stupid. But it's evil. Very, very evil. That's why it seeks out the clever ones. It only shows itself to them. It only gains power when a smart person carries it. And then the smart ones become stupid without noticing, because they mistake the power of the demon for their own power. Then they feel invincible, and they smile. Some people shiver at the sight of that smile, the people who carry an angel within them. They're the only ones who can . . ."

At that moment something strange happened. Fritz Hofmann wiped a tear from his cheek, stood up, and asked Dimitru if he would permit Fritz to sit next to him. When Dimitru answered, "But of course, *permanente,* anytime," everyone in the room had the impression that it had gotten a bit brighter.

Fritz knelt down in front of Dimitru and said, "I don't believe in angels. And I don't shiver at people like Stephanescu, I burn with fury. But Dimitru, please tell me, can one kill the demon?"

"Who are you? I know you from somewhere."

"I'm Fritz Hofmann, born in Baia Luna."

Dimitru looked at him. "That's right. It's you, Fritz, the know-it-all. Oh yes, you're a sly fox, even as a boy you were. But you can't kill a demon, Fritz. No one can. Not even the risen Christ sitting at the right hand of the Father. There's only one way to make the demon disappear forever. Only one."

By now Buba, Antonia, and I had all gathered in a half circle around Dimitru, too.

"Do you know what it is?" I asked.

"Yes, I know about it. But I never took that path. You can only kill the demon by redeeming it. First you have to force it to reveal its face. But if you are hollow within, the demon slips into you. The demon is only redeemed when it sees an angel. As you should know, my dears, an angel has big white wings. He flies away with the demon."

"Where does he fly to, Uncle Dimi? To heaven?"

"Easy, easy, dear Buba. The gates of heaven stay closed even to the most powerful angel if he has a demon in his luggage. First you have to go through purgatory. There the demon is purified. When all the evil in him is burned away, then he himself becomes an angel. He is free. He can fly wherever he likes: up to heaven, to humanity, to the mountains, depending on what his assignment is."

"One more question, if you don't mind, Uncle Dimi. How do you get an angel to enter into you?"

Everyone's eyes were on Dimitru in tense and reverent anticipation. We saw a remarkable transformation. Dimitru not only seemed to grow larger, he really did get a little bigger as he said in a strong voice, "I don't know how to open the door to an angel. I always closed myself off from them. They scared me. They were too shimmery and disembodied. And that's not good for someone as frivolous as me. I was afraid of losing myself. And so I looked for another way, and I thought I had found it. The path to a being who carried all wisdom within, the knowledge of heaven and knowledge of the world. It had to be made of light, like the angels, but also have a body. It could only be a redeemed being of both spirit and flesh and blood. And that could only be the Mother of God. She was the person I assumed had ascended to heaven in bodily form. That was the point of my studies: where is she? I had to know, and I found out. Or so I thought. I was convinced she was on the moon, in the Mare Serenitatis. That was my *error fatal.* I'm the one who understood nothing. Absolutely nothing. And the worst thing is that I dragged my one true friend in life into the same error. Borislav Ilja Botev. Pavel, I had to ask your grandfather for forgiveness. I looked long and hard for Ilja, but I never found him. I'm asking you to help me, Pavel. I'm asking you all to help me! I won't be able to die otherwise."

Dimitru said the Lord's Prayer. When he finished, we all said "Amen." Antonia stood up and got out the Bible that Pastor Johannes Baptiste had once given Ilja Botev.

"I'm not a smart woman," she said, "but my dear husband Dimitru is not to blame. I've told him that hundreds of times, but he won't listen to me. I told him thousands of times it's all the fault of Saint John the Apostle, the one who wrote the Bible. He's to blame because he went crazy in his old age. When he was young, he still had all his wits about him and wrote in his Gospel that no one ascended into heaven except the Son of Man—not Mary, Jesus's mother. Not her. And then John spent his whole life waiting for his Lord Jesus Christ to return to earth after the Crucifixion to establish the kingdom of God. But Jesus didn't come back, and that made John go crazy. Before he passed away, he had that revelation and saw all that crazy stuff and the evil beasts spewing fire." Antonia tapped the Bible. "I read all about it, it's all in there. At the end of his days, the old evangelist claims to have seen a woman on the moon, adorned with the sun and a crown of stars. First there's no Assumption, then all of a sudden there is one after all. Now you see it, now you don't. That's what drove my poor Dimi so crazy."

"Let me see that." Fritz Hofmann took the Bible.

"It's way in the back, chapter twelve," said Antonia.

Fritz read it to us: "'And there appeared a great wonder in heaven, a woman clothed with the sun, and the moon under her feet, and upon her head a crown of twelve stars. And she being with child cried . . .' And before, this John claimed that no woman, just Jesus, ascended into heaven?"

"That's right," said Dimitru. "But that's when John was still right in the head."

"I don't see the problem," Fritz said. "Assuming—purely hypothetically, of course—what's in the Bible is right, then maybe John could have spoken the truth both times."

Dimitru jumped up. "What do you mean, Fritz?"

"It's completely logical. Think dialectically! Thesis: Mary did not ascend to heaven. Period. Antithesis: On the moon John sees a woman with a crown of twelve stars. Period."

"And the synthesis?" The Gypsy was vibrating with excitement. "What's the synthesis, Fritz?"

"The woman Johannes saw with the moon under her feet wasn't Mary."

Dimitru beamed. I saw that not only were his eyes flashing as they used to, but the size of his body had also increased again by a considerable amount.

"Fritz, my son, that's the cleverest if-then *conclusio* I've ever heard from the mouth of a heathen. I have to tell you all that I saw her once, that woman on the moon. When my friend Ilja and I were on the Mondberg in Baia Luna and looking through our telescope. What did the woman look like? I can't remember. It was a long time ago. All I know is she was beautiful. But maybe it wasn't Mary, John wasn't crazy, and I saw a different woman. But who? I don't know. And my friend knows absolutely nothing about it either. Ilja!" Dimitru cried out in desperation. "My beloved Ilja, there's something I have to tell you. Ilja, it wasn't Mary. Ilja, where are you? I can't see you. Show yourself! Won't you tell me where you are?"

I took Buba's hand. "Can you see my grandfather? Could you try to see him?"

Buba rose. "My second sight never worked in Italy." Then she went over to the window, looked out, and closed her eyes. She folded her hands. There wasn't a sound except for the distant, thin wail of a siren.

Buba stood there motionless for an hour. Then she said, "In

the background are tall buildings. They reach the sky and touch the clouds. The clouds are ashes and smoke. There's a woman, a gigantic woman. She holds a torch in her hand. Ilja sits at her feet, looking up at her, but she's not looking at him. She's staring toward the tall buildings. They're collapsing. The woman weeps. The sun is shining, but it's cold. Ilja is freezing. He, he isn't real. The sun is shining brightly, but Ilja casts no shadow."

Buba opened her eyes and sank to the floor.

"In America?" I asked skeptically. "Is Grandfather supposed to be in New York with the Madonna of the Torch?"

"Then Buba would have seen a shadow," Dimitru responded. "Where would Ilja not cast a shadow? The key to the door that will lead us to him is the answer to that question."

"What if the shadow is just an image," conjectured Fritz, "a sort of symbol for darkness or for evil, for all I know?"

"Then the one without a shadow would be the one who carries nothing evil within him," I replied. "Someone who's innocent or cannot be guilty. Maybe a child."

"Or all the people who are sick in the head," Antonia piped up, "the poor lunatics all over this cou—"

"I know where Grandfather is!" Everyone's eyes turned to me. Even Buba awoke from her trance. "'You're crazy! Psychotic!' That's what Stephanescu told Fritz and me this morning. 'You belong in Vadului,' he said, 'with the loonies.'"

"The demon couldn't keep its mouth shut. I told you it was dumb as a doorknob!" Dimitru clapped his hands. "Riu Vadului. I know that name. That's the village my cousin Salman always made a big detour around when he was traveling on business. Vadului, that's where Ilja is!"

"We have a German Volkswagen in the city," I said. "Who wants to come along?"

In a flash, four times "I do" became "We all do." Dimitru wanted to set off immediately, but since it was evening already, Fritz and I decided to spend the night in the Interconti. Fritz volunteered to organize gasoline with the help of some connections and his cache of dollars, while I tried to find Petre Petrov.

As Fritz and I entered the hotel, there was only one topic of conversation among the gaggles of foreign correspondents, namely,

that the Conducator was certainly not going to return. The video-
tapes of the couple's execution were genuine. The fact that the most
promising candidate for the office of the new prime minister was
also among the latest victims of the continuing revolutionary skirmishes was more of a footnote for the representatives of the international media. We learned that the Kronauburg regional secretary
Stefan Stephanescu had been murdered by masked gunmen during
the storming of the Athenee Palace. An American photographer
who had been at the scene related in revulsion that the Presidential
Suite had obviously been the murderers' explicit target and that
they had not just shot their victim but mutilated his body savagely
and beyond recognition.

I set out in search of Petre but couldn't find him in the darkness. To my relief he showed up at the Interconti in the middle of
the night, at first castigating me for always disappearing somewhere
while he was risking his ass for the revolution. But Petre calmed
down and was ecstatic at the news that there was a good chance
the Virgin of Eternal Consolation would be found among the stolen church treasures in the cellars of the Securitate in Kronauburg.
Petre said he would make his way to Kronauburg the next day and
if necessary carry the Madonna to Baia Luna on his own back.

Before I retrieved the priest Antonius Wachenwerther's Volkswagen the next morning from where Petre and I had left it days
ago, Fritz purchased the latest edition of the *Voice of Truth*. We were
relieved to discover that the editor in chief had foregone publishing
the photo of the naked Stephanescu. Instead, there was an earlier
portrait of Dr. Stephanescu with a smiling face. The editor had let
the dead rest in peace, done without an obituary, but had specu-
lated at length about the nebulous identity of the perpetrators. Nor
did the following days and weeks clear up whether a faction of
the splintered Salvation Front or clandestine counterrevolutionary
forces from the Securitate had been behind the murder. Despite
Stephanescu's death, the ministerial council of the provisional government had appointed a prime minister that afternoon. It was a
name I had never heard before. The new head of state promised
to appoint an investigative commission to look into the murder
of Stephanescu, but the country never learned if that commission
ever met.

# Chapter Fifteen

●

*THE PLACE WITHOUT SHADOWS, A SAVIOR FROM AMERICA,*

*AND DIMITRU'S SECRET*

On Wednesday, December 27, 1989, I steered the Volkswagen through the lonely Carpathians. Aunt Antonia sat next to me, and Fritz Hofmann, the Gypsy Dimitru, and Buba were in the backseat. Fritz's luggage was in the trunk along with his photo equipment, Petre's carbine, and Dimitru's white box with the bones of his father Laszlo. No one said a word during the drive. At first an occasional truck or a Dacia would pass us going the other direction and now and then a horse-drawn cart, but for the last half hour before we reached the village of Riu Vadului we encountered nothing and no one.

The barracks stood at the far edge of town. I stopped in front of a closed gate. A rusty tin sign informed us that beyond the gate was a neurologic and psychiatric hospital.

"Wait here a second!" I got out, pushed open the gate, and entered. I couldn't see a soul, only the yellow stone barracks and a large, vacant field to the left. A half-dozen mongrel dogs started growling when they saw me. Despite that, I went nearer. Then I saw the wooden crosses. There were many crosses, some overgrown with weeds, some new. The longer I looked, the more I discovered, all without names. I was standing in a cemetery. The Place Without Shadows. I beseeched heaven that my grandfather not be among those buried here. The dogs were tugging something out of the ground. They were fighting over an arm from a child's corpse.

I returned to the car. Fritz and Buba had gotten out.

"Can we go in?" asked Buba.

"Yes, but just Fritz and me. Not you, Buba."

She started to protest, then she looked into my face. "Is it that bad?"

"Yes."

"No entrance without an appointment," barked a guard at the gate. Fritz and I couldn't tell from his appearance if he was an inmate or one of the staff.

Fritz handed him ten dollars.

The man snatched the bill and held it up to the light. "What's this? Swindler! It's old money!" He tore up the bill and demanded, "Real money!" Fritz gave him some local currency and in a flash the man put it in his pocket.

"You can go in, but not him!" He pointed to me.

I ignored the prohibition and started to push past the guard when suddenly a few figures in rags appeared from nowhere. I froze. Before me stood wretchedness incarnate.

"Food?" asked one.

At our harsh no, the man began to howl like a wolf. The sound pierced me to the quick.

"I'm from Germany," Fritz said quietly. The howling ceased immediately. "I'll see that you get something to eat soon. You'll have enough, you'll always have enough from now on. Not today, but soon. I promise."

"He's a German!" someone yelled, and they all started screaming. "The Germans are here. They haven't forgotten us. They're bringing food. The Germans don't forget!"

"But that one's not a German!" The orderly was putting in his two cents again, and when the howling started up anew, I withdrew.

"Fritz, I can't go into this place."

"Okay, Pavel. I'll give it my best try."

I returned to the car while Fritz asked after a certain Ilja Botev from Baia Luna. The orderly said no, as did the men, who apparently knew nothing of first names or family names.

"Are you really a German?"

Fritz turned around and found himself face-to-face with a young man who introduced himself as Dr. Adrian Bacanu, the director of the hospital, and beseeched Fritz, "Please help us."

Bacanu explained that he had taken over the place only two weeks ago. His predecessor Dr. Pauker had gotten himself transferred to the army. For his part, Bacanu never imagined in his worst nightmares what horrors would await him in Vadului.

"I wanted to be a doctor, not a gravedigger," he said, and Fritz could see he was telling the truth. When Fritz introduced himself as a photojournalist, Bacanu almost hugged him. "Please photograph the wretched people here! Show the Germans what miserable conditions they live in."

"No! I'm not here to take pictures now. But I give you my word I'll send my colleagues from the capital up here in three days at the most."

"Three days? Okay, we can wait that long."

When Fritz Hofmann saw Adrian Bacanu's quiet satisfaction, he knew that he would never again in his life press the shutter release of a camera. Then he explained that the man he was looking for, Ilja Botev, would be very old by now if he was still alive at all—well over eighty and possibly living here for more than twenty years.

But Bacanu also denied knowing the name Ilja Botev. There were certainly some very elderly men among the three hundred patients, but he couldn't imagine that anyone would have been able to survive two decades in Vadului.

"There was hardly anything to eat, thin soup at the most. No medications. No heat in the winter. Even if patients survived their illnesses, they died from the lack of kindness. They dried up like flowers without water. No one wanted them. They have no home, no sense to their lives, no goal, not even to arouse our sympathy. Some have left the world entirely and spun themselves into a cocoon of their own invention as if protecting themselves against a doctor pulling them back into this reality."

"Like the blind guy in the bunker," the orderly interjected, "the crazy New Yorker."

It had been only a few days since Fritz Hofmann had said in the Interconti, "When I see the pain of others, I feel alive." As he descended the steps to the cellar hole in Vadului, he felt ashamed to have said it.

"Don't be shocked," Dr. Bacanu said and pushed open the door to an empty coal bunker. Fritz stepped inside. "I've been with him a few times already," whispered Bacanu, "but he won't talk. I'll leave you alone with the gentleman. Maybe you'll find the magic word to release him from silence."

"Okay!"

And with that, Fritz Hofmann had uttered the magic word.

The bundle of rags turned its head toward him. "Are you from America?"

The man sat in the shadows. From behind him, a ray of light fell from the narrow slit of a shaft onto the blackness of the opposite wall. Long ago something had been scratched onto the naked stone: the outline of the Statue of Liberty. When Fritz's eyes had adjusted to the semidarkness, he saw that the silhouettes of skyscrapers had also been scratched on the walls to Ilja's right and left.

"You haven't answered. Speak! Are you from America?"

"Yes, I'm from America, from New York."

"Can I trust you? Do you know my name? Do you know where I'm from?"

"You are the tavern owner Ilja Botev from Baia Luna. Your grandson Pavel is here. He wants to take you home. I'm his friend. My name is Fritz, and you can trust me."

"I can't see you, but I recognize your voice. Pavel's not going to take me home. He is tired. I don't trust you. You want to spoil my mission."

"Your friend Dimitru is here, waiting for you, too."

"Dimitru will never abandon me. Never. We are friends. But you! You know too much. You want to know my secrets, but I'll never tell them to you."

"Trust me, Ilja. The Conductor is dead. You're free. You can go home, Ilja. Everyone's waiting for you: Dimitru, Pavel, Kathalina, and your daughter Antonia, too. You've completed your mission."

"The Conductor is dead, you say? No, no. He's alive. He is a Titan! You're trying to trick me. The Vatican sent you, the Fourth Power. They want to destroy the Madonna, the Jewess, the resurrected."

"Forget about the Fourth Power. It's lost all its might. The Mother of God is much, much stronger. She's doing fine."

"What about the Conducator? Did the American president help him? Did they save the Madonna? Did my letter reach him?"

"Of course. Your letter reached the right hands. Everything's okay. Believe me. Before he died the Conducator took care of everything. What can the Fourth Power do to a man who outshines the sun? The Conducator even installed a new pope in the Vatican, a Pole. He's made the protection of the Mother of God a priority. Believe me, the woman on the moon is doing fine. Everything's tip-top. The Virgin of Eternal Consolation will soon return to Baia Luna. And the Eternal Flame is shining again."

"You're lying. Wachenwerther sent you. You're a spy from Rome. Can you prove you're from America?"

Fritz reached into his jacket and took out a couple of dollar bills. As he went to hand them to the old man, something fell on the floor, something silvery. Hofmann put the money back in his pocket and picked up the stick of chewing gum, which he pressed firmly into Ilja's outstretched hands.

Ilja Botev fingered the silver wrapper like a precious stone. Then he slowly bent the strip of gum back and forth, unwrapped and sniffed it. He nodded, put it in his mouth, and chewed.

Then Ilja Botev stood up and said, "America. What a country! The best. Take me home."

When people could move around Transmontania freely again and hordes of reporters from all over the world were filing stories from the Realm of Shadows, a French journalist even found his way to Baia Luna. It must have been in March or April 1990 that the man sat down at our kitchen table to interview my aunt Antonia.

"You came all the way from Paris? Well, I'm going to disappoint you. I can't imagine I have anything smart to say into the microphone of a reporter from Paris. But if you insist, I'll be happy to answer your questions as best I can.

"My name is Gabor, Antonia Carolea Gabor. I'm sixty years old and was born here in Baia Luna. Maybe you noticed a wayside cross on the bank of the Tirnava on your way here? No? But you can't miss it! The tragedy at the river happened in 1935. Today I think my fate was determined on that day. I was six years old and it was winter when my mother Agneta and I fell into the Tirnava in our wagon. My father Ilja and my future husband, the Gypsy Dimitru Gabor, pulled us out of the icy water. Dimitru's father Laszlo died trying to save us. Mother died later of pneumonia. Isn't it strange that I lost my mother in the accident and

Dimitru lost his father? But it took a long time until Dimitru and I became a couple. I slept through half of my life. Why? Something inside me was so heavy that I had no desire to bestir myself. What was it, you ask? I don't know. But I think it was my disposition. I'm doing better today. When Pavel goes to Italy with his wife in the spring, I'll see to the tavern business. You know, Socialism, Communism, democracy—in Baia Luna it's all the same thing. *Zuika* is *zuika*. And the men always need it. Oh, forgive me! I haven't offered you a glass of schnapps."

"*Non, non, merci,* Madame Gabor," the journalist declined. "I want to 'ave a clear 'ead."

"If you're sure, monsieur. At any rate, after the tragedy at the Tirnava my father Ilja and Dimitru became friends and stayed friends their whole lives until they died. My father died on December twenty-eighth, 1989, and my husband Dimitru followed him three days later, on New Year's Eve. They had lost sight of each other for two decades, but the bonds of friendship were strong. No power on earth could tear them apart. I traveled cross-country many years with Dimitru. He was looking for his friend, and I was searching for my papa. Then my Dimi became melancholy because the story about the Mother of God was wrong. It's in the Bible, pretty near the end, in Revelation. Lord knows what it is with that woman with the moon under her feet, but she's sure not Mary, the Queen of Heaven. When Dimi died, I think he had an idea who the woman on the moon might be. But he never talked to me about such things. I always left him to his secrets. It was enough for me to be near him. We didn't find my father until very late, when Dimi had almost given up hope. How could we have known that they locked Ilja away with the crazies in Vadului?

"People here in the village also said my father was sick in the head, because he was always dreaming of America. But he wasn't crazy. He just got on the wrong track. And, monsieur, would you like to know why he lost his way? Because he believed the pope and the story about the Assumption of the Mother of God. Mary was supposed to have been assumed body and soul into heaven, right? But in Scripture it says something quite different. Only Jesus was resurrected, no one else. Shall I read you the passage in the Bible?"

"*Non, non,* madame. I don't think people are interested in these tales."

"What a shame. They could find out how little there is to put their trust in nowadays. The apostle John writes that only the Son of Man ascended into heaven. But the pope declares that Mary the Mother of God did, too. So who's right? Can you tell me whom to believe? My father believed the pope, at any rate. That's why he and Dimitru were looking for the Madonna in the sky. On the moon! You find that absurd? No, no, young man! My father Ilja and Dimi were no more crazy than John the Evangelist. My Dimitru was a smart man. It may be that my father's brain waves lost the beat from time to time, but only because he had epilepsy and ran out of pills.

"On the Wednesday after the revolution, December twenty-seventh in the year '89, we found Ilja. That is, Hofmanns' Fritz found him. Just imagine, my father lived in a dark cellar hole for twenty years. We were terribly shocked when we found him. I scrubbed him for hours until he started to look like a human being again, and Fritz gave him some of his clothes.

"My Dimitru was heartbroken. His friend Ilja didn't recognize him at first. Father was blind and couldn't remember anything or anyone, not even me or his daughter-in-law Kathalina or his grandson Pavel. At least Father pretended not to know us. He was skeptical. But one day after he got back to the village a miracle happened. What? You don't believe in miracles? Then let me tell you about it.

"Precisely on December twenty-eighth—Holy Innocents' Day, that is—our Virgin of Eternal Consolation came back to the village. Petre Petrov carried her back on his own shoulders. And she's heavy, let me tell you. She'd been lost for more than thirty years. But eventually, everything comes to light. The Securitate in Kronauburg had stolen the Madonna. But I guess she wasn't valuable enough for some rich man to pay money for her. Petre found her all covered with dust in the cellar of the Security Service. When he entered the village with Mary that afternoon, you wouldn't believe the commotion it caused. There was no end of rejoicing. Pastor Wachenwerther instructed Petre to carry the Madonna into the church. Then my nephew Pavel stepped in. He snatched up Petre's carbine, held it under Wachenwerther's chin, and said, 'Your time's run out here. I'll give you an hour to get out.' Pavel told me afterward that the carbine wasn't even loaded because Petre had used up all his ammunition during the revolution in the capital. In any case, Wachenwerther was in his Volkswagen within the hour and away he went in the general direction of Austria. Then first off, Petre Petrov set up the Madonna on the counter in our old tavern. That's when the miracle happened."

"*Oui*, Madame Gabor. And now you're going to tell me that your father Ilja suddenly regained his sight."

"No, no such luck. Where'd you get that idea? He stayed blind, and he died blind that night. But he died happy. He was redeemed, on account of the Madonna. Once she was set up in our shop, Dimitru took Ilja by the hand and led him over to her. For what seemed like an eternity, my father very carefully ran his hands all over her. I think he was checking to make sure she was the genuine article: first her face, then her gigantic breasts, then the little Baby Jesus, and finally the crescent moon under her feet. I don't know if you can imagine it, but when my father felt that funny sickle, he began to beam. He recognized the Madonna. And at that very moment, he called us all by name: Pavel, Kathalina, me, even Hofmanns' Fritz and Buba Gabor. And his Dimitru, of course. The two of them fell into each other's arms, and Ilja said that now he could set off on his final journey. Mission accomplished. But if you ask me what mission Ilja and Dimitru were on, I don't really know what to tell you. If it had anything to do with Mary, the two of them could be real mystery mongers, the way two old friends are when they always . . ."

The tape ended in midsentence. The reporter from Paris had forgone recording any more of Antonia Carolea Gabor.

On the evening of Holy Innocents' Day my grandfather Ilja expressed a last wish. He asked his family and his friend Dimitru to let him die under the open sky, on the very spot where everything had started early on the morning of his fifty-fifth birthday. Fritz and I carried Ilja's bed outside onto the veranda in front of the tavern. On the night of November 6, 1957, Grandfather had stood right there with a tin funnel to his ear, trying to catch the sound of Sputnik beeping through space. Antonia and Kathalina brought out blankets and pillows and bedded Ilja down beneath the cold, starry night sky. All of us sat around Grandfather: I and my Buba, Fritz Hofmann, Ilja's daughter-in-law Kathalina, Antonia, and Dimitru. Dimi held Ilja's hand. I think it was the first time since the accident on the Tirnava that the cold didn't make Dimitru shiver.

I went into the taproom, opened the old cash register, and got out the wooden box that hadn't been opened for an eternity. Then I gave Fritz and Dimitru each a cigar and also lit the last of the Cubans for myself and my grandfather.

"America," sighed Ilja. The moon rose above the mountains. Ilja pressed Dimitru's hand and asked softly, "Do you still remember the nights we spent looking through our telescope on the Mondberg?"

"I don't just remember them, Ilja my friend! It's as if it were yesterday."

"Good. Very good. And Dimitru? Did you really see the Queen of Heaven back then? The woman with the crown of sunbeams?"

"Absolutely I saw her! Only briefly, mind you. But I saw her clearly. Brighter than a thousand suns, just like Saint John the Evangelist saw her. Exactly like that!"

"And was she beautiful?"

"Beautiful? She was more than that. Believe me, she was wonderful, *magnifica maxima*."

"I would have liked to see her—very much. Not just white dots on black paper." Ilja's breathing was labored. The Cuban slipped from his fingers. Buba leaned closer to him and laid her hands on his blind eyes. In the light of the moon, we saw that Grandfather was smiling.

"You see her now, don't you, my friend?"

Ilja nodded slightly. "Yes." He sighed again. "I see her, Dimitru. And I see more. She's not alone."

"Who else is there?"

"Many people, very many."

"Do you recognize any of them?"

"Yes, of course. I can see my son Nicolai. Your father Laszlo. Papa Baptiste. And my dear Agneta. She's waving to me. And I see many, many other women."

"And the Queen? What is she doing? How does she look?"

"She's smiling. A child is sitting on her lap, a boy. Or a girl, I can't tell which. The child is blond, just like its mother. Her hair is blowing in the wind. She smells of roses. And she's wearing a lovely dress covered in sunflowers. I know her. I know her from somewhere, but I can't remember where."

"That's her! That's exactly how she looked when I saw her in the Sea of Serenity. So she is doing well."

"Yes, Dimitru, she is."

The Gypsy kissed his friend's forehead and whispered, "You go on ahead, Ilja. I have one more thing to take care of, then I'll join you."

On the morning of December 29, Dimitru asked me to carry the red chaise longue back into the library, the one that Antonius Wachenwerther had ordered stowed away in the cellar two decades ago. Then the Gypsy had me throw open all the doors and windows of the rectory.

For the last time Dimitru entered the library where he had once pursued his studies in Mariology. He lay down on the couch and asked his niece Buba, Fritz Hofmann, and me to gather round.

"I have one final song to sing. Then you can bury me and the bones of my father next to my friend Ilja. And see to it that Papa Baptiste also gets a nice place. And please, also a grave in our midst for the teacher Angela Barbulescu, one with a white cross. You'll find a good place, I know you will. And now sit down, all of you, because I have a confession to make.

"I spent many, many nights here in this library. I studied. Oh yes, I read a lot of books. But that's not all I did. There were nights when I wasn't alone. Man needs warmth, and I got some for myself from a woman who also needed warmth. And yet we were never man and wife. I didn't want to commit myself to her, and Angela couldn't commit herself to me either. My angel, that's what I called her, but that was a lie. It was only flesh. And after pleasure, an empty sadness that longs for more pleasure so it won't have to confront itself."

"What? You, you and Angela Barbulescu were lovers in secret?" I uttered the question before I had grasped its enormity.

"Yes, we were."

"But Uncle Dimi, you never loved her." Buba was trembling.

"No, I used her. And when I began to love Angela, it was too late. In our nocturnal encounters we didn't say much to each other. But I always sensed that something had happened to her. Something dark, earlier, before she came to Baia Luna. I saw the shadow, but I closed my eyes. I didn't want to see it. I wanted her to keep her heart to herself. Until our last night before my friend Ilja's fifty-fifth birthday. It was almost winter already, and Angela came to me through the cold. She was freezing, and we made love, but it didn't warm us up. She put her clothes back on and all she said was 'Dimitru, I'm not going to come anymore. I'm going down into the black water.' "

Dimitru was weeping. "At that moment I would have given anything to save her from that final step. Anything. But it was too late. When Angela showed me her heart, her time had run out. She had touched me, but I saw a heart without blood. It lay dying, wounded long, long ago. When I finally felt my love, I learned what guilt means. She was lost. And I had not stood by her. She would die and take the dark secret of her past with her."

"Uncle Dimi, Angela kept a diary that—"

"I know, dear Buba, I know. Let me talk. I was desperate. I could think of nothing but Angela. At the same time, it was my friend Ilja's birthday. When I brought the television into the taproom that afternoon, I had already been drinking *zuika*. I didn't want to burden my friend on his special day with my own bad conscience. So I kept on drinking. Our conversation about Korolev's Sputnik and the Virgin Mary with Papa Baptiste went right past me. I was so drunk that I fell down the steps in front of Ilja's tavern on my way home. Pavel and Fritz, do you remember dragging me home?"

"Oh yes, Dimitru," said Fritz. "I'll never forget that night."

"I was drunk, believe me, but I wasn't blind or deaf. I heard the steeple clock strike nine thirty and saw there was no light burning in Angela's house. But there was always a light on at that time. I knew then she was on her way to the black water. I fell asleep then, but I woke up in the middle of the night. I was terribly cold. I thought I heard a voice calling softly, Dimitru, Dimitru! I'm cold, I'm so cold. I got up and looked, but there was no one out there. I pleaded with God to send Angela to the rectory library. Although I knew that such prayers are never answered, I went to the rectory. And so the disaster took its course. If I hadn't gone there, those criminals wouldn't have murdered Papa Baptiste."

Now Dimitru was crying steadily. Buba put her hand on his shoulder. "What happened, Uncle Dimi?"

"My curiosity was to blame. An envelope was sticking out of the rectory's mailbox. Although it wasn't addressed to me, I took it out and locked myself in the library. There were photographs in the envelope."

"My father Heinrich took them," Fritz interrupted the Gypsy. "My father put the letter into the mailbox."

"I guessed that was the case. The pictures were of Angela and some men. They were doing things to her, things no one should do to another person. I can't talk to you about them. But now I knew why Angela's heart had bled to death. She was a brave woman. She kept on living although they had killed her long ago."

"Those pictures," I asked, "what happened to them, Dimitru?"

"What could I do? I burned them and scattered the ashes in the Tirnava. That's why Papa Baptiste had to die. The thugs who killed him thought he had hidden the photographs in the rectory, and that's why they turned everything upside down. But Papa Baptiste had no idea. He couldn't tell them anything because he knew nothing about them."

"Maybe he did know something about Angela's past?" I ventured. "Kora Konstantin claimed that Angela had been with the pastor on the afternoon of Grandfather's birthday, wanting to confess. Fernanda the housekeeper had listened at the door and told Kora that Johannes Baptiste refused Angela absolution."

"Yes, Pavel, that old Konstantin woman told the truth. Or what she thought was the truth. But that's another story. It's true that Angela was in the rectory with Papa Baptiste and then in the library. When I entered the library on the day after Ilja's birthday, I noticed right away that she had been back again. It smelled of roses. Angela must have left me a message. I searched and I found the green diary."

"What?" both Buba and I cried out in shock and surprise.

"You read the diary? So it was only playacting when you did a headstand against the bookcase and afterward said you had to turn the world upside down?" My astonishment was mixed with anger. "You tricked me. You wanted me to find the book so you wouldn't need to have anything to do with it."

"You're right, Pavel. But you're also wrong. Yes, I wanted the diary to be found, and I wanted you to find it. But let me talk. I holed up for days in the library, and believe me, I read Angela's book hundreds of times. It seared my soul. I was guilty of not helping her, and I also wanted justice. I passed sentence and decided to kill the man who had killed Angela. Stephanescu had to die. He had to fall when he reached the top. Like in the Bible, like in Mary's Magnificat. And it was up to me, Dimitru Carolea Gabor, who only saw Angela's flesh when she was still alive. It was up to me to make sure that at least her prophecy would be fulfilled."

"But Angela was wrong," I interrupted the Gypsy. "In her farewell letter she wrote that Stephanescu's last hour had struck. But that hour lasted more than thirty years."

"Pavel, my boy, when will you ever learn how to read properly? Always *exactamente*! Angela didn't predict 'Your last hour has already struck.' She wrote, 'Your last hours have been rung in.' There's a difference. The course for his fall had been set. It was a question of timing when he would be thrown off course. First, he had to reach the top. But you're right, Pavel. The moment of truth was long in coming."

"And that moment arrived when the Conducator fell and Stephanescu was celebrating his guaranteed succession," Fritz added. "Dimitru, what I don't understand is how you could be sure that Pavel, Buba, and I would be able to topple Stephanescu from his throne. And besides, you declared war on the man, but you sent us into battle against him. You used us for your purposes."

Dimitru didn't answer immediately. He looked at the ceiling and murmured in a low monotone, *"Mea culpa, mea culpa, mea maxima culpa."* Then: "Yes, you were my tools. And yet you fought your own battle. What was I supposed to do? I saw no other way except for one, but I was unable to follow it. After Angela had been buried behind the cemetery, everyone in the village thought I had locked myself up in the library. But I hadn't. I walked through the snow all the way to Kronauburg. I acquired a pistol from the Gypsies who hung around the train station, and I intended to shoot Stephanescu. I waited for him on the market square for three days, but he never showed up. Then I went up to his villa on the Klosterberg under cover of darkness and rang the doorbell. He answered the door and stood before me. I drew the pistol, but I couldn't shoot. I was overcome by a terrible fear I've never felt before or since. Stephanescu looked at me. He wasn't horrified or frightened, no, he was smiling. All I needed to do was pull the trigger, and Stephanescu would have been dead. But not the smiling demon. It would have entered me. Everything inside me was pain and hatred, but nothing that would have protected me from the demon: no angel, no saints, no Mother of God, nothing. I threw the pistol away and ran and ran . . .

"I wasn't the right one to bring down Stephanescu. Someone else had to do it, someone whose eye could see the invisible and ear hear the inaudible, the mute scream of grief. The person had to be smart. And courageous, for he had to get so close to Stephanescu that the demon would be forced to show its face. It couldn't possibly be me. Don't forget, I'm only a Black. A person like Dr. Stephanescu doesn't even consider me worthy to wipe his behind. Stephanescu would only feel comfortable with a white, with one of his own kind, and then he could be lured into a trap. That *gajo* was you, Pavel. You were different from all the other *gaje* I knew. You knew what it meant to turn the world upside down, you and my niece Buba. You two were young and were just falling in love. I was born an old man. But now that my music is ending, I wonder, would it have been better if you'd never come across Angela's diary? I don't know the answer."

Buba took his hand. "But I do," she said. "Your music was wonderful. Without your song I would have forgotten that I'd forgotten. Without you, Dimi, Pavel and I would never have lost each other but never found each other either."

"Is that really true, Pavel?"

"*Completamente* true! And because it is, your niece's name is Buba Botev from now on."

Dimitru sat up. His eyes were shimmering, and he looked quite youthful. "That is good news. But you really could have thought of it earlier. You're not the youngest anymore. Pavel, it's high time for you to start thinking about offspring. Time passes in a flash, and before you know it you're out of juice. But don't worry. Abraham was a hundred when Sarah bore him Isaac. And the old guy was just warming up and went on to be a mighty progenitor. You too, Fritz, you should be thinking of the future, too, not just living from day to day, running hither and yon. Like the Gypsies."

"I'll try." Fritz Hofmann laughed. "But I've got to get one thing off my chest: Dimitru Carolea Gabor, you're the slyest fox I've ever run across."

"Now, now, now, my boy. Even your advanced age doesn't save you from error. You have absolutely encountered a slyer person than me. But know-it-all that you were, you didn't realize it, of course. Yes, I was always a fox, and do you know why, Fritz? Because I had a teacher who was even slyer. Much, much slyer."

"Your father?"

"No, no. My father Laszlo was certainly a genius. Without him I never would have gotten into the relics business. But as far as brains go, my father—may he rest in peace—could never hold a candle to Papa Baptiste. Papa was really sly. I would never have gotten wise to him if he himself hadn't given me the necessary tools, the *instrumentum intellectatilibus,* or something like that. Papa taught me the language of the Latins, which, by the way, came in very handy in selling my milk to the Orthodox. But I'm getting ahead of myself. When I was only a young man, temptation in the form of woman kept crossing my path—*permanente.* So I was also regularly kneeling in the confessional with Papa Baptiste. I hadn't learned enough Latin yet to understand which formulas Papa Johannes was murmuring, but one year on Good Friday I noticed what he didn't say. At the absolution he never said *Ego te absolvo.*

"And that's why what the housekeeper Fernanda Klein overheard and Kora Konstantin spread around is true: Papa Baptiste really didn't absolve Angela after her confession. He would pray for her—that's what he's supposed to have said to Angela—but he couldn't speak the words *Ego te absolvo*."

"Were Angela's sins really so great?"

"That's a question I'm not qualified to answer, Pavel. The deciding factor was that Papa was not able or allowed to forgive sins because he wasn't a priest!"

*"What?"*

"More precisely, when he came to Baia Luna he wasn't a priest anymore. Papa Baptiste had been excommunicated, that is, he had been stripped of the office of priest and banned from the Benedictine order and the flock of the faithful."

"But why? I can't believe it!"

"But it's true. When I asked Papa Baptiste why he never granted me an *Ego te absolvo* he explained it all to me over a glass of *zuika*. In the early thirties, Papa had been a secret agent in Soviet Russia, working underground for the Vatican as a priest on a clandestine mission. He was constantly on the go between Odessa, Moscow, and some town with a name no one can pronounce, trying to convert the unbelieving Soviets. He was even about to be consecrated as a secret bishop when some Judas betrayed him. Papa was able to escape back to Rome, but some underground Catholic priests were exposed. They got transported to a prison on a nameless island in the White Sea. To free the poor fellows the Vatican had to send an entire freight car full of church treasures to Moscow, where some of the loot was melted down and some illegally sold back to the West for hard currency. Papa told me that then he'd gotten a new assignment from the Vatican. All I remember is that he was supposed to help arrange complicated treaties between the German Hitlerists and the Catholics. Instead, Baptiste wrote a paper explaining why one must never sign a pact with the devil. But Pope Pius tore up the paper, and Papa Baptiste was sent back to the Benedictines in Austria where they put him to work in the monastery library filling out catalog cards and sorting old books. Papa did that for a while, but then he'd had enough. He refused to submit any longer to the authority of the pope and his abbot. That's when they handed him the certificate of excommunication."

I shook my head. "I still can't believe it. He said Mass and preached sermons here. The old folks still say that Johannes Baptiste was the best pastor Baia Luna ever had."

"Absolutely correct, except he wasn't a Catholic anymore. Why the pope and the bishop in Kronauburg let him stay here I can only guess."

"I bet Johannes Baptiste knew too much about some people in the church," Fritz Hofmann remarked.

"*Exactamente.* That must have been it. They probably thought that up here in Baia Luna, Papa Baptiste wouldn't cause any trouble. Let him preach what he wants. But I'm telling you, Papa Johannes was an upright man. He baptized children, consecrated the host, blessed marriages, led processions to the Mondberg, buried Gypsies in sacred ground, and it was all a point of honor. The only thing he never did was to forgive sins. And do you know what he said to me over that glass of *zuika* right here in this library? 'Dimitru,' he said . . ."

"Pavel, I think a little glass would help refresh my memories of Papa's words."

I laughed. "You can always count on a tavern keeper from the House of Botev." I fetched four glasses and uncorked a bottle of *zuika*. Buba, Fritz, and I clinked glasses with Dimitru.

"Innkeeper, my glass has a hole in it!" I refilled it for him. "Well, here's how it was. Papa Baptiste sat here with me on the chaise longue and said, 'Dimitru, I forgive everything you did, but not in the name of the Lord. I'm not authorized to do that . . .' And that, that tortures me to this very day. Because I've never been absolved. I mean, really absolved. And now I'm scheduled to appear at the Last Judgment. And what then? I want so much to go to the Sea of Serenity and join Ilja there. I promised him I would. But what if they won't let me in without absolution? What if God turns thumbs-down on me? What then?"

The Gypsy got up from the red chaise longue. He went to the window and looked up at the sky. He closed his eyes.

We weren't looking at an old man, but at a small, shy boy who raised his index finger for quiet.

"What are you doing, Dimitru?"

"Shh," said Buba. "I think Uncle Dimi is rehearsing his appearance before the throne of the Almighty."

From the small boy's mouth came a deep bass voice: "The Gypsy Dimitru Carolea Gabor! Please stand before the court! Let us look into the book of your life! Sins, sins, and more sins! How dare you appear before me? What's this I read? You sold the Orthodox bottles of milk supposedly from the breasts of my Son's mother! Shame on you, Dimitru Carolea Gabor! Do you repent?"

"Not bottles, just tiny little flasks," answered a higher boy's voice. "Believe me, Lord. It wasn't my fault. My father Laszlo had the idea with the milk. What could I do, Lord? Was I supposed to deny my father? Leave him in the lurch? Like you left your Son so long ago? Didn't Jesus complain bitterly about you as he hung on the cross? 'My God, my God, why hast thou forsaken me?' Did you really expect the same from me? To forsake my father? Why did you put me into the world in the first place? . . . As a Gypsy!"

Dimitru turned from the window, picked up his glass, and drank his very last swallow of *zuika* with the deepest satisfaction.

"That's just what I'll say this evening. Believe me, if the Old Man up there falls for it, he'll let me through to Ilja." Then Dimitru threw off all the warm blankets he was wrapped in. "My God, I'm hot. Take me to my Antonia, my dears. After all, Abraham was already a hundred when he . . ."

## A Note About the Author

Rolf Bauerdick was born in 1957 in Lehnhausen and now lives in Hiddingsel, Westphalia. After studying literature and theology in Münster, he taught German, religion, and politics in schools in the Ruhr Valley until 1985. Since 1987, he has worked as a journalist and photographer and has traveled to more than sixty countries. His award-winning articles and photo essays have appeared in European newspapers and magazines. *The Madonna on the Moon* is his first novel.

## A Note About the Translator

David Dollenmayer is a literary translator and professor of German at the Worcester Polytechnic Institute in Worcester, Massachusetts. He has translated works by Bertolt Brecht, Elias Canetti, Peter Stephan Jungk, Michael Kleeberg, Perikles Monioudis, Anna Mitgutsch, Mietek Pemper, Moses Rosenkranz, and Hansjörg Schertenleib. He is the recipient of the 2008 Helen and Kurt Wolff Translator's Prize and the 2010 Austrian Cultural Forum Translation Prize.